InvestiGATORS
All Tide Up

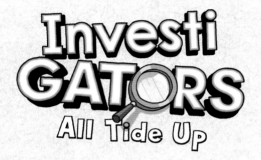

Investi GATORS
All Tide Up

written and illustrated by
John Patrick Green

with color by **Wes Dzioba**

:01
First Second
New York

To Dr. Stanley Goldstein, MD, for all the fresh air

:01

First Second

© 2023 by John Patrick Green. INVESTIGATORS and related designs are trademarks of John Patrick Green.

Penciled on plain typing paper, then printed and inked on Strathmore Smooth Bristol paper with Sakura Pigma Micron and Staedtler Pigment Liner pens. Digitally colored in Photoshop and lettered in InDesign.

Published by First Second
First Second is an imprint of Roaring Brook Press,
a division of Holtzbrinck Publishing Holdings Limited Partnership
120 Broadway, New York, NY 10271
firstsecondbooks.com
mackids.com
All rights reserved

Don't miss your next favorite book from First Second! For the latest updates go to firstsecondnewsletter.com and sign up for our enewsletter.

Library of Congress Control Number: 2022920388

ISBN: 978-1-250-84989-2 (Hardcover)
ISBN: 978-1-250-90887-2 (Special Edition)
ISBN: 978-1-250-90886-5 (Special Edition)
ISBN: 978-1-250-90885-8 (Special Edition)

Our books may be purchased in bulk for promotional, educational, or business use. Please contact your local bookseller or the Macmillan Corporate and Premium Sales Department at (800) 221-7945 ext. 5442 or by email at MacmillanSpecialSales@macmillan.com.

FIRST
EDITION

First edition, 2023
Edited by Calista Brill and Dave Roman
Cover design by John Patrick Green, Molly Johanson, and Kirk Benshoff
Interior book design by John Patrick Green
Production editing by Dawn Ryan and Arik Hardin
Color by Wes Dzioba
Printed in China by Toppan Leefung Printing Ltd., Dongguan City, Guangdong Province

10 9 8 7 6 5 4 3 2 1

Prologue

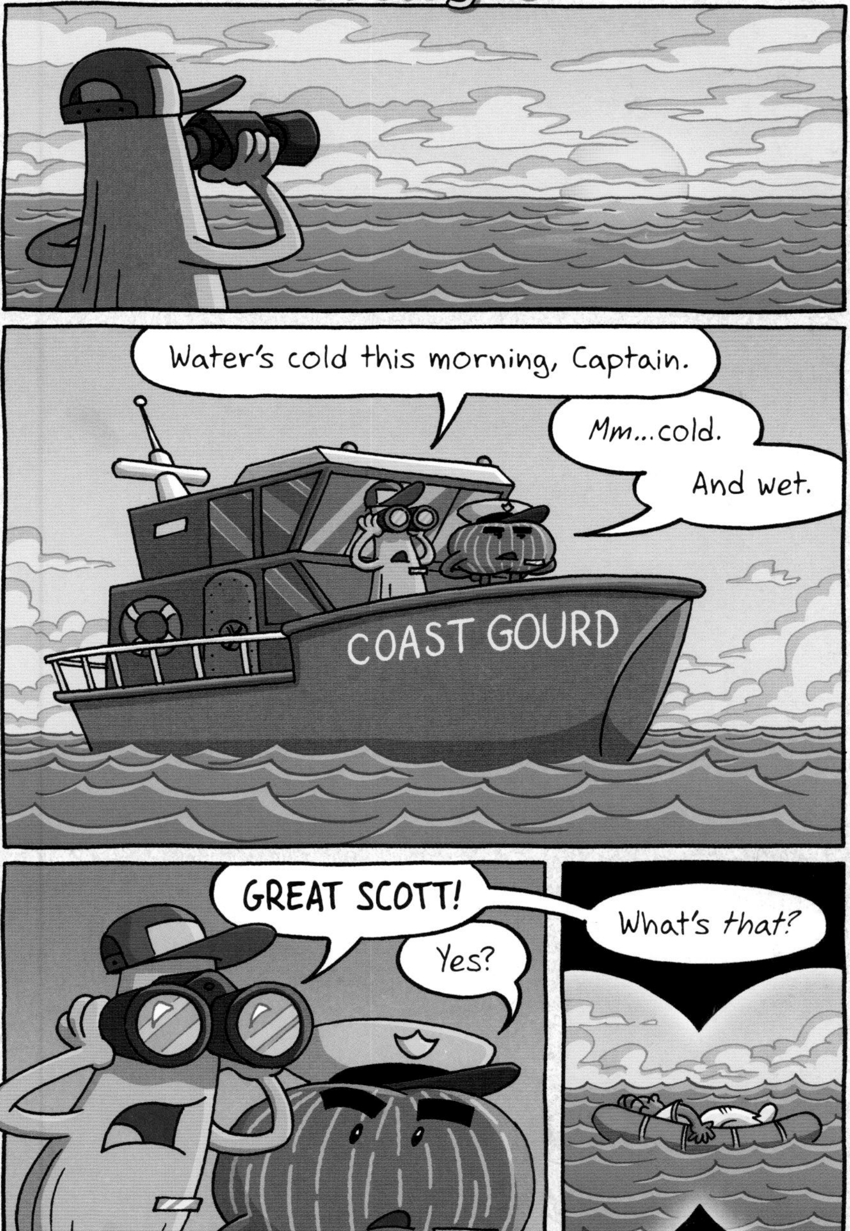
Water's cold this morning, Captain.
Mm...cold.
And wet.
COAST GOURD
GREAT SCOTT!
Yes?
What's that?
SCOTT

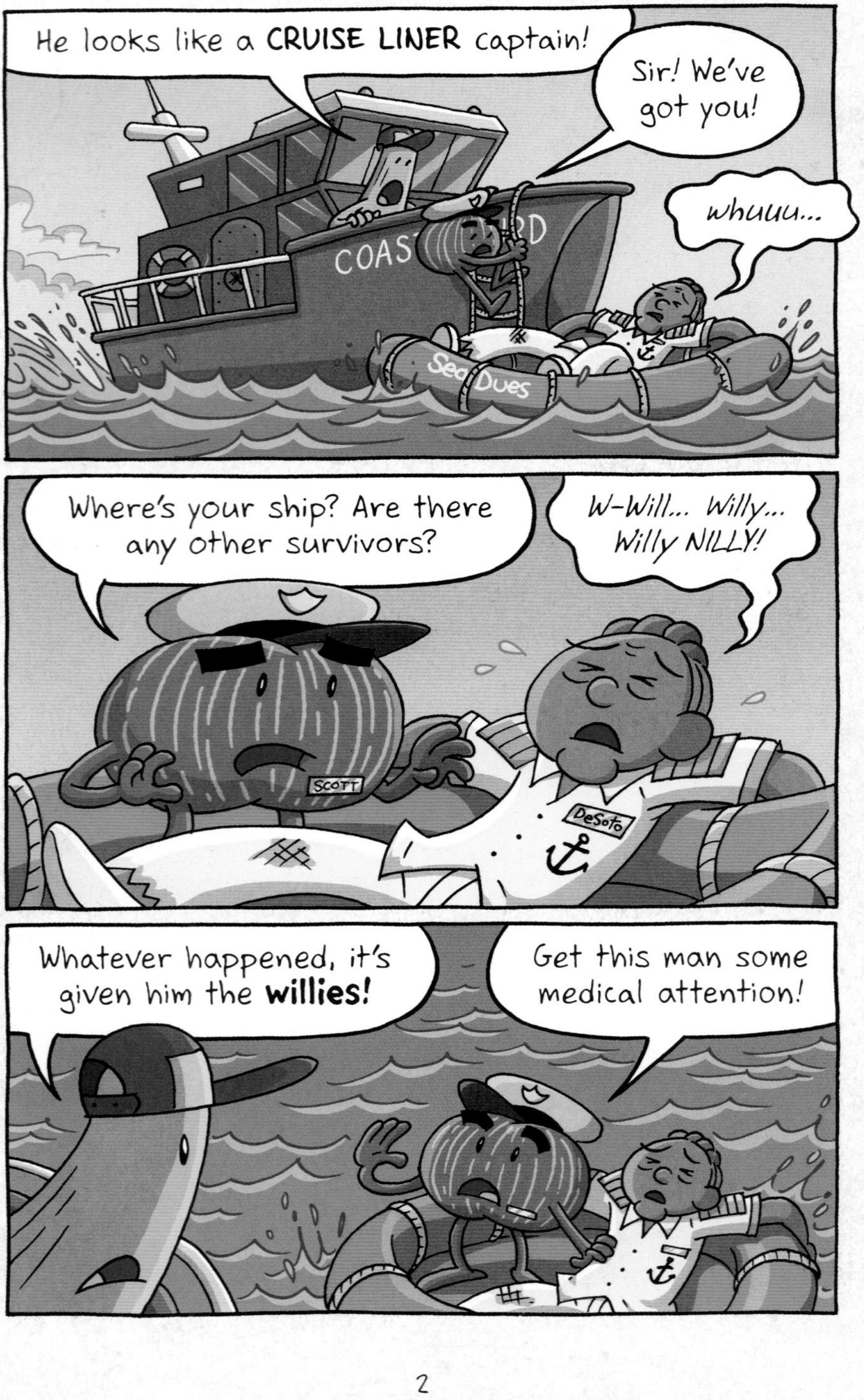
He looks like a **CRUISE LINER** captain!
Sir! We've got you!
whuuu...
COAST
RD
Sea Dues
Where's your ship? Are there any other survivors?
W-Will... Willy... Willy NILLY!
SCOTT
DeSoto
Whatever happened, it's given him the **willies!**
Get this man some medical attention!

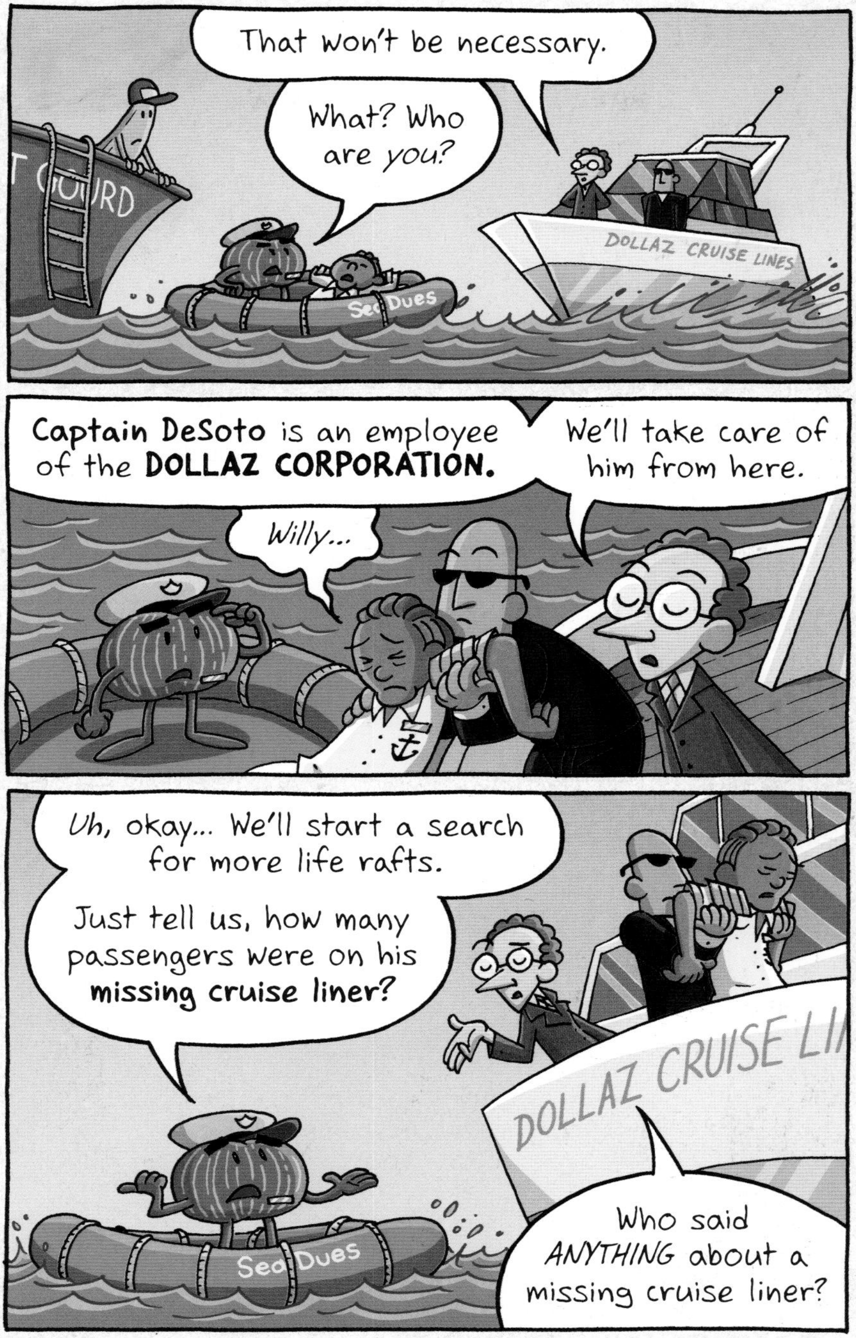
That won't be necessary.
What? Who are *you?*
T GOURD
DOLLAZ CRUISE LINES
Sea Dues
Captain DeSoto is an employee of the **DOLLAZ CORPORATION.**
We'll take care of him from here.
Willy...
Uh, okay... We'll start a search for more life rafts.
Just tell us, how many passengers were on his **missing cruise liner?**
DOLLAZ CRUISE LI
Sea Dues
Who said *ANYTHING* about a missing cruise liner?

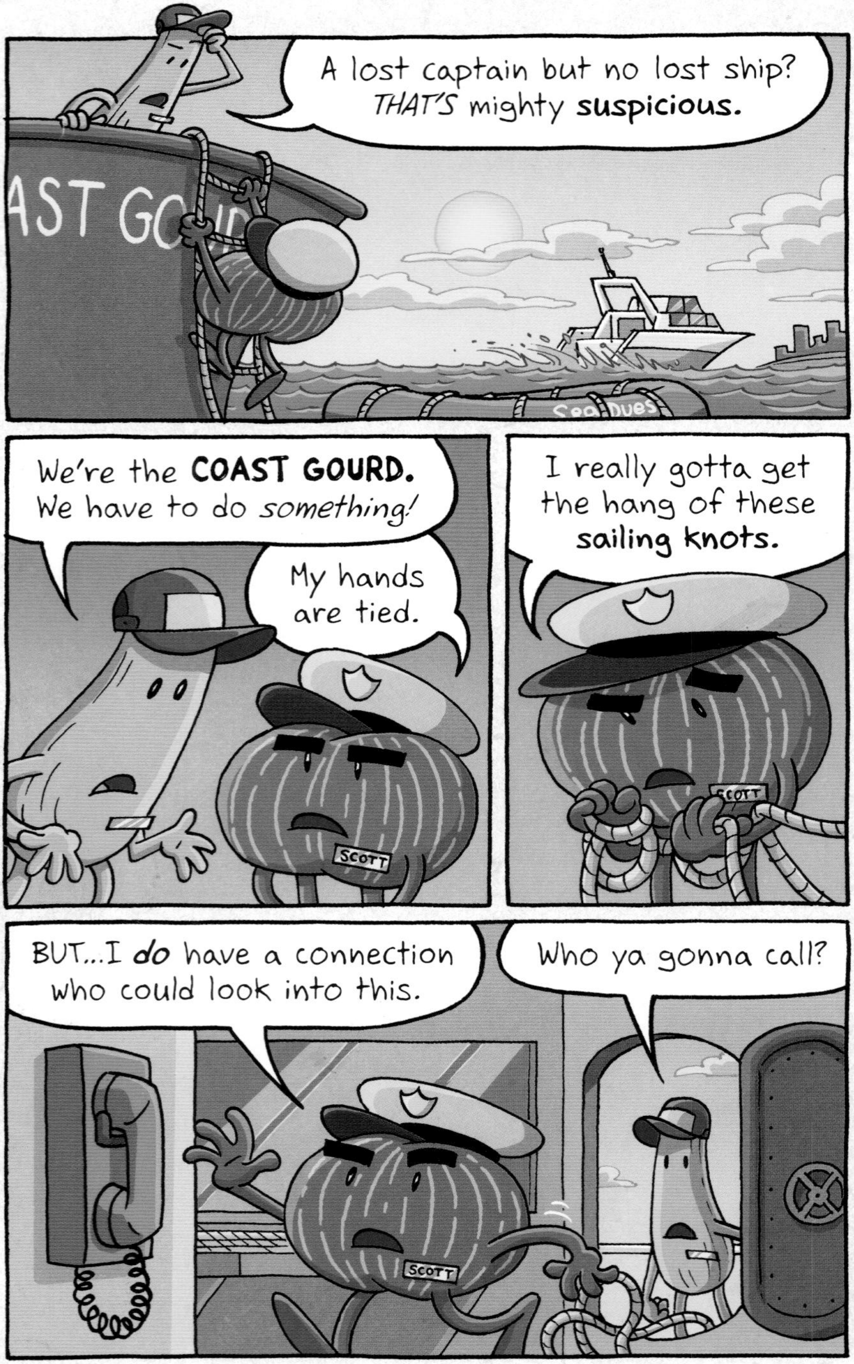

A lost captain but no lost ship? *THAT'S* mighty **suspicious.**
AST GO
Sea Dues
We're the **COAST GOURD.** We have to do *something!*
My hands are tied.
SCOTT
I really gotta get the hang of these **sailing knots.**
SCOTT
BUT...I ***do*** have a connection who could look into this.
Who ya gonna call?
SCOTT

Chapter 1

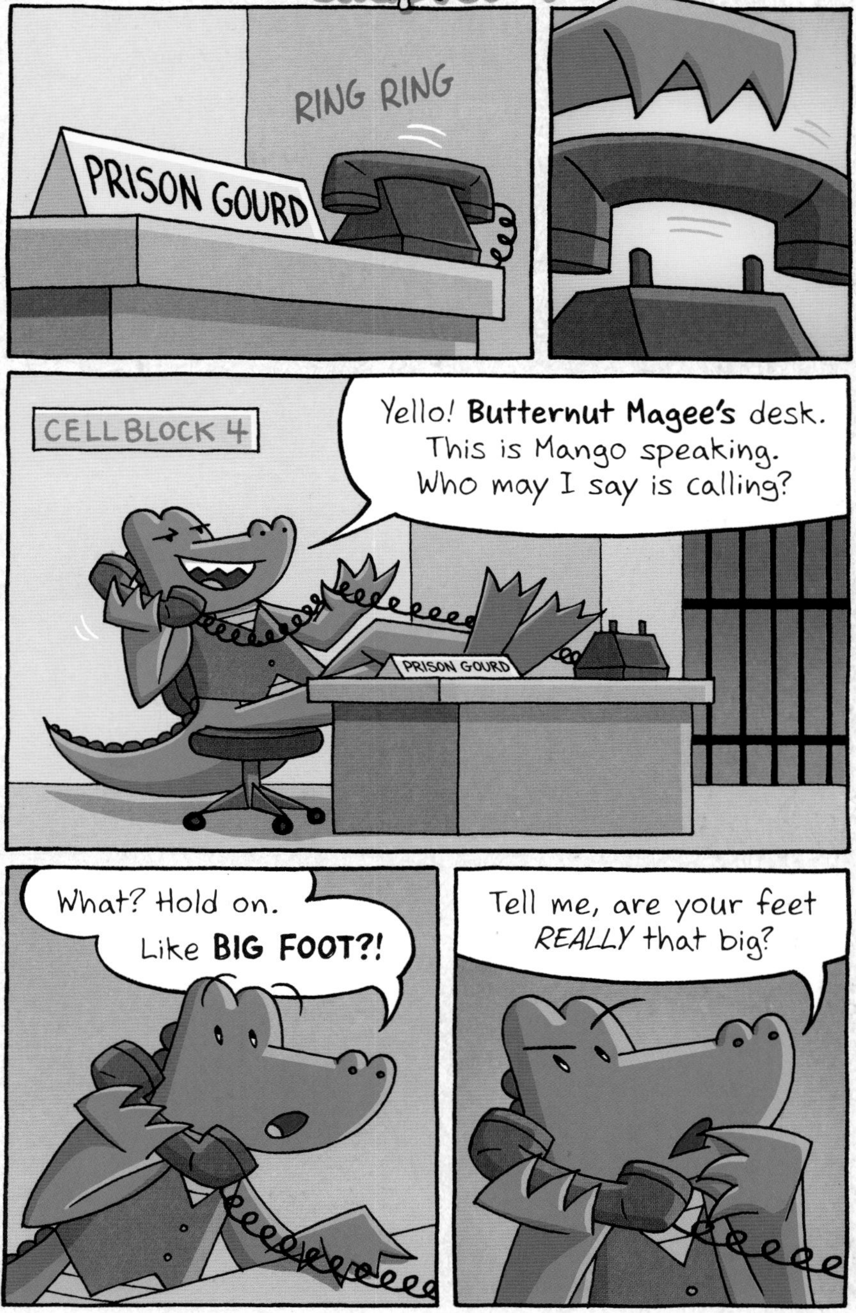
RING RING
PRISON GOURD
CELLBLOCK 4
Yello! **Butternut Magee's** desk. This is Mango speaking. Who may I say is calling?
PRISON GOURD
What? Hold on. Like **BIG FOOT?!**
Tell me, are your feet *REALLY* that big?

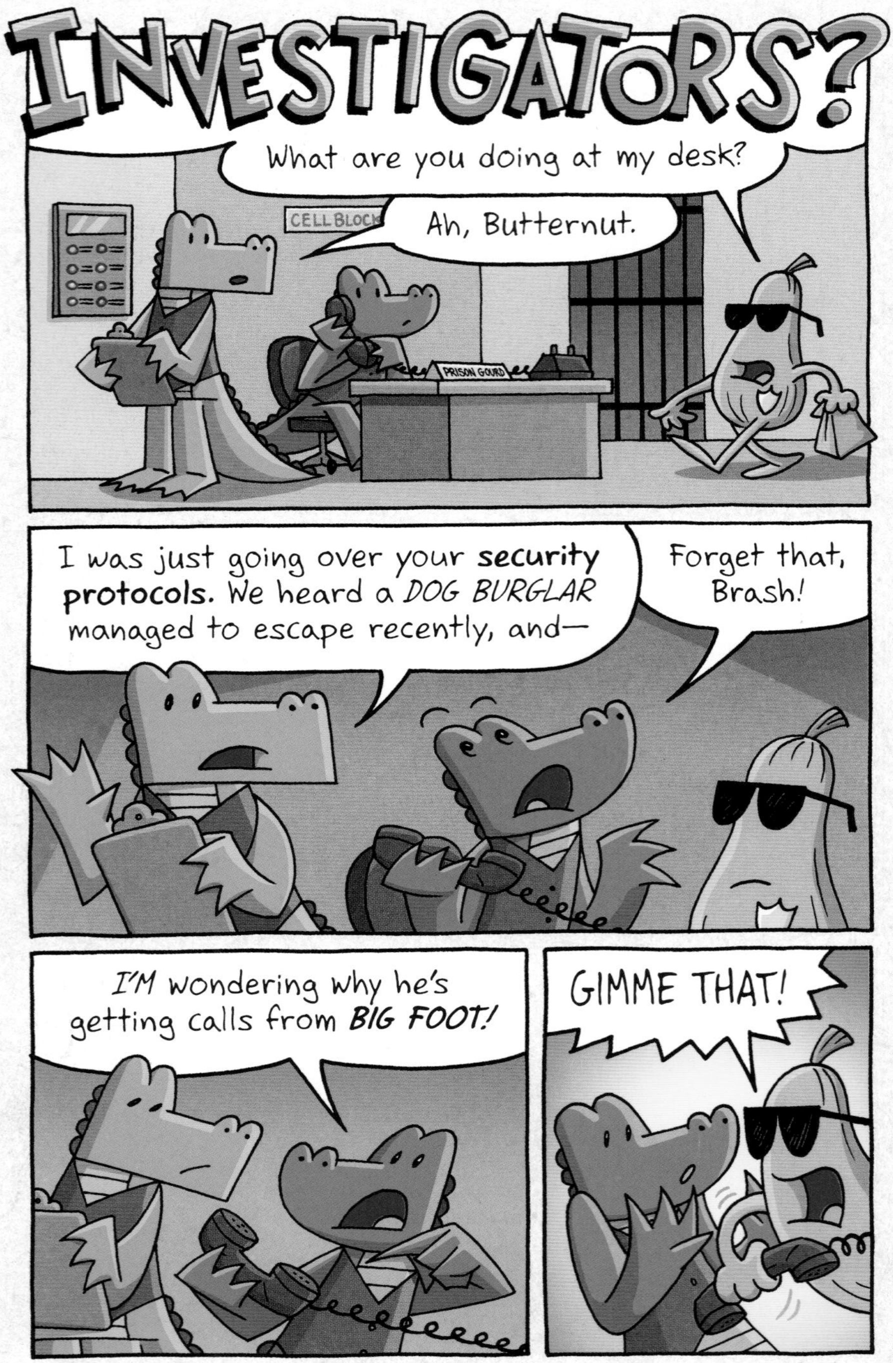
INVESTIGATORS?
What are you doing at my desk?
CELL BLOCK
Ah, Butternut.
PRISON GOURD
I was just going over your **security protocols.** We heard a *DOG BURGLAR* managed to escape recently, and—
Forget that, Brash!
I'M wondering why he's getting calls from ***BIG FOOT!***
GIMME THAT!

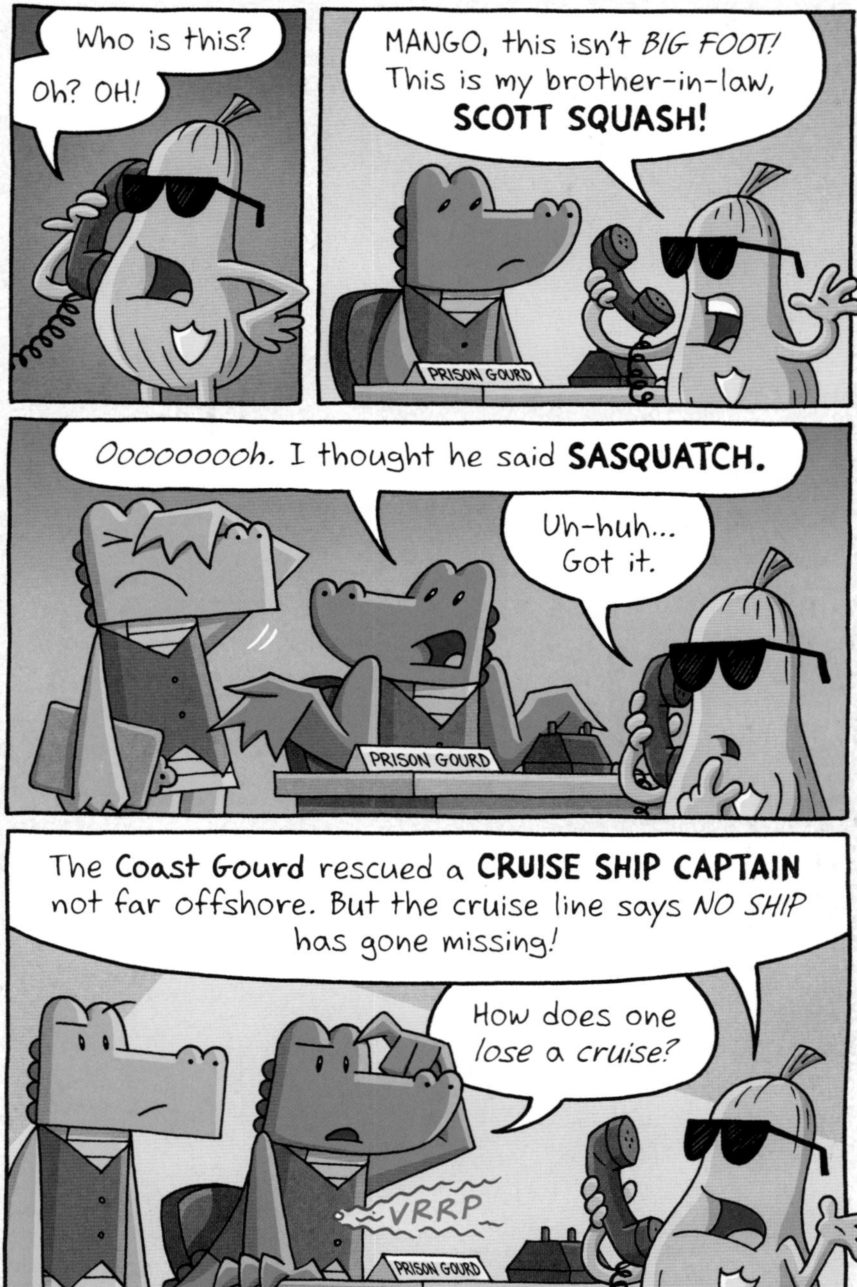
Who is this?
Oh? OH!
MANGO, this isn't *BIG FOOT!* This is my brother-in-law, **SCOTT SQUASH!**
PRISON GOURD
Oooooooh. I thought he said **SASQUATCH.**
Uh-huh... Got it.
PRISON GOURD
The **Coast Gourd** rescued a **CRUISE SHIP CAPTAIN** not far offshore. But the cruise line says *NO SHIP* has gone missing!
How does one *lose* a *cruise?*
VRRP
PRISON GOURD

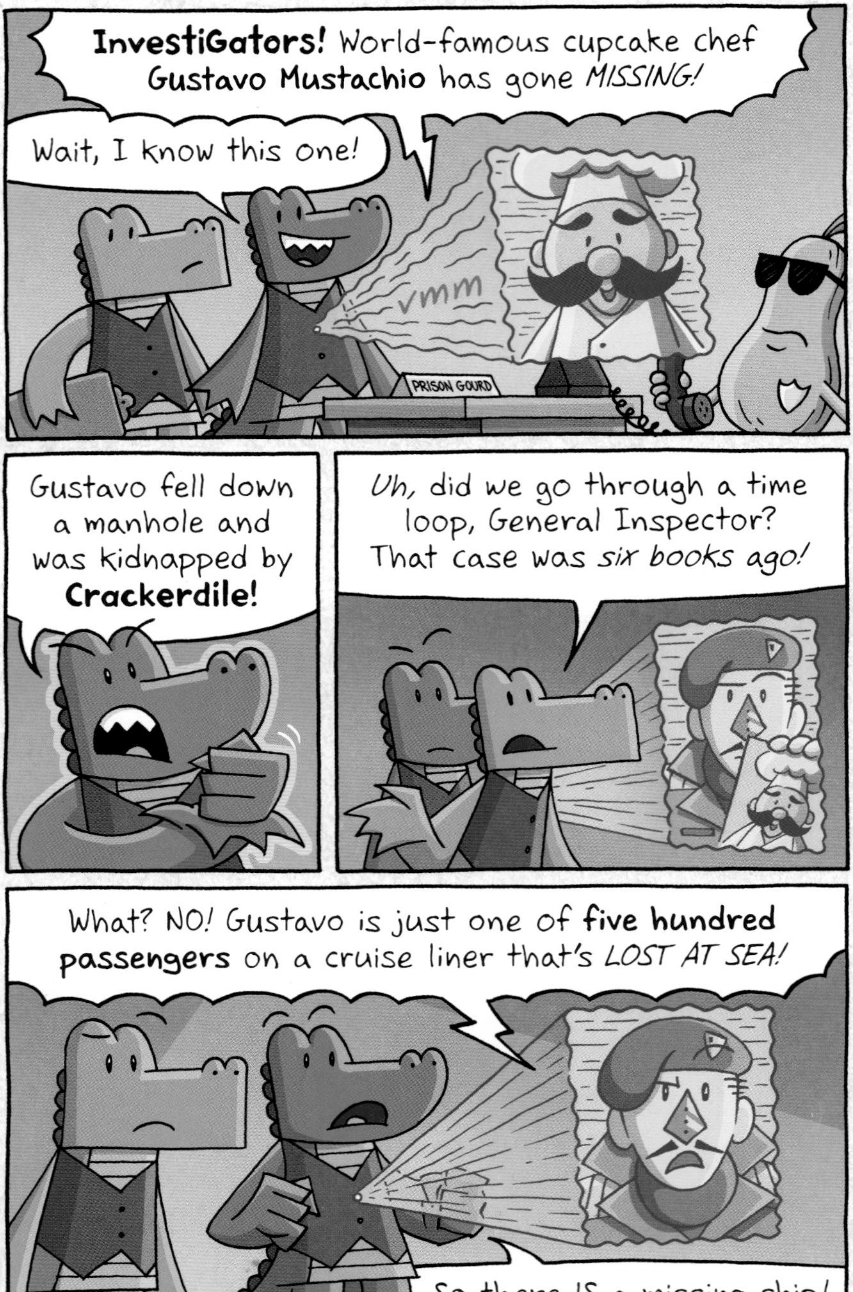
InvestiGators! World-famous cupcake chef **Gustavo Mustachio** has gone *MISSING!*
Wait, I know this one!
vmm
PRISON GOURD
Gustavo fell down a manhole and was kidnapped by **Crackerdile!**
Uh, did we go through a time loop, General Inspector? That case was *six books ago!*
What? NO! Gustavo is just one of **five hundred passengers** on a cruise liner that's *LOST AT SEA!*
So there IS a missing ship!

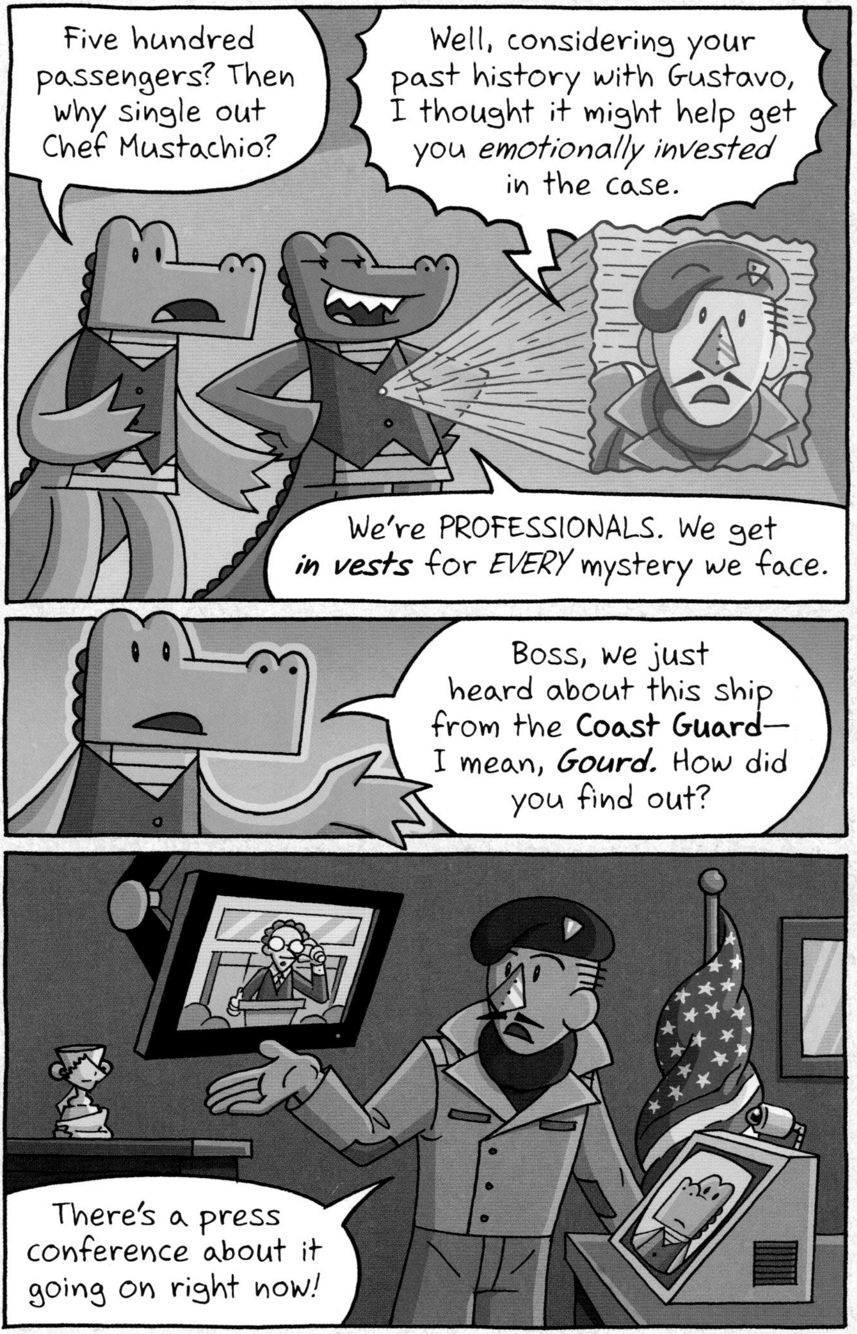
Five hundred passengers? Then why single out Chef Mustachio?
Well, considering your past history with Gustavo, I thought it might help get you *emotionally invested* in the case.
We're PROFESSIONALS. We get ***in vests*** for *EVERY* mystery we face.
Boss, we just heard about this ship from the **Coast Guard**— I mean, ***Gourd.*** How did you find out?
There's a press conference about it going on right now!

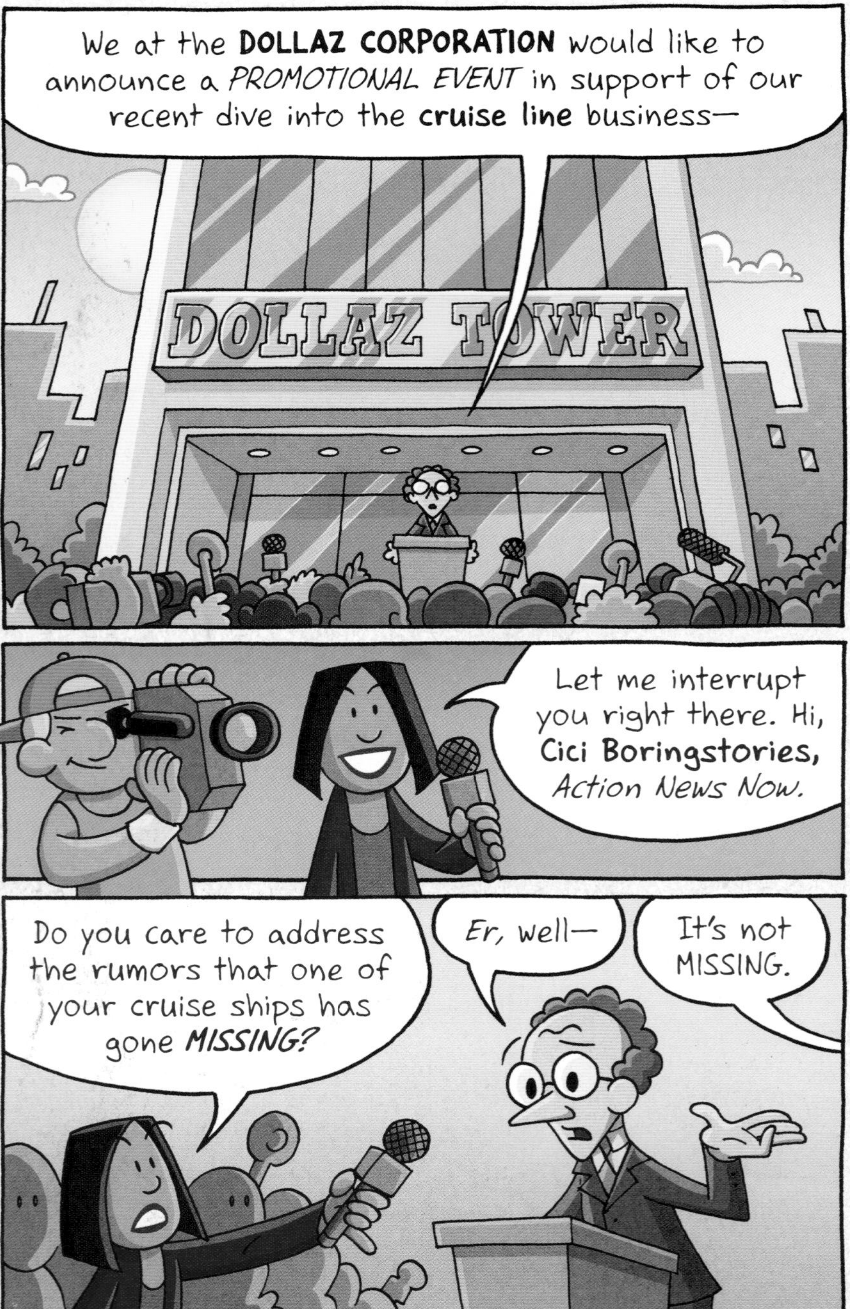
We at the **DOLLAZ CORPORATION** would like to announce a *PROMOTIONAL EVENT* in support of our recent dive into the **cruise line** business—
DOLLAZ TOWER
Let me interrupt you right there. Hi, **Cici Boringstories,** *Action News Now.*
Do you care to address the rumors that one of your cruise ships has gone ***MISSING?***
Er, well—
It's not MISSING.

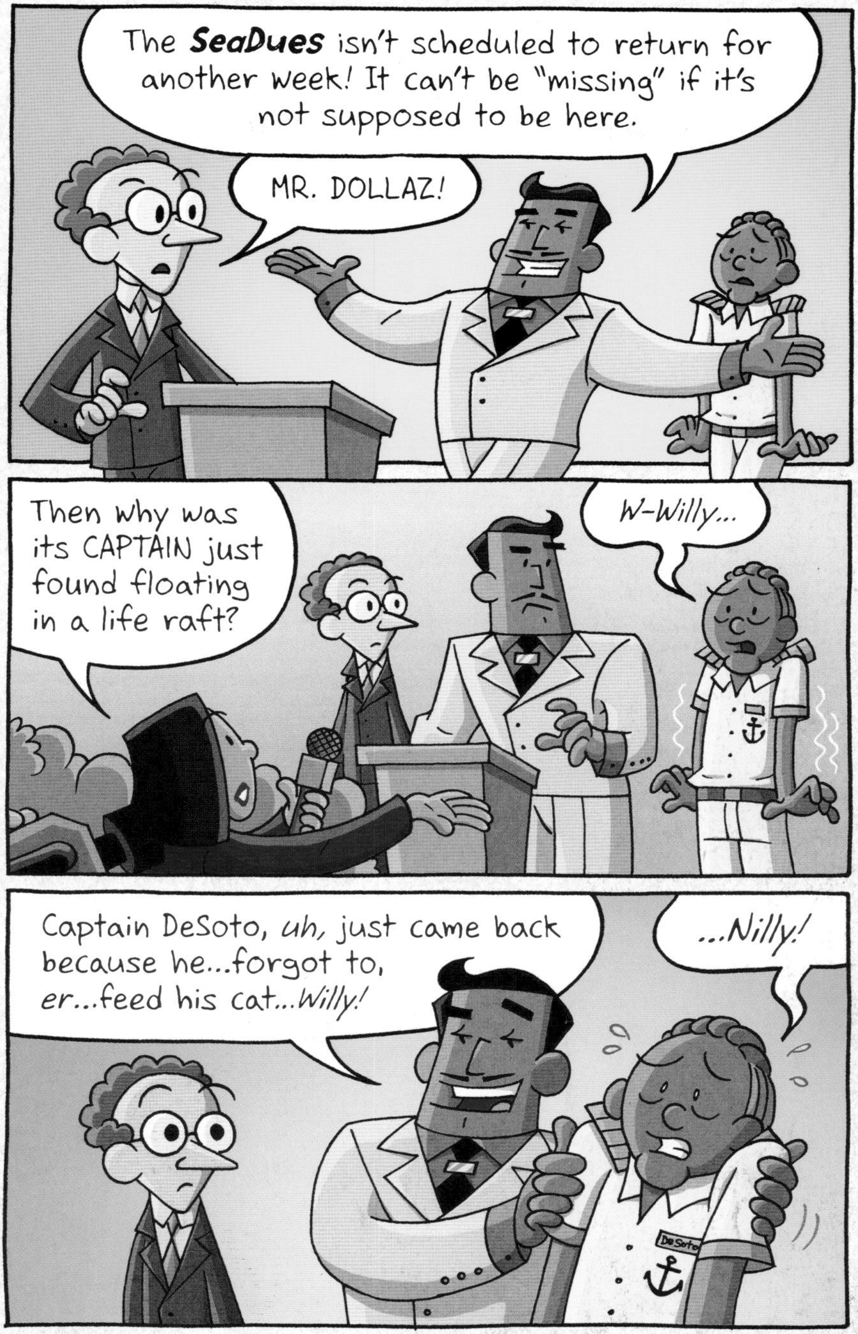
The **SeaDues** isn't scheduled to return for another week! It can't be "missing" if it's not supposed to be here.
MR. DOLLAZ!
Then why was its CAPTAIN just found floating in a life raft?
W-Willy...
Captain DeSoto, *uh,* just came back because he...forgot to, er...feed his cat...*Willy!*
...Nilly!
DeSoto

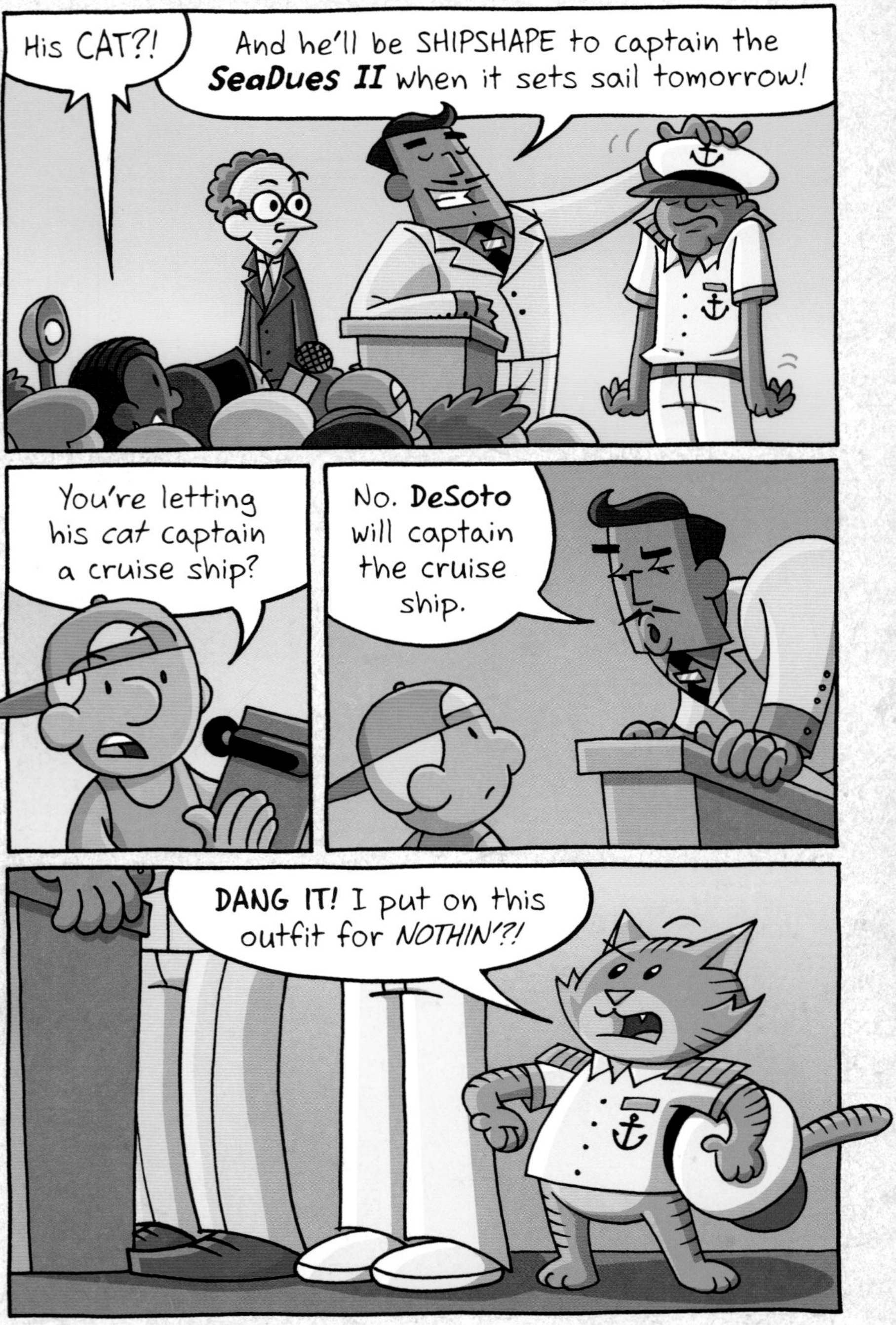
His CAT?!
And he'll be SHIPSHAPE to captain the **SeaDues II** when it sets sail tomorrow!
You're letting his *cat* captain a cruise ship?
No. **DeSoto** will captain the cruise ship.
DANG IT! I put on this outfit for *NOTHIN'?!*

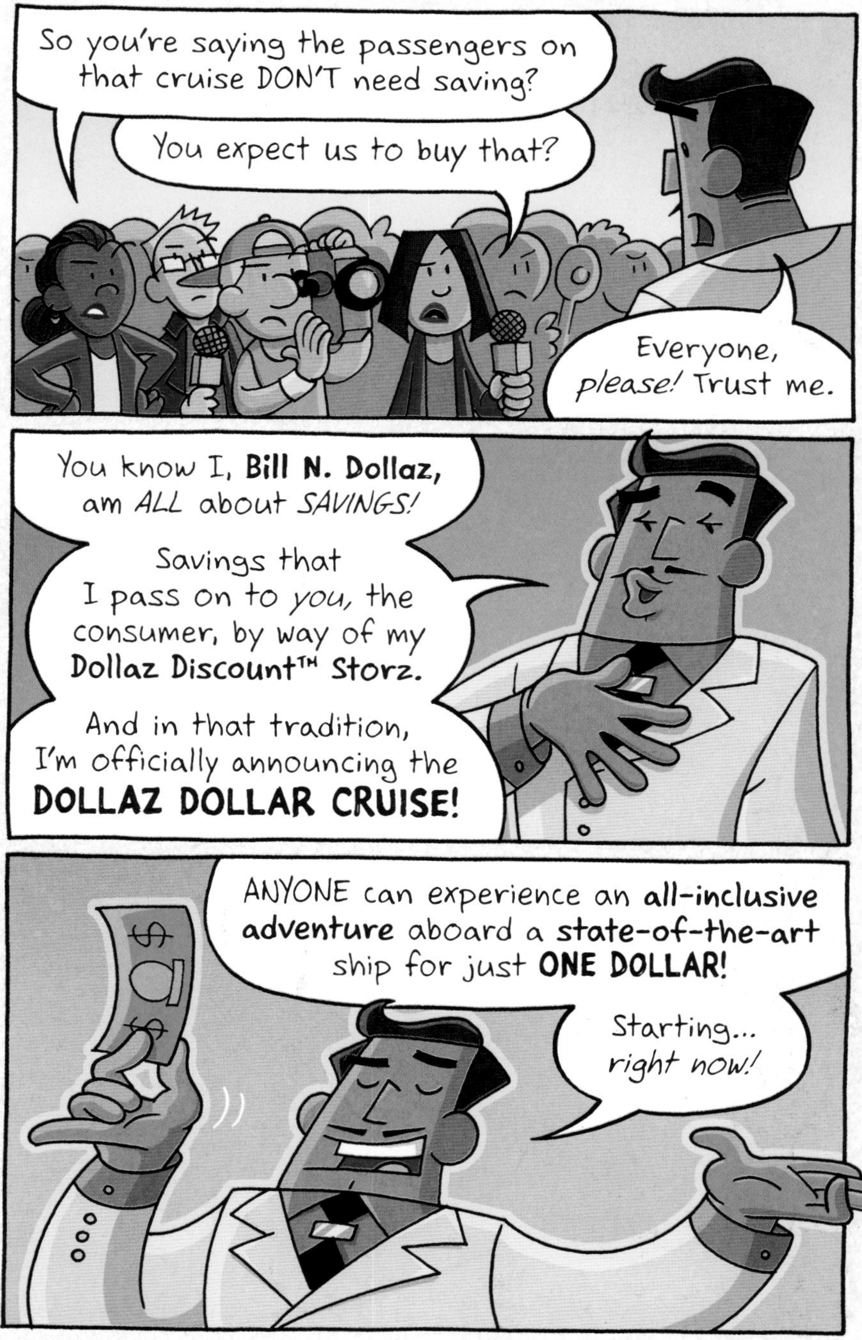
So you're saying the passengers on that cruise DON'T need saving?
You expect us to buy that?
Everyone, *please!* Trust me.
You know I, **Bill N. Dollaz,** am *ALL* about *SAVINGS!*
Savings that I pass on to *you,* the consumer, by way of my **Dollaz Discount™ Storz.**
And in that tradition, I'm officially announcing the **DOLLAZ DOLLAR CRUISE!**
ANYONE can experience an **all-inclusive adventure** aboard a **state-of-the-art** ship for just **ONE DOLLAR!**
Starting... *right now!*

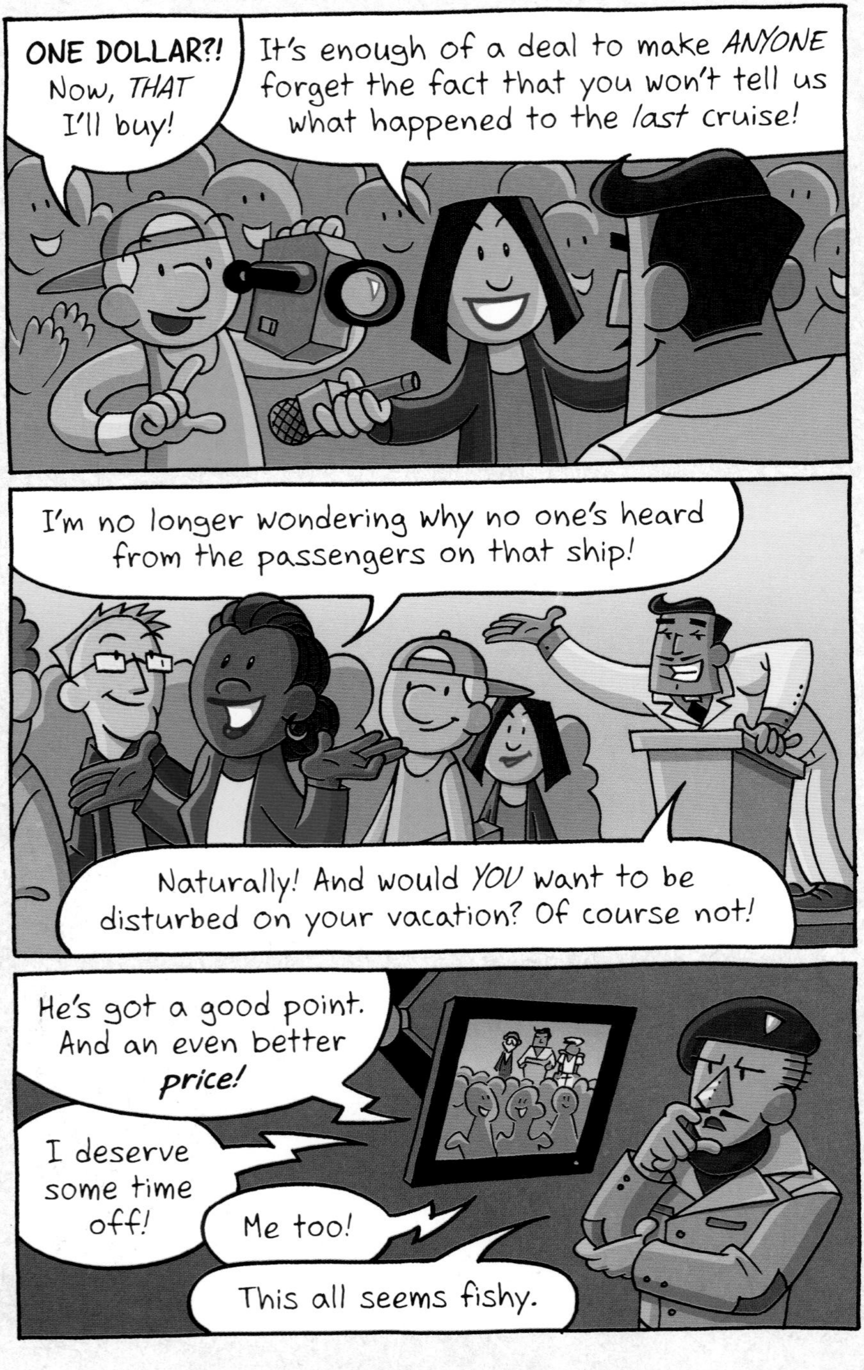
ONE DOLLAR?! Now, *THAT* I'll buy!
It's enough of a deal to make *ANYONE* forget the fact that you won't tell us what happened to the *last* cruise!
I'm no longer wondering why no one's heard from the passengers on that ship!
Naturally! And would *YOU* want to be disturbed on your vacation? Of course not!
He's got a good point. And an even better ***price!***
I deserve some time off!
Me too!
This all seems fishy.

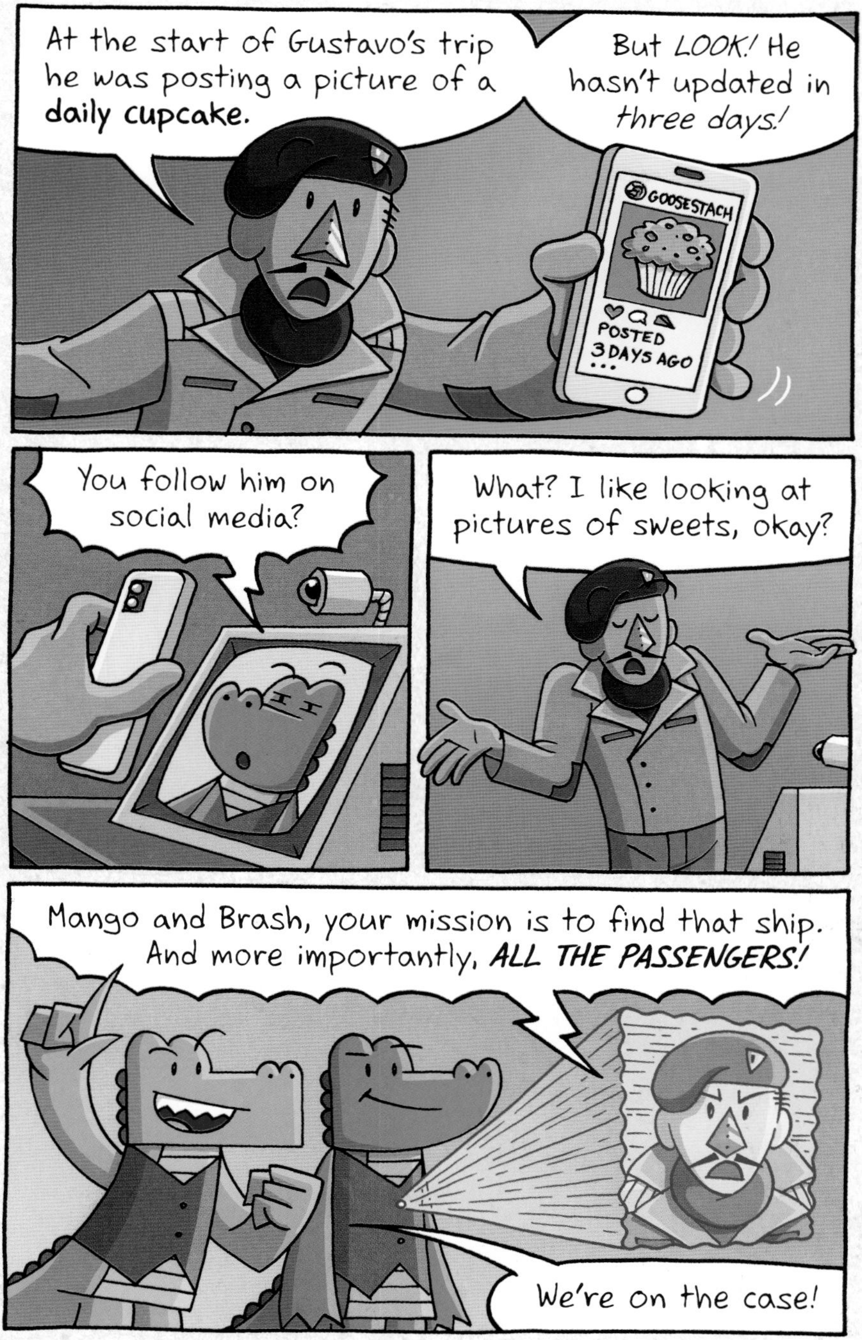
At the start of Gustavo's trip he was posting a picture of a **daily cupcake.**
But *LOOK!* He hasn't updated in *three days!*
GOOSESTACH
POSTED
3 DAYS AGO
You follow him on social media?
What? I like looking at pictures of sweets, okay?
Mango and Brash, your mission is to find that ship. And more importantly, ***ALL THE PASSENGERS!***
We're on the case!

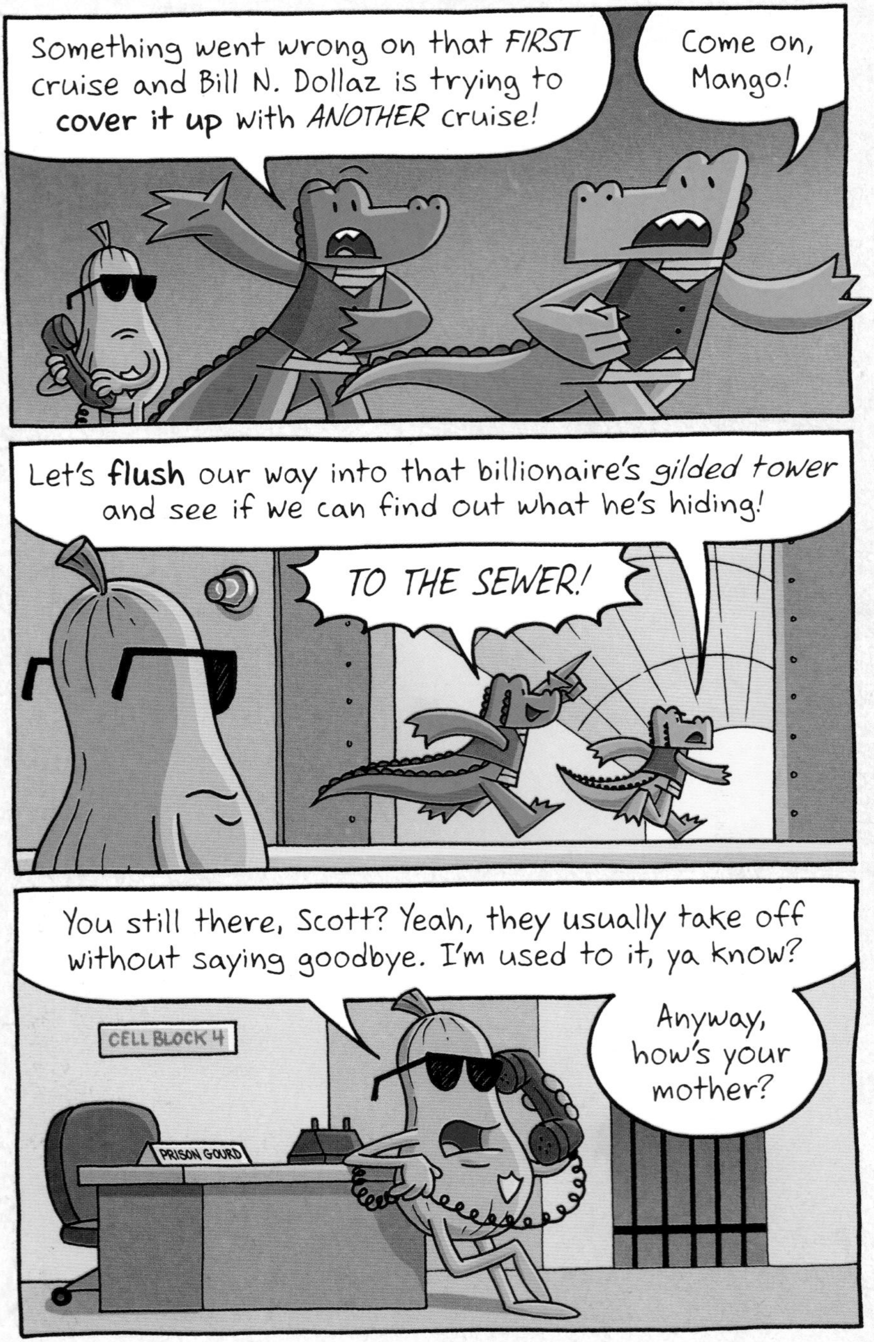
Something went wrong on that *FIRST* cruise and Bill N. Dollaz is trying to **cover it up** with *ANOTHER* cruise!
Come on, Mango!
Let's **flush** our way into that billionaire's *gilded tower* and see if we can find out what he's hiding!
TO THE SEWER!
You still there, Scott? Yeah, they usually take off without saying goodbye. I'm used to it, ya know?
CELL BLOCK 4
Anyway, how's your mother?
PRISON GOURD

Chapter 2

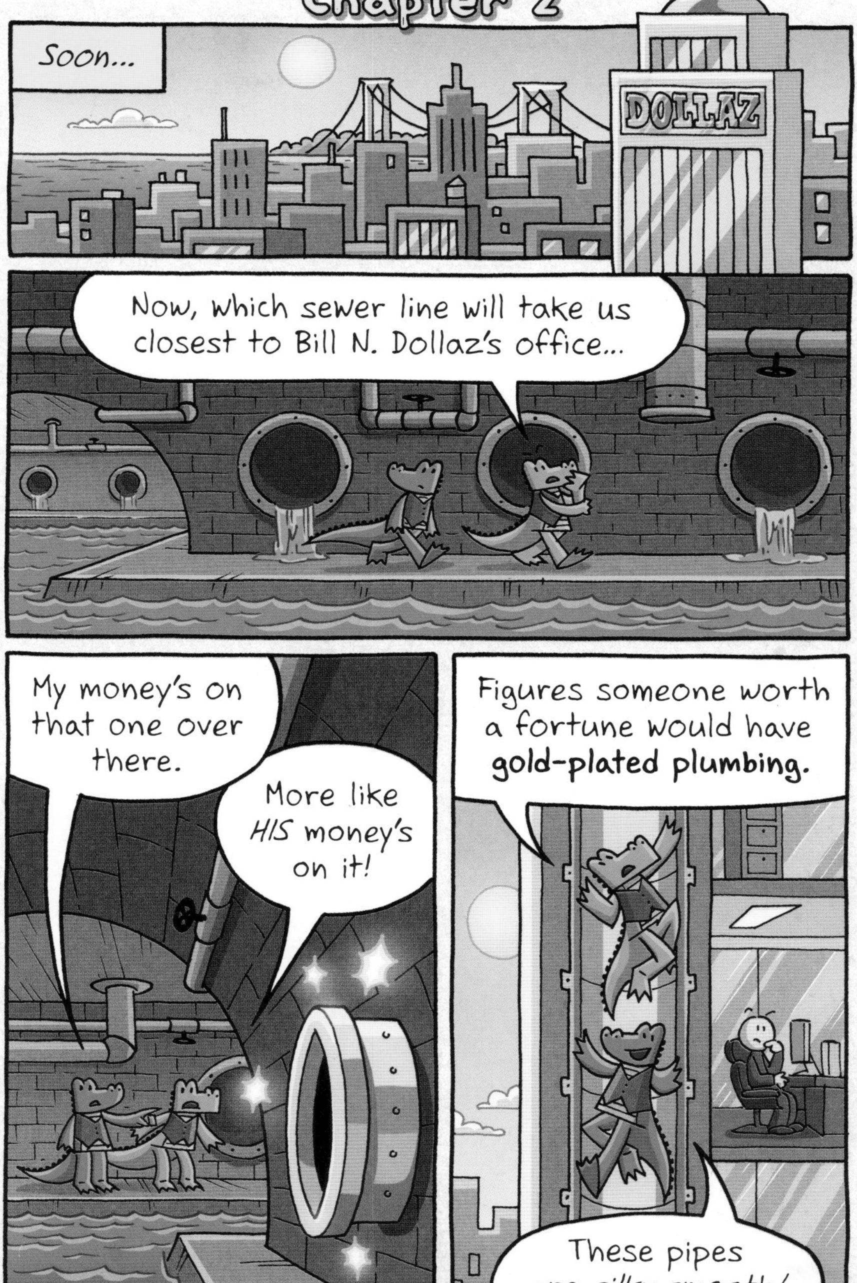

Soon...
DOLLAZ
Now, which sewer line will take us closest to Bill N. Dollaz's office...
My money's on that one over there.
More like *HIS* money's on it!
Figures someone worth a fortune would have **gold-plated plumbing.**
These pipes are *silky smooth!*

Wow, that was *nice.* A gator could get used to traveling in style like this.

No one's here. Good!

There's gotta be details about the first cruise somewhere.

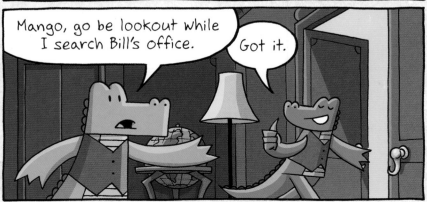

Mango, go be lookout while I search Bill's office.

Got it.

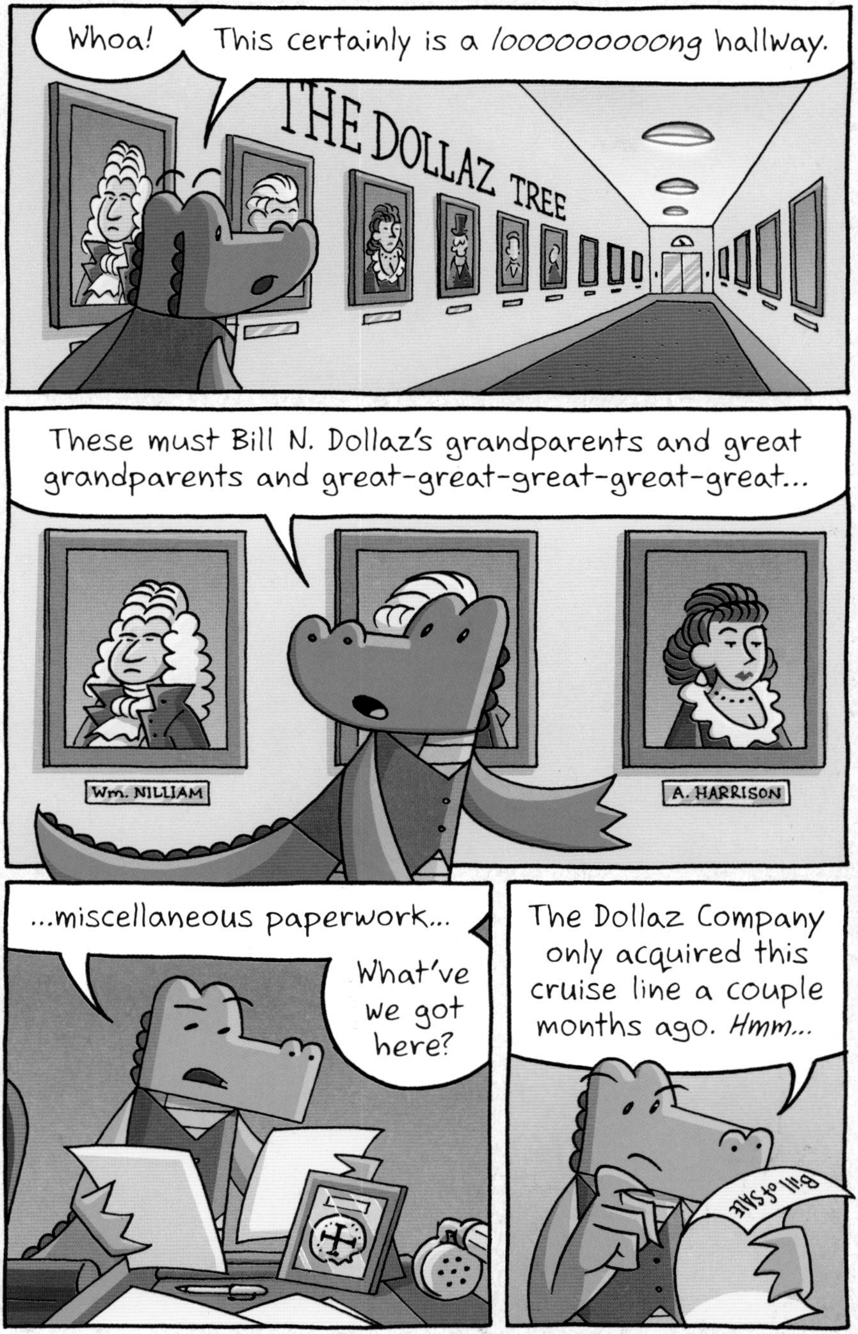
Whoa!
This certainly is a *looooooooong* hallway.
THE DOLLAZ TREE
These must Bill N. Dollaz's grandparents and great grandparents and great-great-great-great-great...
Wm. NILLIAM
A. HARRISON
...miscellaneous paperwork...
What've we got here?
The Dollaz Company only acquired this cruise line a couple months ago. *Hmm...*
Bill of SALE

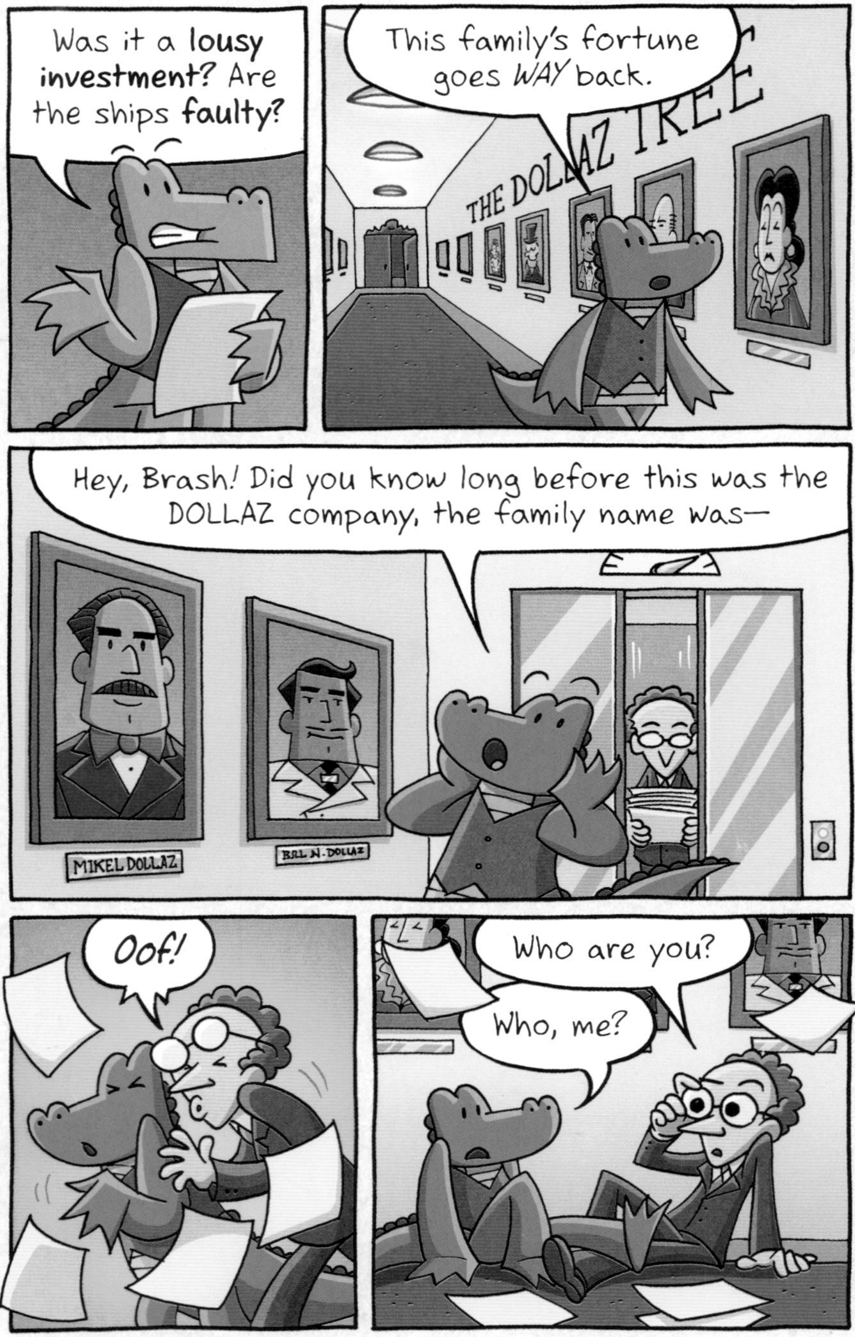
Was it a **lousy investment?** Are the ships **faulty?**
This family's fortune goes *WAY* back.
THE DOLLAZ TREE
Hey, Brash! Did you know long before this was the DOLLAZ company, the family name was—
MIKEL DOLLAZ
BILL N. DOLLAZ
Oof!
Who are you?
Who, me?

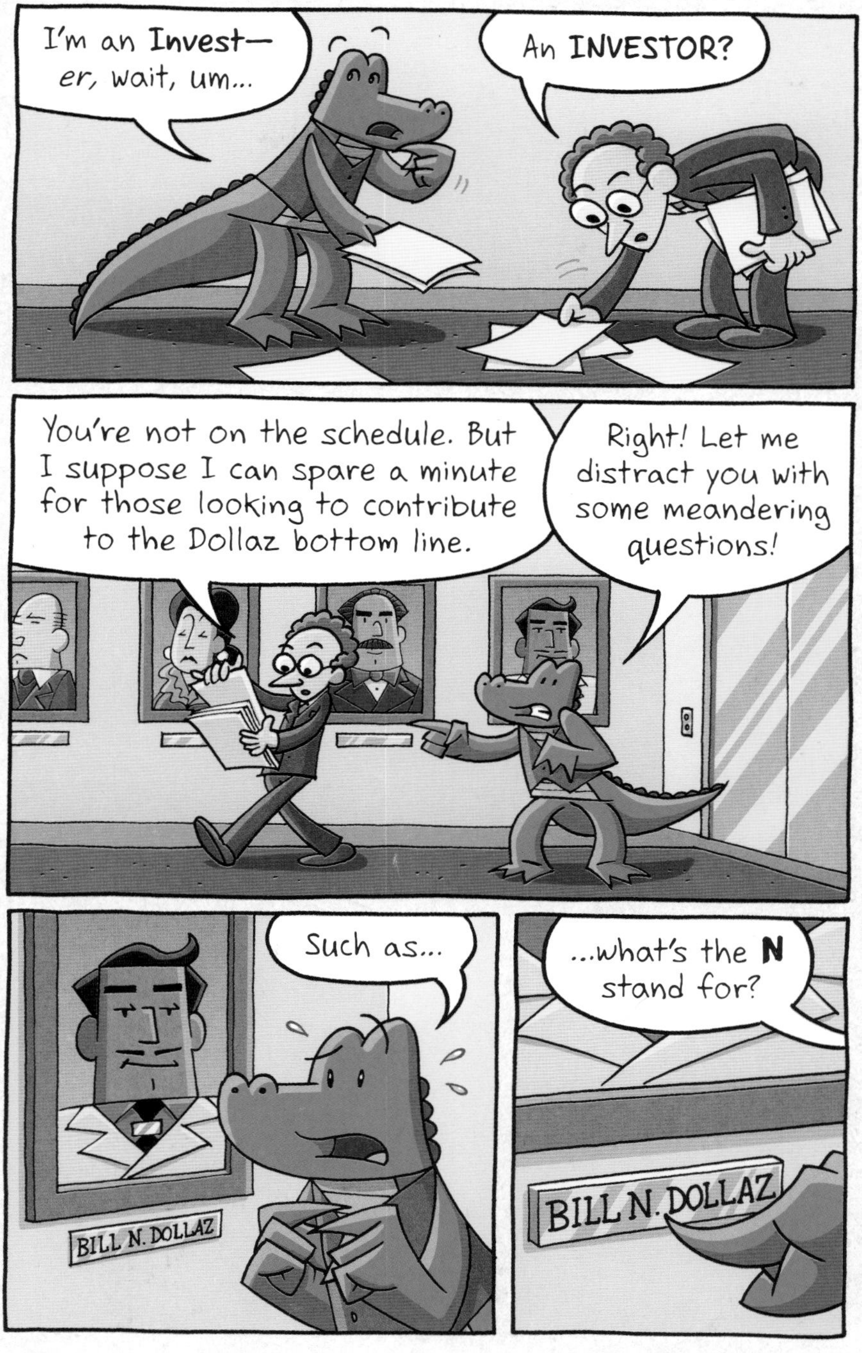
I'm an **Invest—** er, wait, um...
An **INVESTOR?**
You're not on the schedule. But I suppose I can spare a minute for those looking to contribute to the Dollaz bottom line.
Right! Let me distract you with some meandering questions!
BILL N. DOLLAZ
Such as...
...what's the **N** stand for?
BILL N. DOLLAZ

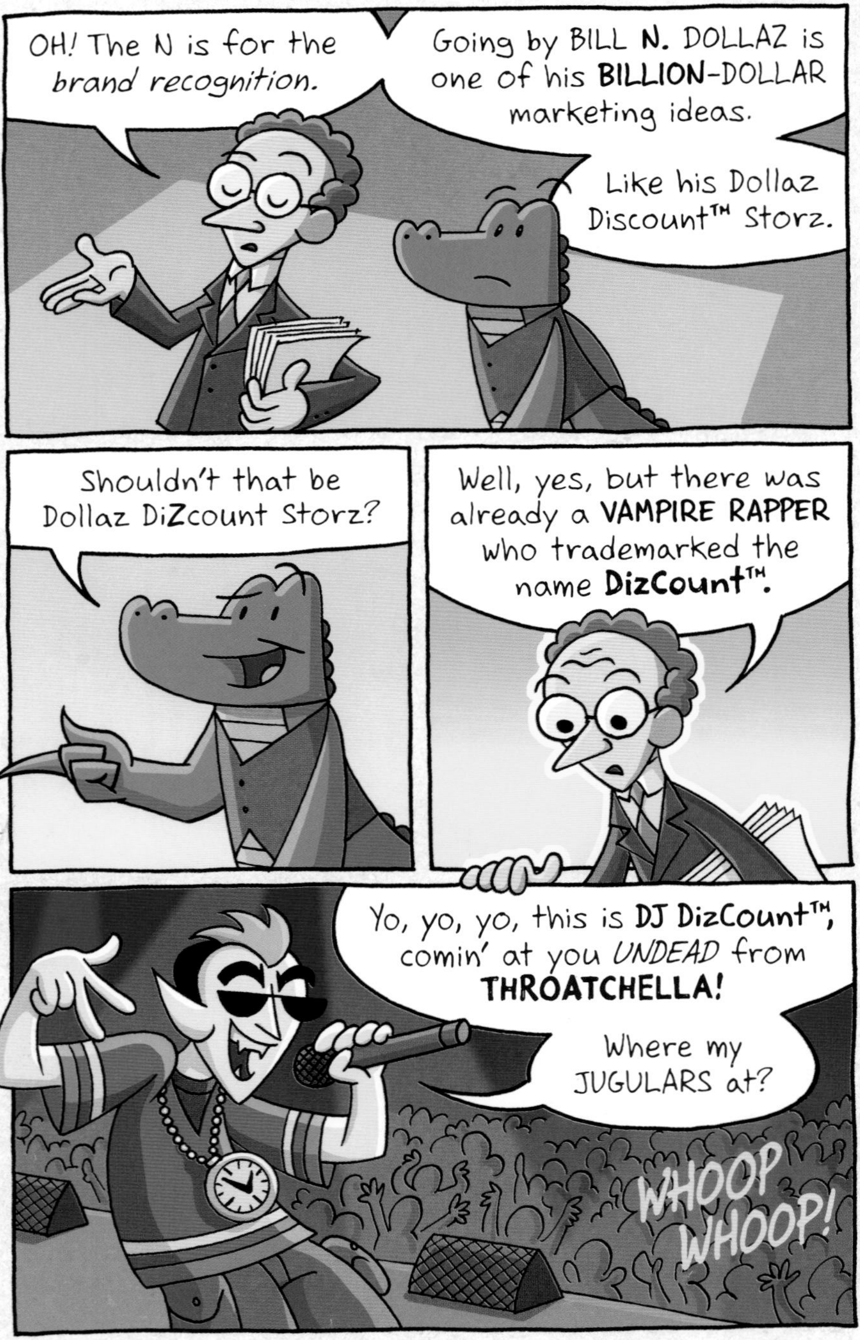
OH! The N is for the *brand recognition.*
Going by BILL **N.** DOLLAZ is one of his **BILLION**-DOLLAR marketing ideas.
Like his Dollaz Discount™ Storz.
Shouldn't that be Dollaz DiZcount Storz?
Well, yes, but there was already a **VAMPIRE RAPPER** who trademarked the name **DizCount™.**
Yo, yo, yo, this is **DJ DizCount™,** comin' at you *UNDEAD* from **THROATCHELLA!**
Where my JUGULARS at?
WHOOP WHOOP!

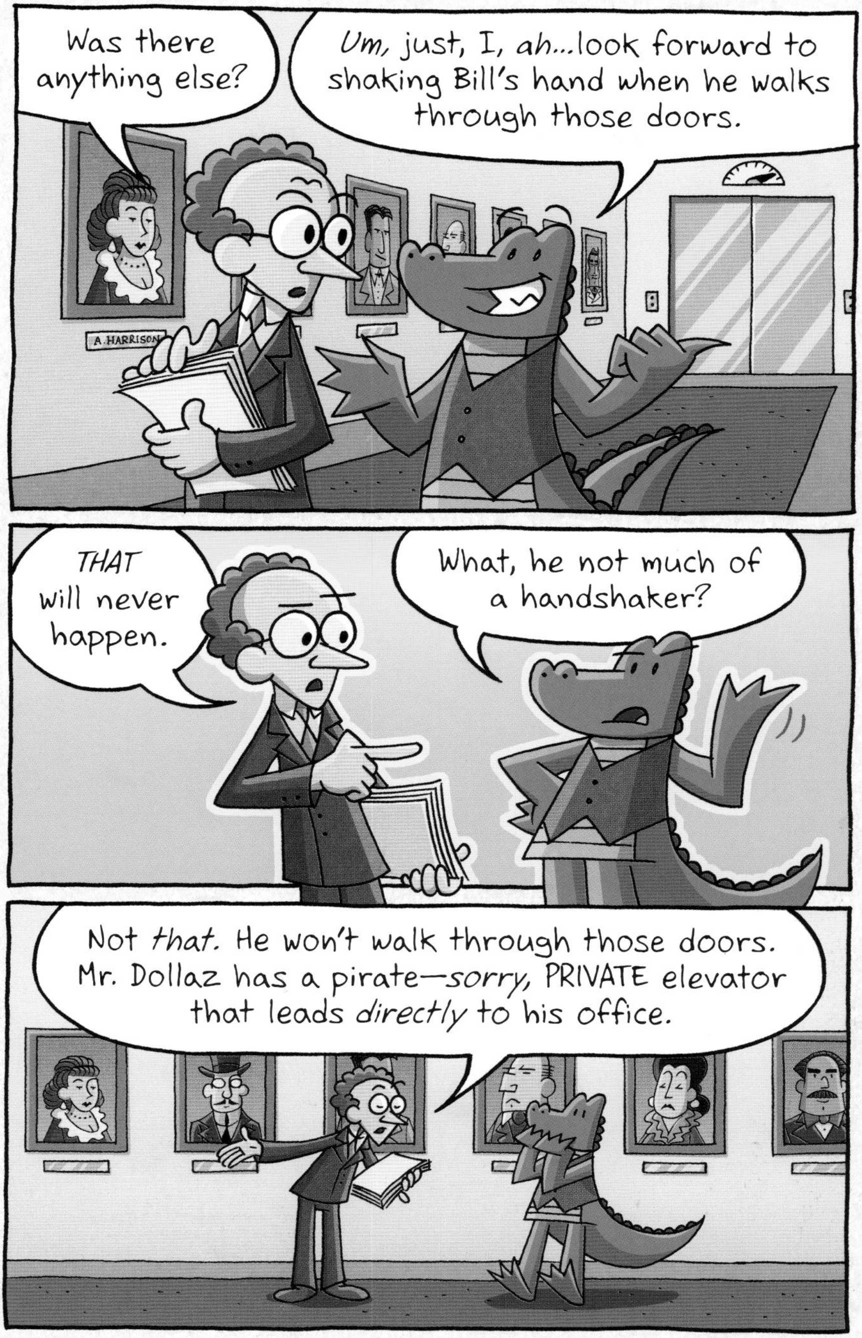
Was there anything else?
Um, just, I, *ah*...look forward to shaking Bill's hand when he walks through those doors.
A. HARRISON
THAT will never happen.
What, he not much of a handshaker?
Not *that.* He won't walk through those doors. Mr. Dollaz has a pirate—*sorry,* PRIVATE elevator that leads *directly* to his office.

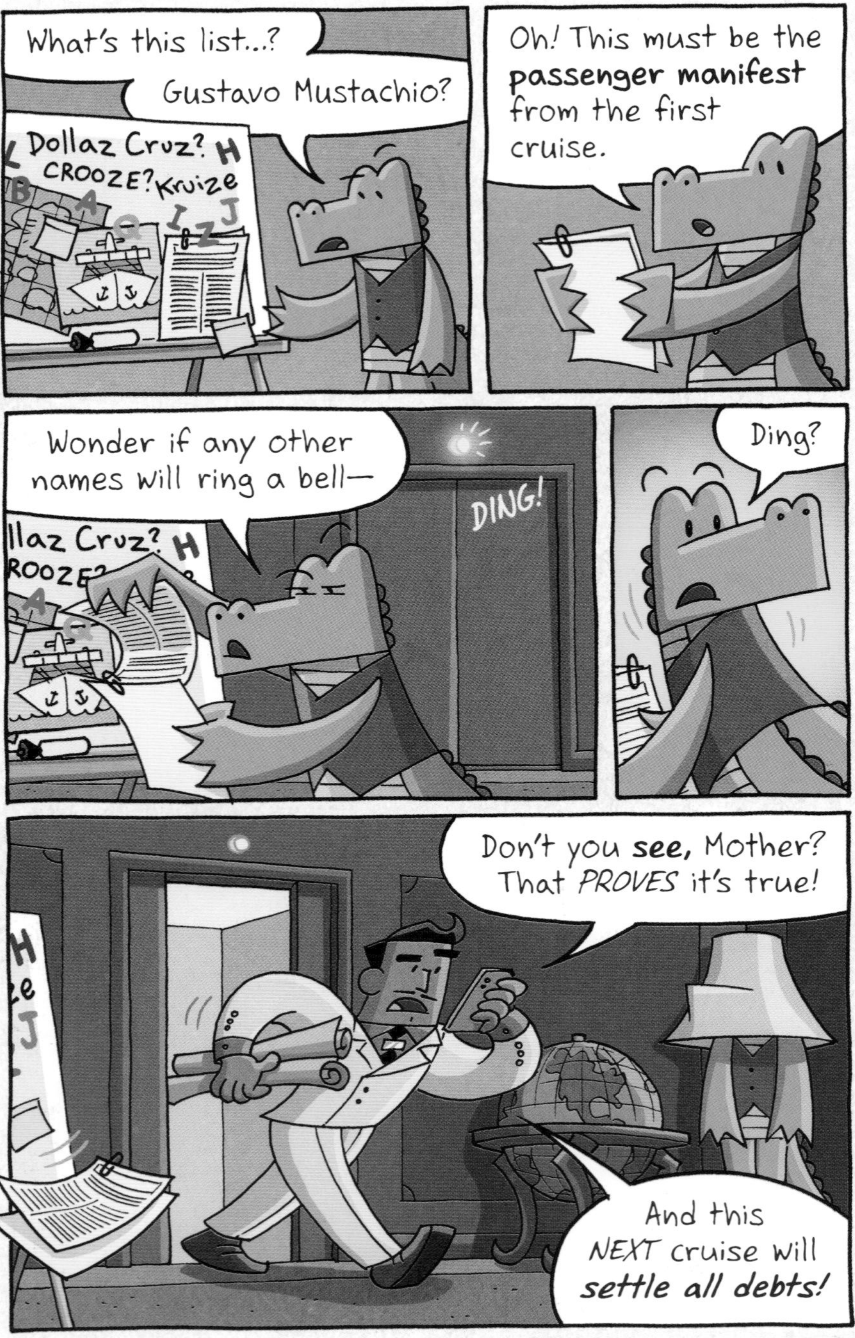
What's this list...?
Gustavo Mustachio?
Dollaz Cruz? CROOZE? Kruize
Oh! This must be the **passenger manifest** from the first cruise.
Wonder if any other names will ring a bell—
DING!
Ding?
Don't you **see,** Mother? That *PROVES* it's true!
And this *NEXT* cruise will ***settle all debts!***

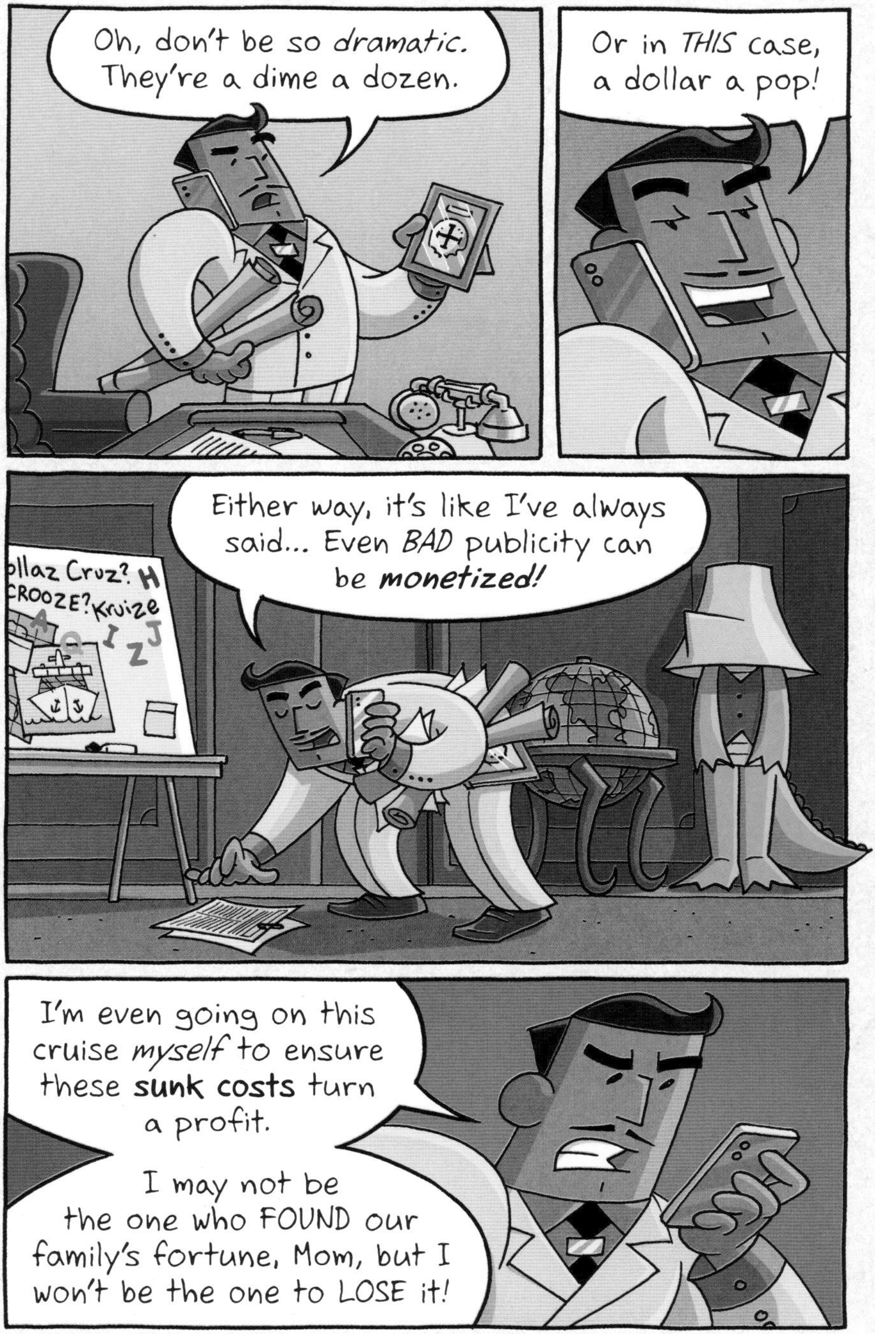
Oh, don't be so *dramatic.* They're a dime a dozen.
Or in *THIS* case, a dollar a pop!
Either way, it's like I've always said... Even *BAD* publicity can be ***monetized!***
llaz Cruz? H
CROOZE? Kruize
I'm even going on this cruise *myself* to ensure these **sunk costs** turn a profit.
I may not be the one who FOUND our family's fortune, Mom, but I won't be the one to LOSE it!

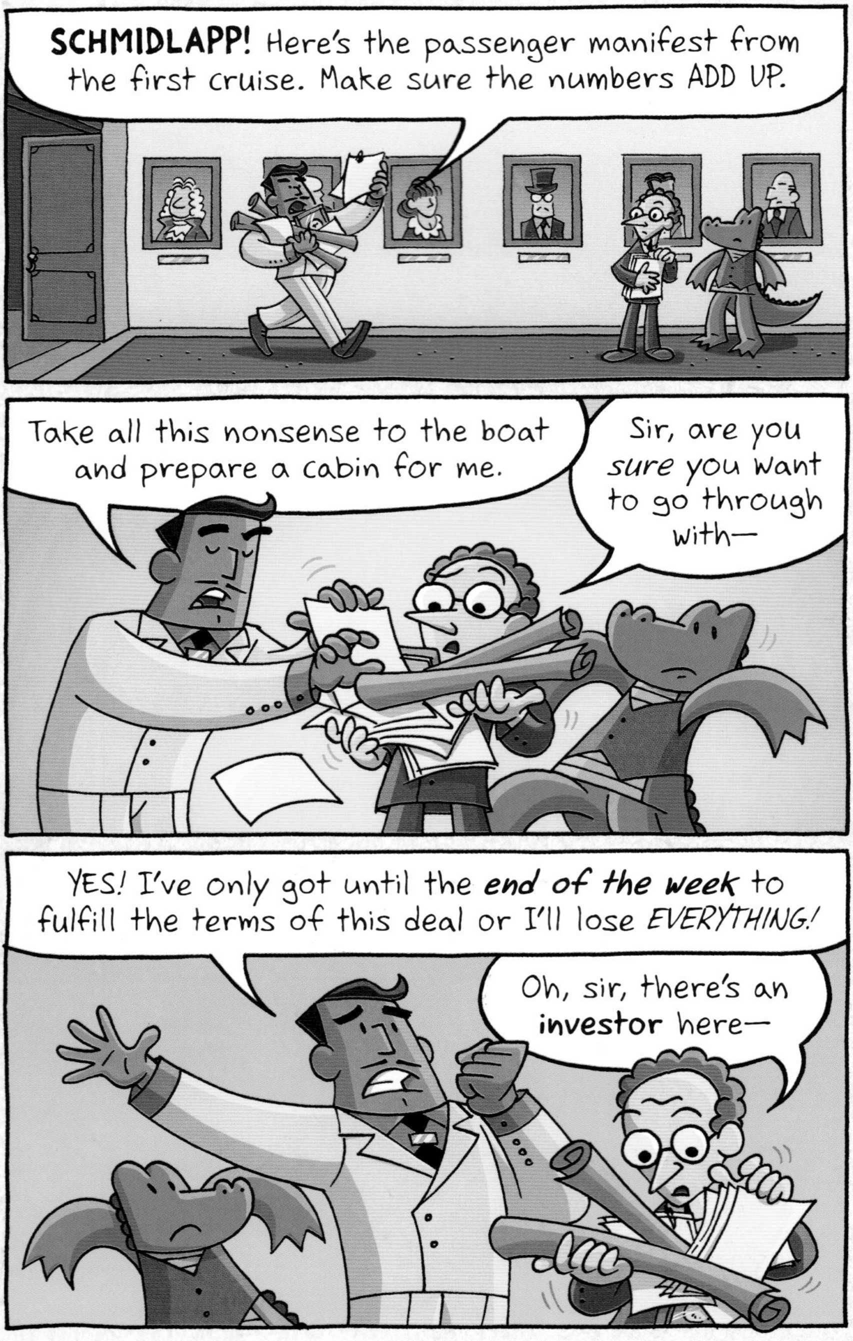
SCHMIDLAPP! Here's the passenger manifest from the first cruise. Make sure the numbers ADD UP.
Take all this nonsense to the boat and prepare a cabin for me.
Sir, are you *sure* you want to go through with—
YES! I've only got until the ***end of the week*** to fulfill the terms of this deal or I'll lose *EVERYTHING!*
Oh, sir, there's an **investor** here—

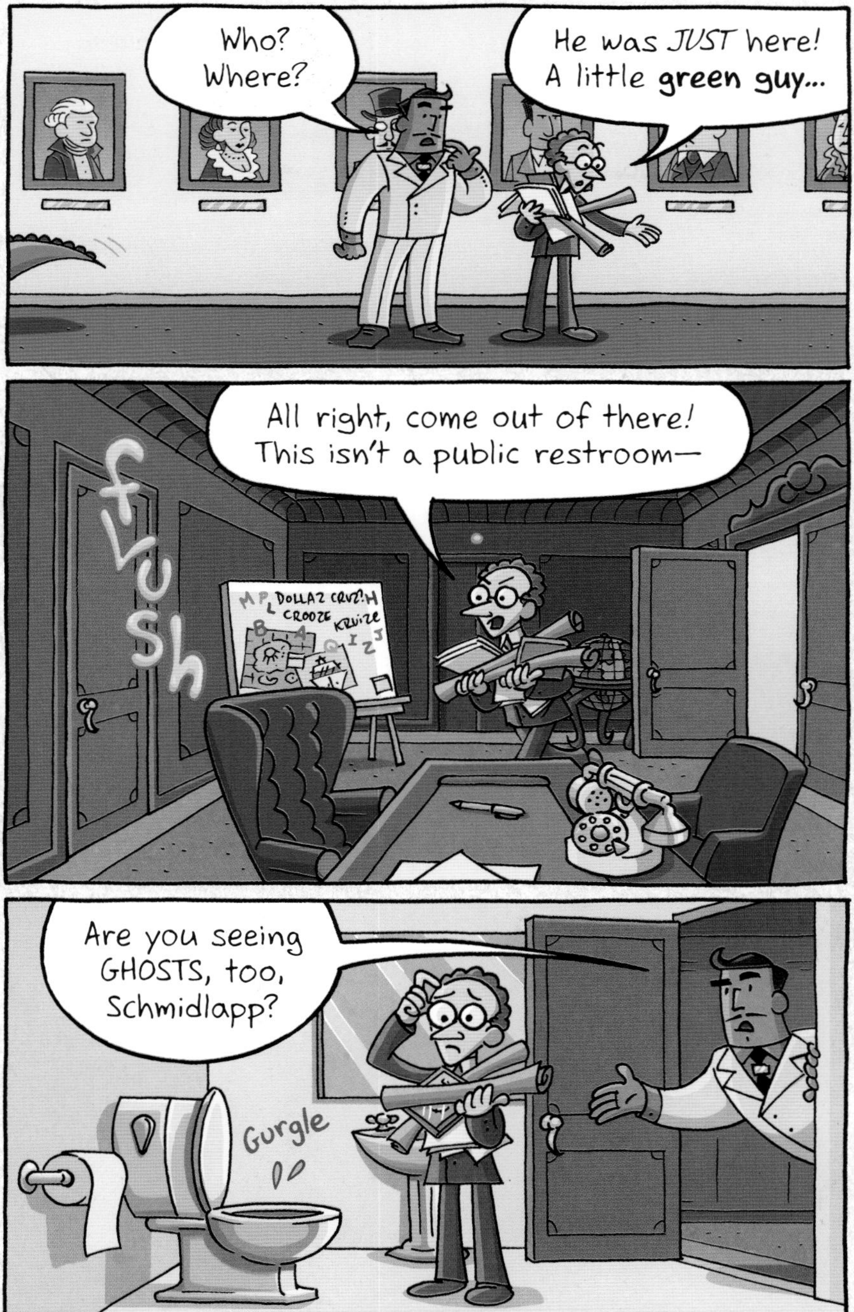
Who? Where?
He was JUST here! A little **green guy...**
flush
All right, come out of there! This isn't a public restroom—
DOLLAZ CRUZ!
CROOZE
KRUIZE
Are you seeing GHOSTS, too, Schmidlapp?
Gurgle

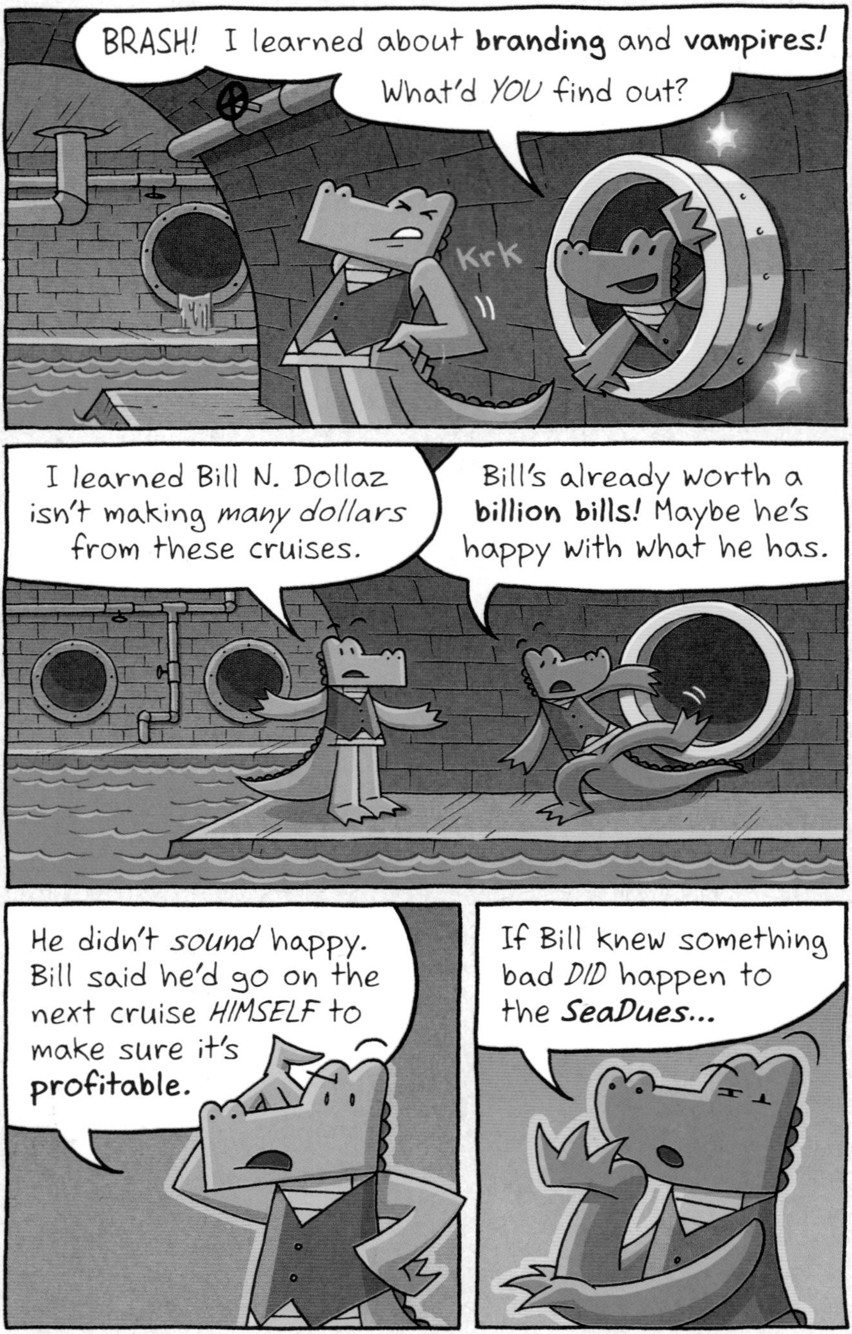
BRASH! I learned about **branding** and **vampires!** What'd *YOU* find out?
KrK
I learned Bill N. Dollaz isn't making *many dollars* from these cruises.
Bill's already worth a **billion bills!** Maybe he's happy with what he has.
He didn't *sound* happy. Bill said he'd go on the next cruise *HIMSELF* to make sure it's **profitable.**
If Bill knew something bad *DID* happen to the ***SeaDues...***

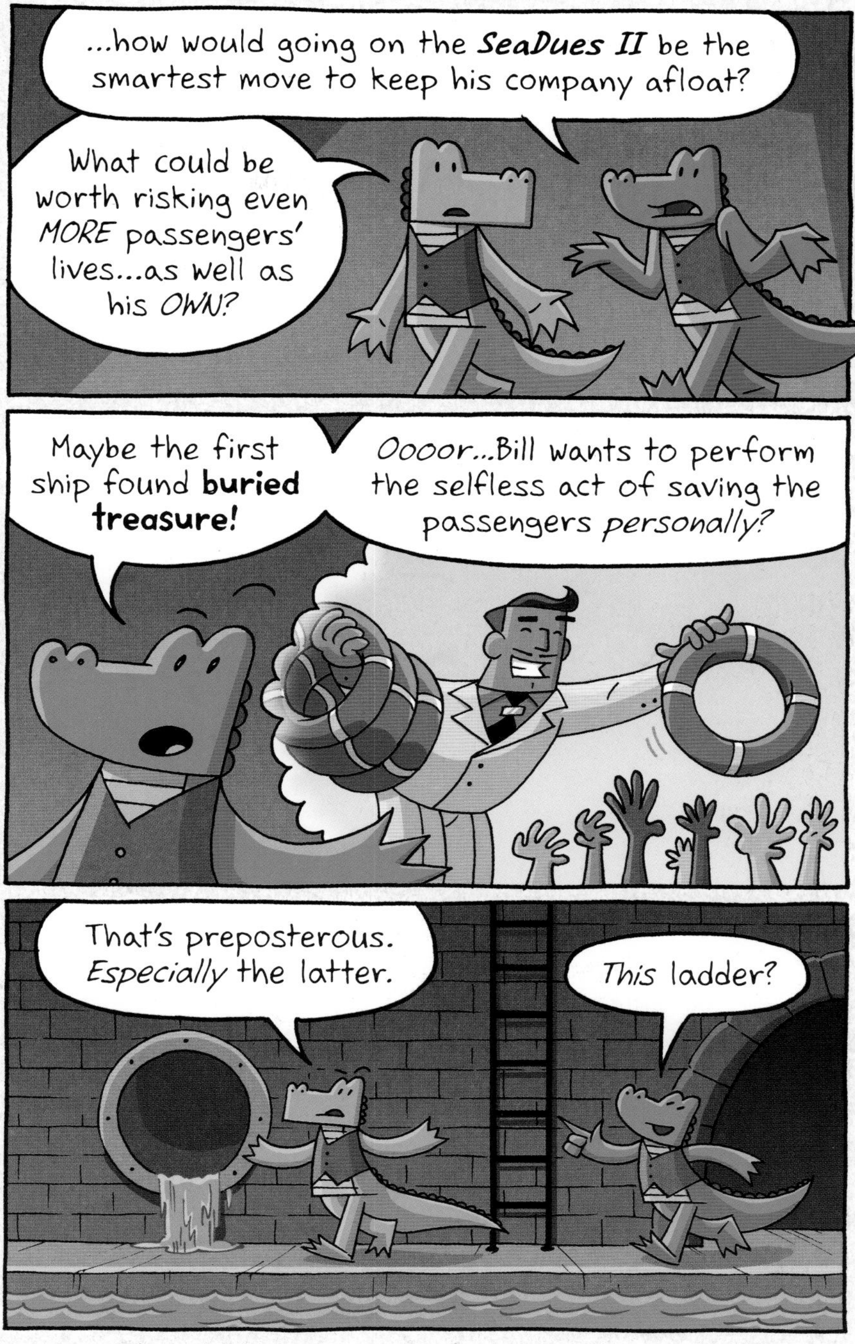
...how would going on the ***SeaDues II*** be the smartest move to keep his company afloat?
What could be worth risking even *MORE* passengers' lives...as well as his *OWN*?
Maybe the first ship found **buried treasure!**
Oooor...Bill wants to perform the selfless act of saving the passengers *personally*?
That's preposterous. *Especially* the latter.
This ladder?

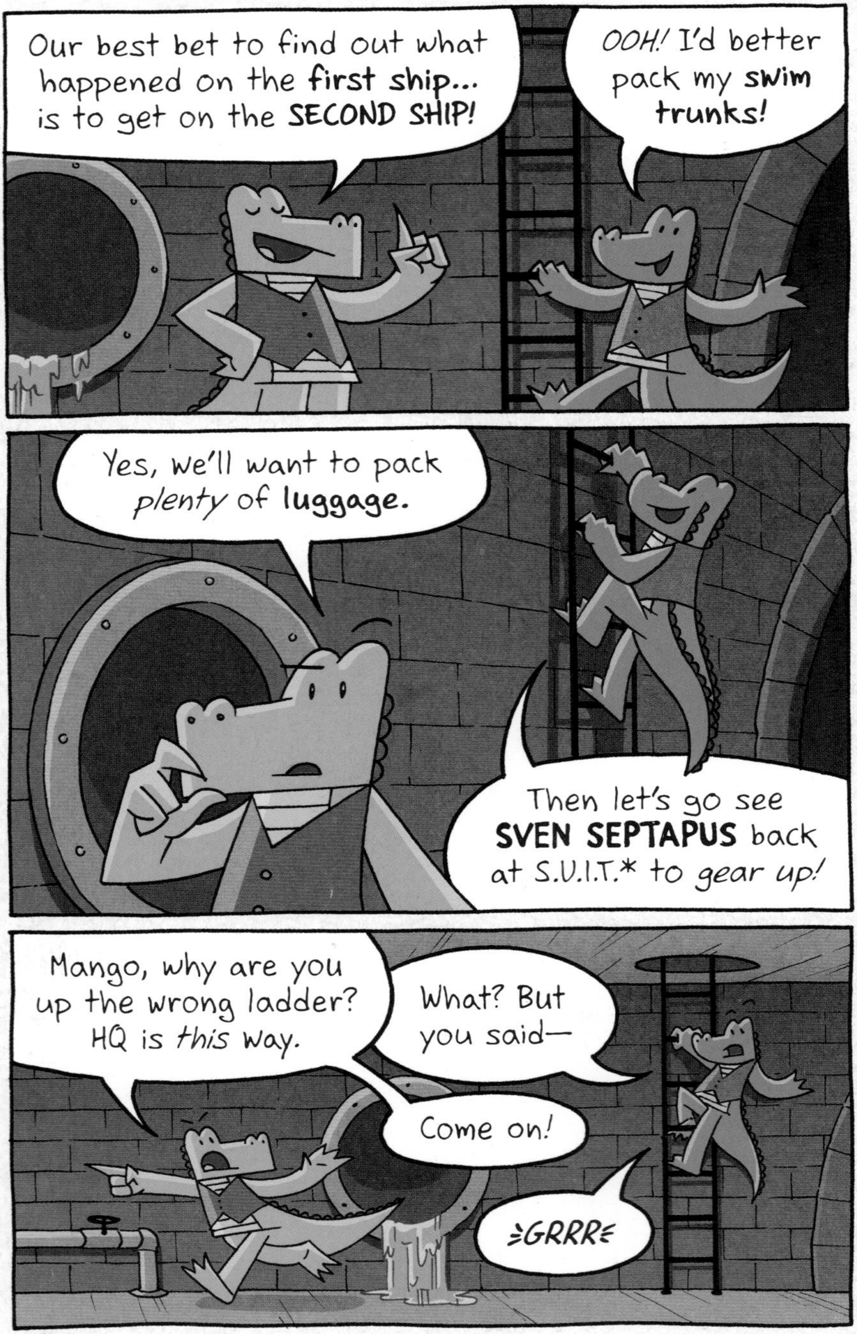
Our best bet to find out what happened on the first ship... is to get on the SECOND SHIP!
OOH! I'd better pack my swim trunks!
Yes, we'll want to pack plenty of luggage.
Then let's go see SVEN SEPTAPUS back at S.U.I.T.* to gear up!
Mango, why are you up the wrong ladder? HQ is this way.
What? But you said—
Come on!
GRRR

*Special Undercover Investigation Teams

Chapter 3

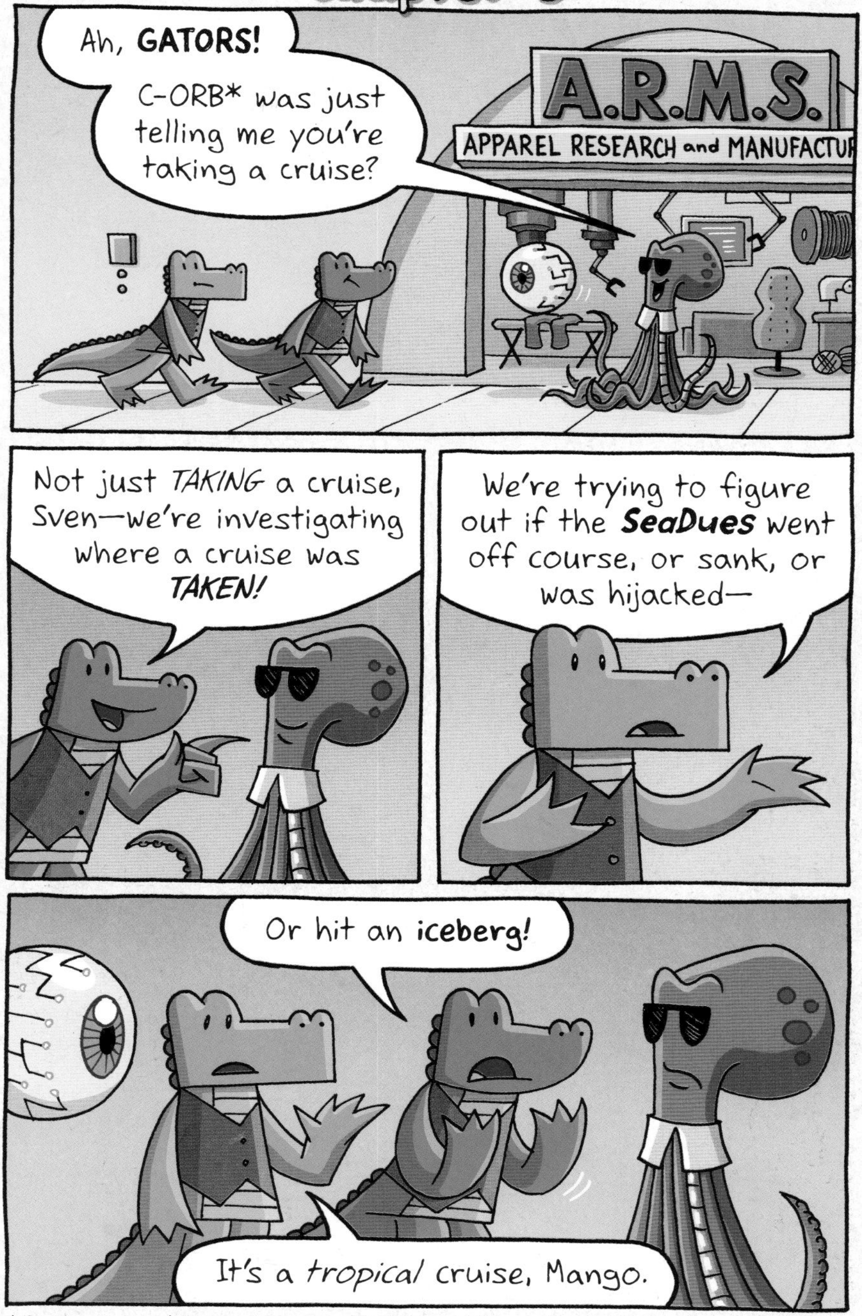
Ah, **GATORS!**
C-ORB* was just telling me you're taking a cruise?
A.R.M.S.
APPAREL RESEARCH and MANUFACTUR
Not just *TAKING* a cruise, Sven—we're investigating where a cruise was *TAKEN!*
We're trying to figure out if the ***SeaDues*** went off course, or sank, or was hijacked—
Or hit an **iceberg!**
It's a *tropical* cruise, Mango.

*Computerized Ocular Remote Butler

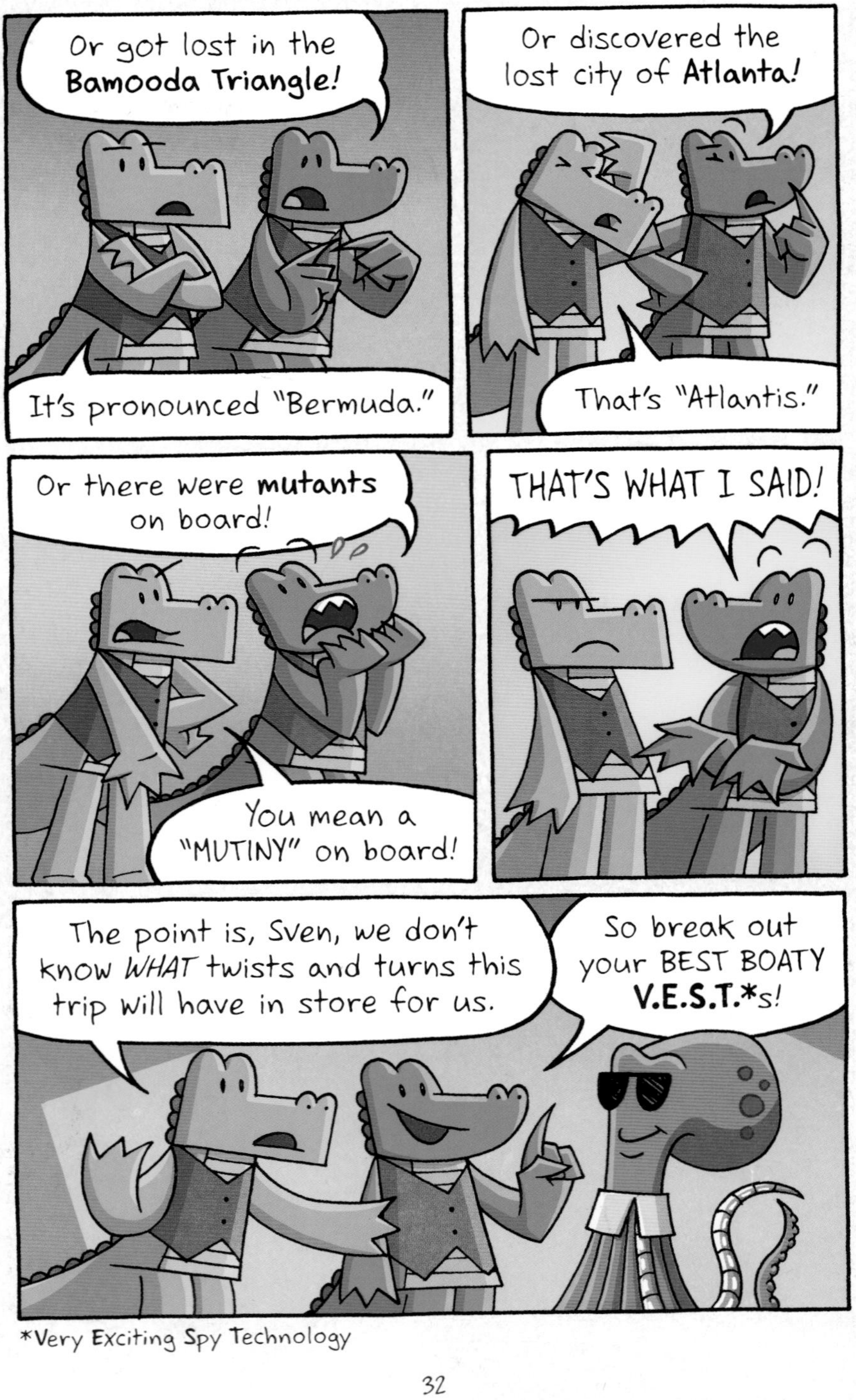
Or got lost in the Bamooda Triangle!
It's pronounced "Bermuda."
Or discovered the lost city of Atlanta!
That's "Atlantis."
Or there were mutants on board!
You mean a "MUTINY" on board!
THAT'S WHAT I SAID!
The point is, Sven, we don't know WHAT twists and turns this trip will have in store for us.
So break out your BEST BOATY V.E.S.T.*s!

*Very Exciting Spy Technology

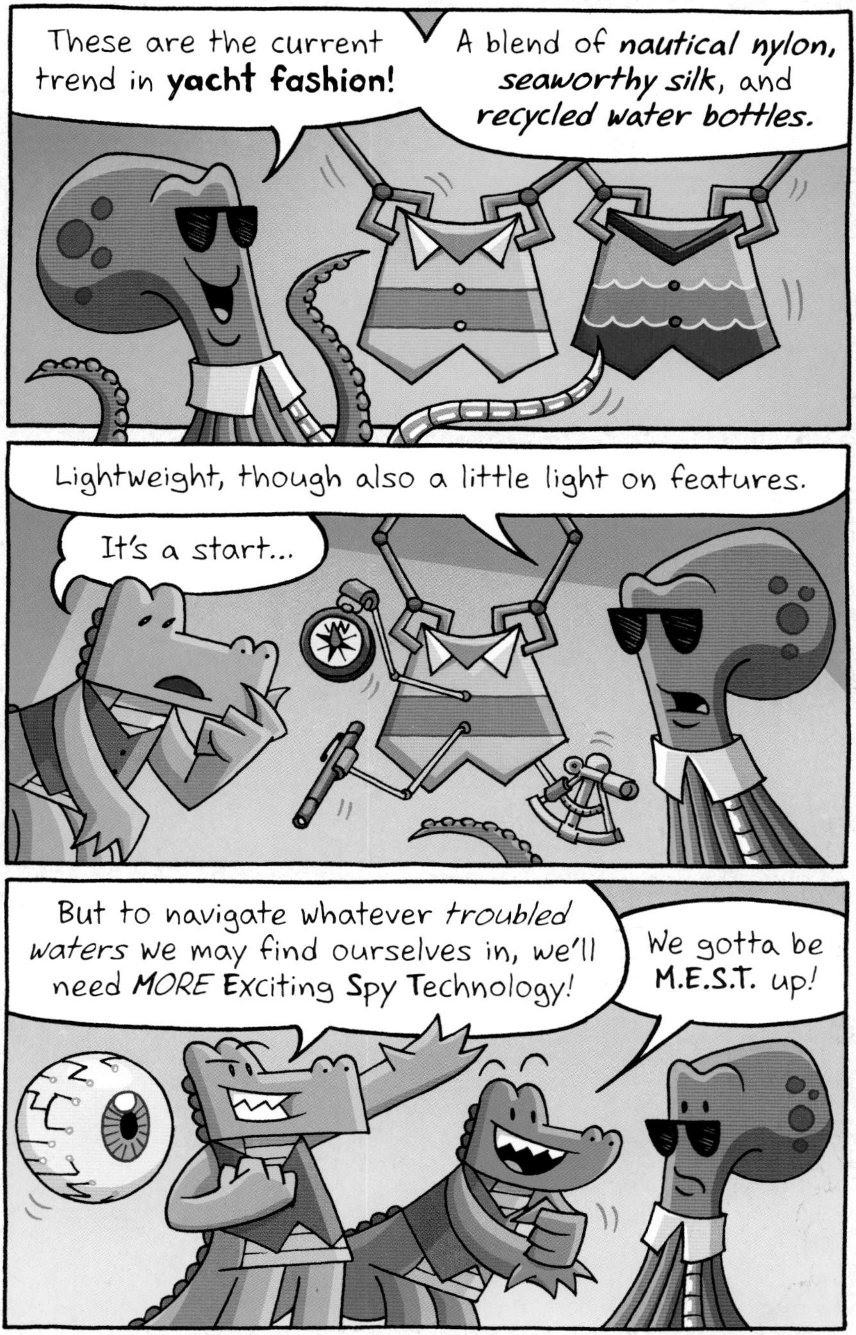
These are the current trend in **yacht fashion!**
A blend of ***nautical nylon, seaworthy silk***, and ***recycled water bottles.***
Lightweight, though also a little light on features.
It's a start...
But to navigate whatever *troubled waters* we may find ourselves in, we'll need *MORE* **E**xciting **S**py **T**echnology!
We gotta be **M.E.S.T.** up!

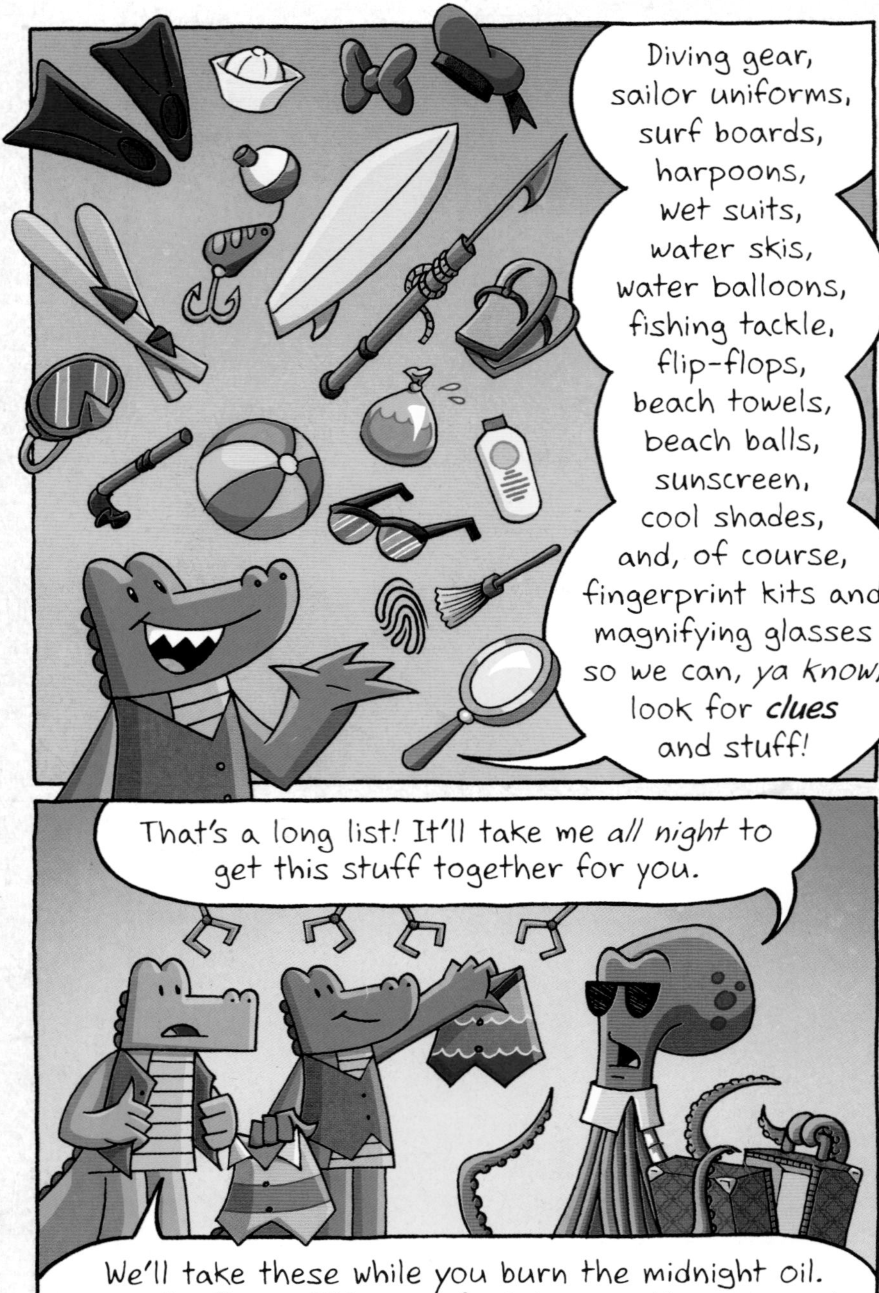
Diving gear, sailor uniforms, surf boards, harpoons, wet suits, water skis, water balloons, fishing tackle, flip-flops, beach towels, beach balls, sunscreen, cool shades, and, of course, fingerprint kits and magnifying glasses so we can, *ya know*, look for ***clues*** and stuff!
That's a long list! It'll take me *all night* to get this stuff together for you.
We'll take these while you burn the midnight oil. The ***SeaDues II*** leaves *first thing in the morning!*

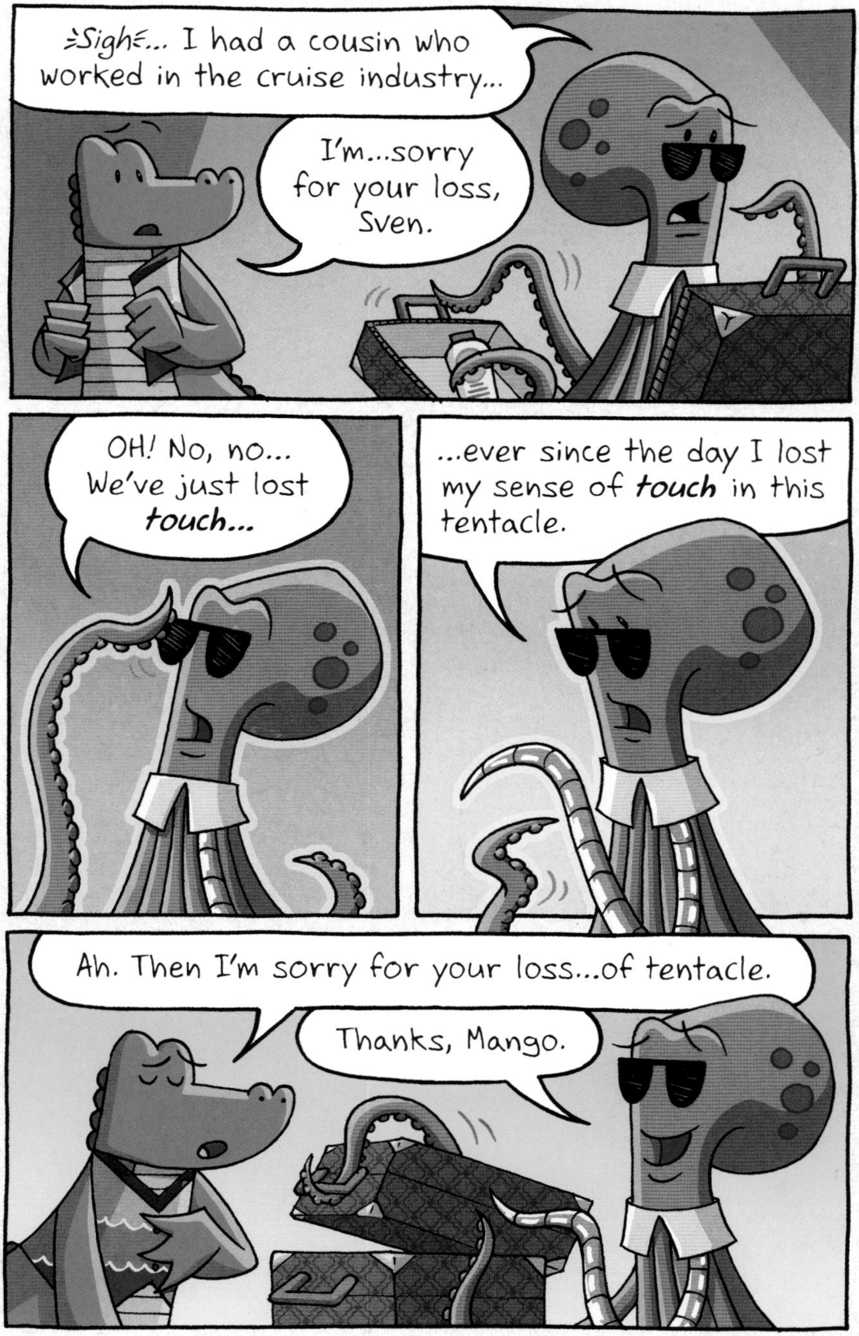

Sigh... I had a cousin who worked in the cruise industry...
I'm...sorry for your loss, Sven.
OH! No, no... We've just lost ***touch...***
...ever since the day I lost my sense of ***touch*** in this tentacle.
Ah. Then I'm sorry for your loss...of tentacle.
Thanks, Mango.

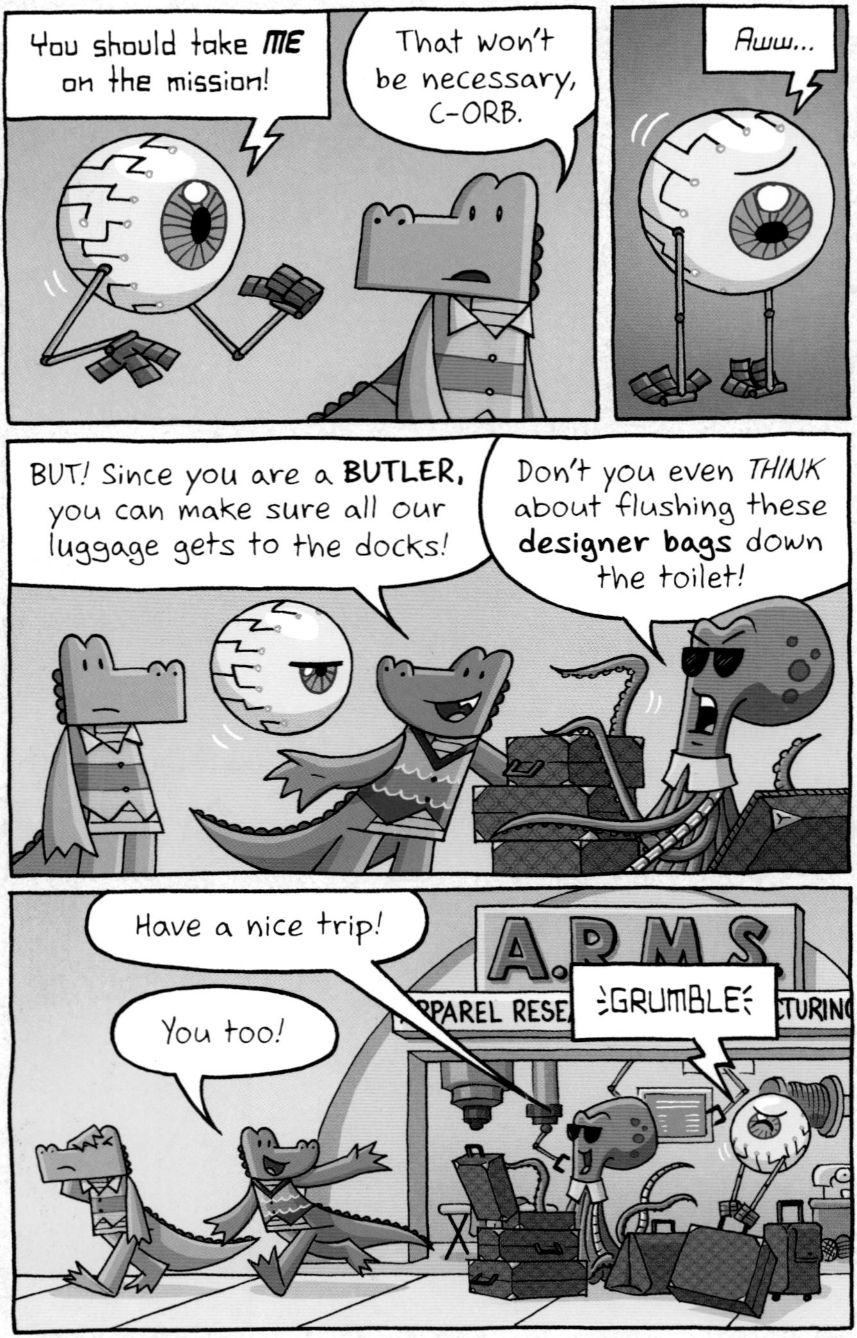
You should take **ME** on the mission!
That won't be necessary, C-ORB.
Aww...
BUT! Since you are a **BUTLER,** you can make sure all our luggage gets to the docks!
Don't you even *THINK* about flushing these **designer bags** down the toilet!
Have a nice trip!
You too!
GRUMBLE

Chapter 4

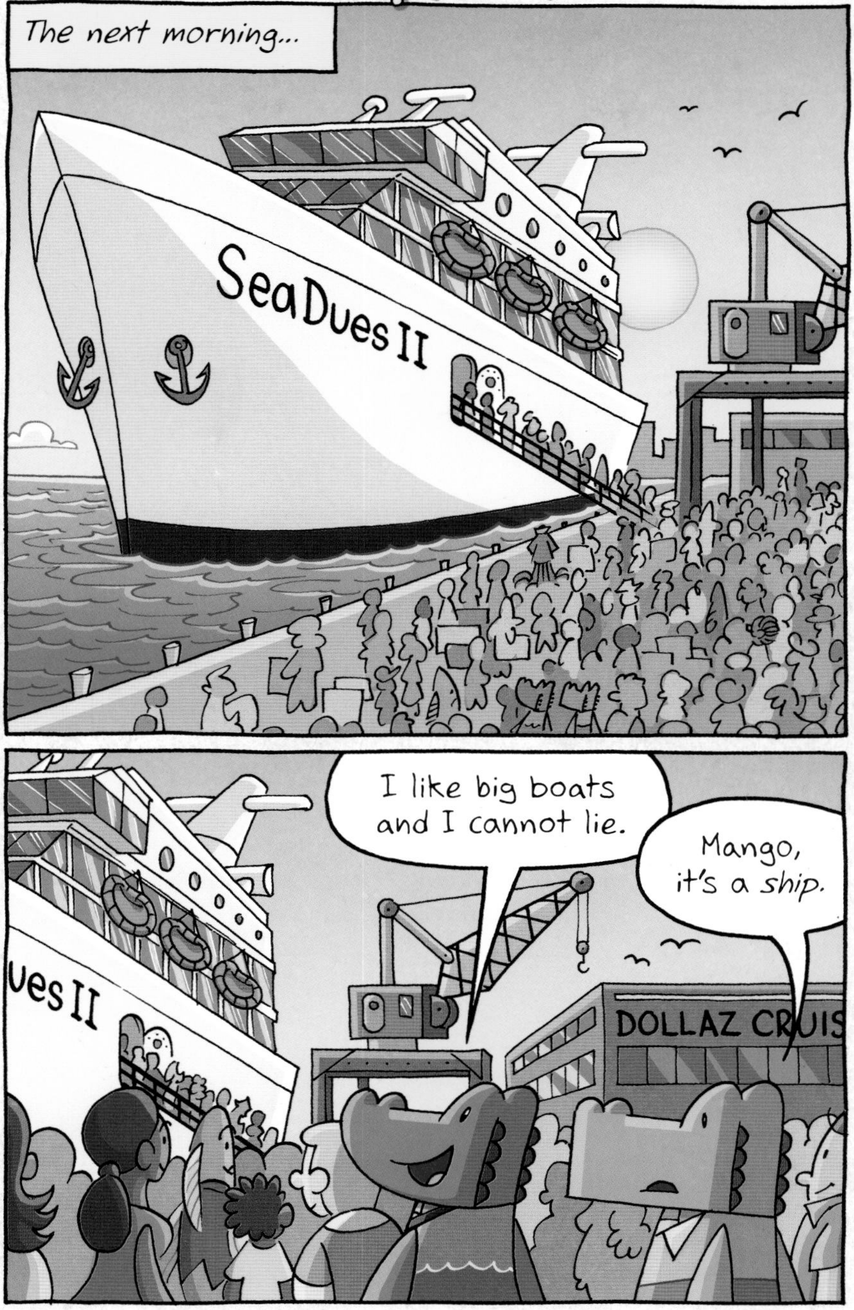
The next morning...
SeaDues II
I like big boats and I cannot lie.
Mango, it's a ship.
DOLLAZ CRUIS

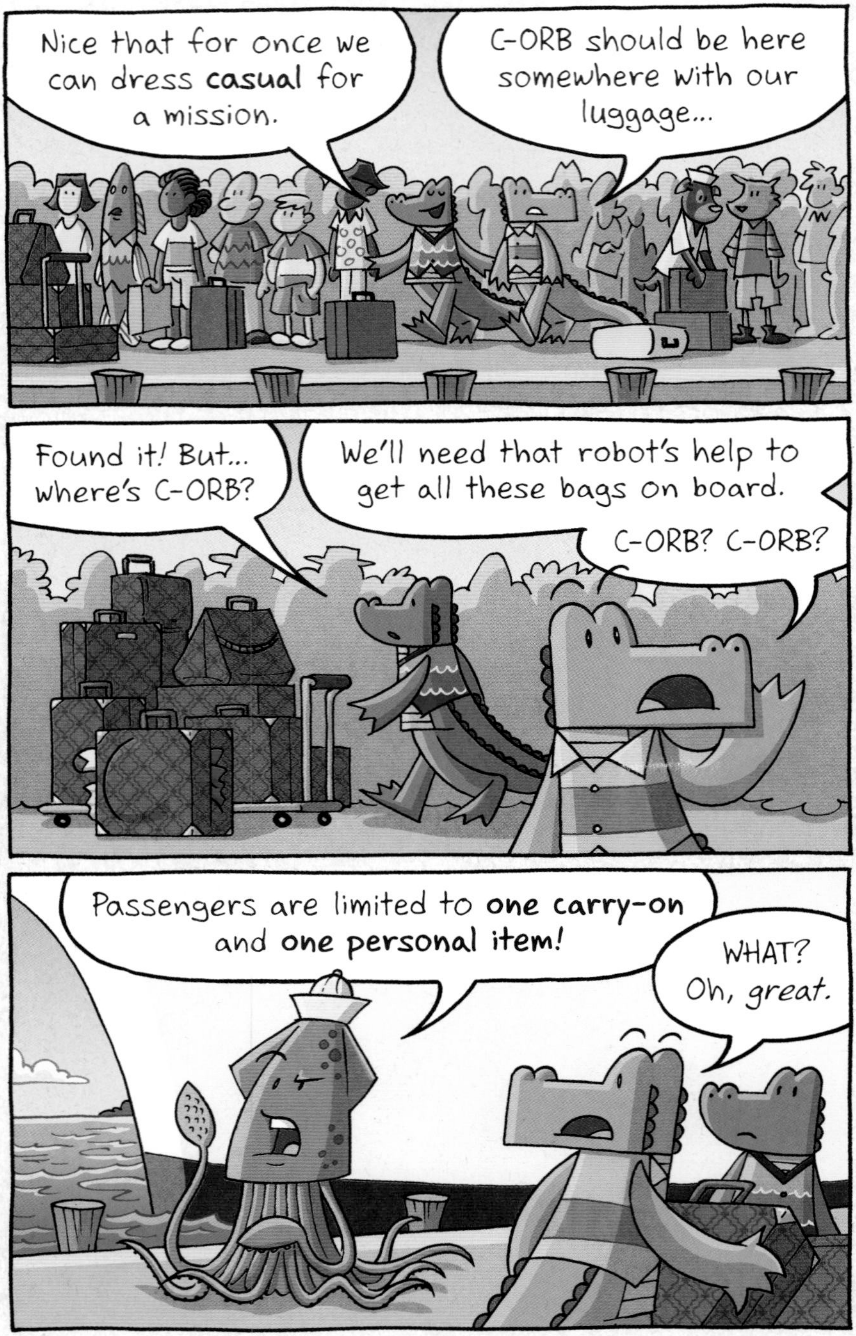
Nice that for once we can dress **casual** for a mission.
C-ORB should be here somewhere with our luggage...
Found it! But... where's C-ORB?
We'll need that robot's help to get all these bags on board.
C-ORB? C-ORB?
Passengers are limited to **one carry-on** and **one personal item!**
WHAT? Oh, great.

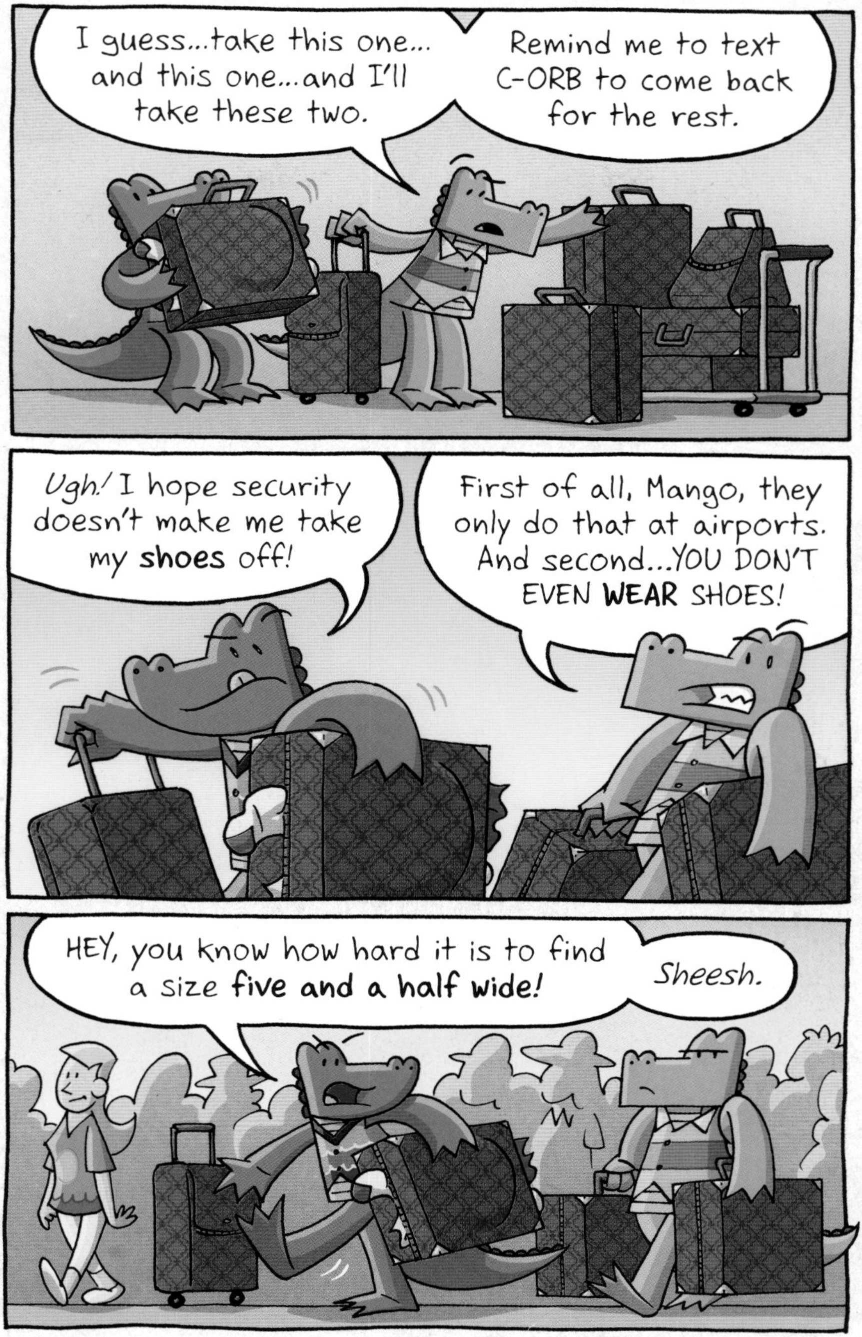
I guess...take this one... and this one...and I'll take these two.
Remind me to text C-ORB to come back for the rest.
Ugh! I hope security doesn't make me take my **shoes** off!
First of all, Mango, they only do that at airports. And second...YOU DON'T EVEN **WEAR** SHOES!
HEY, you know how hard it is to find a size **five and a half wide!**
Sheesh.

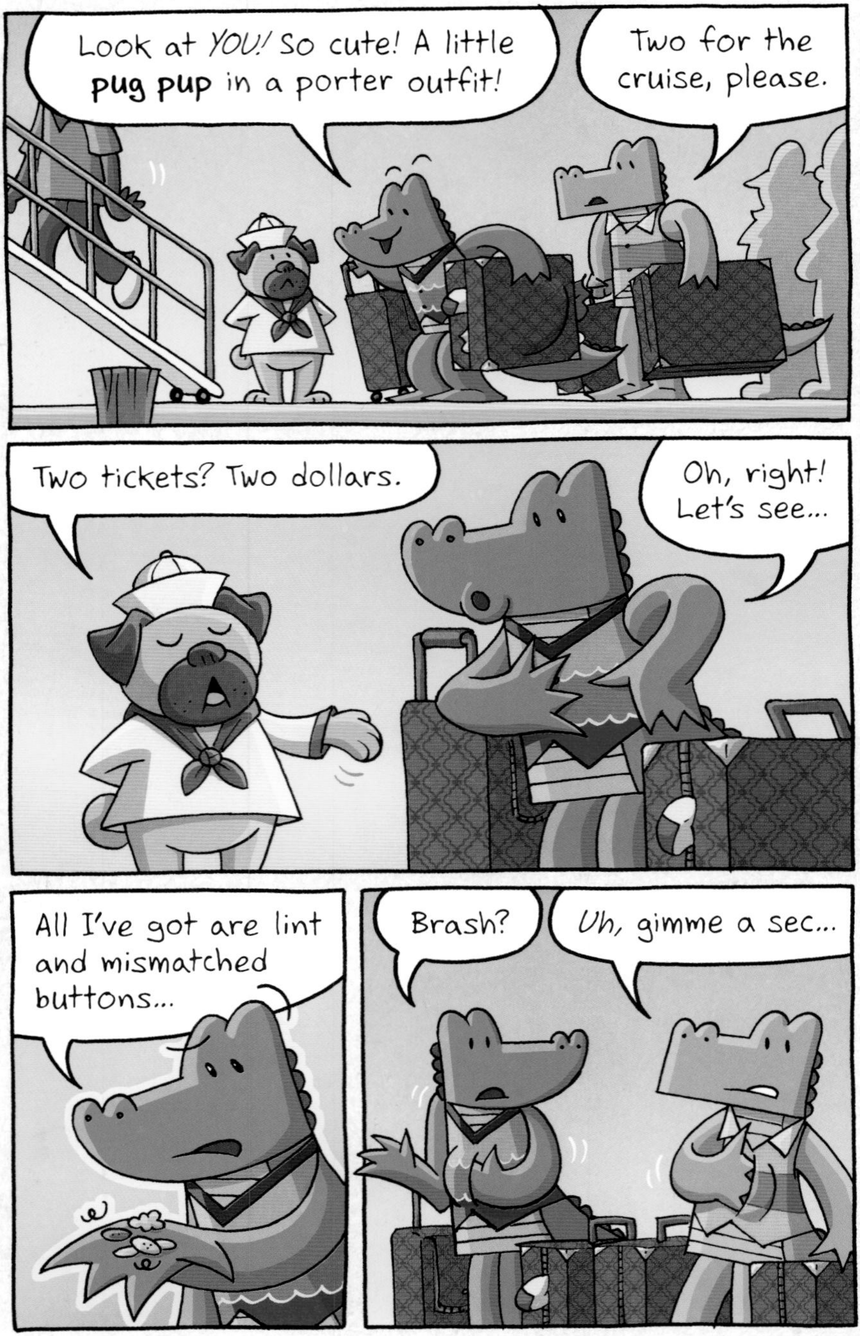

Look at YOU! So cute! A little pug pup in a porter outfit!
Two for the cruise, please.
Two tickets? Two dollars.
Oh, right! Let's see...
All I've got are lint and mismatched buttons...
Brash?
Uh, gimme a sec...

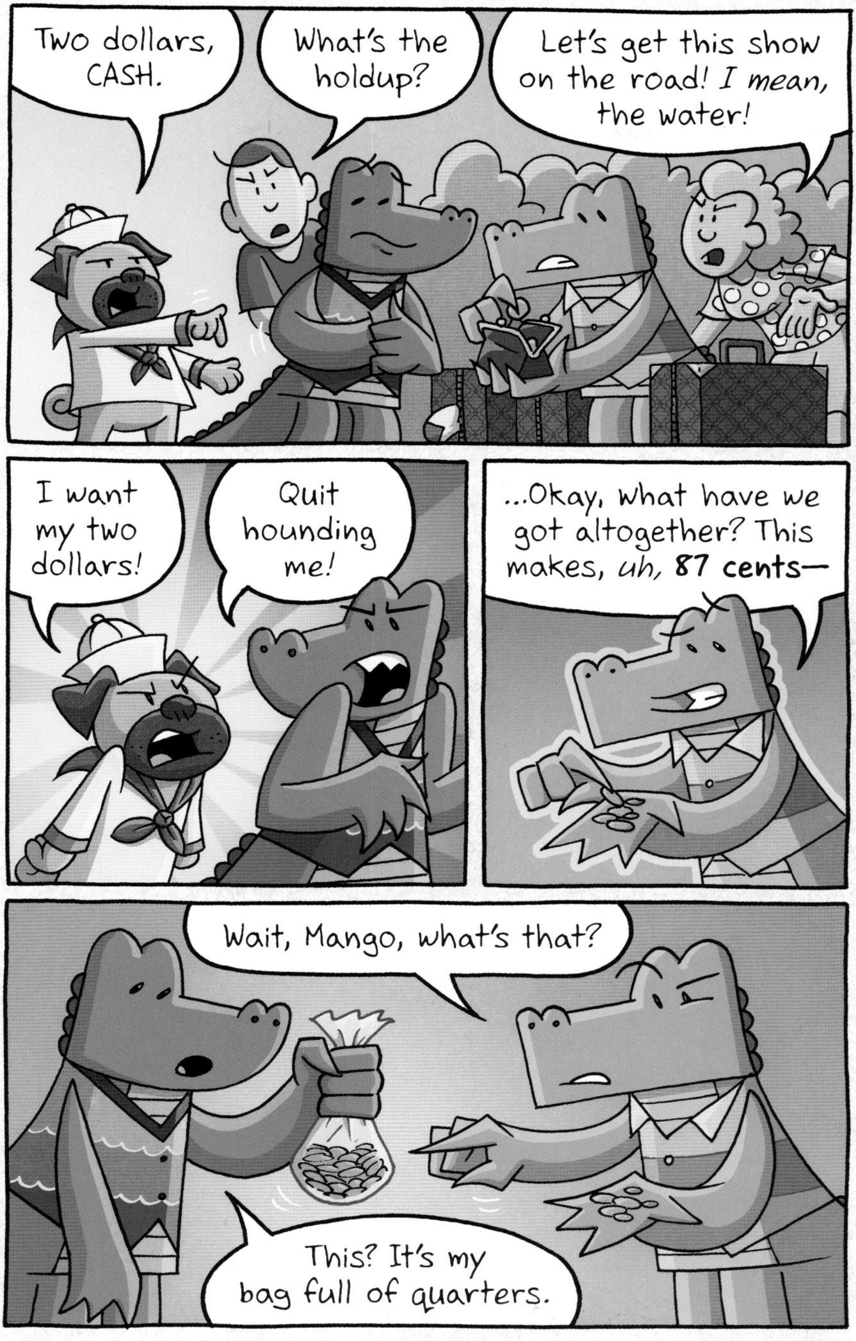
Two dollars, CASH.
What's the holdup?
Let's get this show on the road! *I mean,* the water!
I want my two dollars!
Quit hounding me!
...Okay, what have we got altogether? This makes, *uh,* **87 cents—**
Wait, Mango, what's that?
This? It's my bag full of quarters.

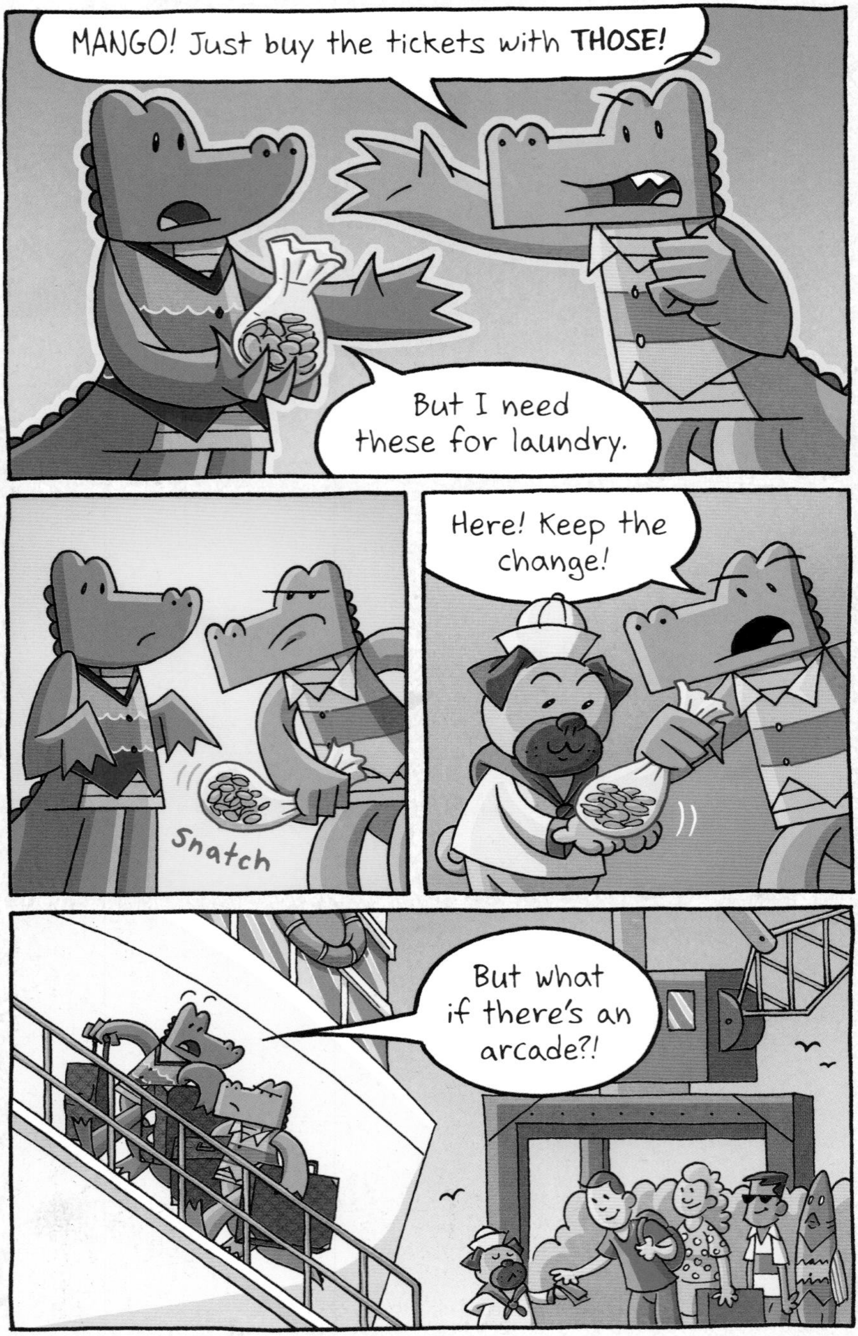
MANGO! Just buy the tickets with THOSE!
But I need these for laundry.
Snatch
Here! Keep the change!
But what if there's an arcade?!

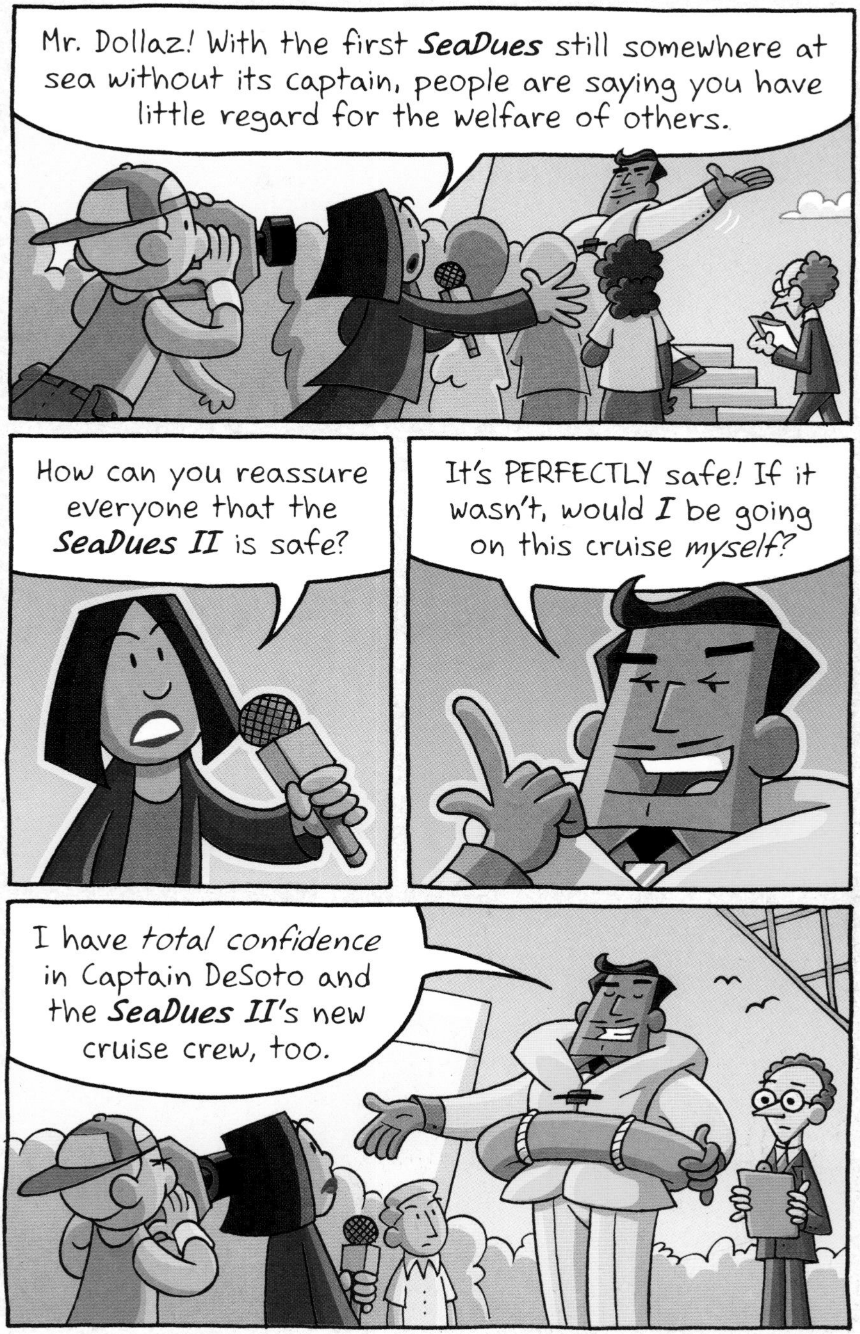
Mr. Dollaz! With the first SeaDues still somewhere at sea without its captain, people are saying you have little regard for the welfare of others.
How can you reassure everyone that the SeaDues II is safe?
It's PERFECTLY safe! If it wasn't, would I be going on this cruise myself?
I have total confidence in Captain DeSoto and the SeaDues II's new cruise crew, too.

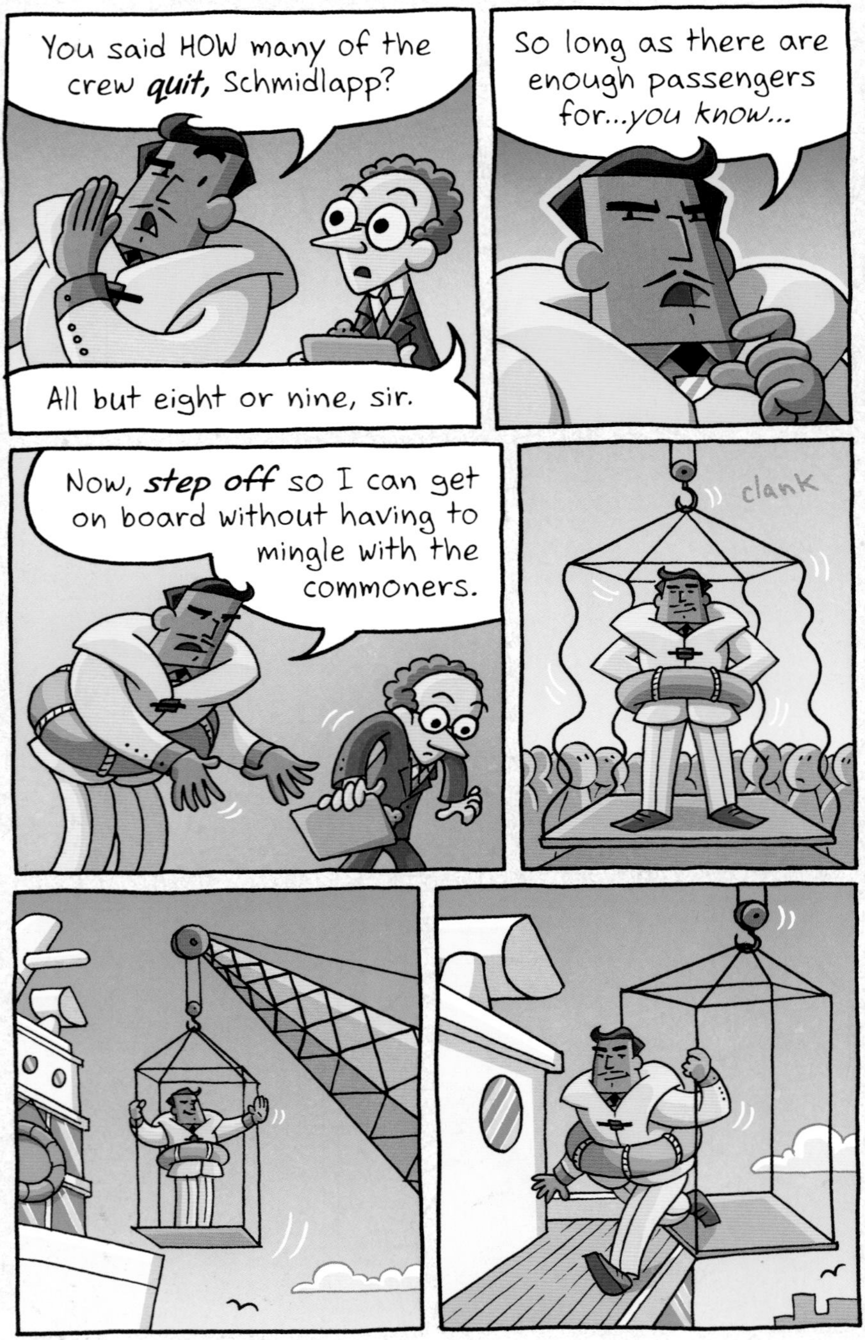
You said HOW many of the crew *quit,* Schmidlapp?
All but eight or nine, sir.
So long as there are enough passengers for...*you know...*
Now, *step off* so I can get on board without having to mingle with the commoners.
clank

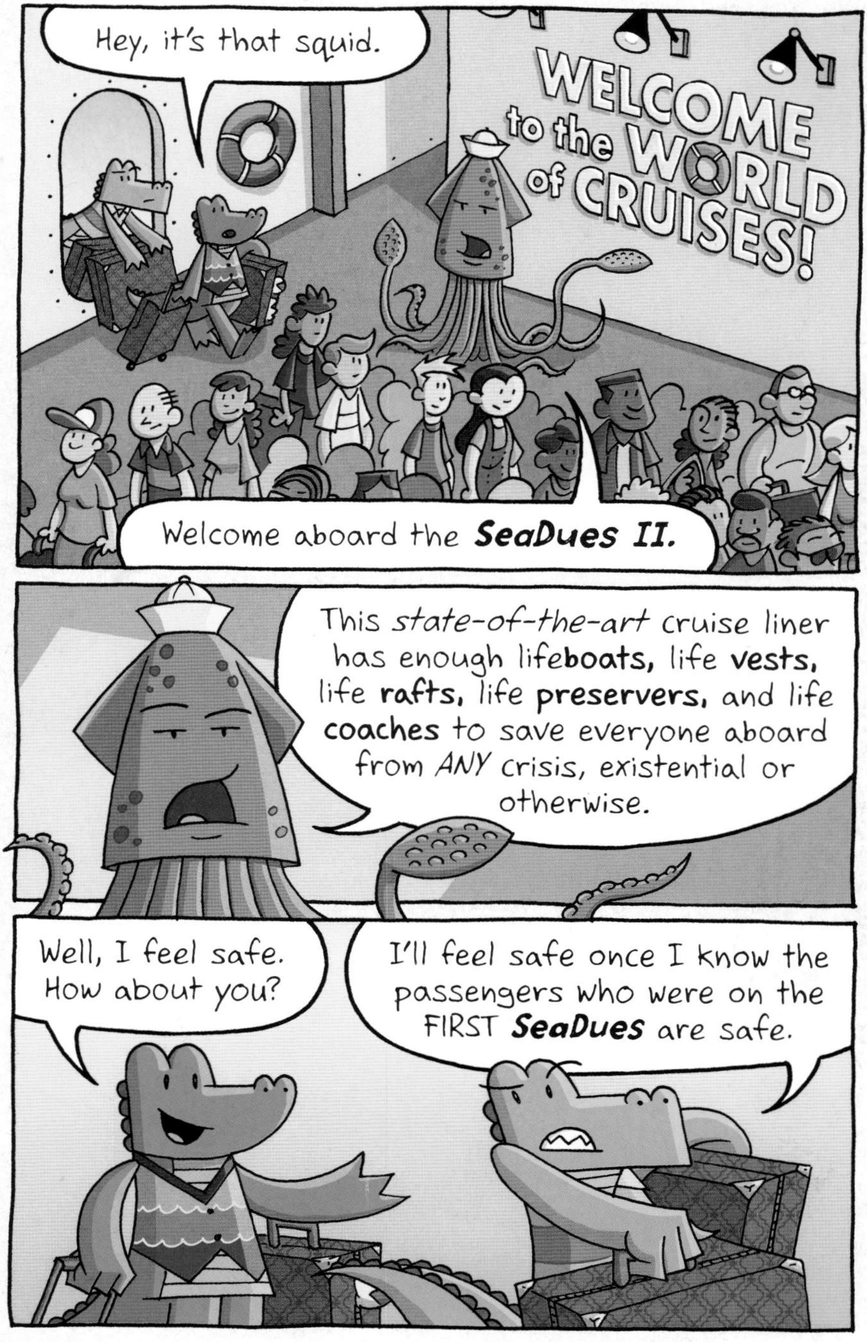
Hey, it's that squid.
WELCOME to the WORLD of CRUISES!
Welcome aboard the **SeaDues II.**
This *state-of-the-art* cruise liner has enough life**boats,** life **vests,** life **rafts,** life **preservers,** and life **coaches** to save everyone aboard from *ANY* crisis, existential or otherwise.
Well, I feel safe. How about you?
I'll feel safe once I know the passengers who were on the FIRST ***SeaDues*** are safe.

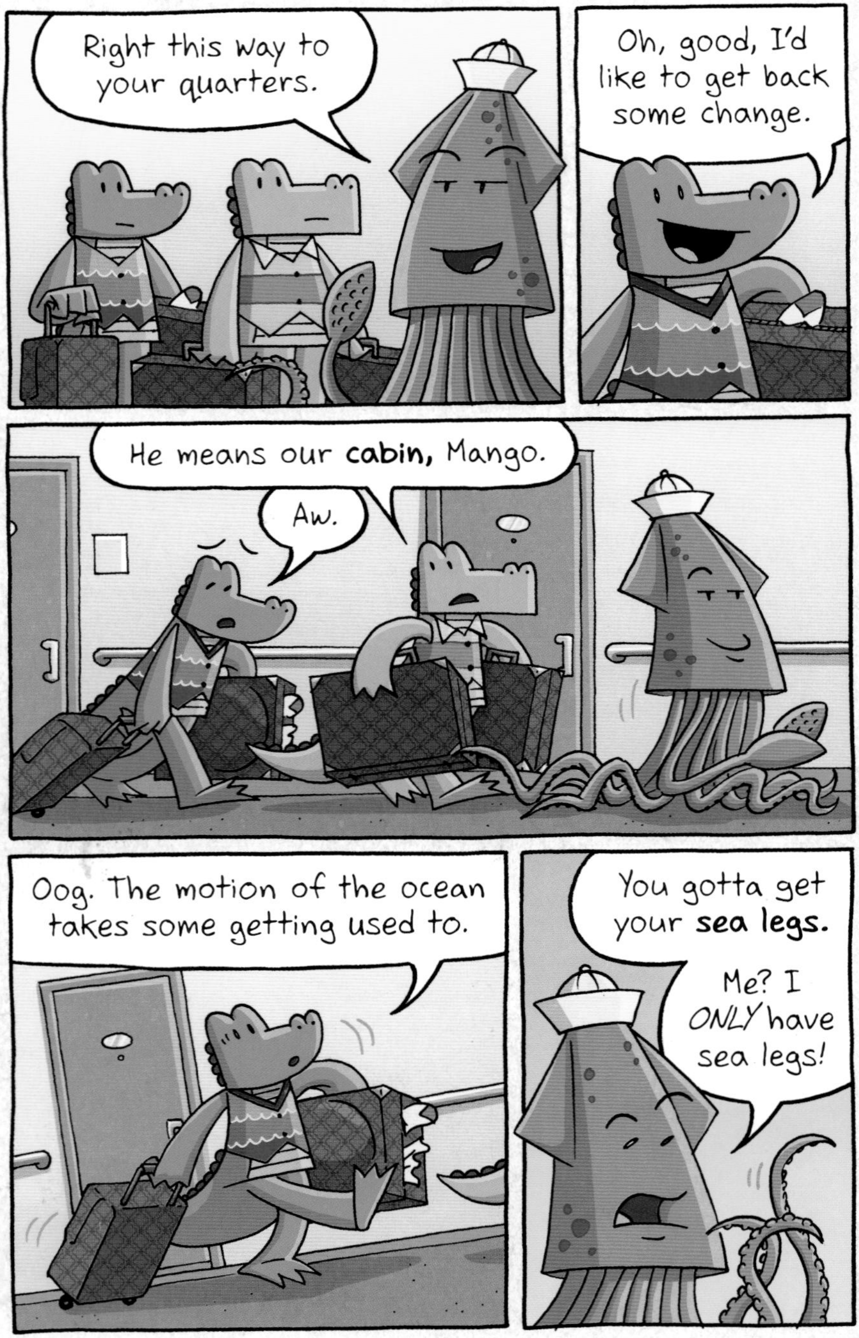
Right this way to your quarters.
Oh, good, I'd like to get back some change.
He means our **cabin,** Mango.
Aw.
Oog. The motion of the ocean takes some getting used to.
You gotta get your **sea legs.**
Me? I *ONLY* have sea legs!

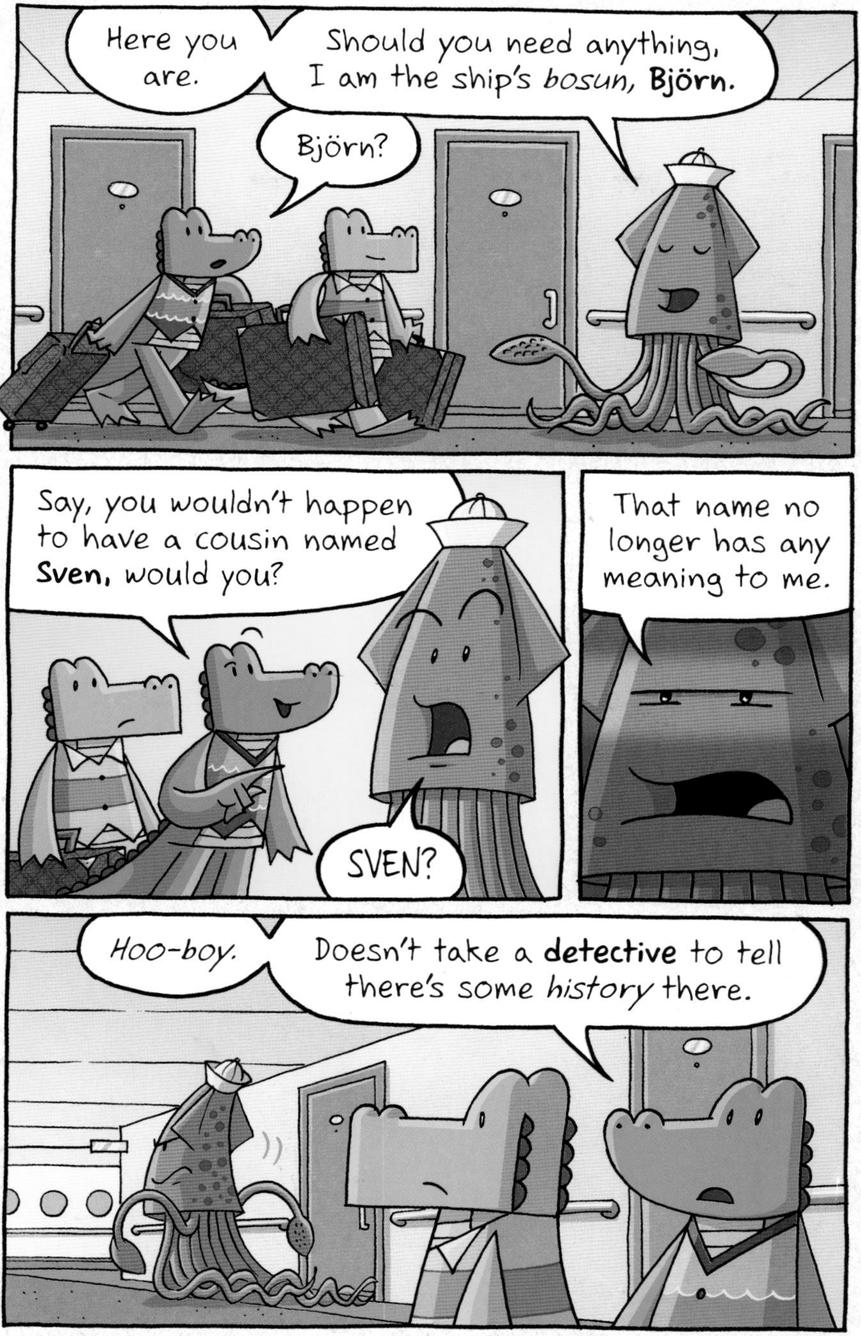

Here you are.
Should you need anything, I am the ship's *bosun*, **Björn.**
Björn?
Say, you wouldn't happen to have a cousin named **Sven,** would you?
SVEN?
That name no longer has any meaning to me.
Hoo-boy.
Doesn't take a **detective** to tell there's some *history* there.

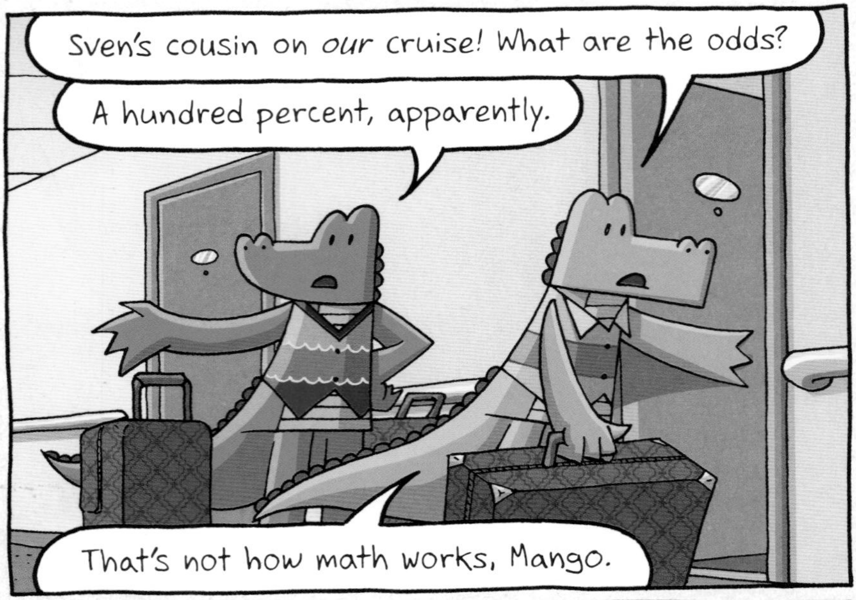
Sven's cousin on *our* cruise! What are the odds?
A hundred percent, apparently.
That's not how math works, Mango.

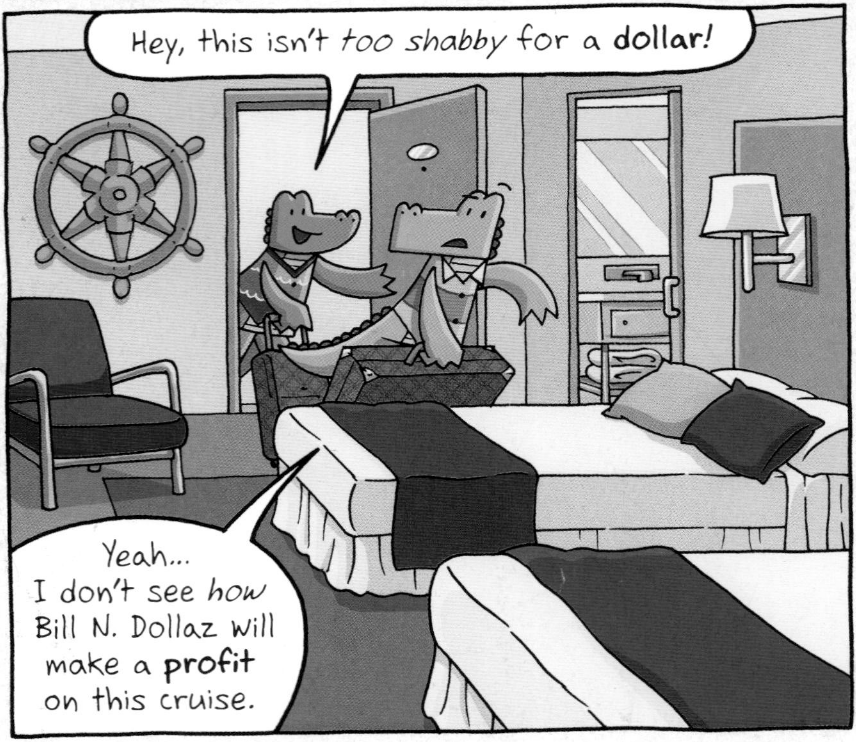
Hey, this isn't *too shabby* for a **dollar**!
Yeah...
I don't see *how*
Bill N. Dollaz will
make a **profit**
on this cruise.

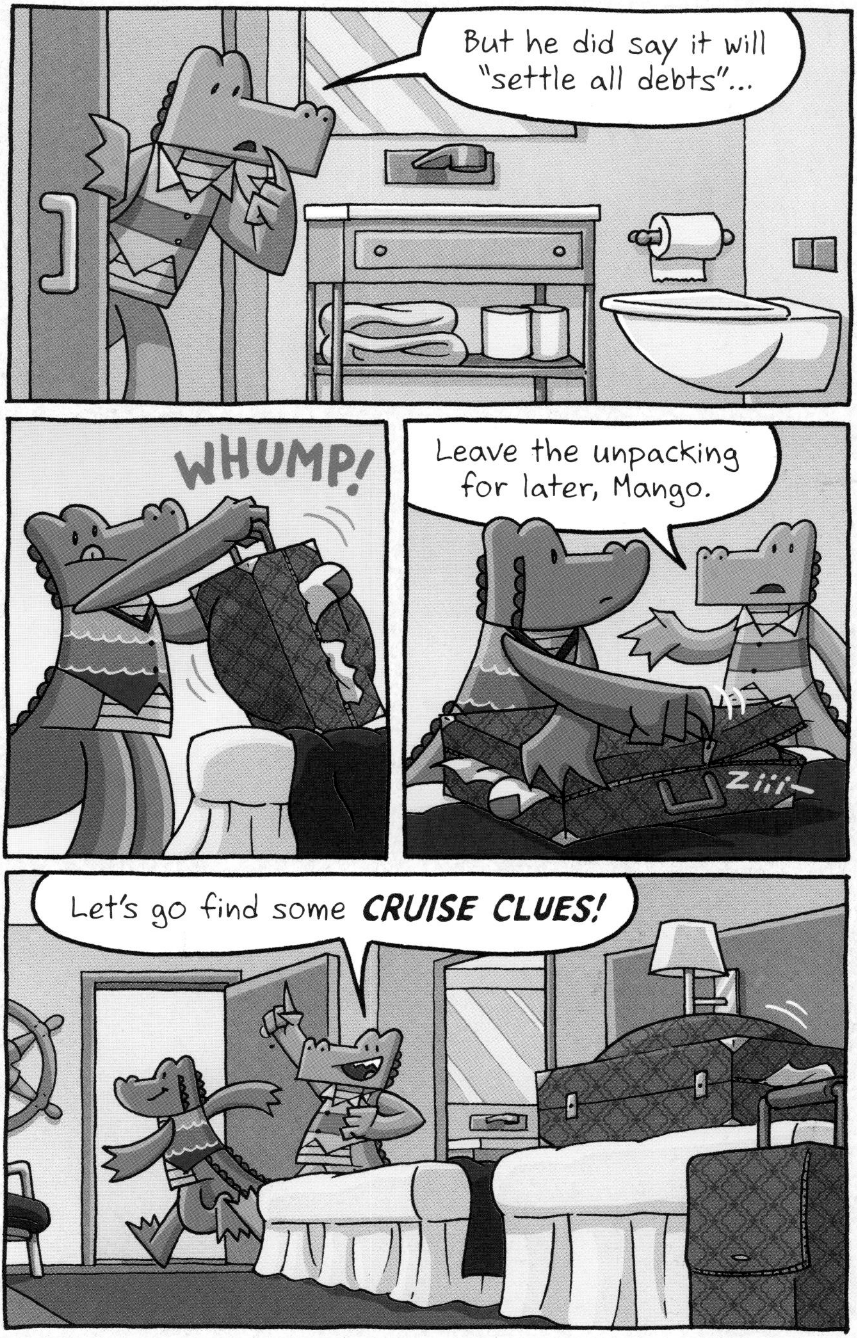

But he did say it will "settle all debts"...
WHUMP!
Leave the unpacking for later, Mango.
Ziii
Let's go find some **CRUISE CLUES!**

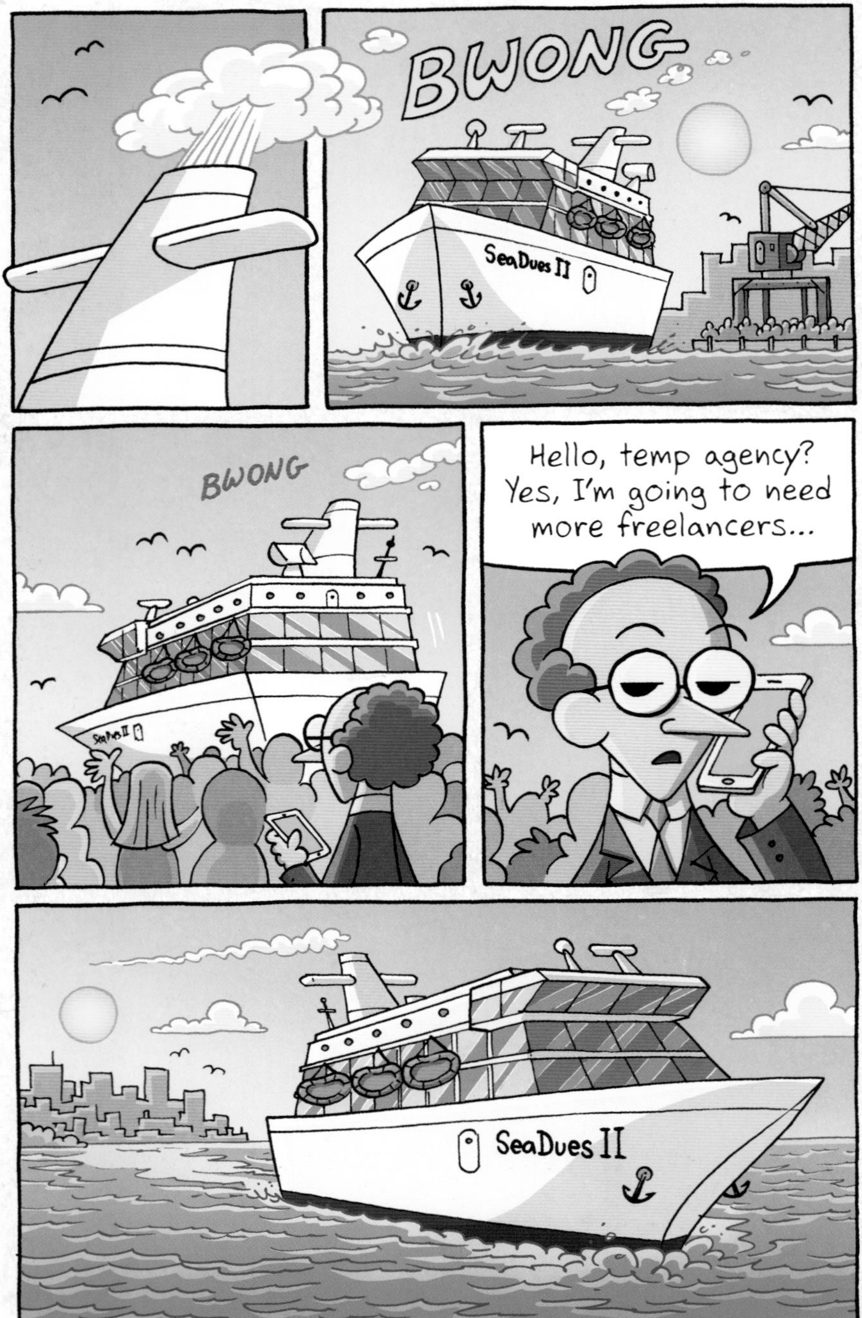
BWONG
SeaDues II
BWONG
SeaDues II
Hello, temp agency? Yes, I'm going to need more freelancers...
SeaDues II

Chapter 5

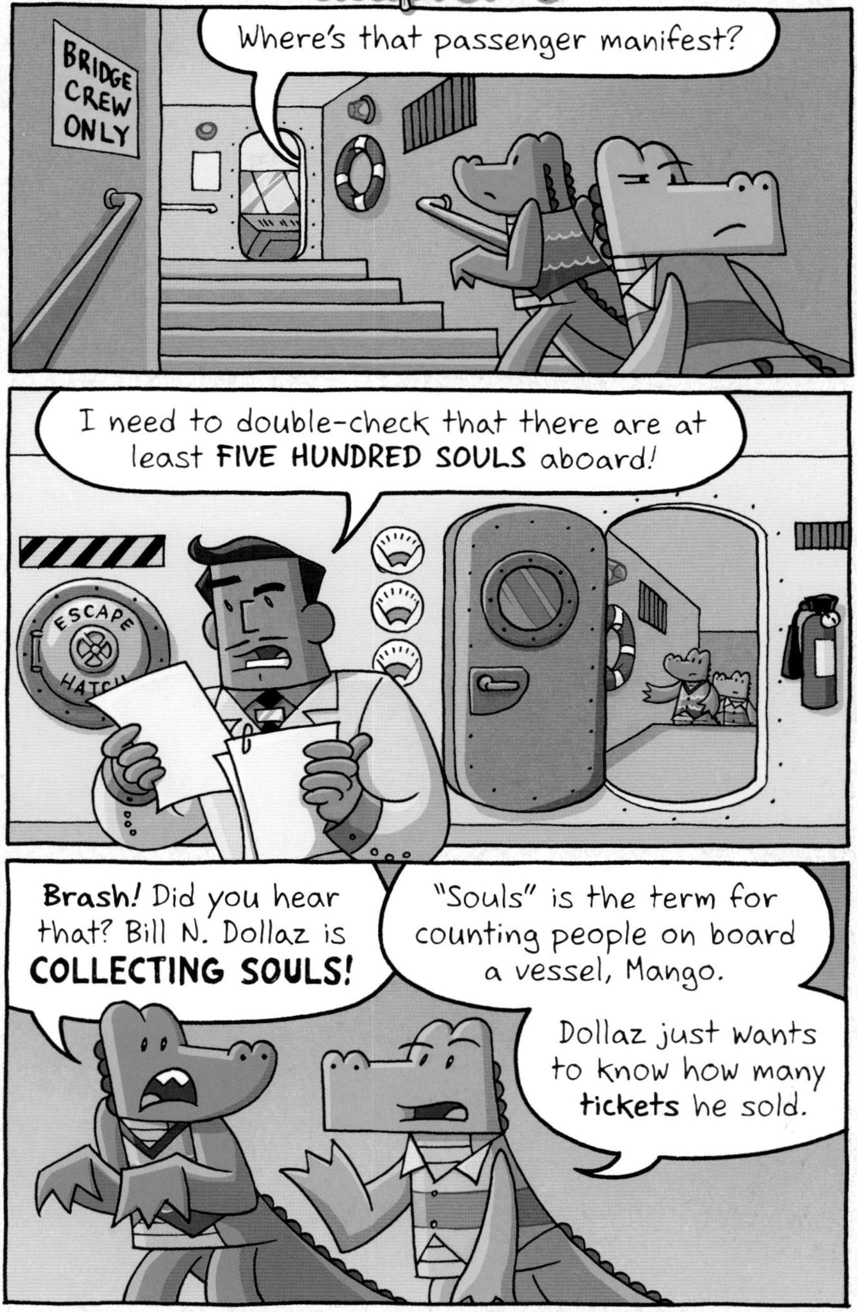

BRIDGE CREW ONLY
Where's that passenger manifest?
I need to double-check that there are at least **FIVE HUNDRED SOULS** aboard!
ESCAPE HATCH
Brash! Did you hear that? Bill N. Dollaz is **COLLECTING SOULS!**
"Souls" is the term for counting people on board a vessel, Mango.
Dollaz just wants to know how many **tickets** he sold.

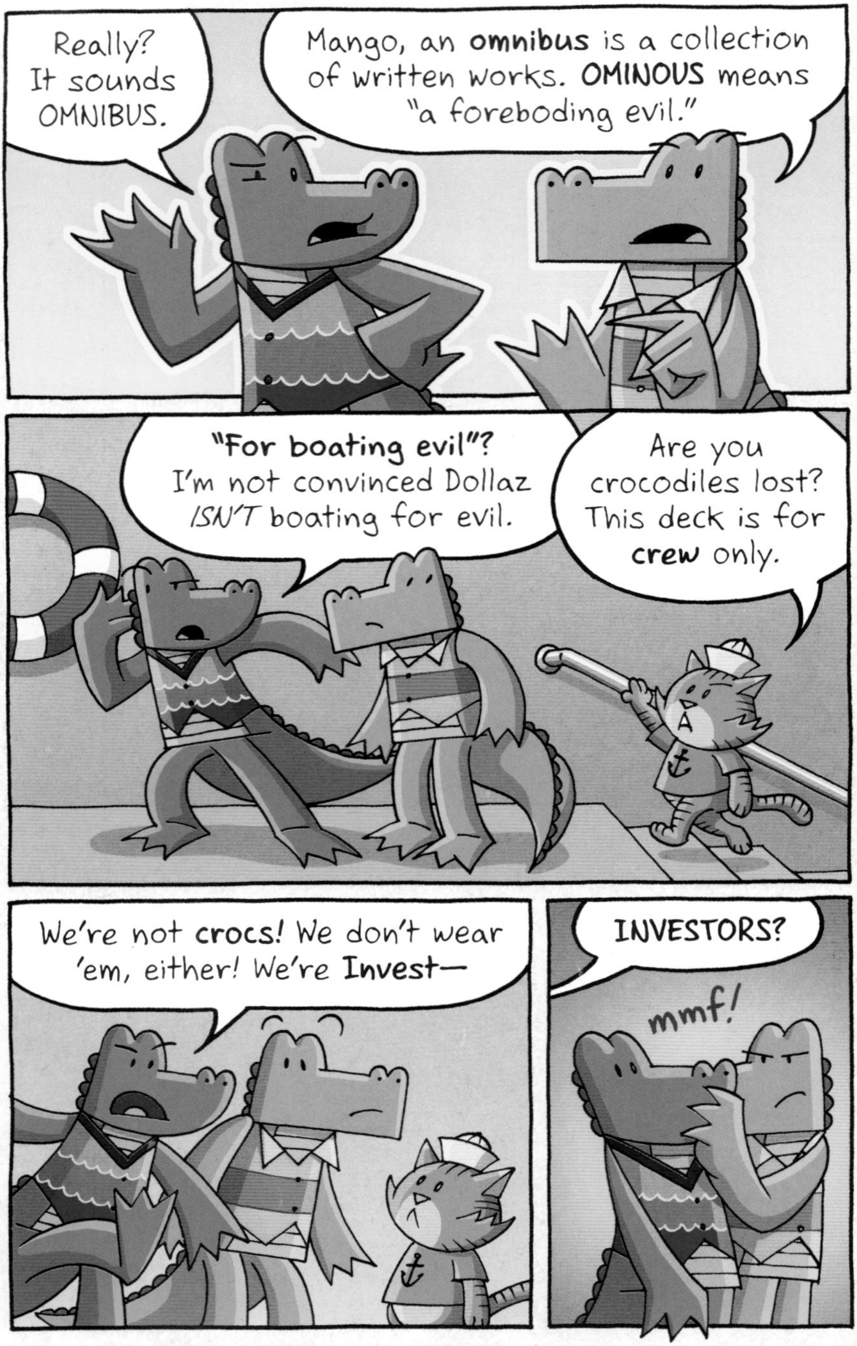
Really? It sounds OMNIBUS.
Mango, an **omnibus** is a collection of written works. **OMINOUS** means "a foreboding evil."
"For boating evil"? I'm not convinced Dollaz *ISN'T* boating for evil.
Are you crocodiles lost? This deck is for **crew** only.
We're not **crocs**! We don't wear 'em, either! We're **Invest**—
INVESTORS?
mmf!

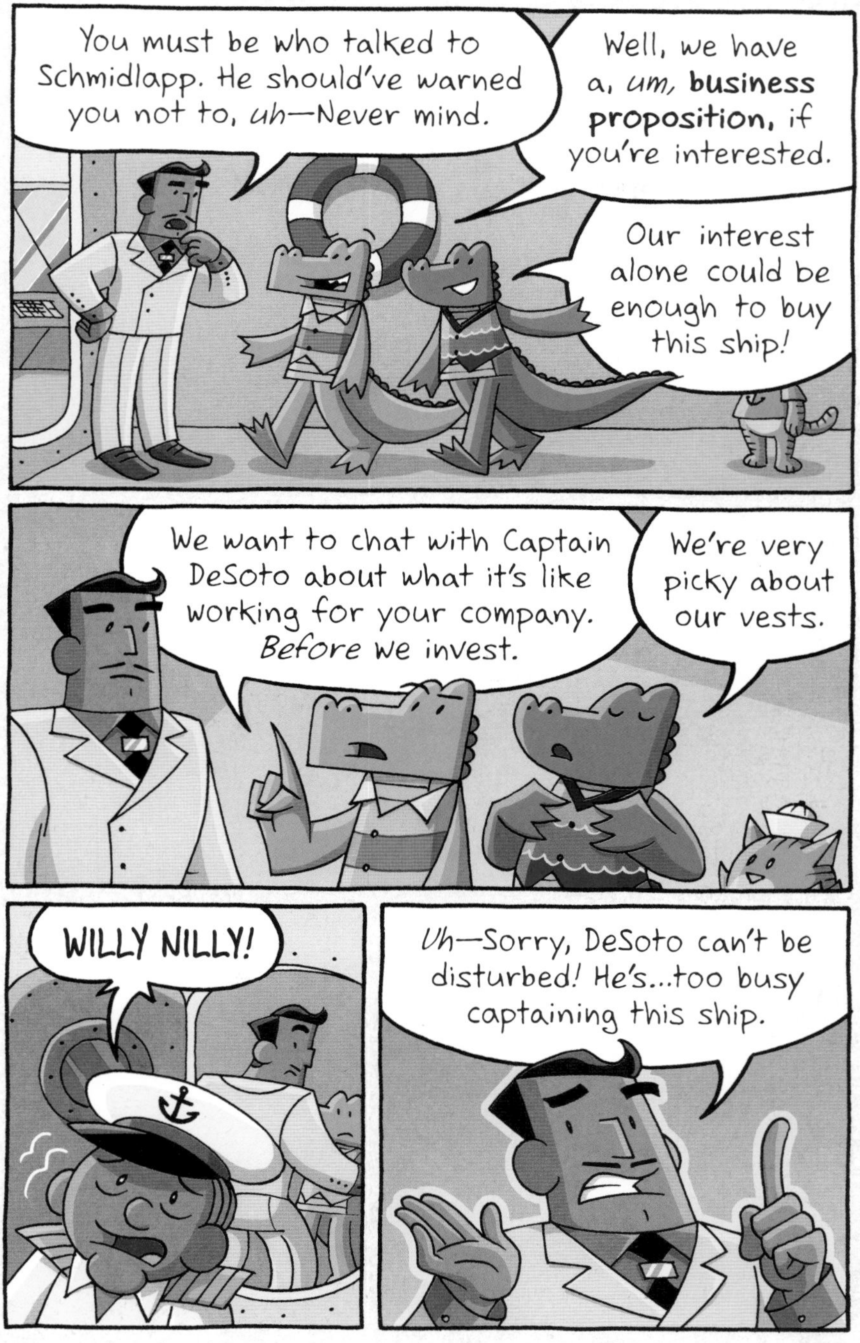
You must be who talked to Schmidlapp. He should've warned you not to, *uh*—Never mind.
Well, we have a, *um,* **business proposition,** if you're interested.
Our interest alone could be enough to buy this ship!
We want to chat with Captain DeSoto about what it's like working for your company. *Before* we invest.
We're very picky about our vests.
WILLY NILLY!
Uh—Sorry, DeSoto can't be disturbed! He's...too busy captaining this ship.

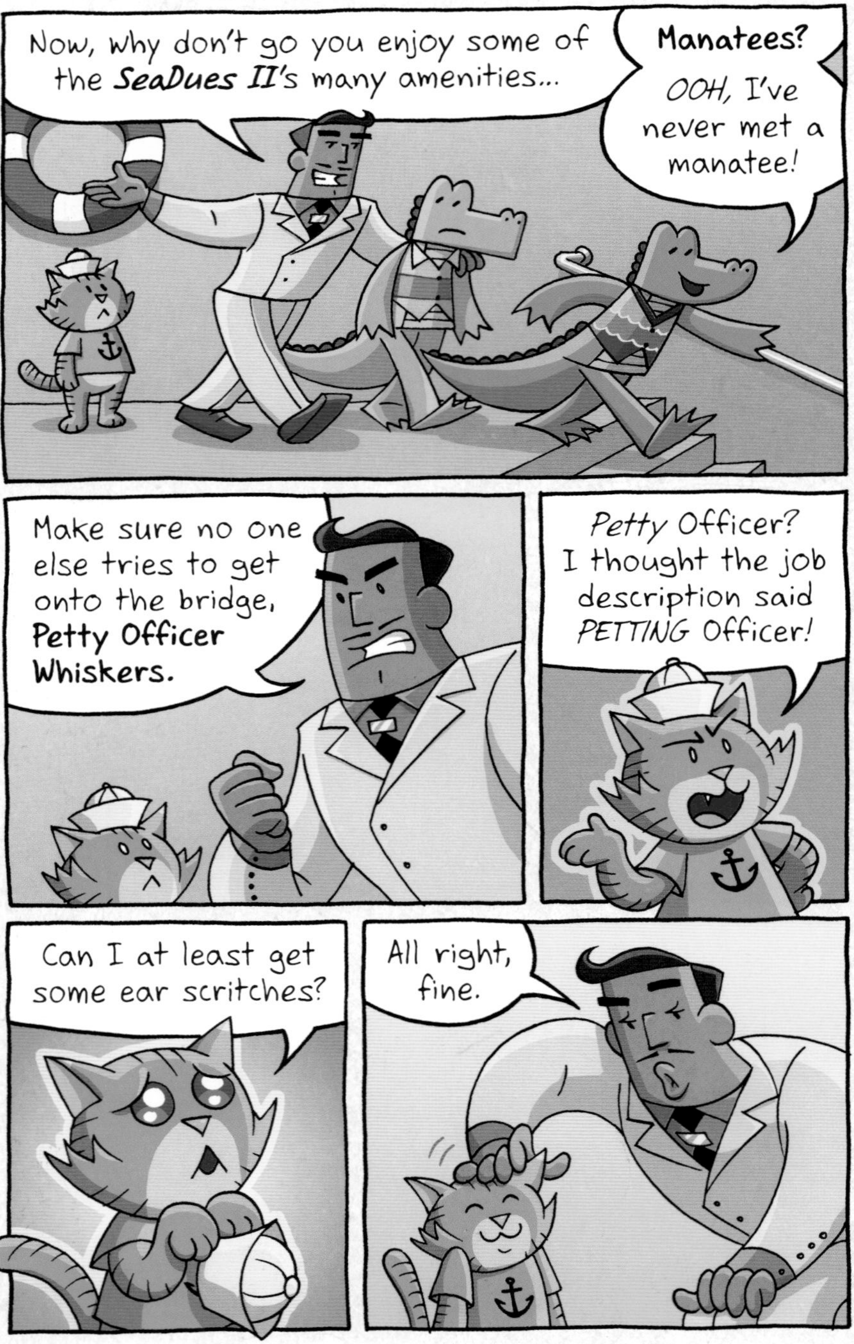
Now, why don't go you enjoy some of the *SeaDues II*'s many amenities...
Manatees?
OOH, I've never met a manatee!
Make sure no one else tries to get onto the bridge, **Petty Officer Whiskers.**
Petty Officer? I thought the job description said *PETTING* Officer!
Can I at least get some ear scritches?
All right, fine.

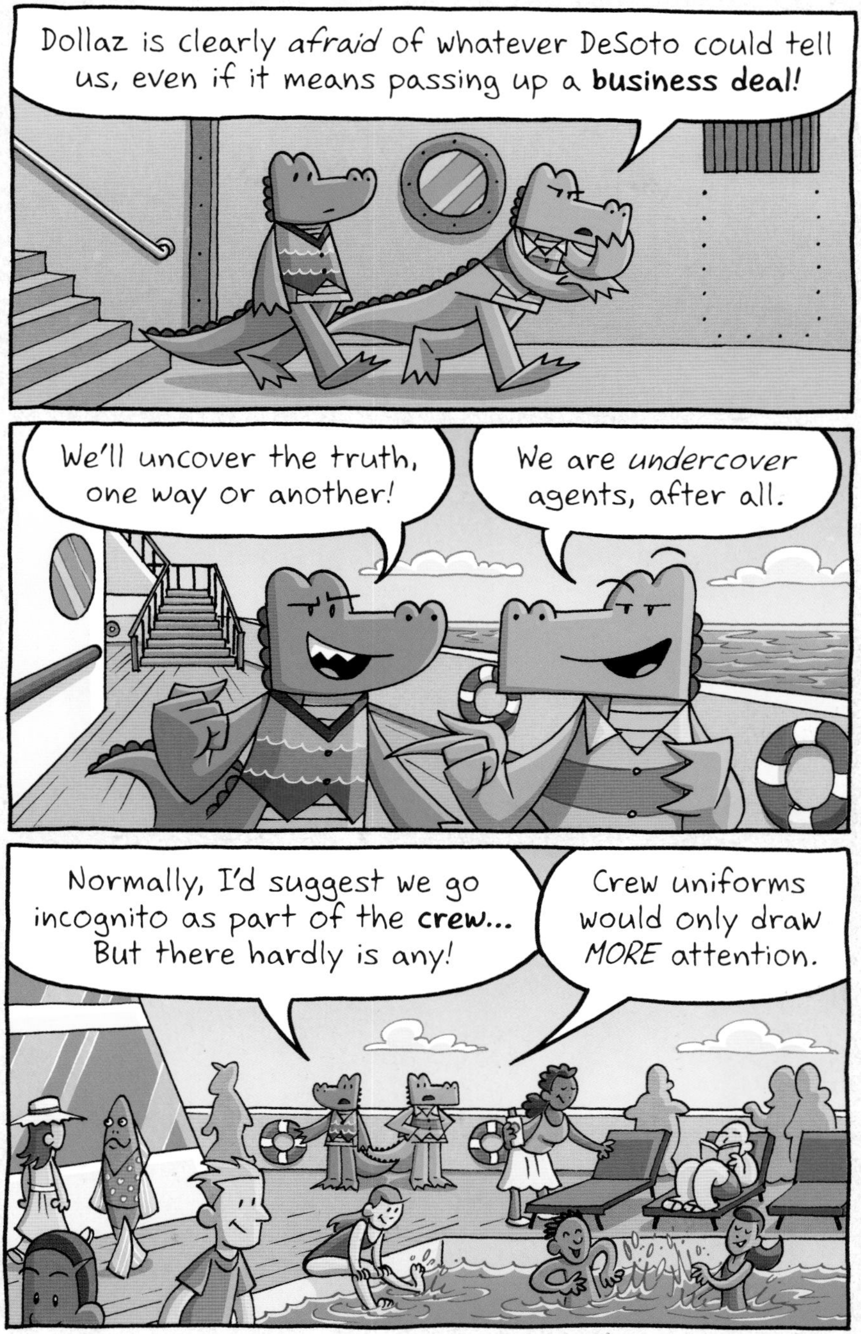
Dollaz is clearly *afraid* of whatever DeSoto could tell us, even if it means passing up a **business deal**!
We'll uncover the truth, one way or another!
We are *undercover* agents, after all.
Normally, I'd suggest we go incognito as part of the **crew**... But there hardly is any!
Crew uniforms would only draw *MORE* attention.

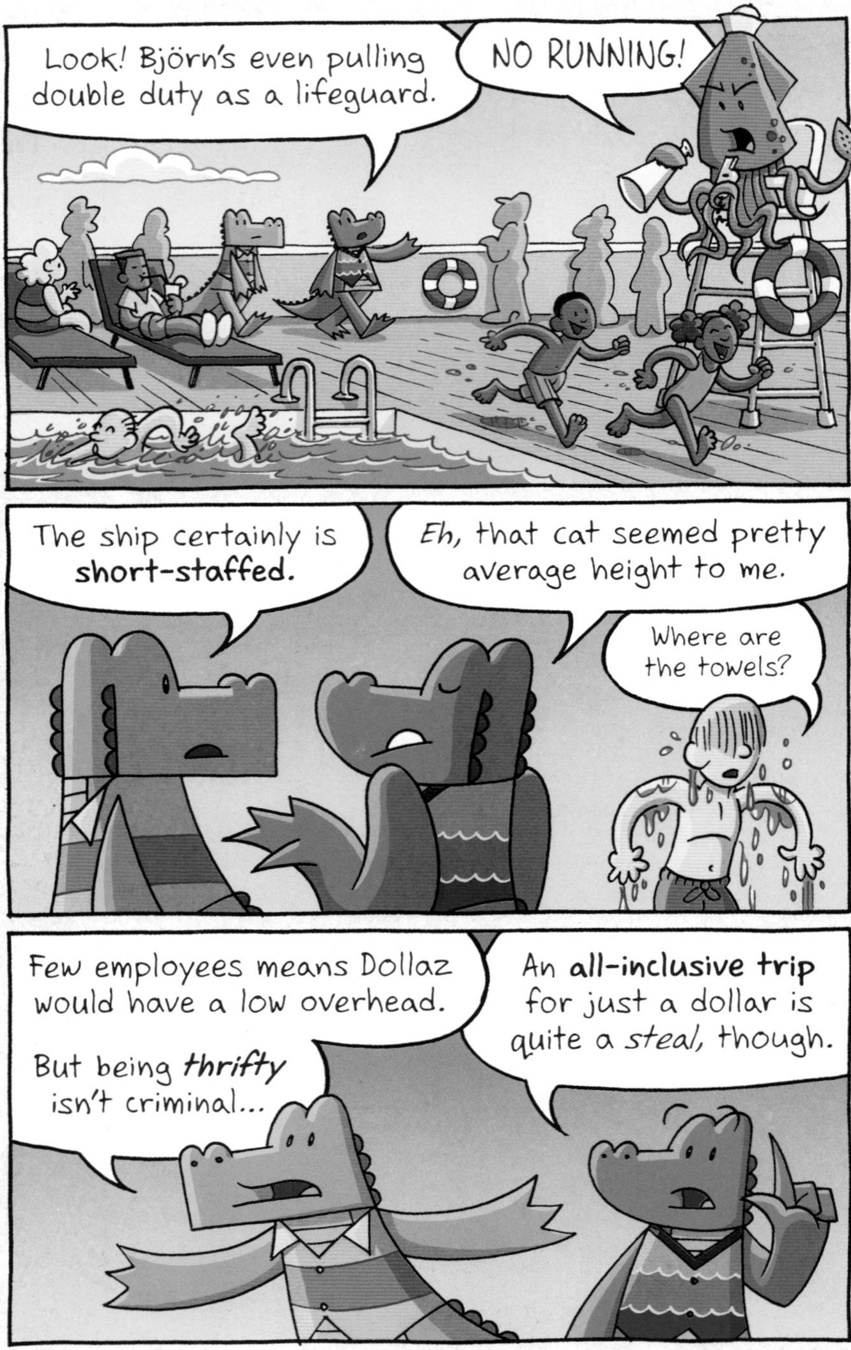
Look! Björn's even pulling double duty as a lifeguard.
NO RUNNING!
The ship certainly is **short-staffed.**
Eh, that cat seemed pretty average height to me.
Where are the towels?
Few employees means Dollaz would have a low overhead.
But being ***thrifty*** isn't criminal...
An **all-inclusive trip** for just a dollar is quite a *steal,* though.

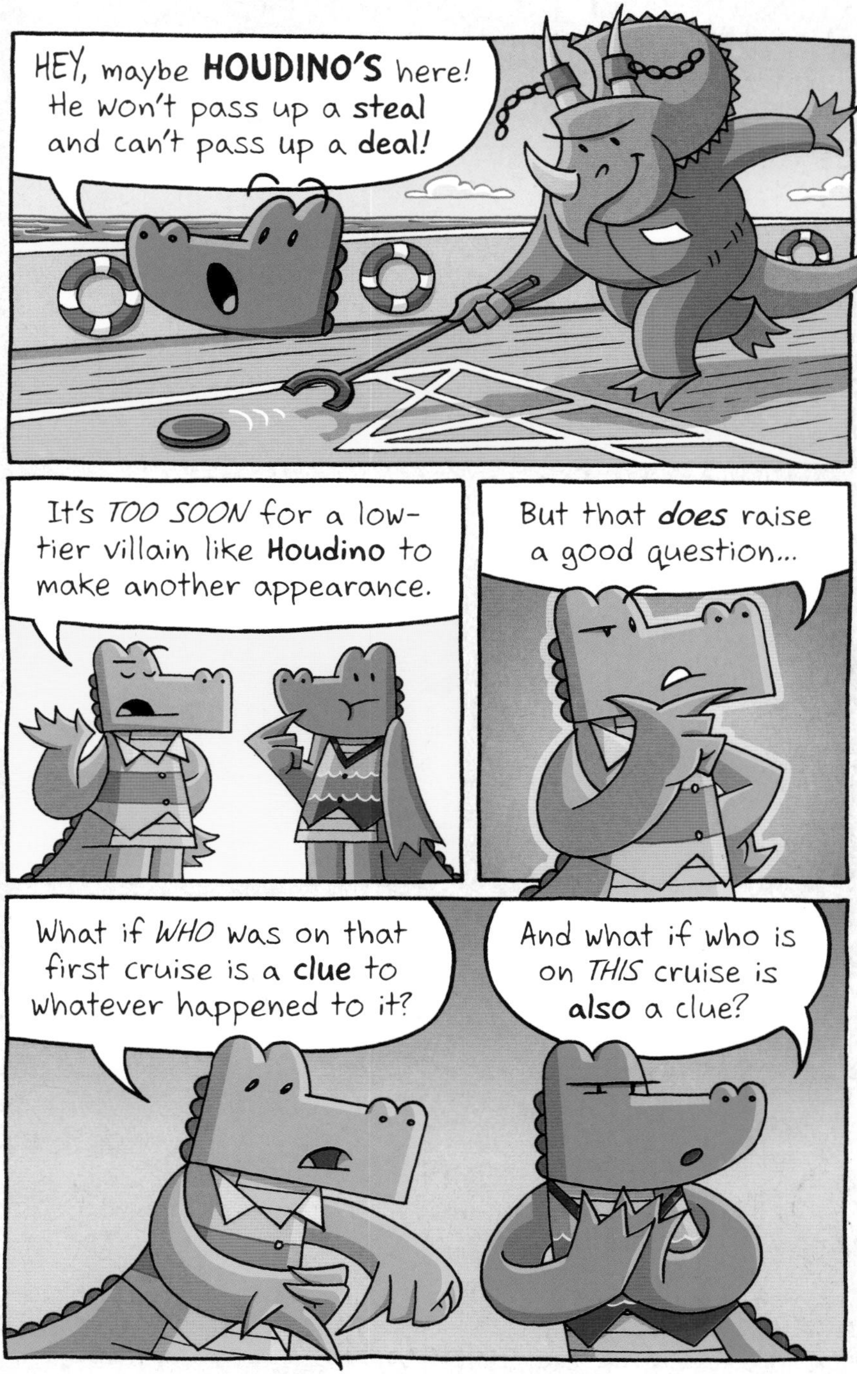
HEY, maybe **HOUDINO'S** here! He won't pass up a **steal** and can't pass up a **deal**!
It's *TOO SOON* for a low-tier villain like **Houdino** to make another appearance.
But that ***does*** raise a good question...
What if *WHO* was on that first cruise is a **clue** to whatever happened to it?
And what if who is on *THIS* cruise is **also** a clue?

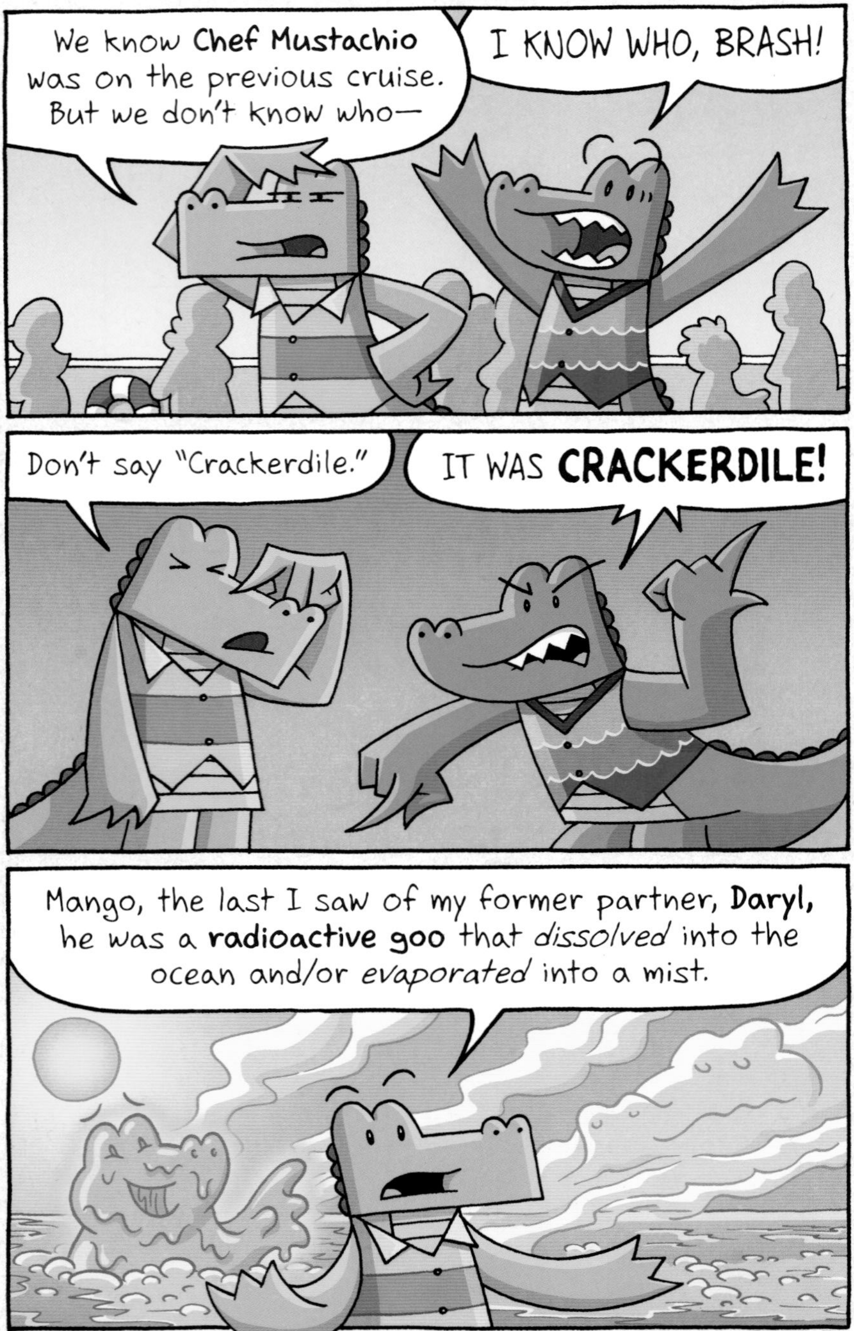
We know Chef Mustachio was on the previous cruise. But we don't know who—
I KNOW WHO, BRASH!
Don't say "Crackerdile."
IT WAS CRACKERDILE!
Mango, the last I saw of my former partner, Daryl, he was a radioactive goo that dissolved into the ocean and/or evaporated into a mist.

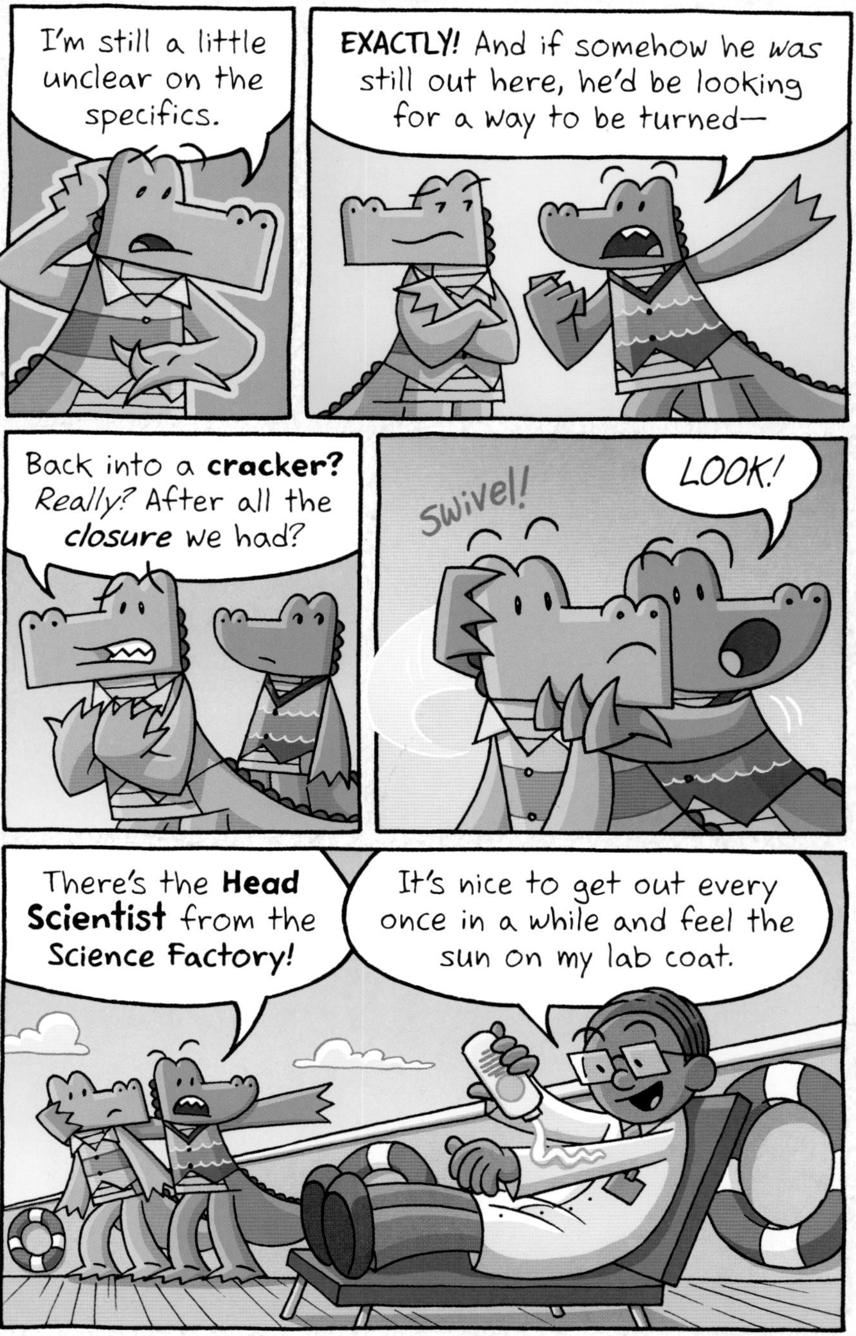
I'm still a little unclear on the specifics.
EXACTLY! And if somehow he was still out here, he'd be looking for a way to be turned—
Back into a cracker? Really? After all the closure we had?
SWIVEL!
LOOK!
There's the Head Scientist from the Science Factory!
It's nice to get out every once in a while and feel the sun on my lab coat.

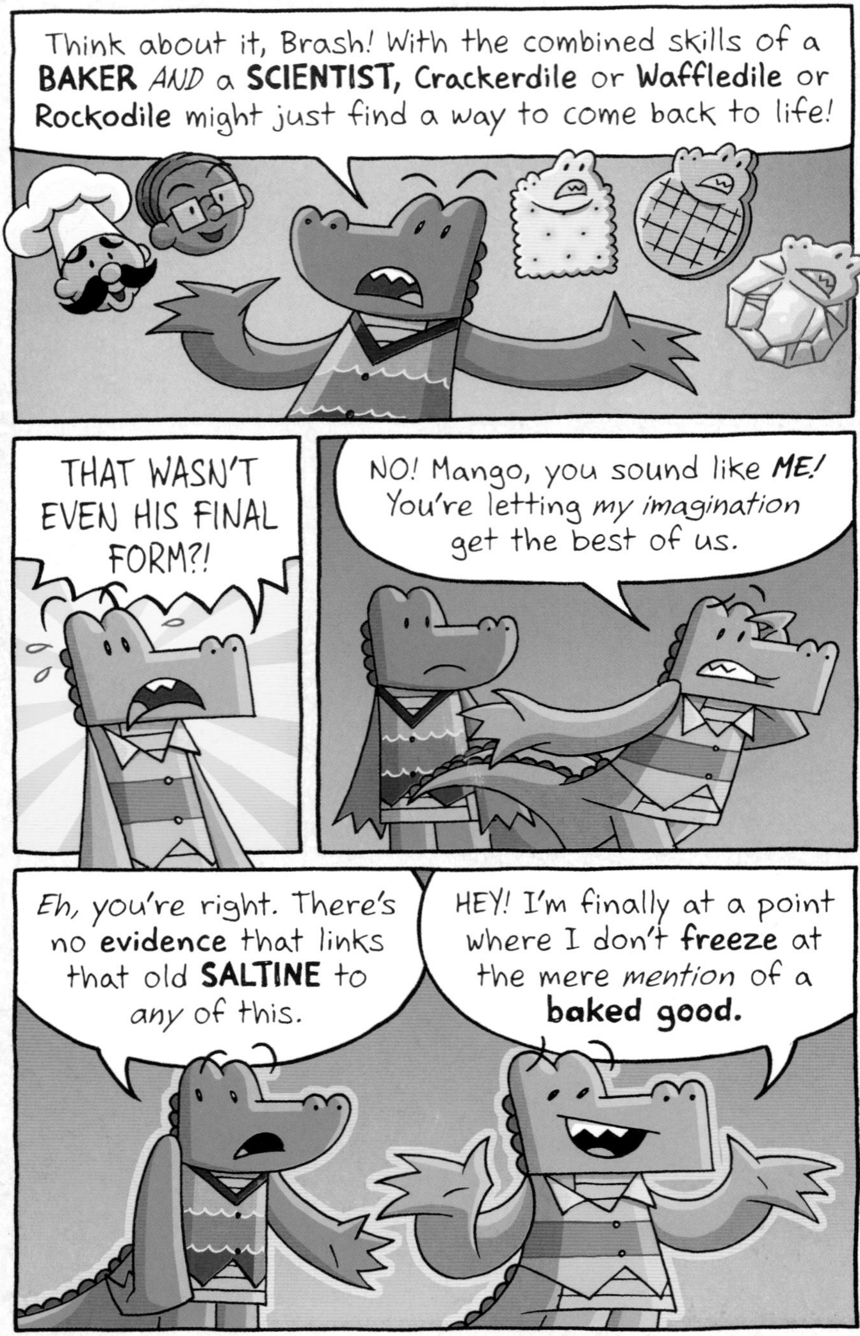
Think about it, Brash! With the combined skills of a **BAKER** *AND* a **SCIENTIST, Crackerdile** or **Waffledile** or **Rockodile** might just find a way to come back to life!
THAT WASN'T EVEN HIS FINAL FORM?!
NO! Mango, you sound like ***ME!*** You're letting *my imagination* get the best of us.
Eh, you're right. There's no **evidence** that links that old **SALTINE** to *any* of this.
HEY! I'm finally at a point where I don't **freeze** at the mere *mention* of a **baked good.**

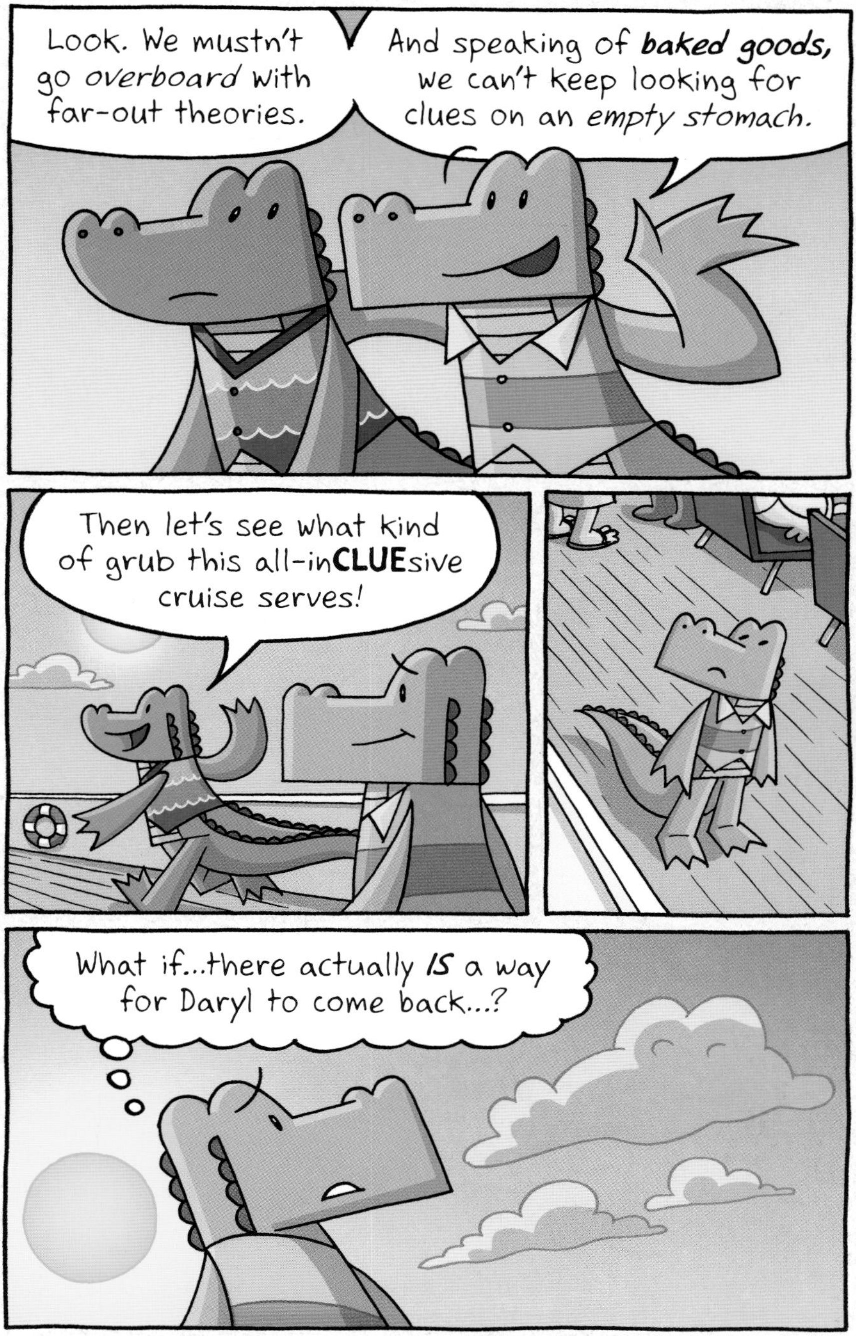
Look. We mustn't go *overboard* with far-out theories.
And speaking of **baked goods,** we can't keep looking for clues on an *empty stomach.*
Then let's see what kind of grub this all-in**CLUE**sive cruise serves!
What if...there actually ***IS*** a way for Daryl to come back...?

Chapter 6

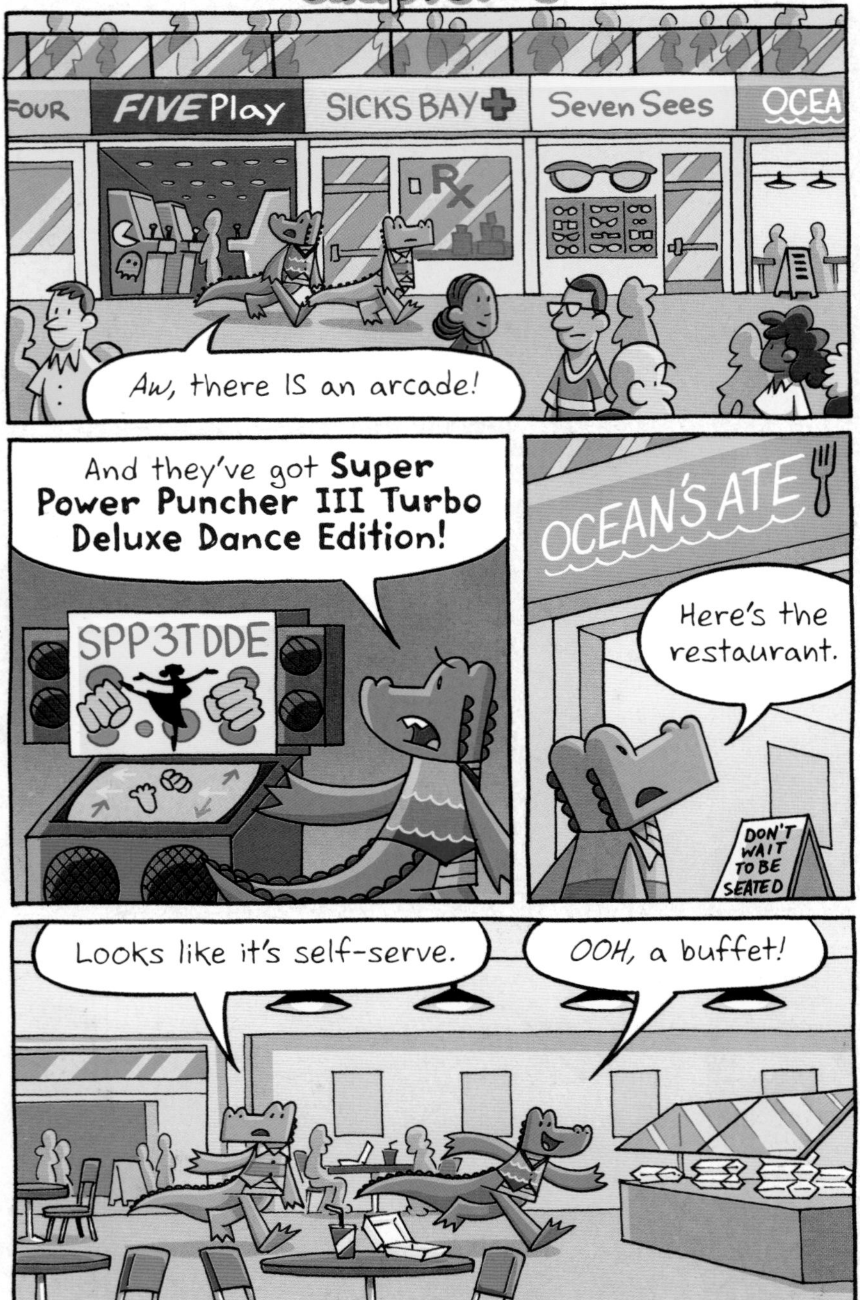
FOUR
FIVE Play
SICKS BAY
Seven Sees
OCEA
Aw, there IS an arcade!
And they've got **Super Power Puncher III Turbo Deluxe Dance Edition!**
SPP3TDDE
OCEAN'S ATE
Here's the restaurant.
DON'T WAIT TO BE SEATED
Looks like it's self-serve.
OOH, a buffet!

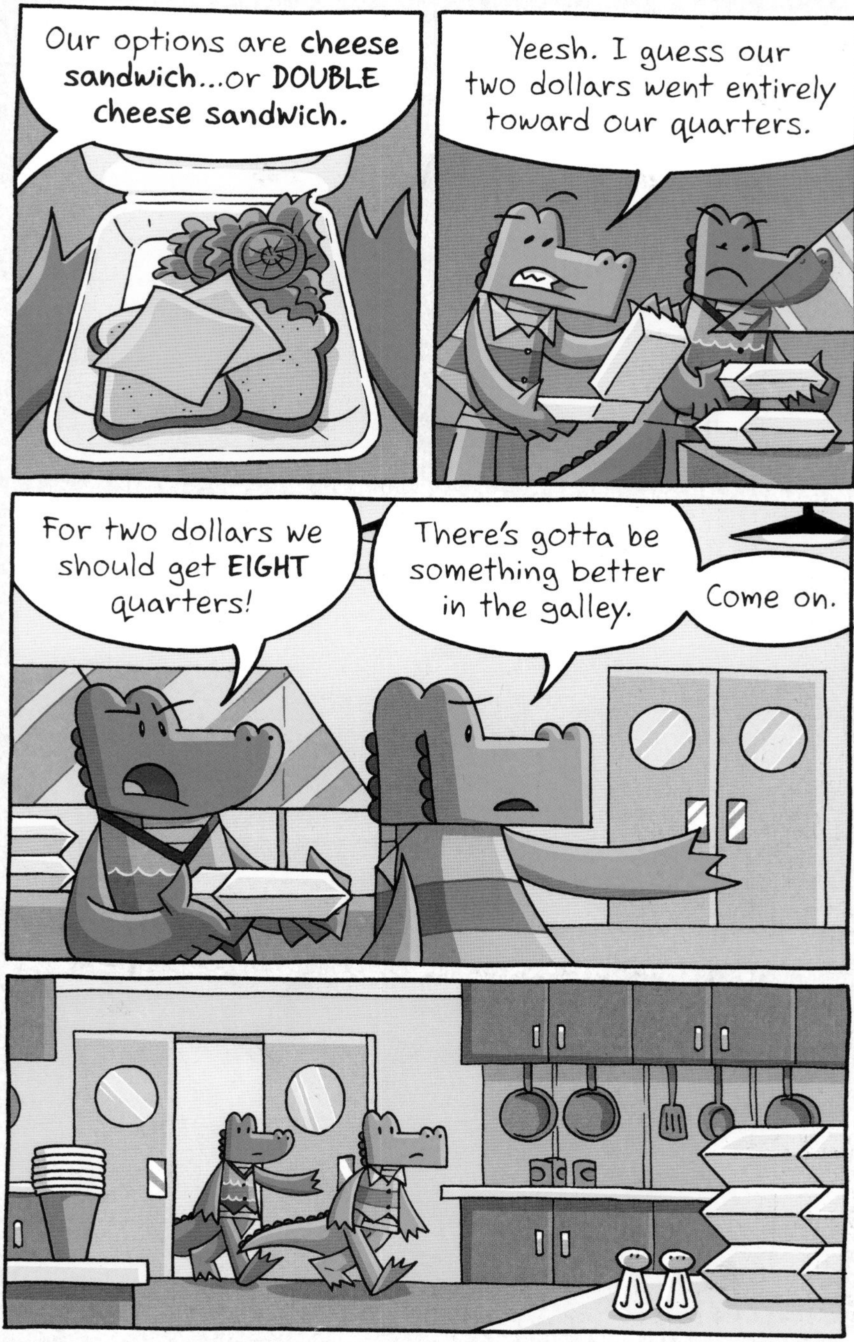
Our options are **cheese sandwich**...or **DOUBLE cheese sandwich.**
Yeesh. I guess our two dollars went entirely toward our quarters.
For two dollars we should get **EIGHT** quarters!
There's gotta be something better in the galley.
Come on.

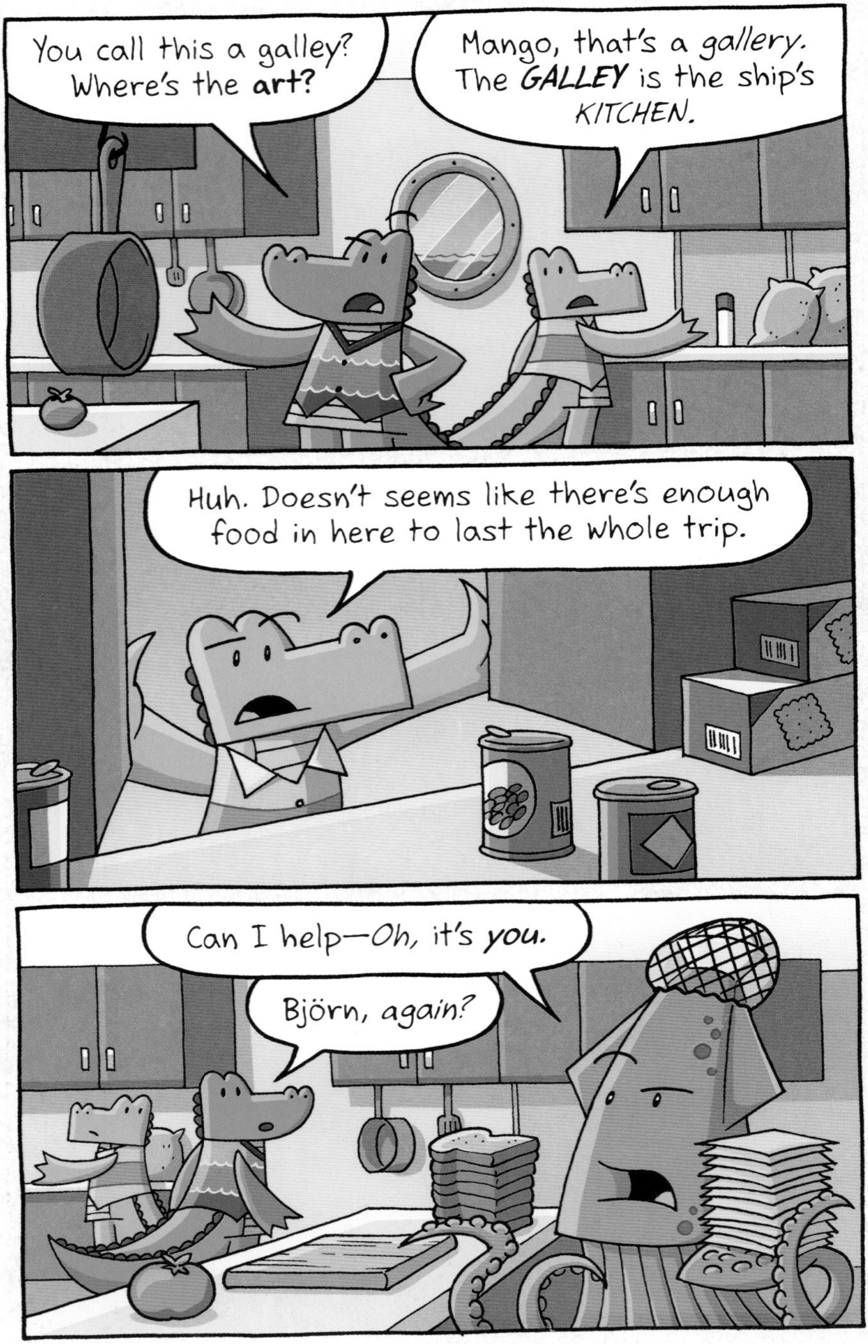
You call this a galley? Where's the **art?**
Mango, that's a *gallery.* The ***GALLEY*** is the ship's *KITCHEN.*
Huh. Doesn't seems like there's enough food in here to last the whole trip.
Can I help—*Oh,* it's ***you.***
Björn, *again?*

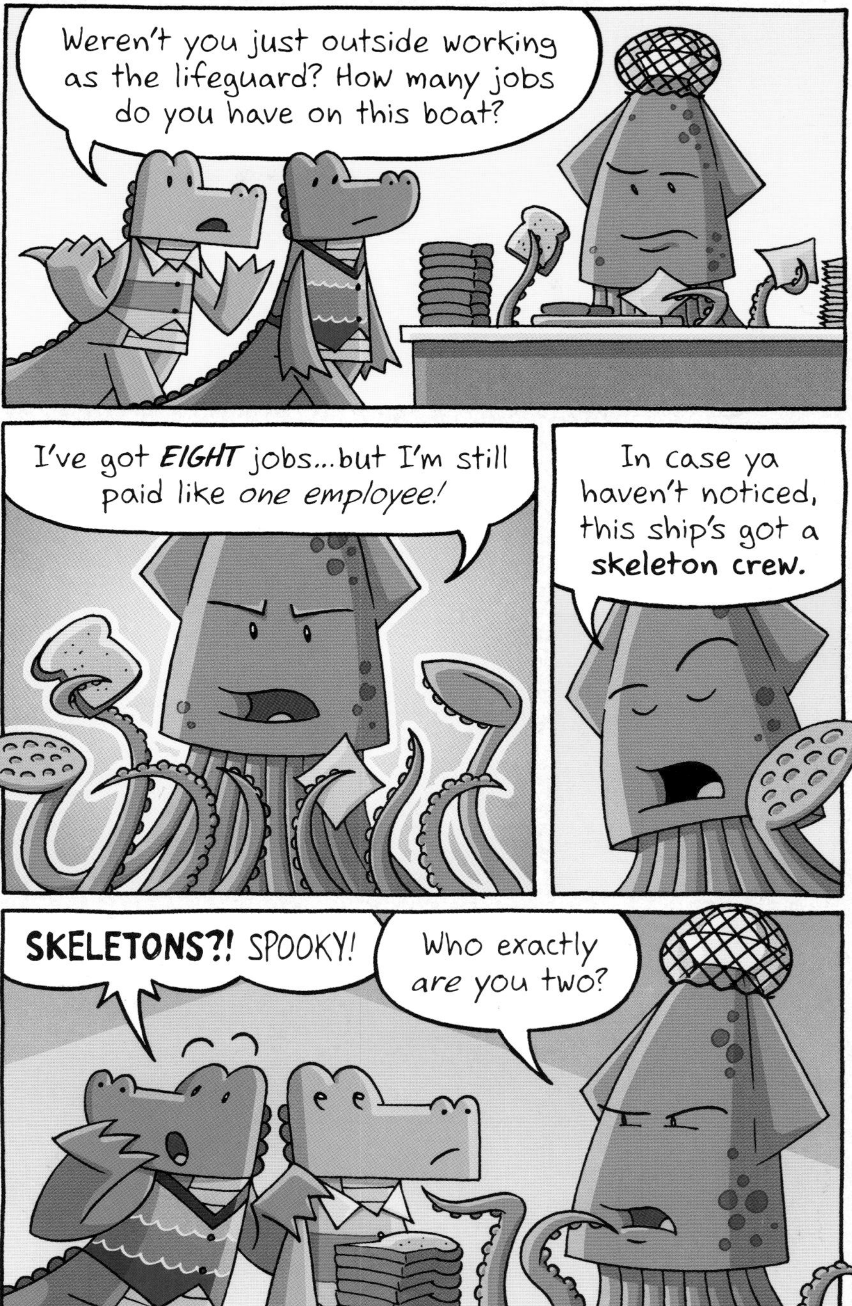
Weren't you just outside working as the lifeguard? How many jobs do you have on this boat?
I've got **EIGHT** jobs...but I'm still paid like *one employee!*
In case ya haven't noticed, this ship's got a **skeleton crew.**
SKELETONS?! SPOOKY!
Who exactly are you two?

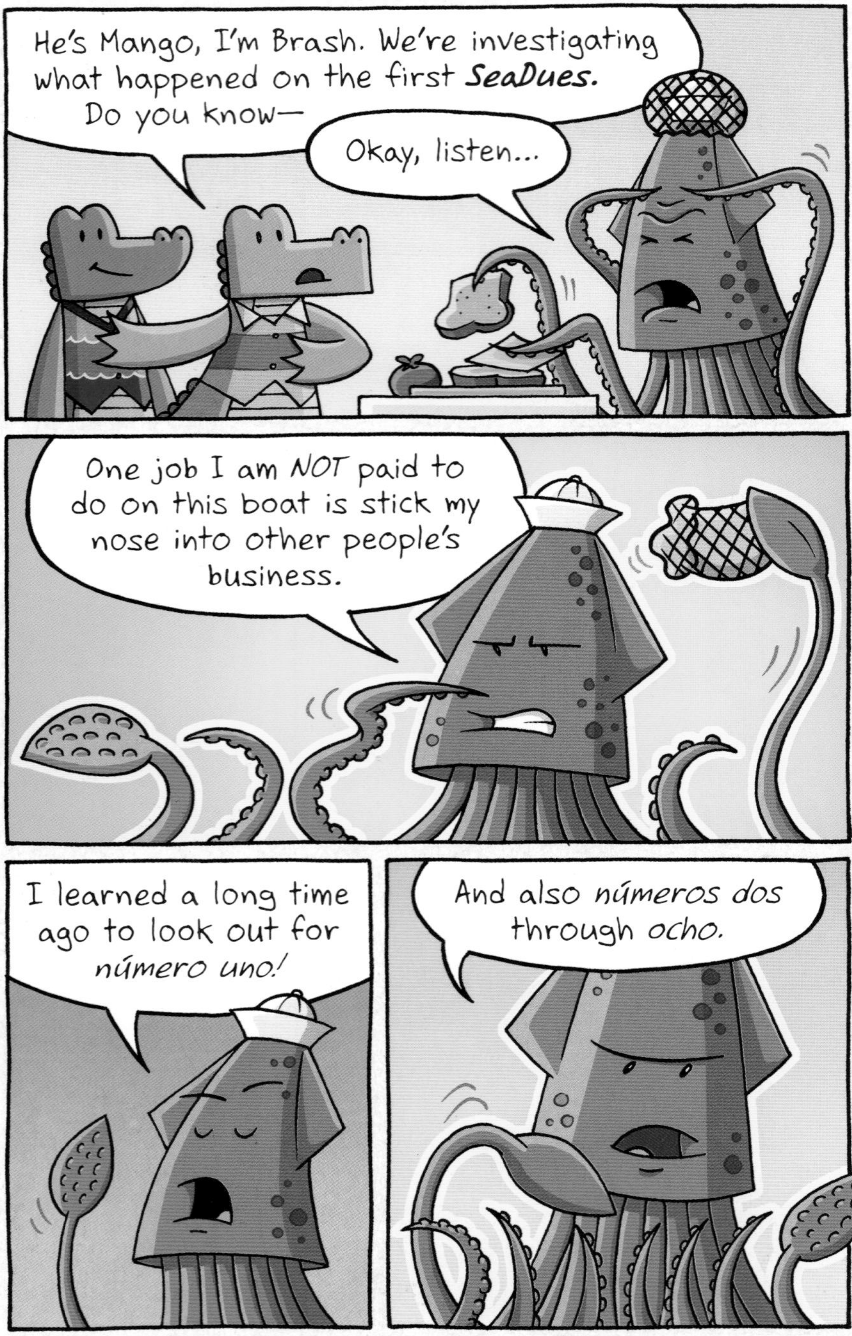

He's Mango, I'm Brash. We're investigating what happened on the first **SeaDues.** Do you know—
Okay, listen...
One job I am *NOT* paid to do on this boat is stick my nose into other people's business.
I learned a long time ago to look out for *número uno!*
And also *números dos* through *ocho.*

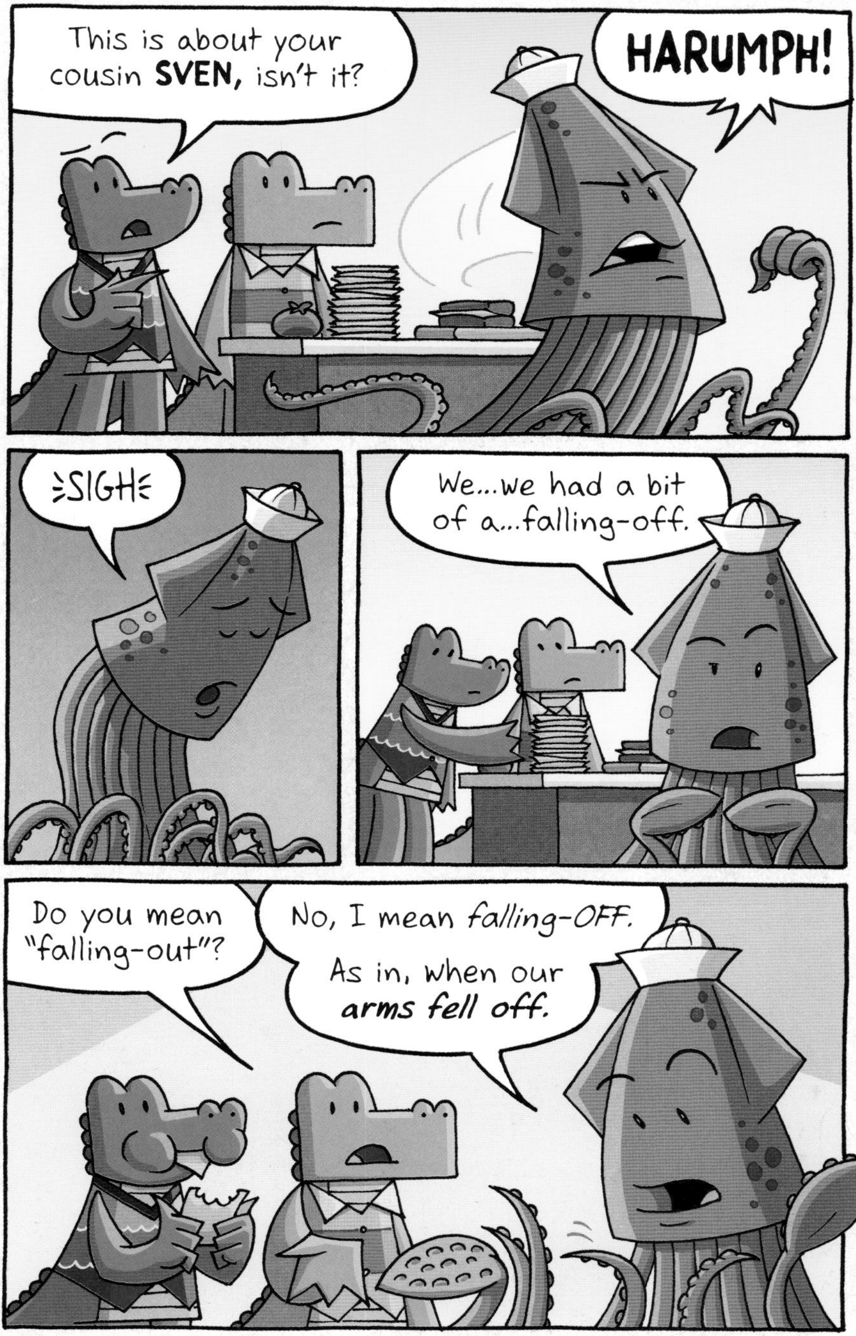
This is about your cousin **SVEN,** isn't it?
HARUMPH!
SIGH
We...we had a bit of a...falling-off.
Do you mean "falling-out"?
No, I mean *falling-OFF.*
As in, when our **arms fell off.**

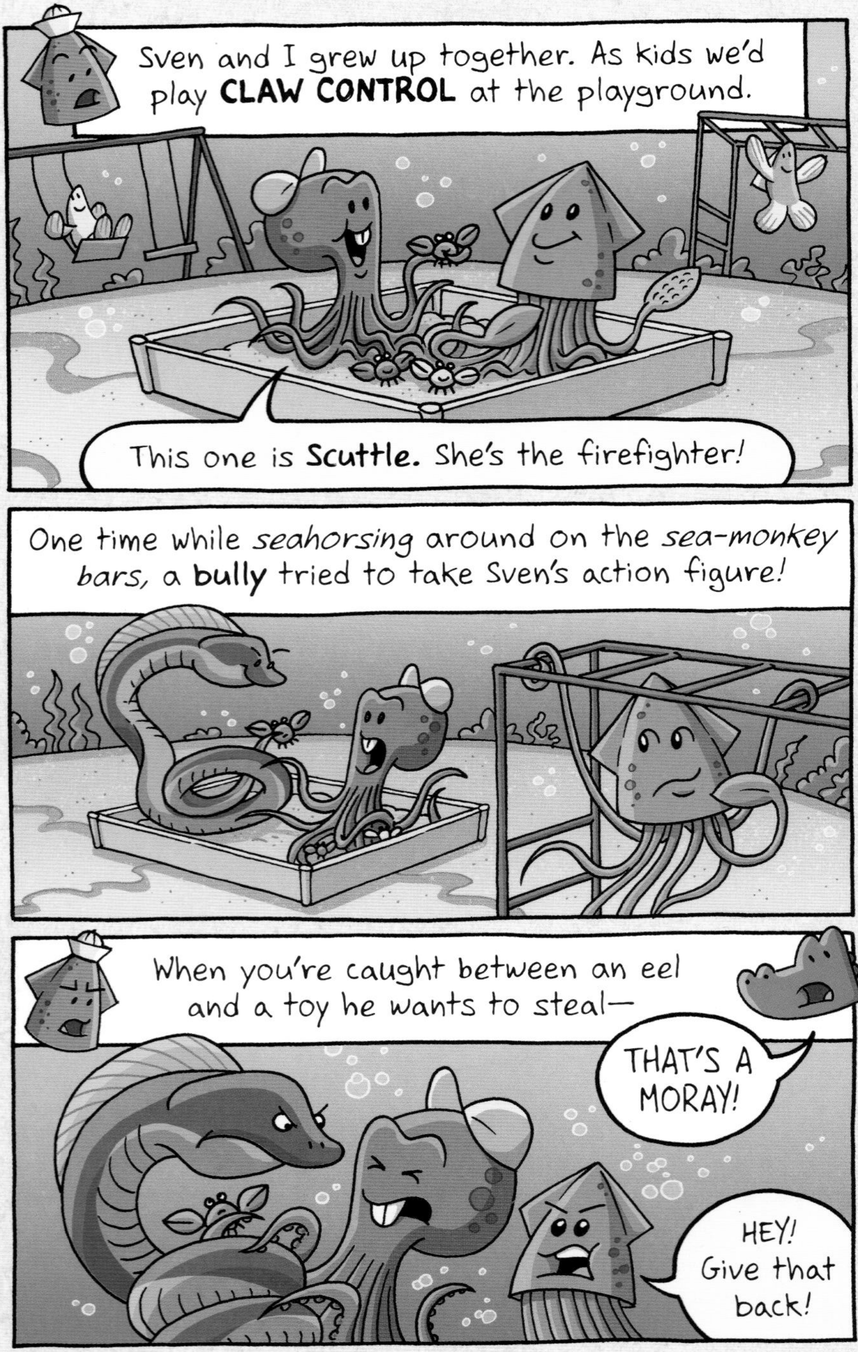

Sven and I grew up together. As kids we'd play **CLAW CONTROL** at the playground.
This one is **Scuttle.** She's the firefighter!
One time while *seahorsing* around on the *sea-monkey bars,* a **bully** tried to take Sven's action figure!
When you're caught between an eel and a toy he wants to steal—
THAT'S A MORAY!
HEY! Give that back!

I *could've* let Sven fight his own battle. But I stepped in, and things got out of hand...*literally!*

At first, we laughed it off as no big deal, because squid and octopus tentacles grow back.

Except, for some reason... Sven's *didn't!*

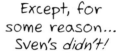

Sven blamed **me** for it! All I did was *help* him! I got back his toy, but *I* was the *BAD GUY?!*

I got *grounded*, and his parents wouldn't let us play together anymore.

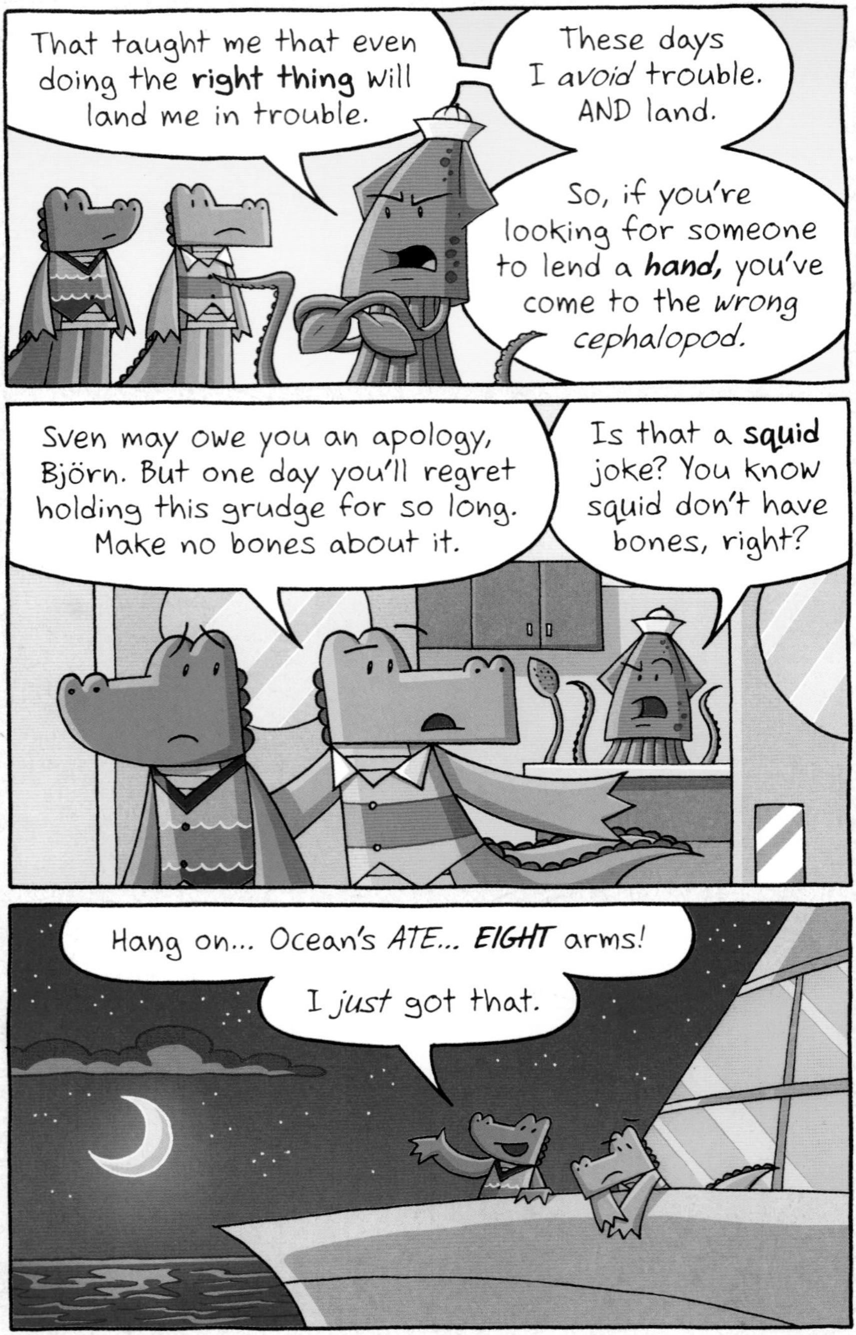
That taught me that even doing the **right thing** will land me in trouble.
These days I *avoid* trouble. AND land.
So, if you're looking for someone to lend a ***hand,*** you've come to the *wrong cephalopod.*
Sven may owe you an apology, Björn. But one day you'll regret holding this grudge for so long. Make no bones about it.
Is that a **squid** joke? You know squid don't have bones, right?
Hang on... Ocean's *ATE*... ***EIGHT*** arms!
I *just* got that.

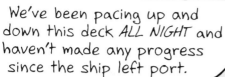

Chapter 7

We've been pacing up and down this deck *ALL NIGHT* and haven't made any progress since the ship left port.

Port? This case is too im**PORT**ant to give up now, Brash!

I'm too tired for jokes, Mango.

I'm not joking. In fact, I'm *done* **KITTEN** around.

Okay, that *was* a joke. But I **meant** it! *FOLLOW ME!*

Beep

BRIDGE

POUNCE!

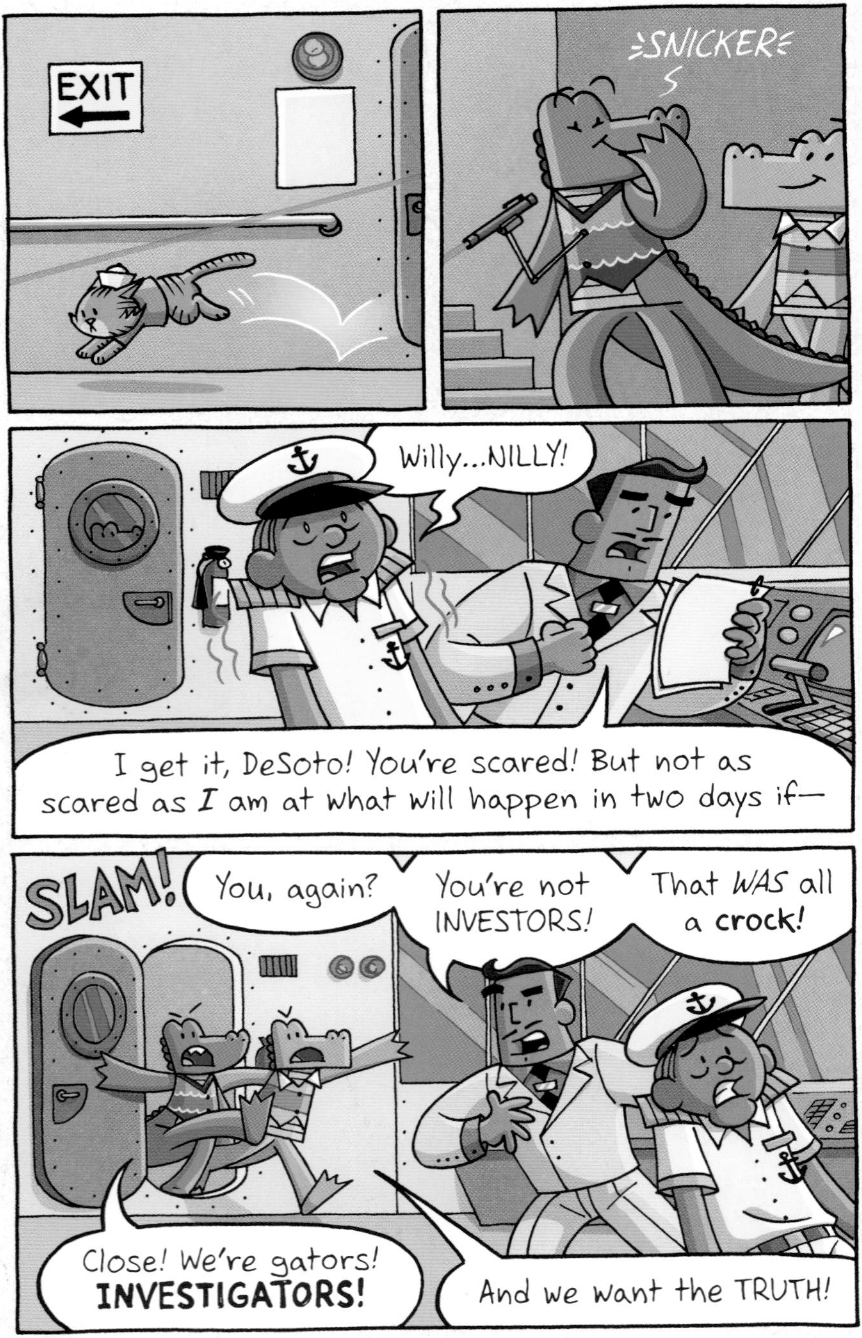
EXIT
SNICKER
Willy...NILLY!
I get it, DeSoto! You're scared! But not as scared as *I* am at what will happen in two days if—
SLAM!
You, again?
You're not INVESTORS!
That *WAS* all a **crock!**
Close! We're gators! **INVESTIGATORS!**
And we want the TRUTH!

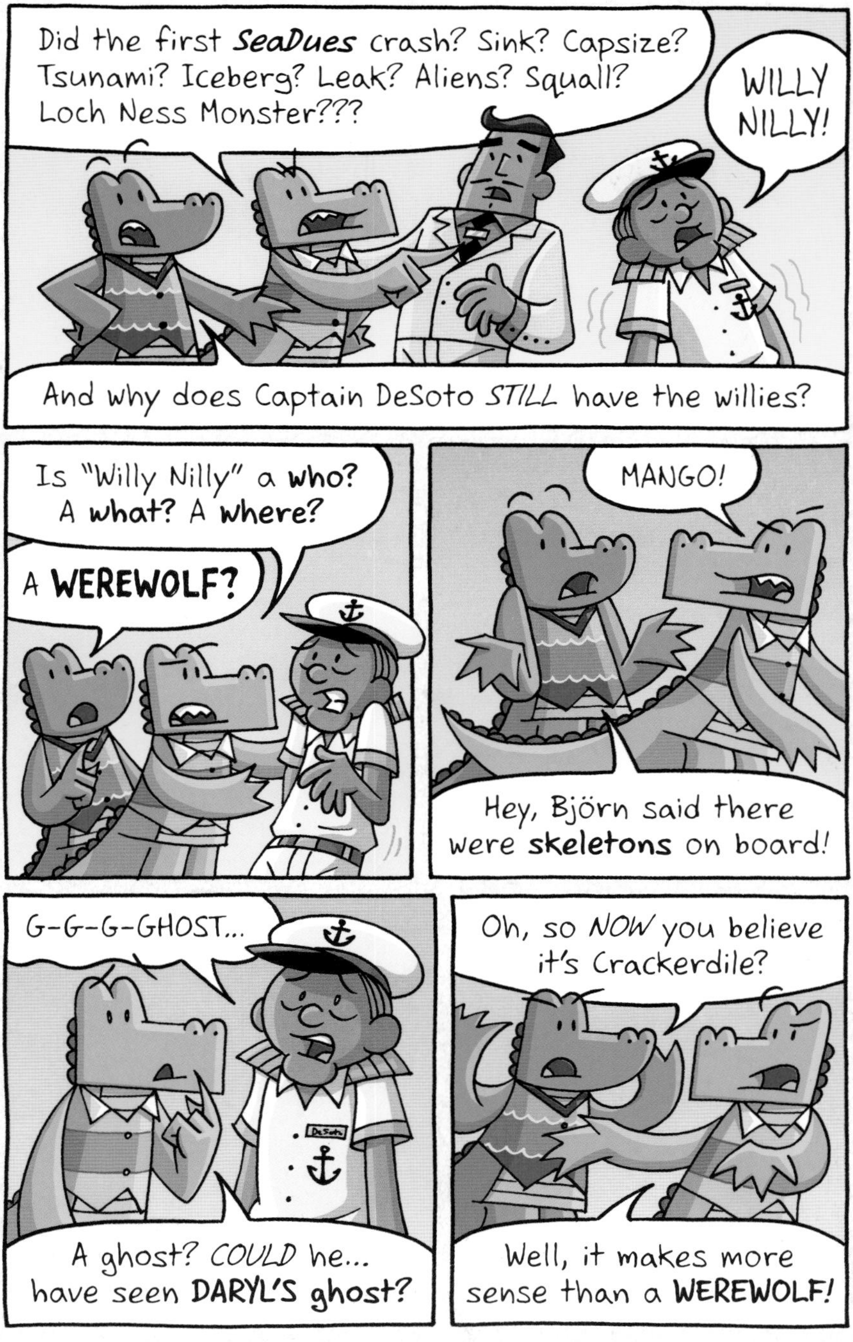

Did the first SeaDues crash? Sink? Capsize? Tsunami? Iceberg? Leak? Aliens? Squall? Loch Ness Monster???
WILLY NILLY!
And why does Captain DeSoto STILL have the willies?
Is "Willy Nilly" a who? A what? A where?
A WEREWOLF?
MANGO!
Hey, Björn said there were skeletons on board!
G-G-G-GHOST...
DeSoto
A ghost? COULD he... have seen DARYL'S ghost?
Oh, so NOW you believe it's Crackerdile?
Well, it makes more sense than a WEREWOLF!

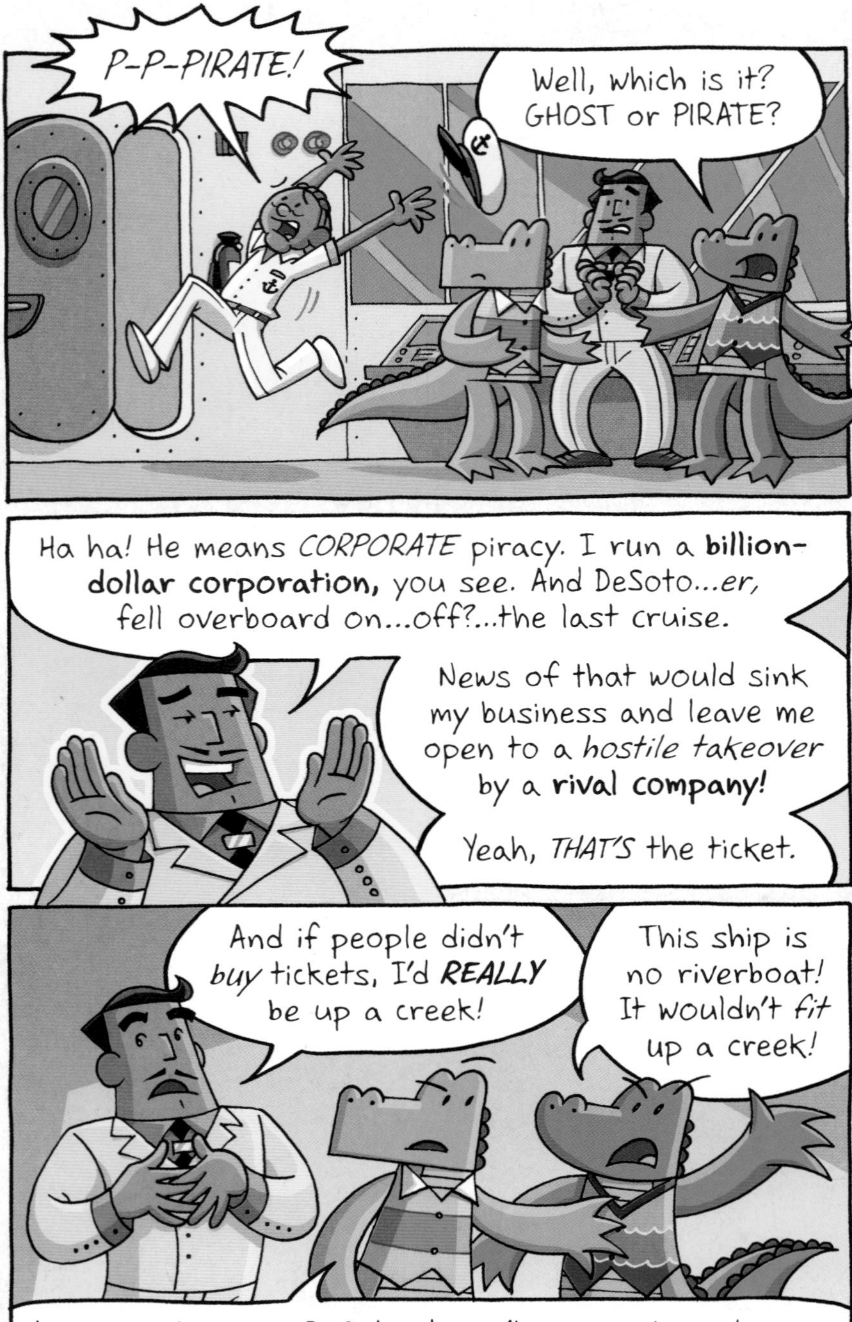
P-P-PIRATE!
Well, which is it? GHOST or PIRATE?
Ha ha! He means *CORPORATE* piracy. I run a **billion-dollar corporation,** you see. And DeSoto...*er,* fell overboard on...off?...the last cruise.
News of that would sink my business and leave me open to a *hostile takeover* by a **rival company!**
Yeah, *THAT'S* the ticket.
And if people didn't *buy* tickets, I'd ***REALLY*** be up a creek!
This ship is no riverboat! It wouldn't *fit* up a creek!
Mango, make sure DeSoto doesn't go overboard again.

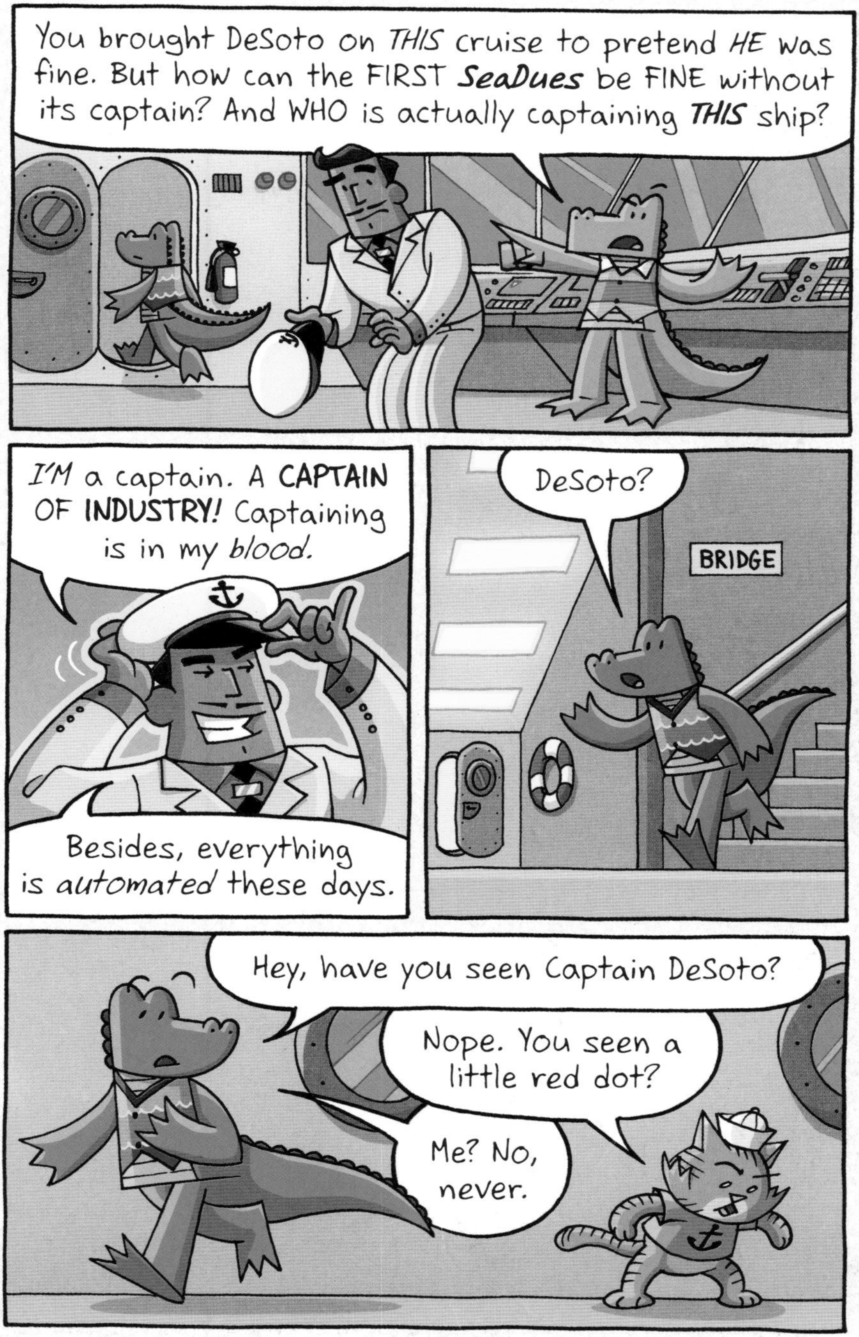
You brought DeSoto on *THIS* cruise to pretend *HE* was fine. But how can the FIRST ***SeaDues*** be FINE without its captain? And WHO is actually captaining ***THIS*** ship?
I'M a captain. A **CAPTAIN OF INDUSTRY!** Captaining is in my *blood.*
Besides, everything is *automated* these days.
DeSoto?
BRIDGE
Hey, have you seen Captain DeSoto?
Nope. You seen a little red dot?
Me? No, never.

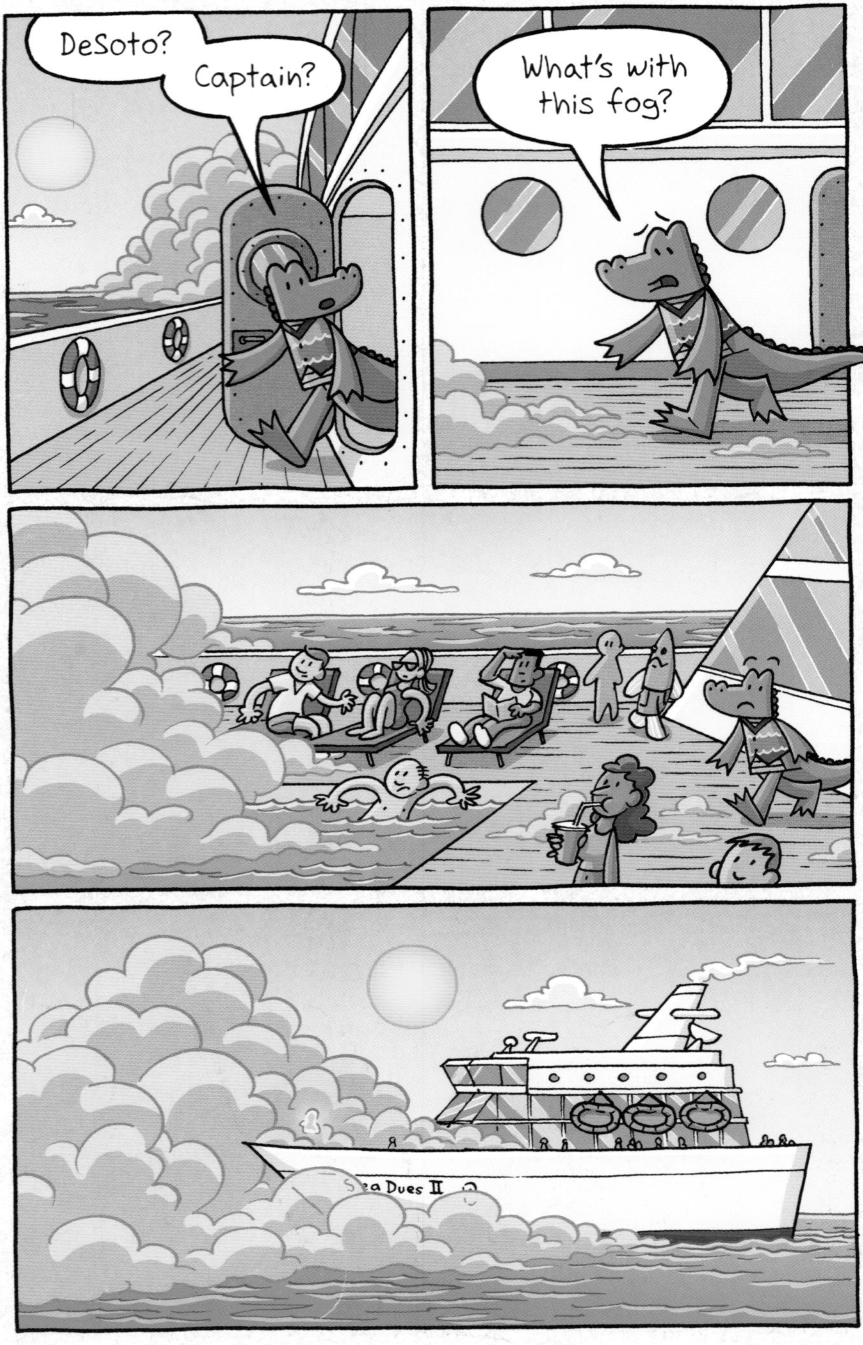
DeSoto?
Captain?
What's with this fog?
Sea Dues II

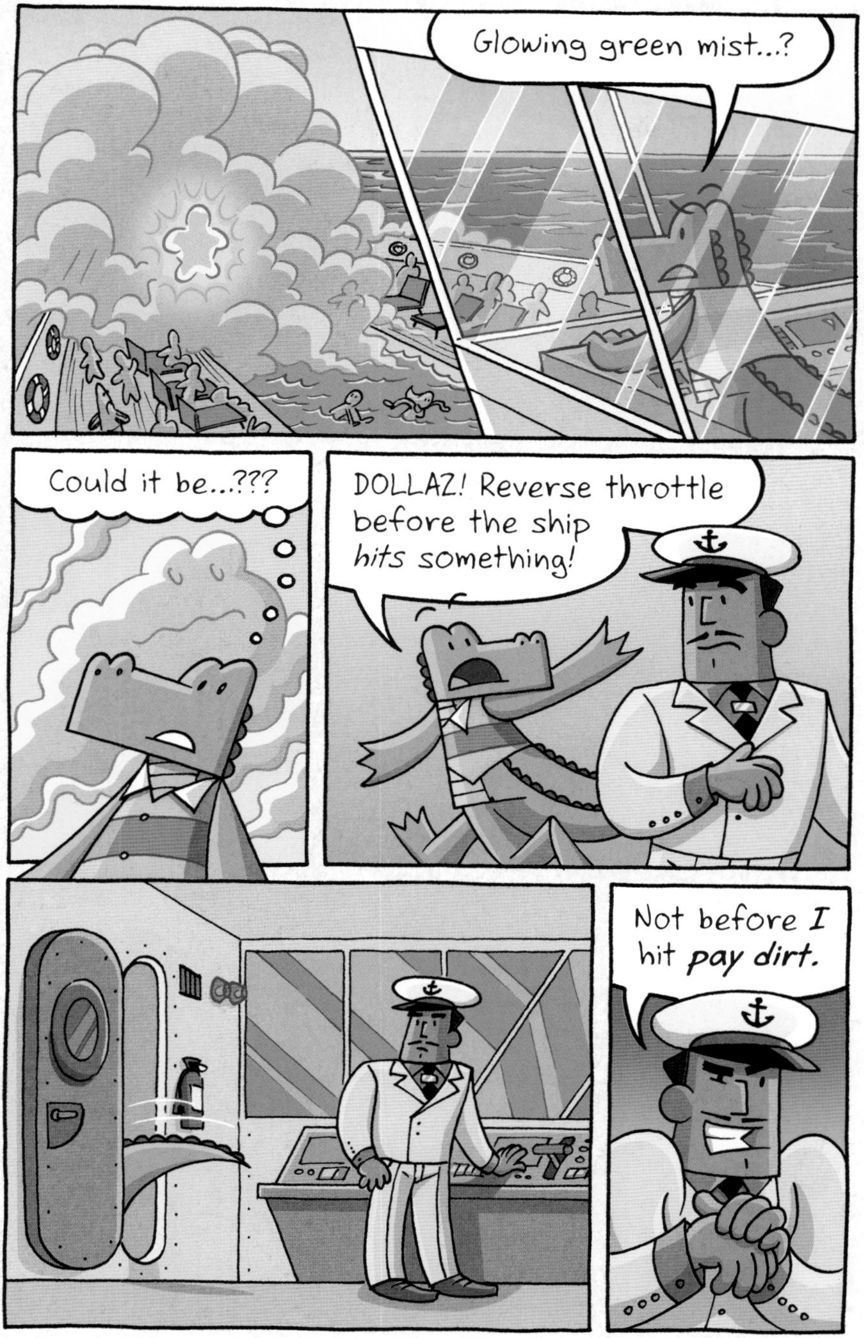
Glowing green mist...?
Could it be...???
DOLLAZ! Reverse throttle before the ship *hits* something!
Not before *I* hit *pay dirt.*

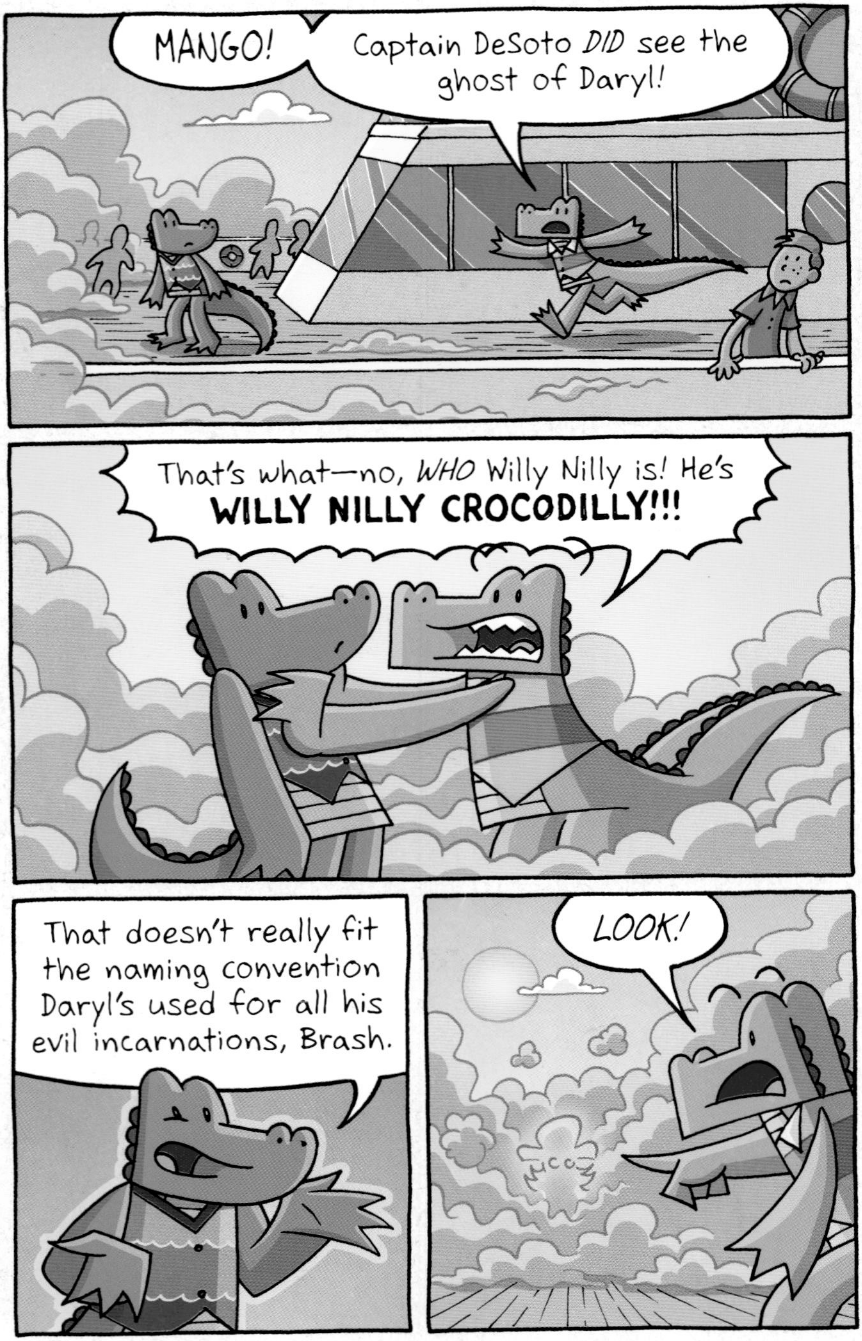
MANGO!
Captain DeSoto *DID* see the ghost of Daryl!
That's what—no, *WHO* Willy Nilly is! He's **WILLY NILLY CROCODILLY!!!**
That doesn't really fit the naming convention Daryl's used for all his evil incarnations, Brash.
LOOK!

Chapter 8

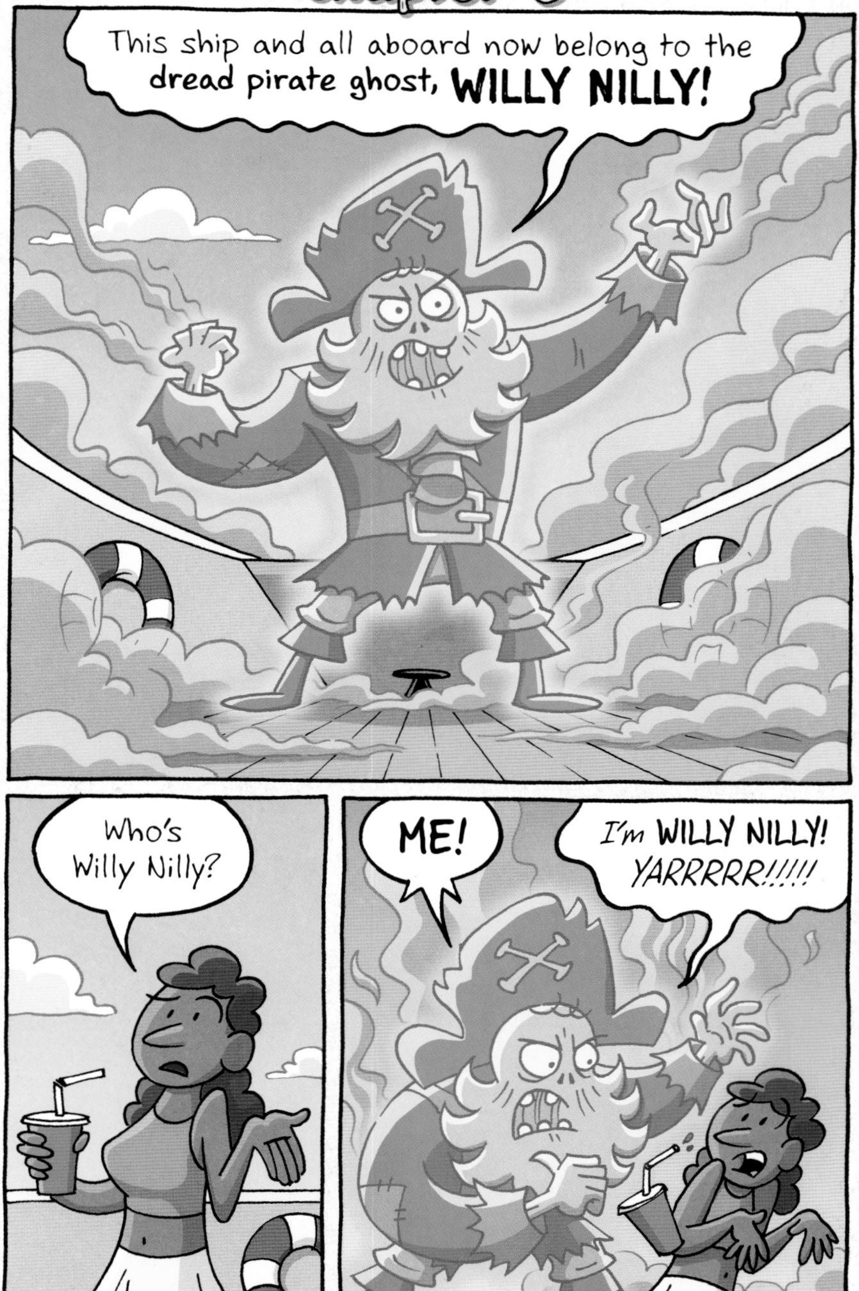

This ship and all aboard now belong to the dread pirate ghost, WILLY NILLY!
Who's Willy Nilly?
ME!
I'm WILLY NILLY! YARRRRR!!!!!

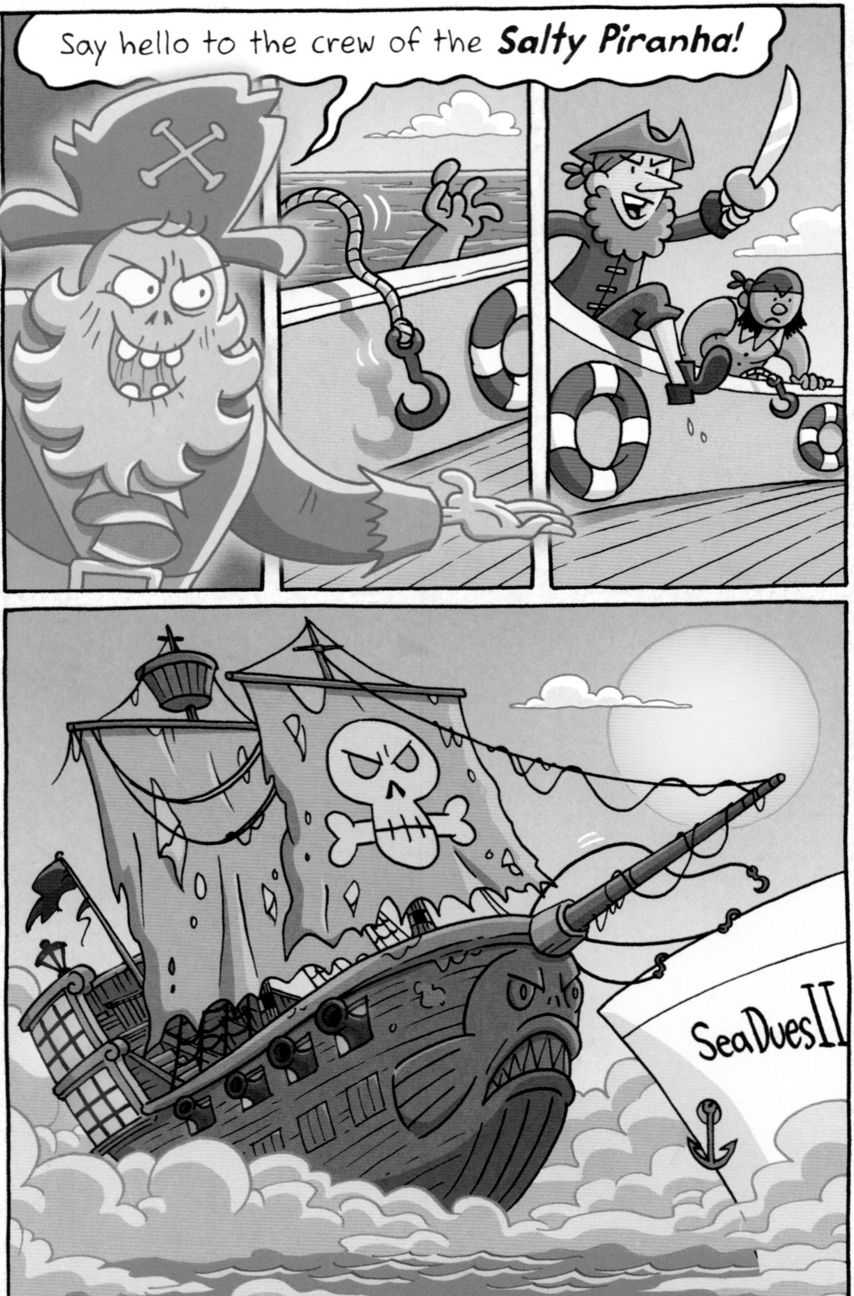
Say hello to the crew of the **Salty Piranha!**
SeaDues II

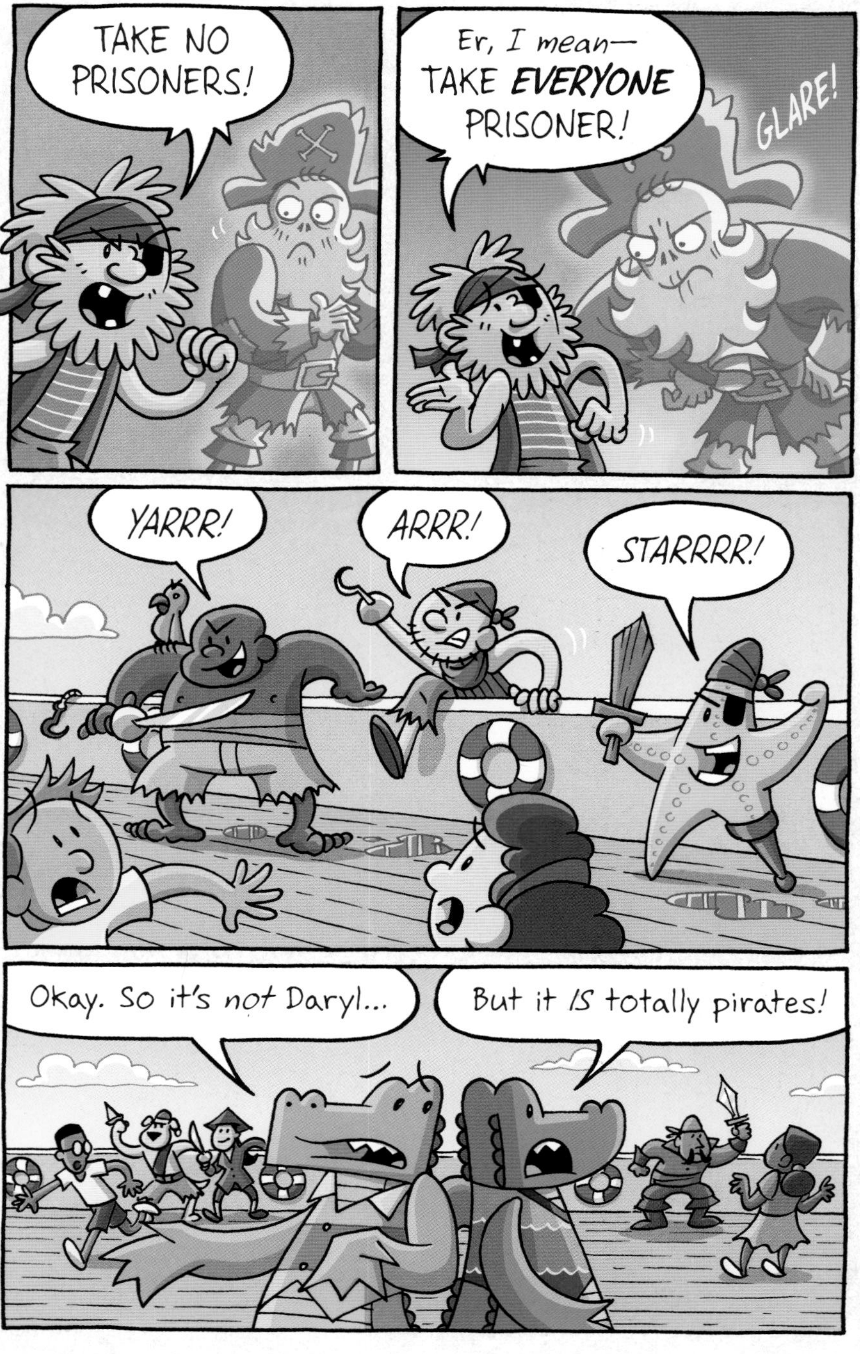
TAKE NO PRISONERS!
Er, I mean— TAKE **EVERYONE** PRISONER!
GLARE!
YARRR!
ARRR!
STARRRR!
Okay. So it's *not* Daryl...
But it *IS* totally pirates!

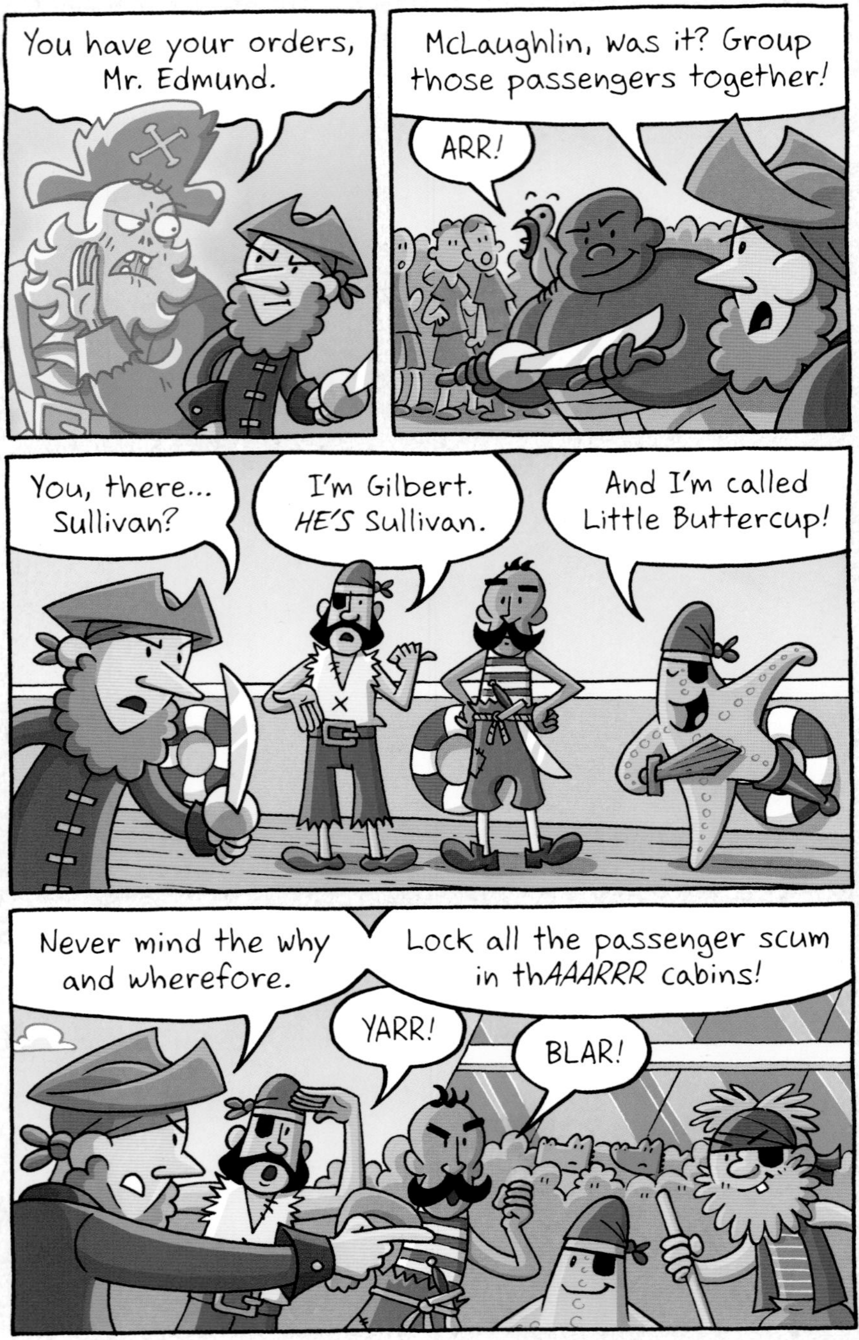

You have your orders, Mr. Edmund.
McLaughlin, was it? Group those passengers together!
ARR!
You, there... Sullivan?
I'm Gilbert. *HE'S* Sullivan.
And I'm called Little Buttercup!
Never mind the why and wherefore.
Lock all the passenger scum in th*AAARRR* cabins!
YARR!
BLAR!

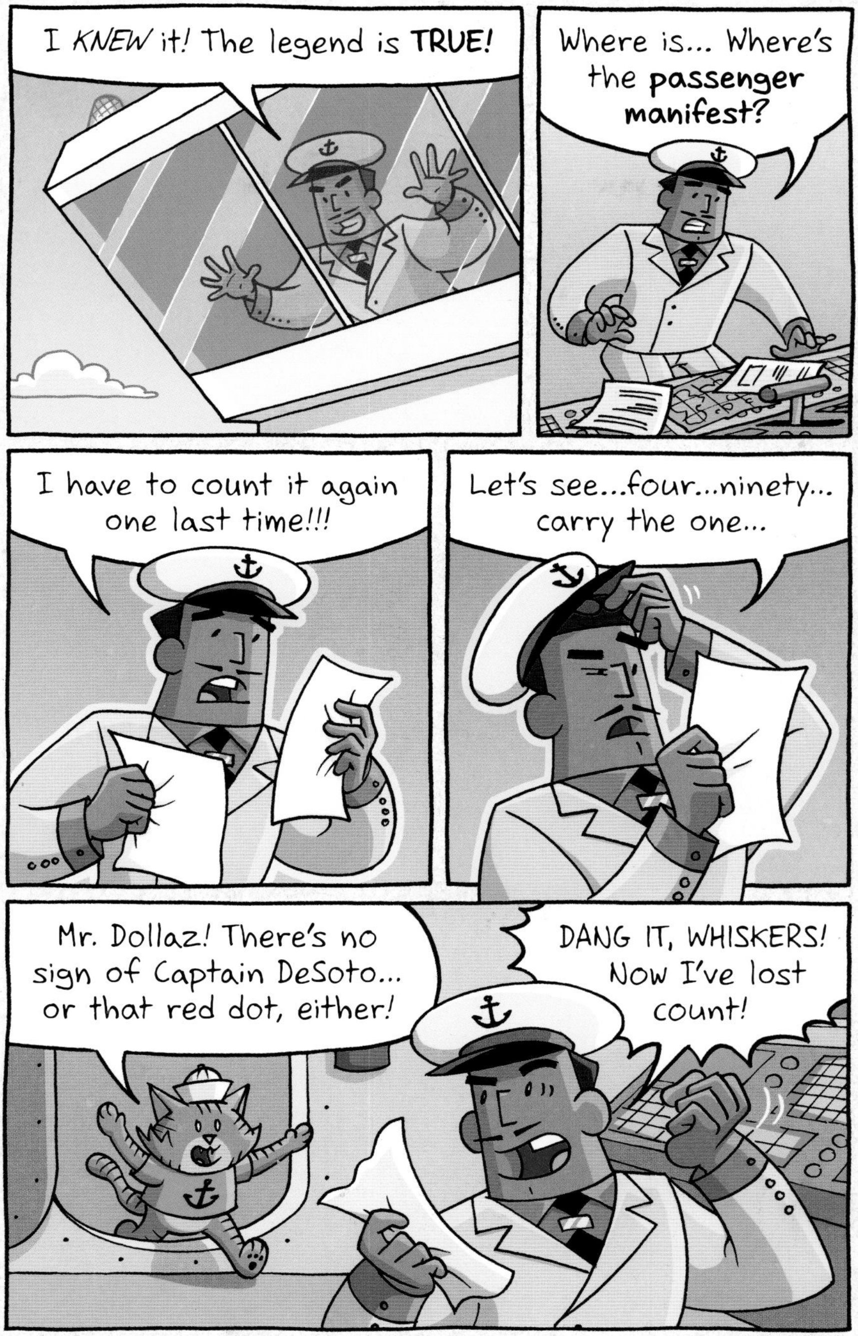
I *KNEW* it! The legend is **TRUE!**
Where is... Where's the **passenger manifest?**
I have to count it again one last time!!!
Let's see...four...ninety... carry the one...
Mr. Dollaz! There's no sign of Captain DeSoto... or that red dot, either!
DANG IT, WHISKERS! Now I've lost count!

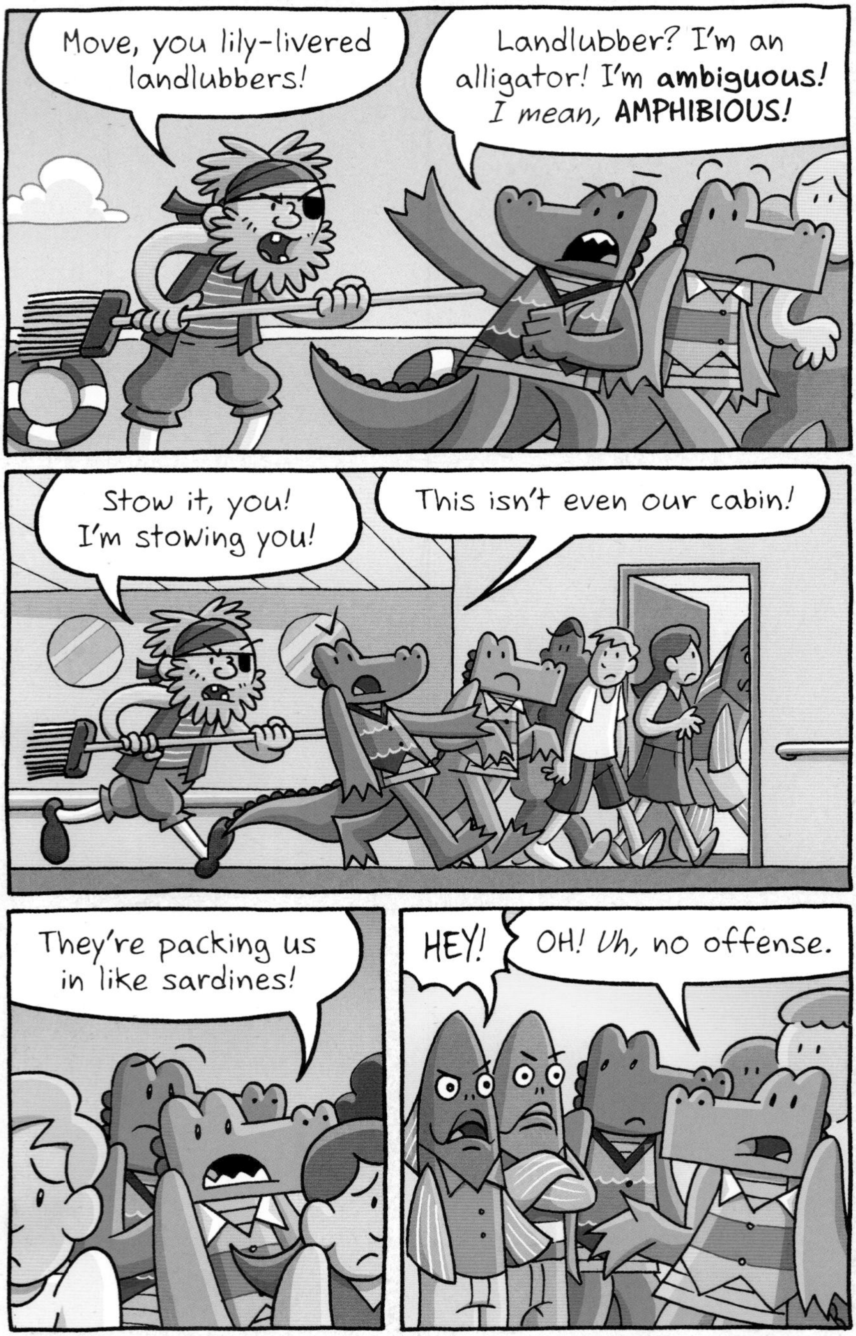
Move, you lily-livered landlubbers!
Landlubber? I'm an alligator! I'm **ambiguous!** *I mean,* **AMPHIBIOUS!**
Stow it, you! I'm stowing you!
This isn't even our cabin!
They're packing us in like sardines!
HEY!
OH! *Uh,* no offense.

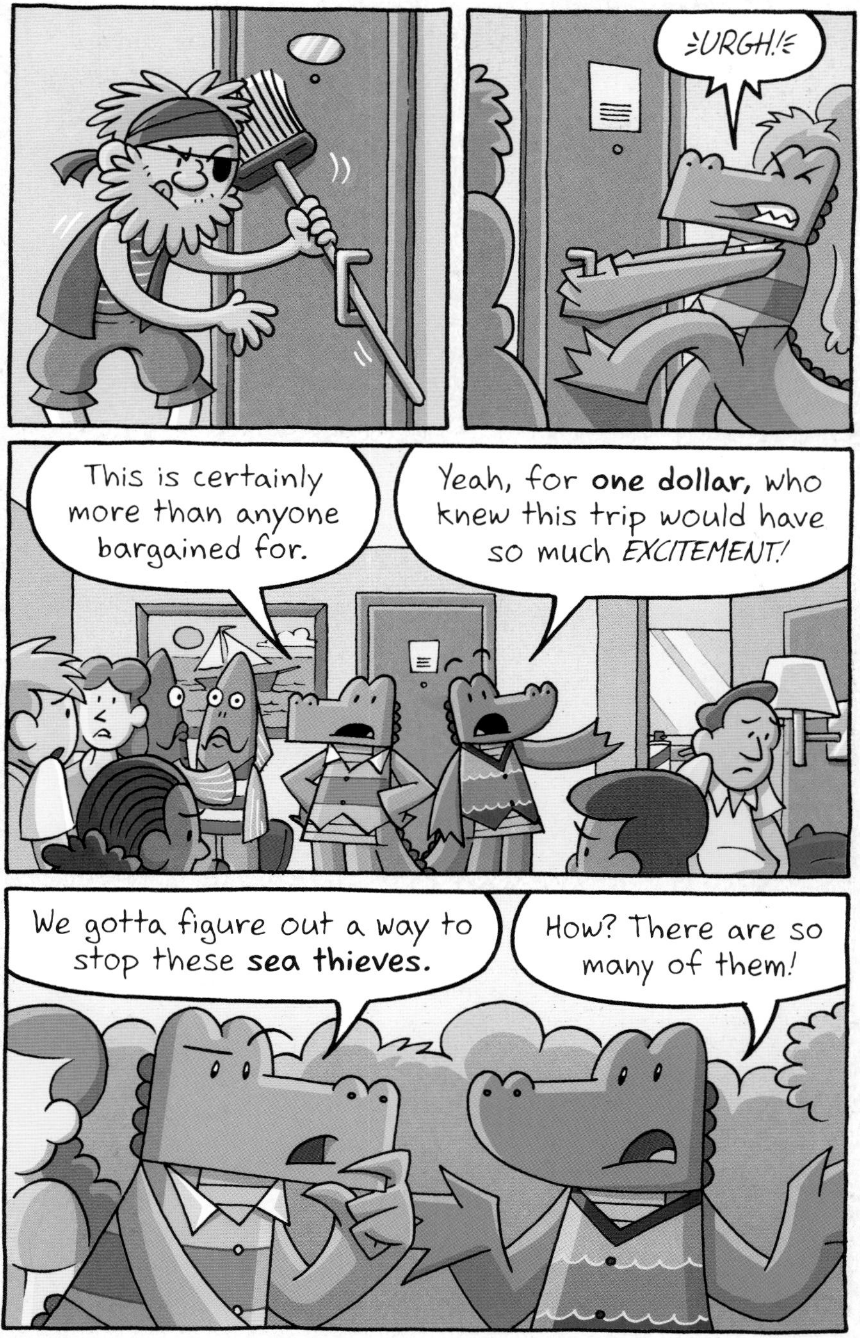
URGH!
This is certainly more than anyone bargained for.
Yeah, for **one dollar,** who knew this trip would have so much *EXCITEMENT!*
We gotta figure out a way to stop these **sea thieves.**
How? There are so many of them!

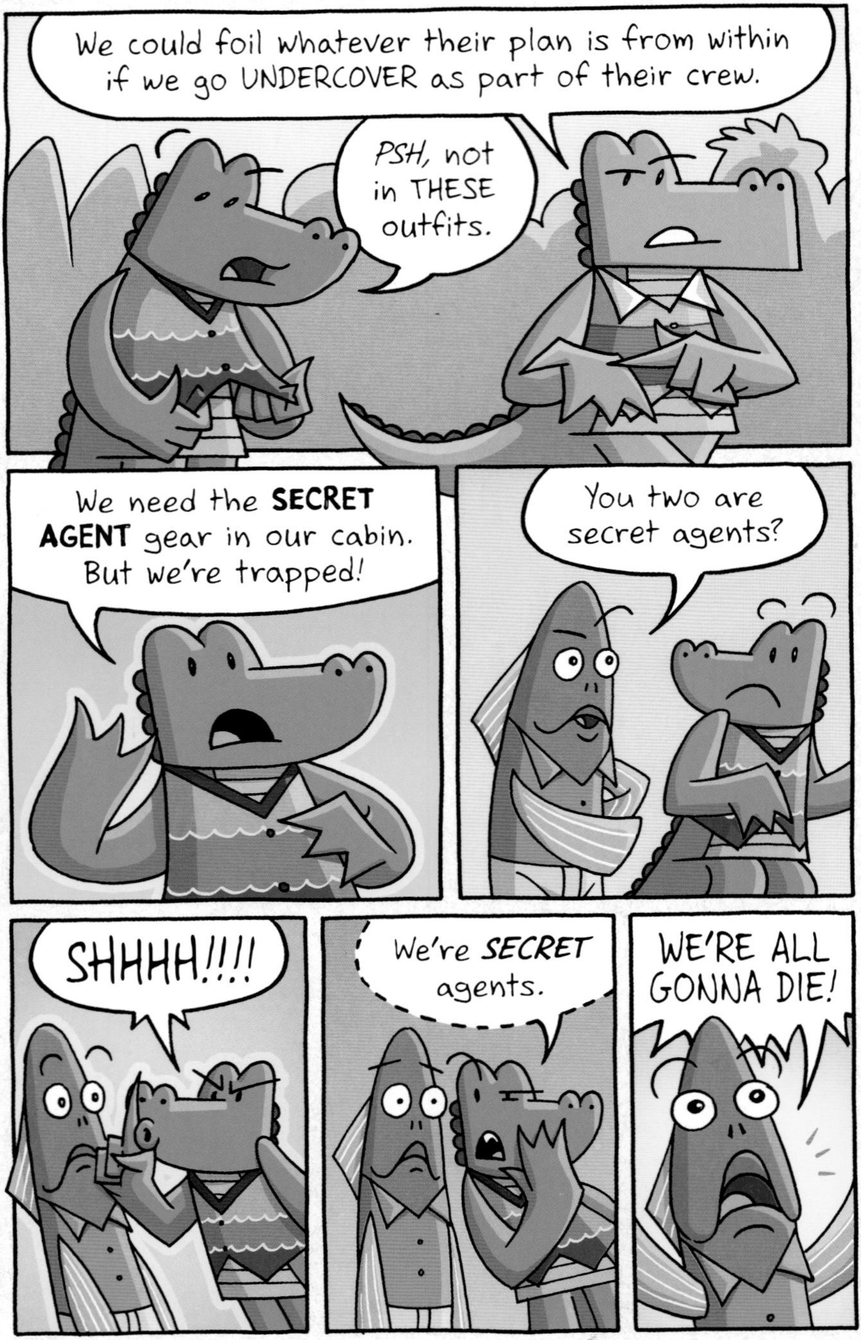
We could foil whatever their plan is from within if we go UNDERCOVER as part of their crew.
PSH, not in THESE outfits.
We need the **SECRET AGENT** gear in our cabin. But we're trapped!
You two are secret agents?
SHHHH!!!!
We're ***SECRET*** agents.
WE'RE ALL GONNA DIE!

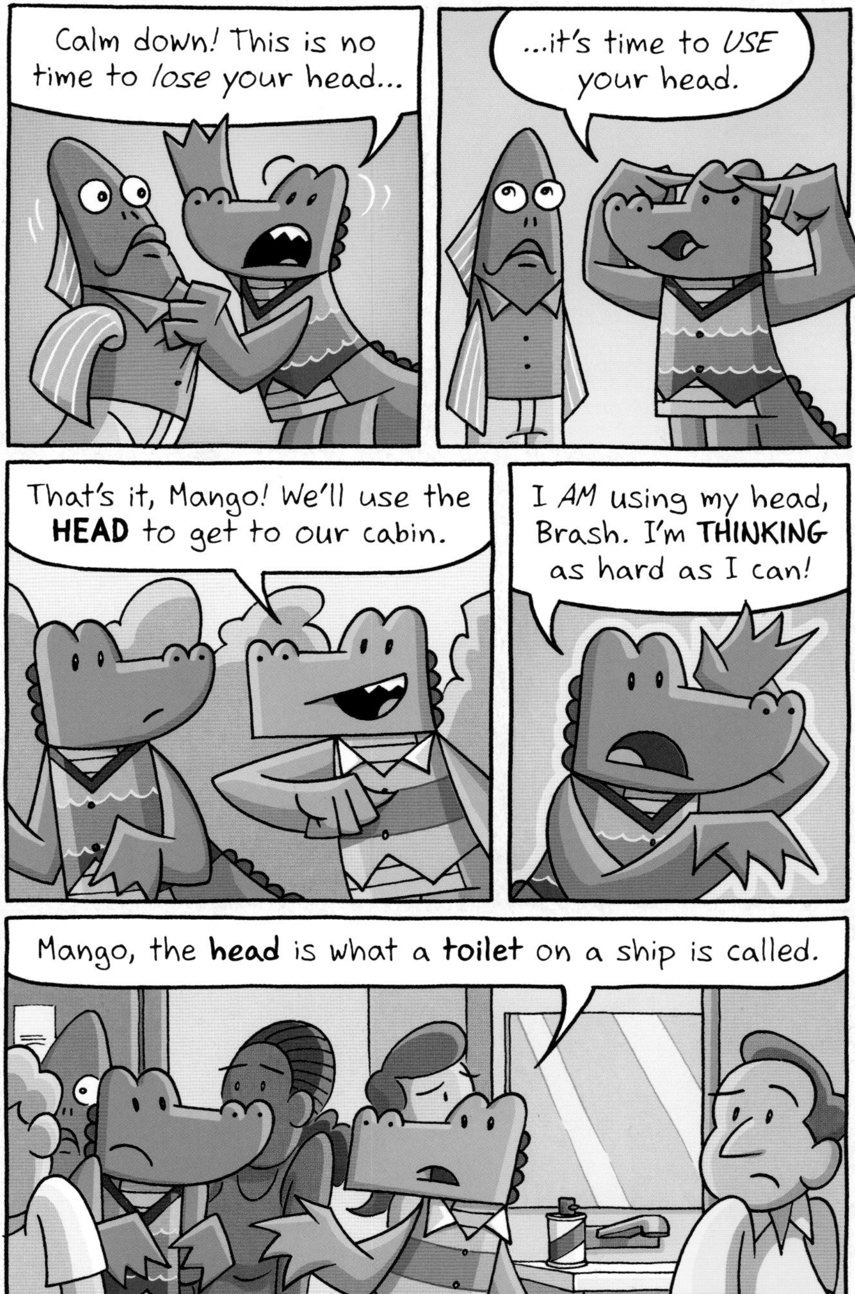
Calm down! This is no time to *lose* your head...
...it's time to *USE* your head.
That's it, Mango! We'll use the **HEAD** to get to our cabin.
I *AM* using my head, Brash. I'm **THINKING** as hard as I can!
Mango, the **head** is what a **toilet** on a ship is called.

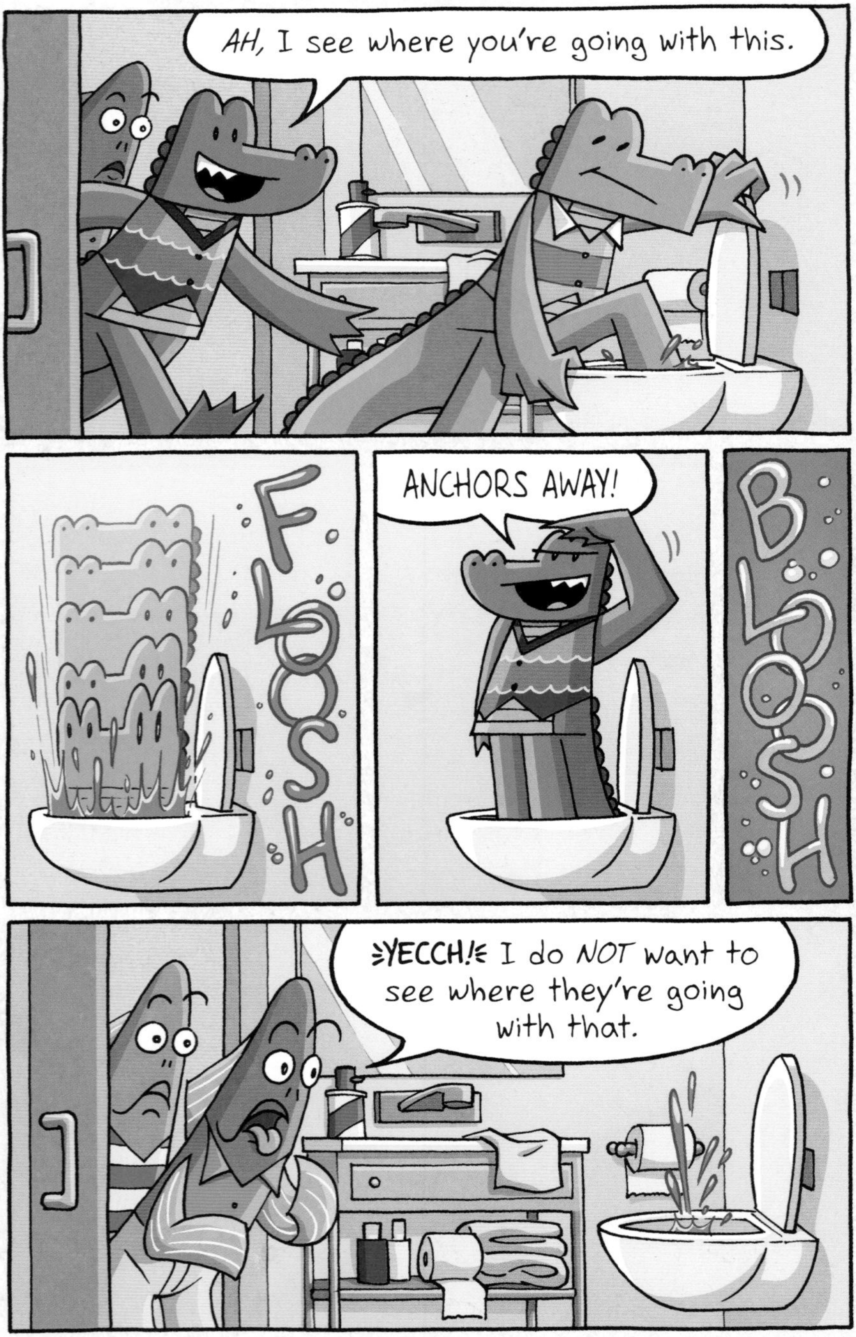
AH, I see where you're going with this.
FLOOSH
ANCHORS AWAY!
BLOOSH
YECCH! I do NOT want to see where they're going with that.

Chapter 9

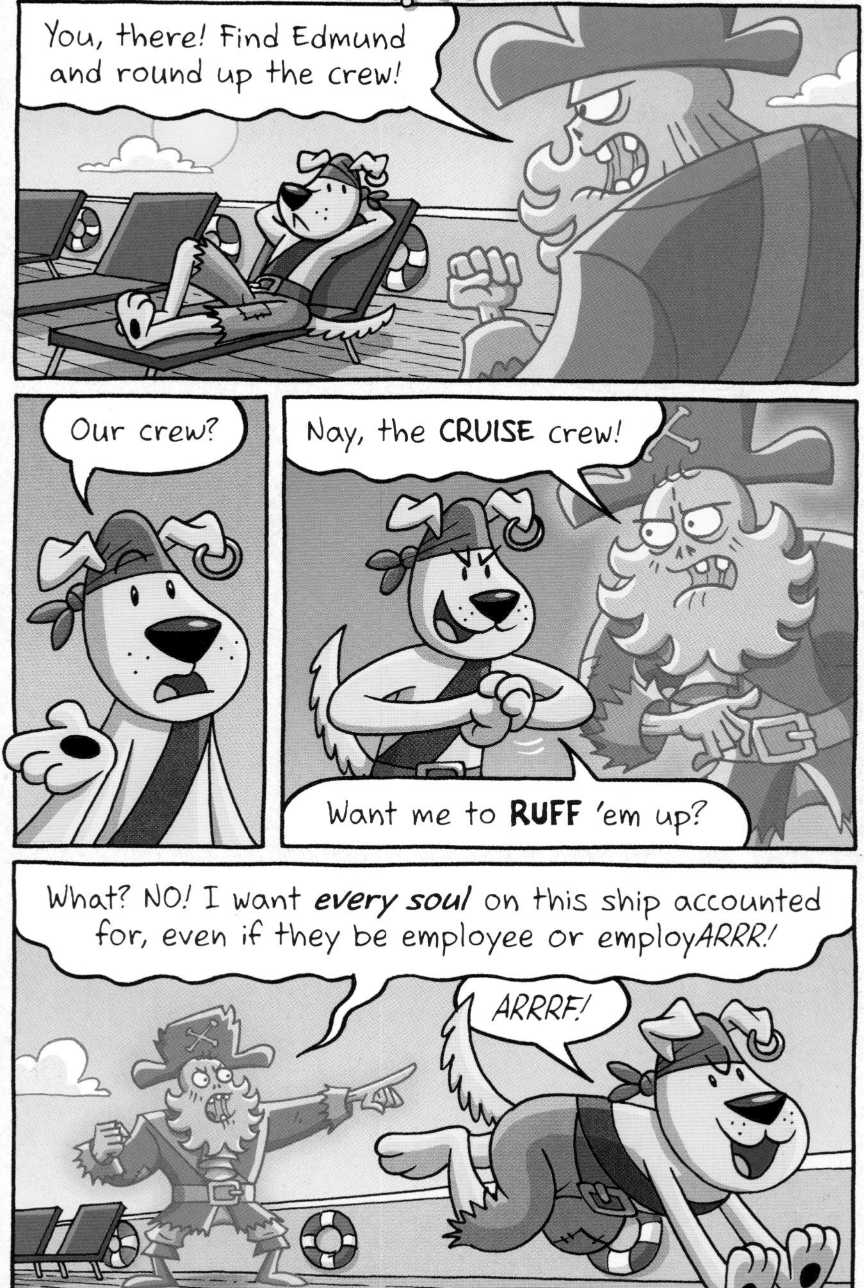
You, there! Find Edmund and round up the crew!
Our crew?
Nay, the **CRUISE** crew!
Want me to **RUFF** 'em up?
What? NO! I want ***every soul*** on this ship accounted for, even if they be employee or employ*ARRR!*
ARRRF!

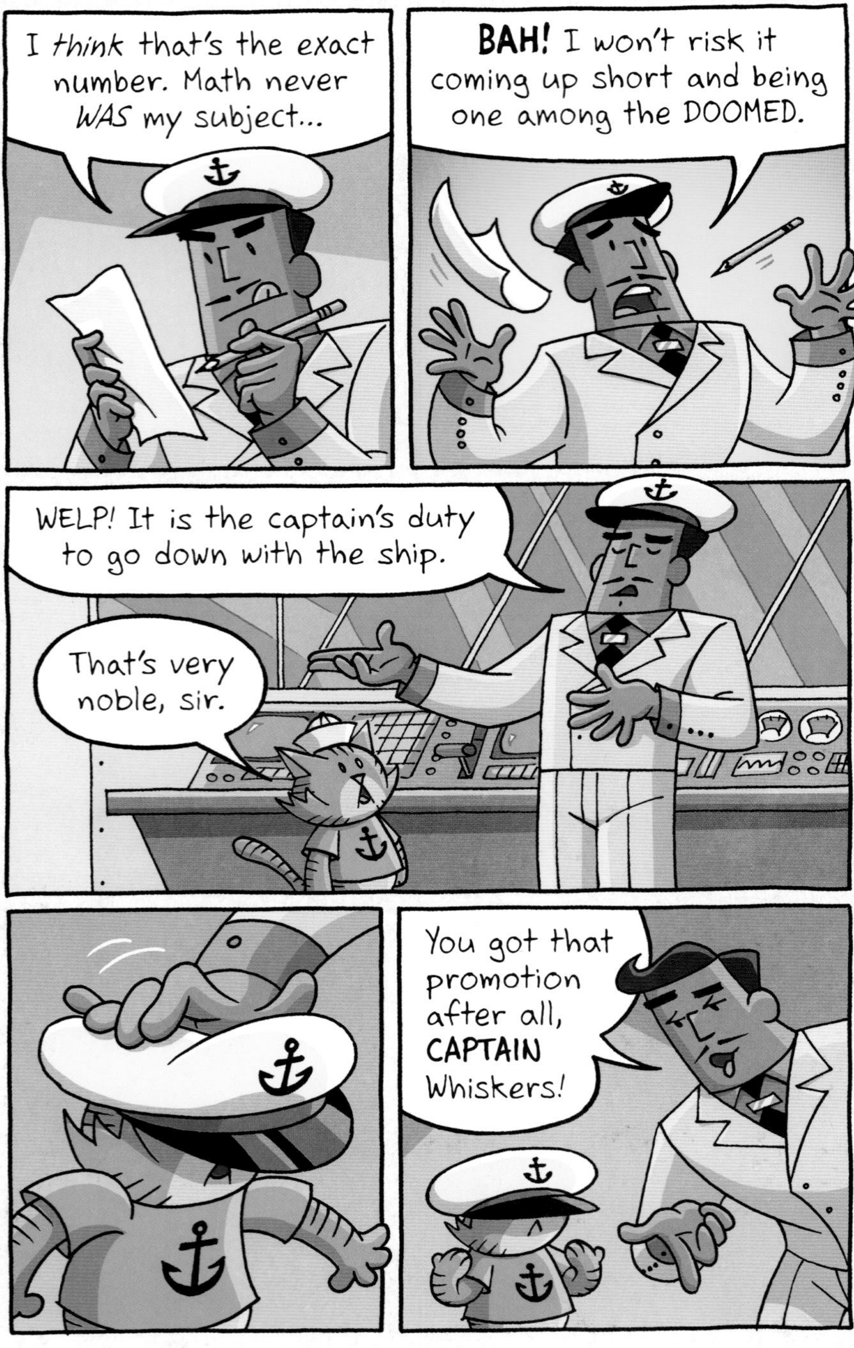
I *think* that's the exact number. Math never *WAS* my subject...
BAH! I won't risk it coming up short and being one among the DOOMED.
WELP! It is the captain's duty to go down with the ship.
That's very noble, sir.
You got that promotion after all, **CAPTAIN** Whiskers!

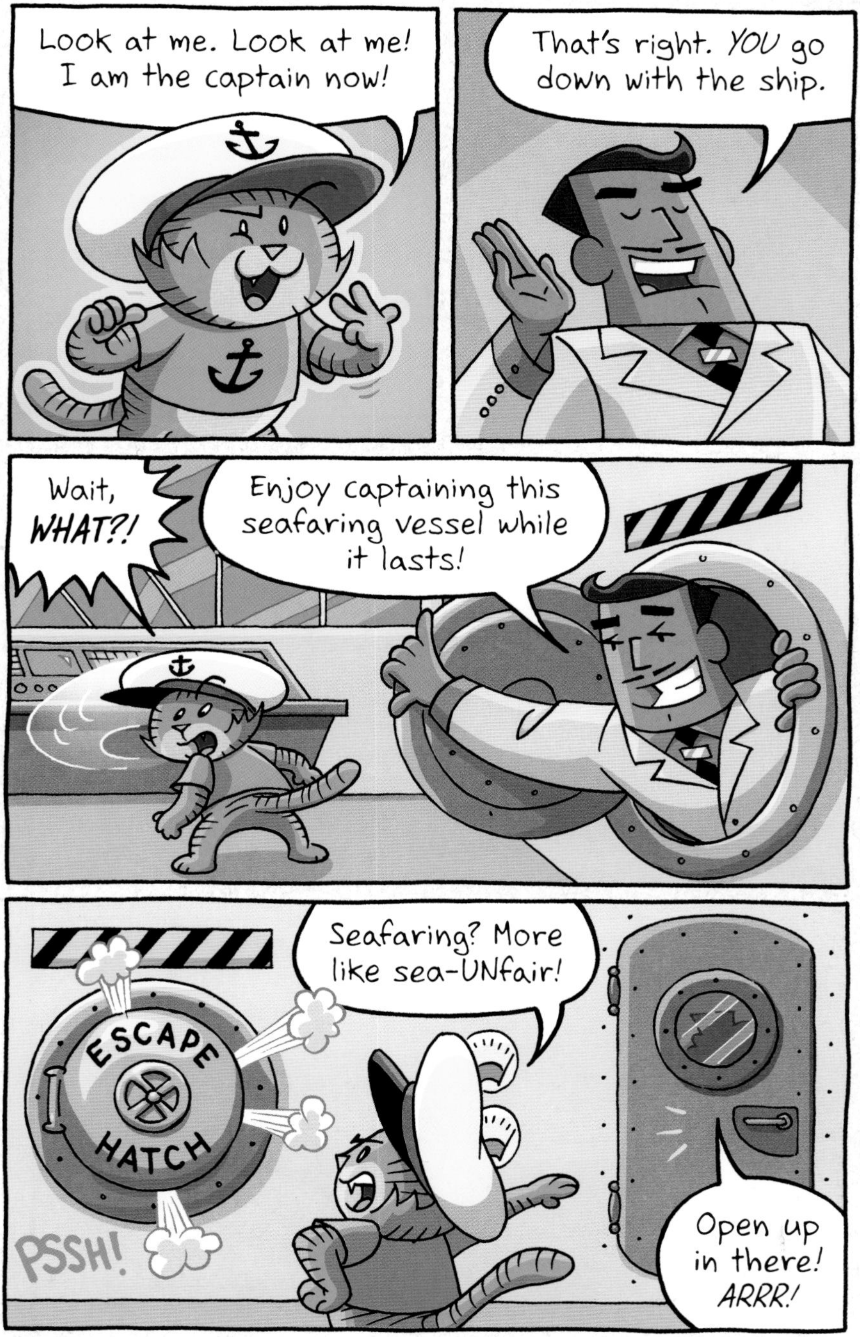
Look at me. Look at me! I am the captain now!
That's right. *YOU* go down with the ship.
Wait, *WHAT?!*
Enjoy captaining this seafaring vessel while it lasts!
Seafaring? More like sea-UNfair!
ESCAPE HATCH
PSSH!
Open up in there! *ARRR!*

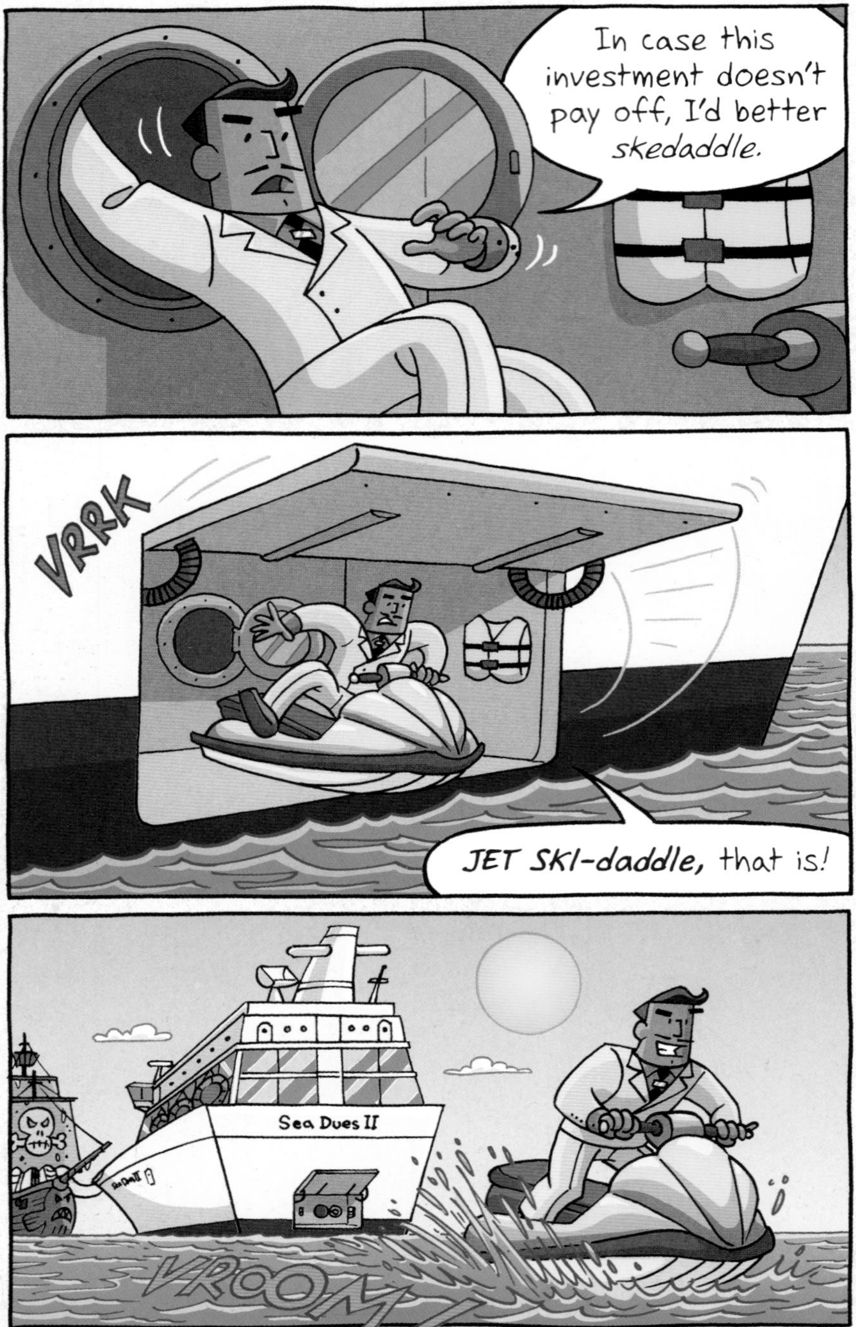
In case this investment doesn't pay off, I'd better *skedaddle.*
VRRK
JET SKI-daddle, that is!
Sea Dues II
VROOM!

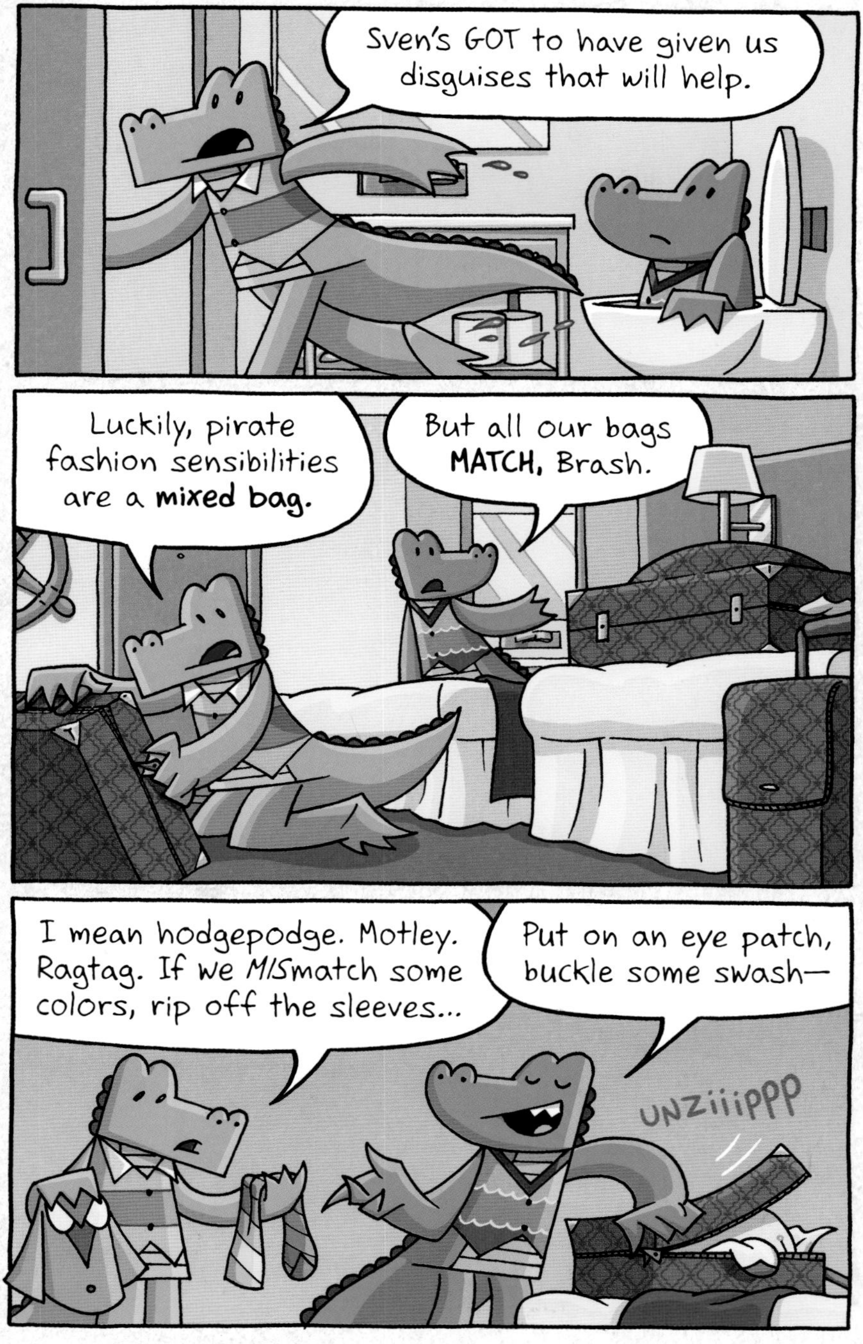
Sven's GOT to have given us disguises that will help.
Luckily, pirate fashion sensibilities are a **mixed bag.**
But all our bags **MATCH,** Brash.
I mean hodgepodge. Motley. Ragtag. If we *MIS*match some colors, rip off the sleeves...
Put on an eye patch, buckle some swash—
UNZiiippp

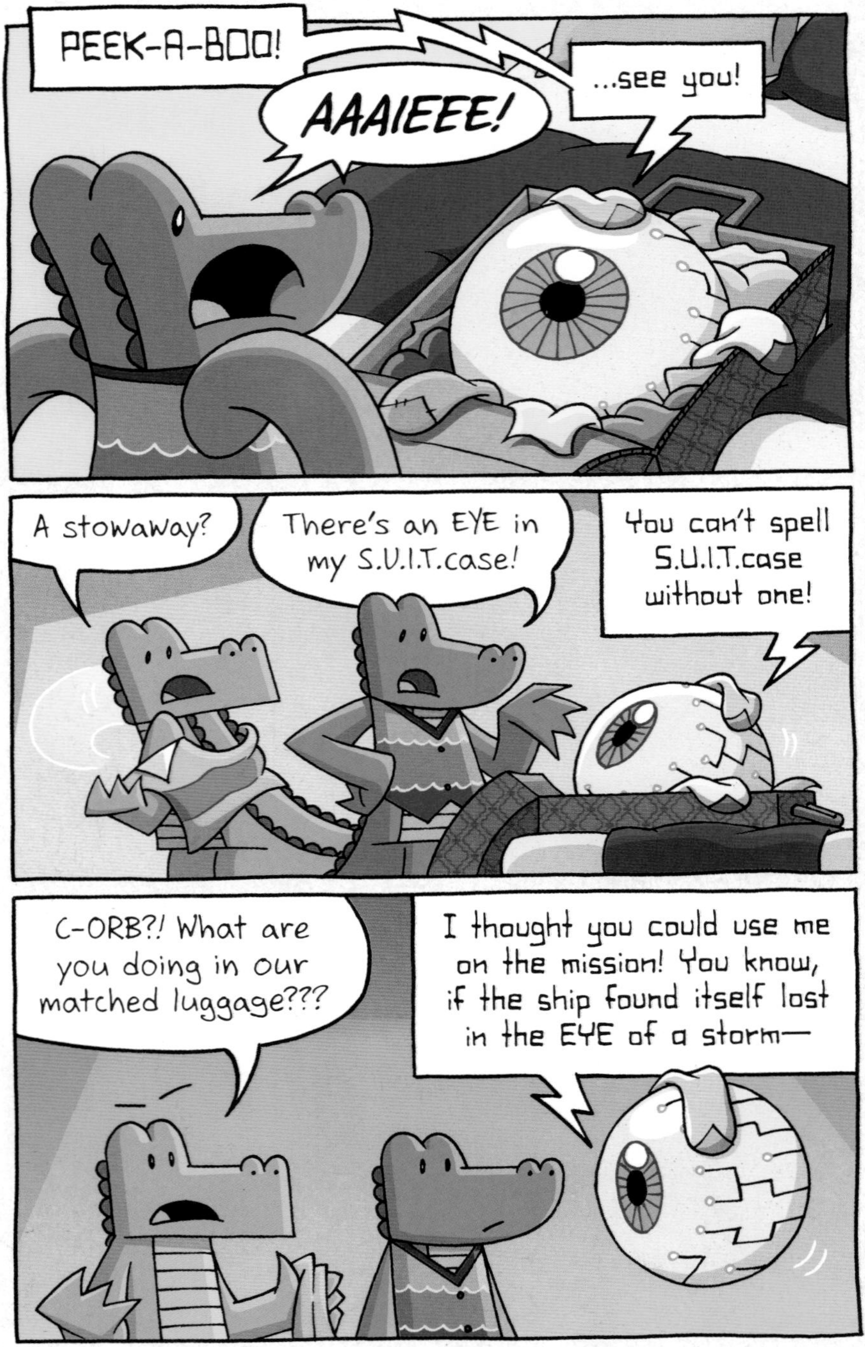
PEEK-A-BOO!
AAAIEEE!
...see you!
A stowaway?
There's an EYE in my S.U.I.T.case!
You can't spell S.U.I.T.case without one!
C-ORB?! What are you doing in our matched luggage???
I thought you could use me on the mission! You know, if the ship found itself lost in the EYE of a storm—

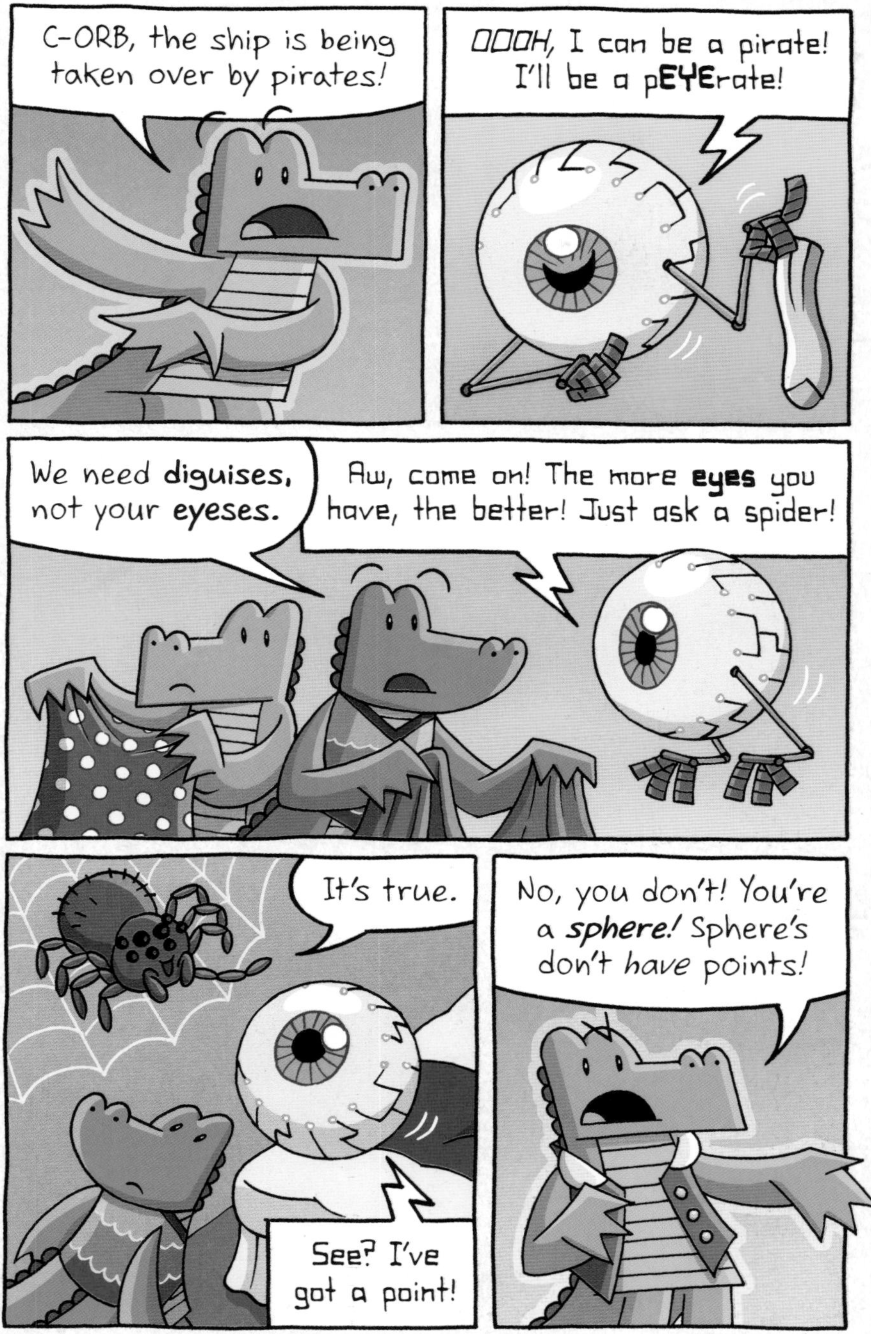
C-ORB, the ship is being taken over by pirates!
OOOH, I can be a pirate! I'll be a pEYErate!
We need diguises, not your eyeses.
Aw, come on! The more eyes you have, the better! Just ask a spider!
It's true.
See? I've got a point!
No, you don't! You're a sphere! Sphere's don't have points!

With all the **eye patches** pirates wear, we'd have an easier time blending in with *FEWER* eyeballs.

I just don't see how a *giant floating one* will give us a **leg up** in this situation.

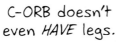

C-ORB doesn't even *HAVE* legs.

So? Plenty of pirates are missing legs! They've got PEG legs.

HOLD ON... I've got an *EYE*dea...

Chapter 10

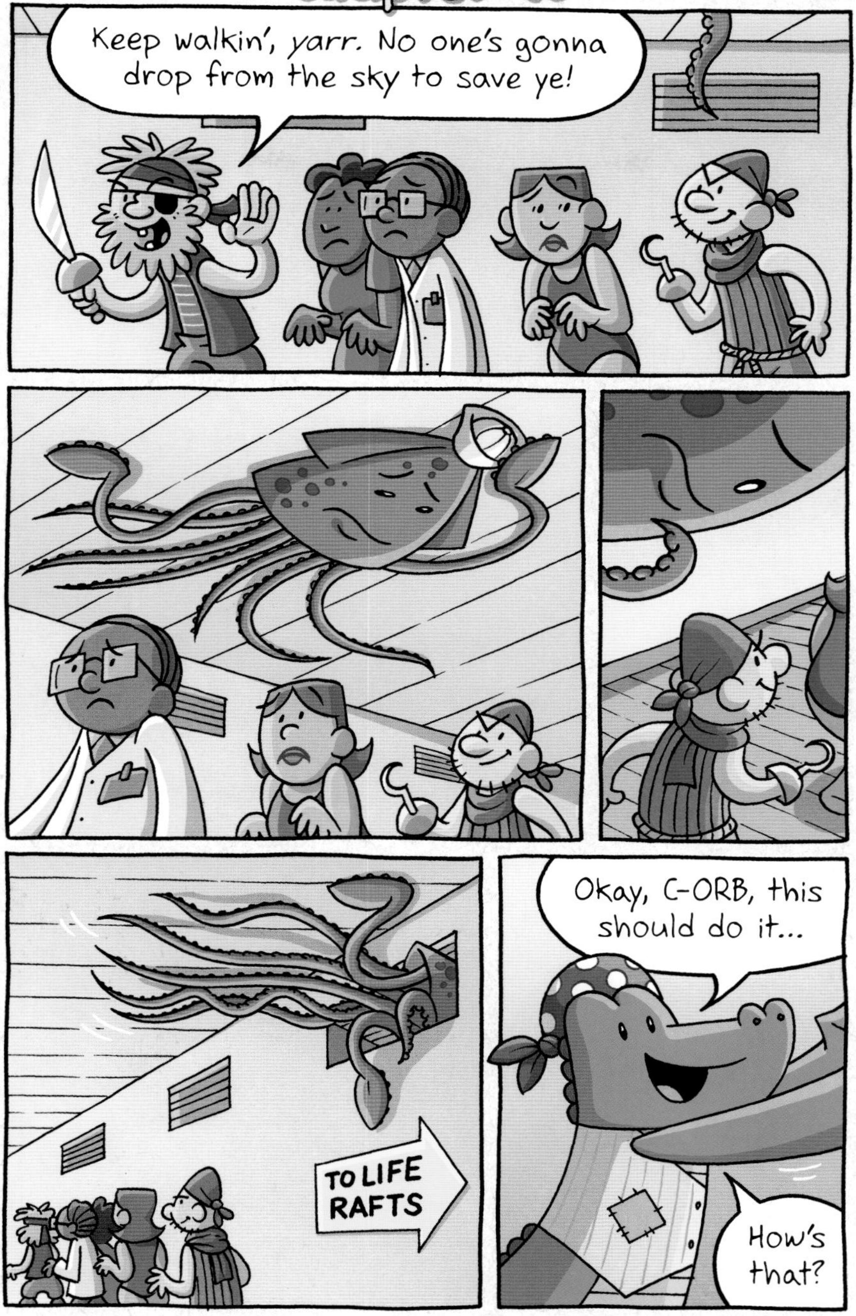

Keep walkin', *yarr.* No one's gonna drop from the sky to save ye!
TO LIFE RAFTS
Okay, C-ORB, this should do it...
How's that?

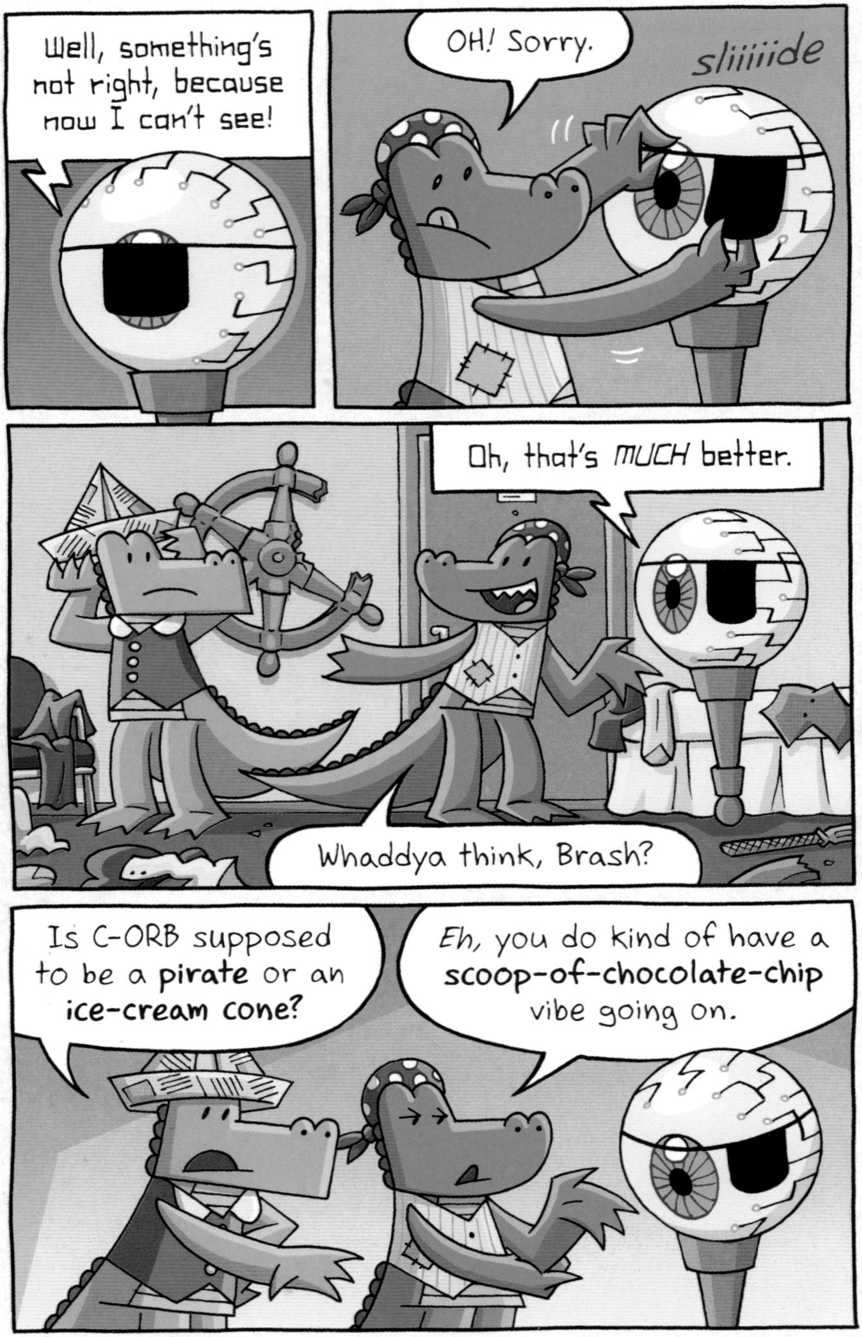
Well, something's not right, because now I can't see!
OH! Sorry.
sliiiiide
Oh, that's MUCH better.
Whaddya think, Brash?
Is C-ORB supposed to be a **pirate** or an **ice-cream cone?**
Eh, you do kind of have a **scoop-of-chocolate-chip** vibe going on.

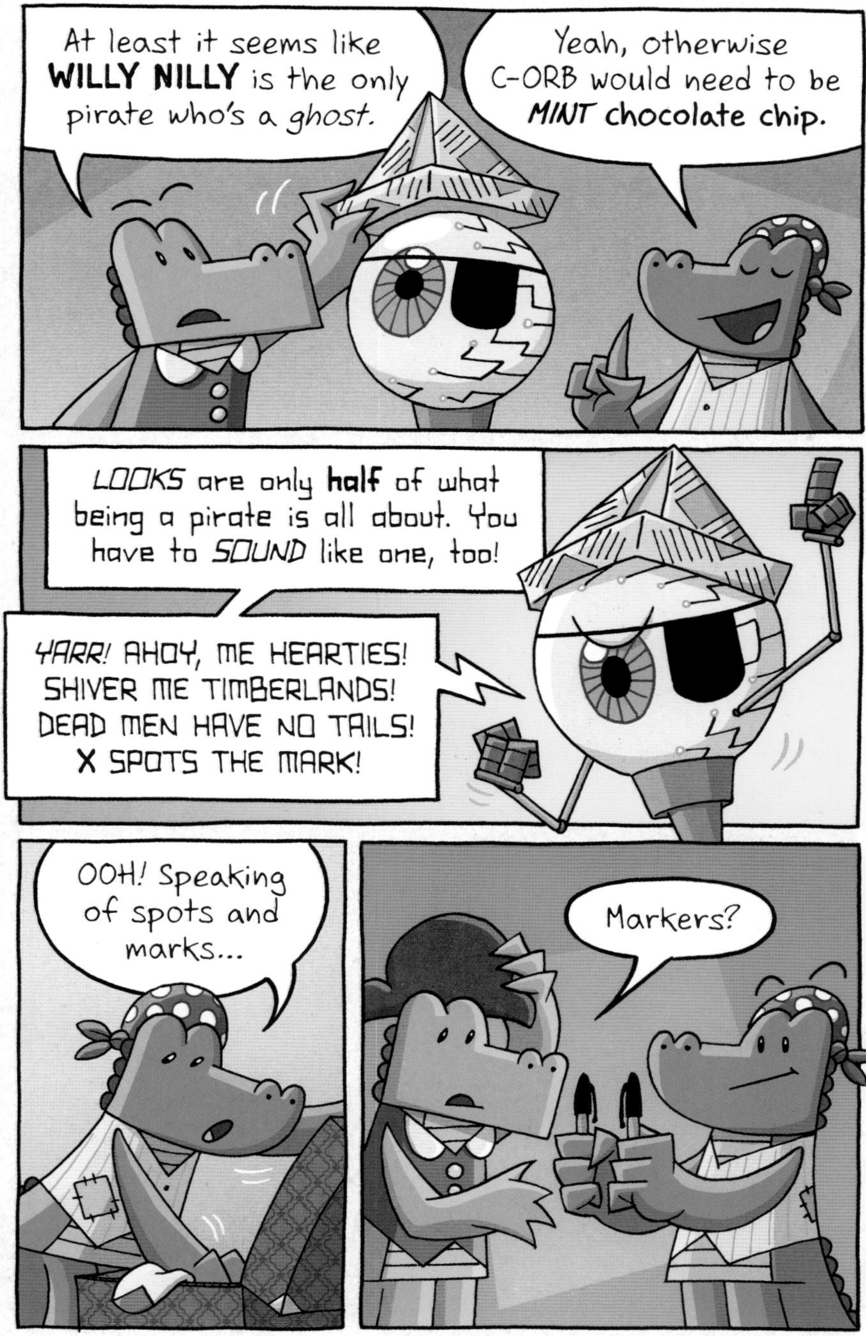

At least it seems like WILLY NILLY is the only pirate who's a ghost.
Yeah, otherwise C-ORB would need to be MINT chocolate chip.
LOOKS are only half of what being a pirate is all about. You have to SOUND like one, too!
YARR! AHOY, ME HEARTIES! SHIVER ME TIMBERLANDS! DEAD MEN HAVE NO TAILS! X SPOTS THE MARK!
OOH! Speaking of spots and marks...
Markers?

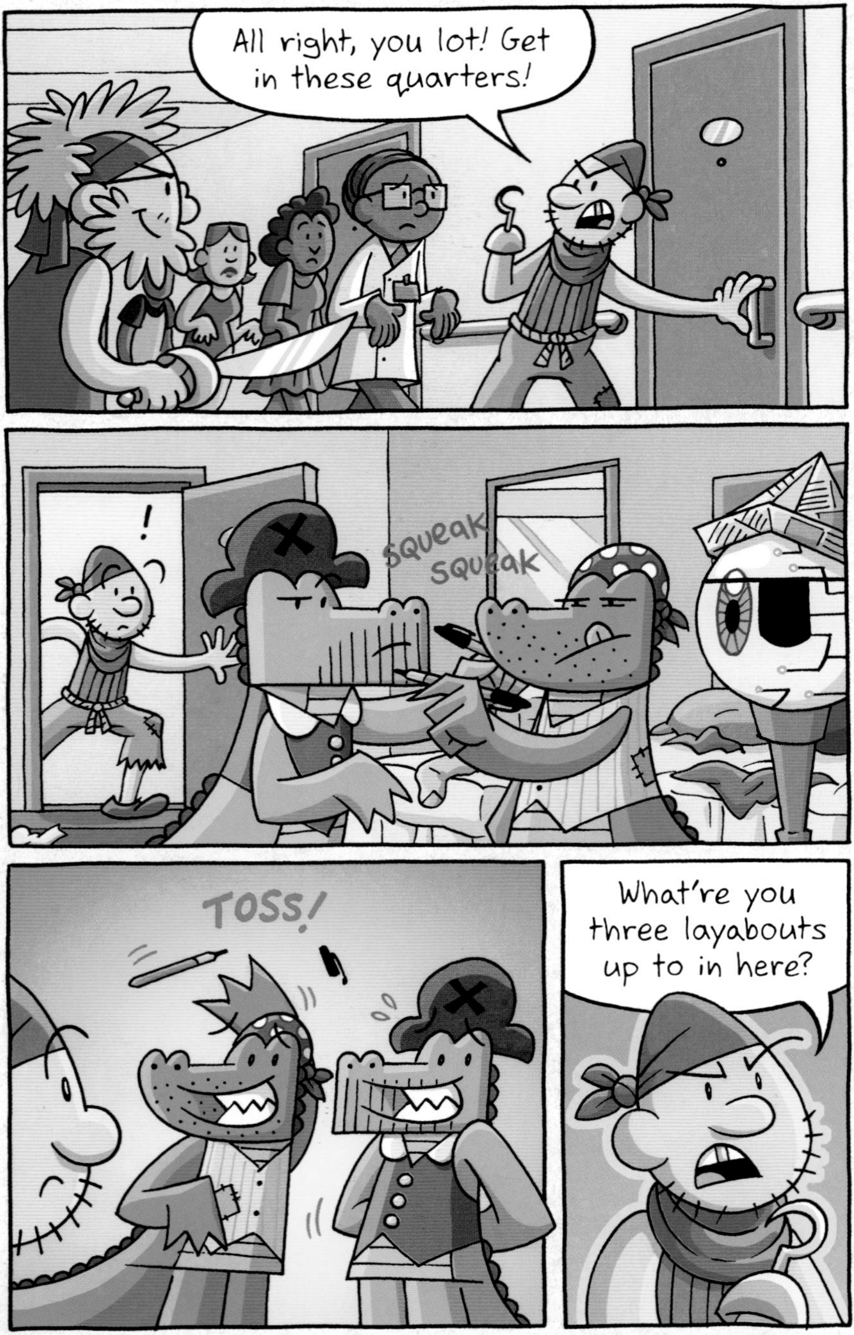
All right, you lot! Get in these quarters!
!
SQUEAK SQUEAK
TOSS!
What're you three layabouts up to in here?

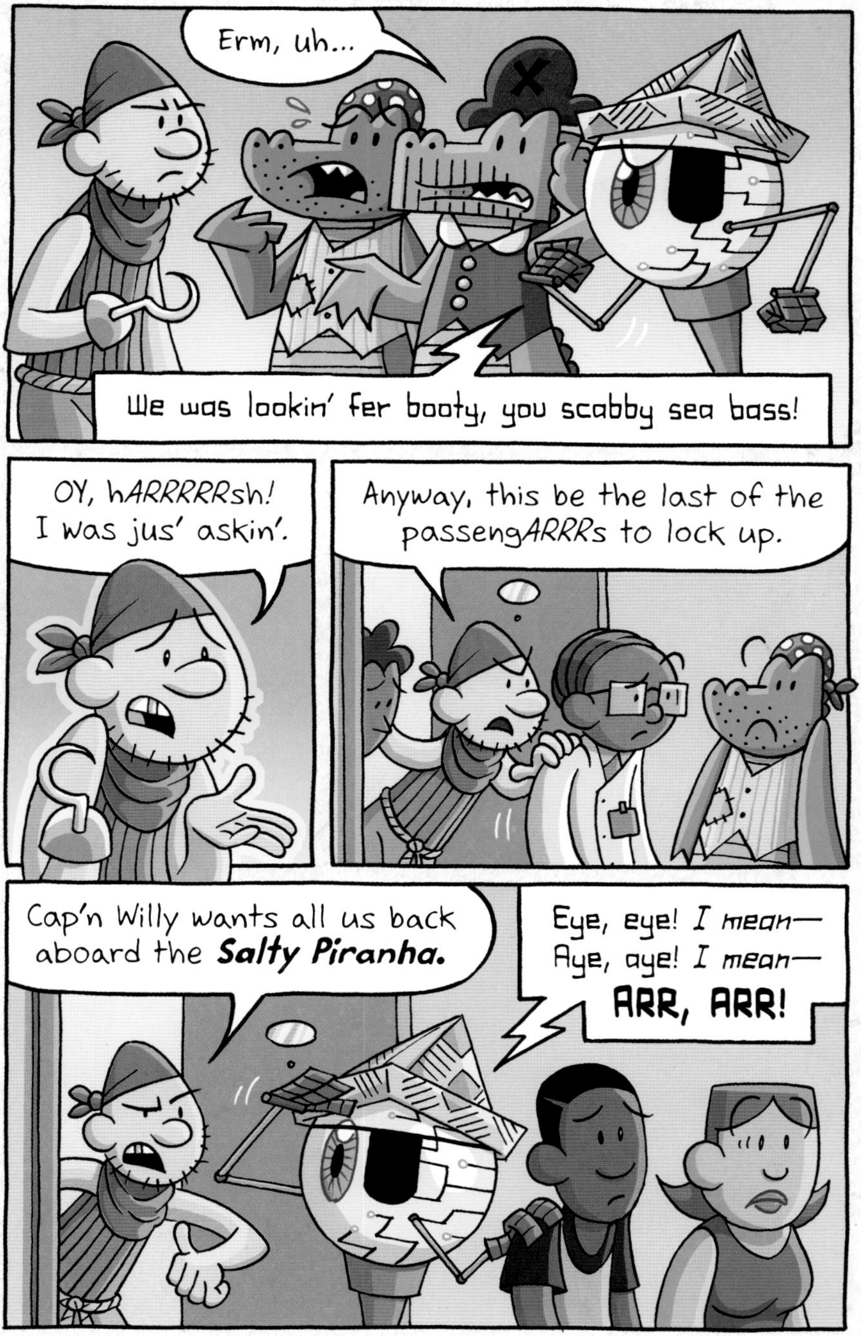
Erm, uh...
We was lookin' fer booty, you scabby sea bass!
OY, hARRRRRsh! I was jus' askin'.
Anyway, this be the last of the passengARRRs to lock up.
Cap'n Willy wants all us back aboard the **Salty Piranha.**
Eye, eye! *I mean—* Aye, aye! *I mean—* **ARR, ARR!**

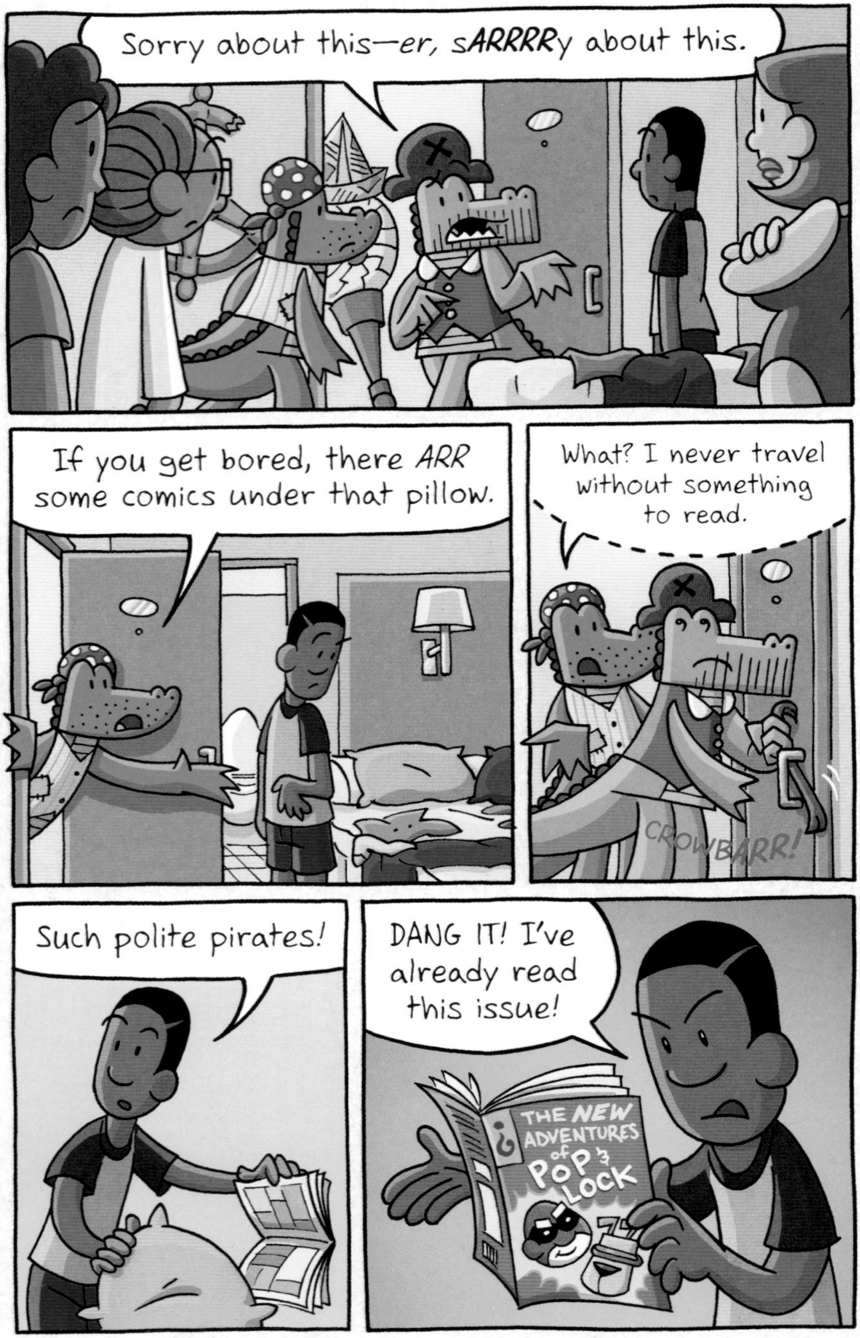

Sorry about this—*er*, s**ARRRR**y about this.
If you get bored, there *ARR* some comics under that pillow.
What? I never travel without something to read.
CROWBARR!
Such polite pirates!
DANG IT! I've already read this issue!
THE NEW ADVENTURES of POP & LOCK

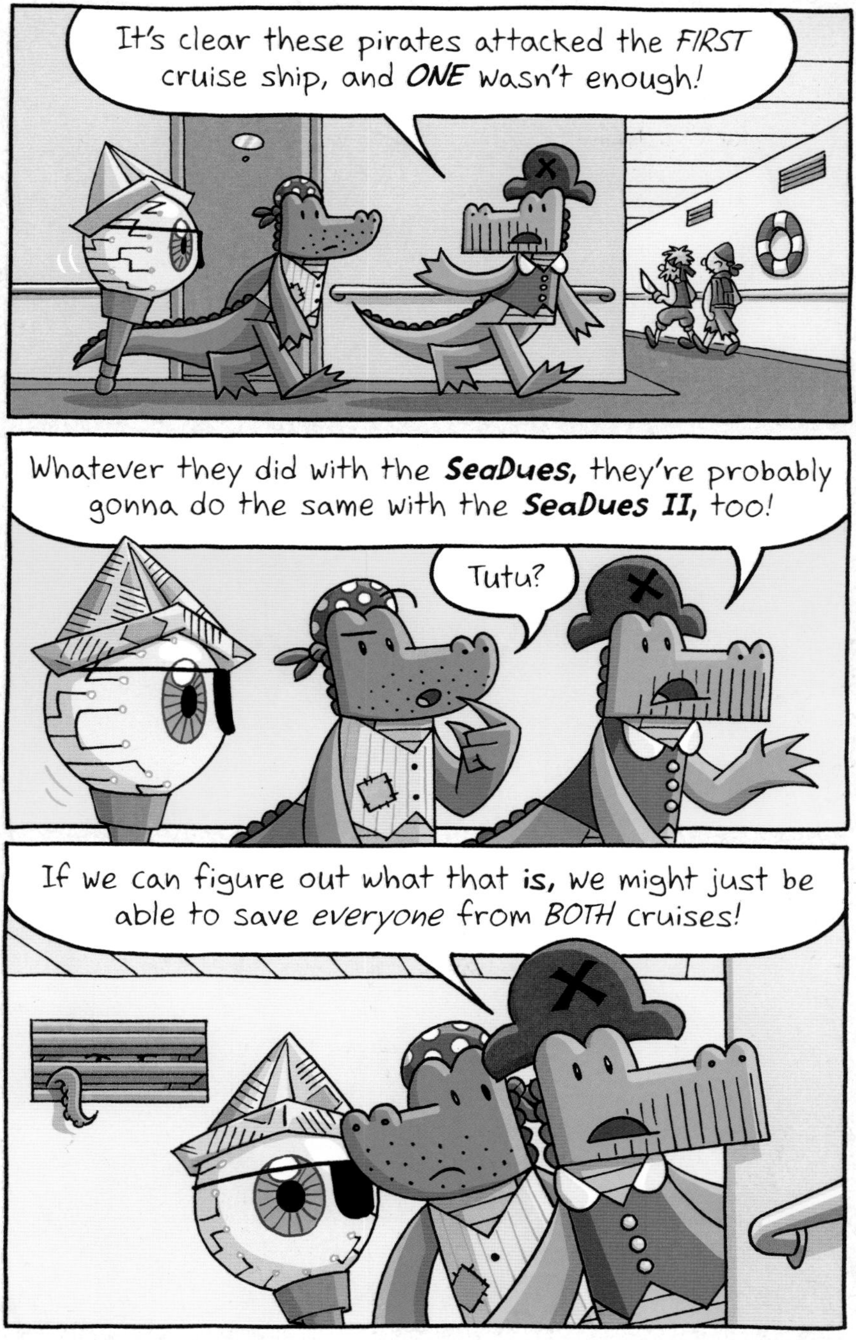
It's clear these pirates attacked the *FIRST* cruise ship, and ***ONE*** wasn't enough!
Whatever they did with the **SeaDues**, they're probably gonna do the same with the **SeaDues II**, too!
Tutu?
If we can figure out what that **is**, we might just be able to save *everyone* from *BOTH* cruises!

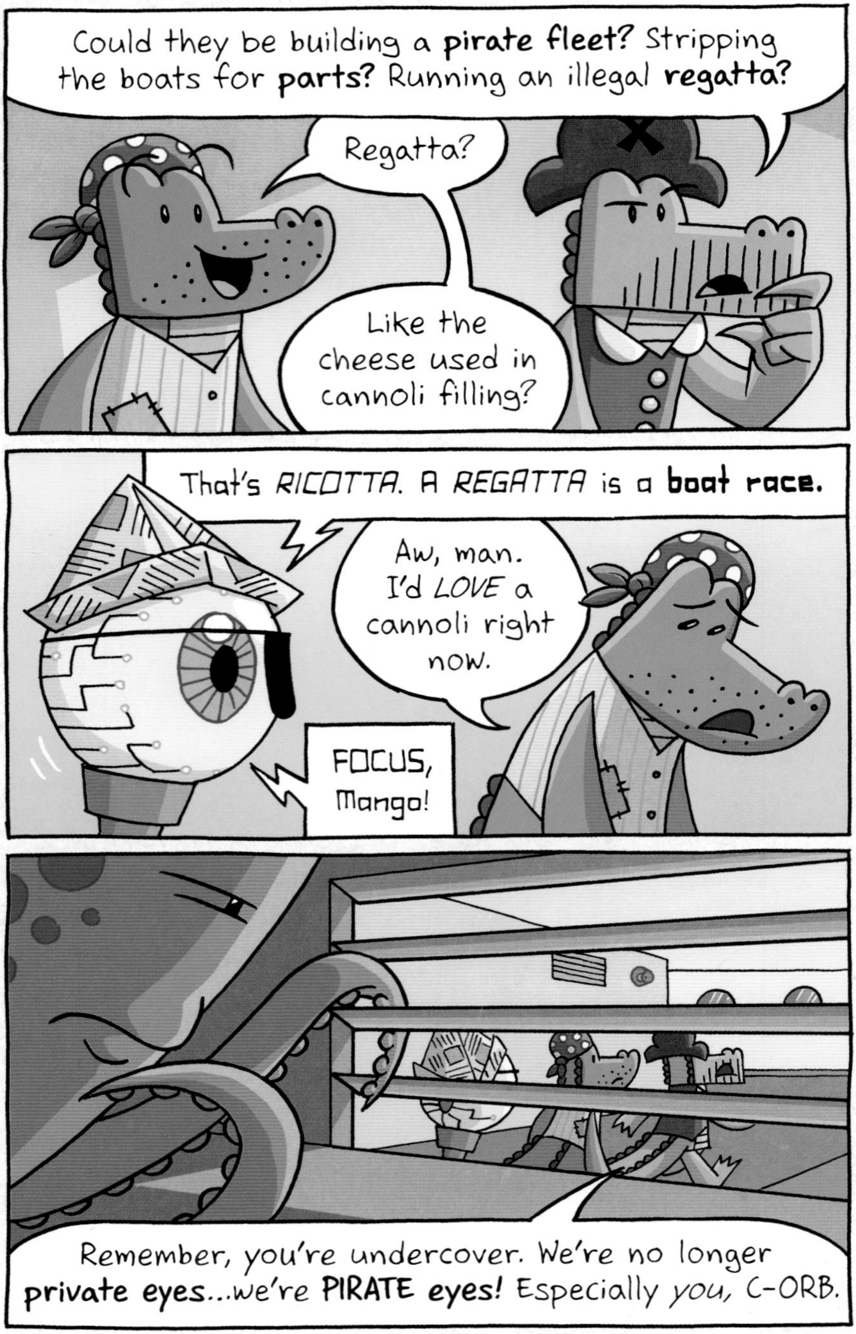
Could they be building a **pirate fleet?** Stripping the boats for **parts?** Running an illegal **regatta?**
Regatta?
Like the cheese used in cannoli filling?
That's *RICOTTA*. A *REGATTA* is a **boat race.**
Aw, man. I'd *LOVE* a cannoli right now.
FOCUS, Mango!
Remember, you're undercover. We're no longer **private eyes**...we're **PIRATE eyes!** Especially *you*, C-ORB.

Chapter 11

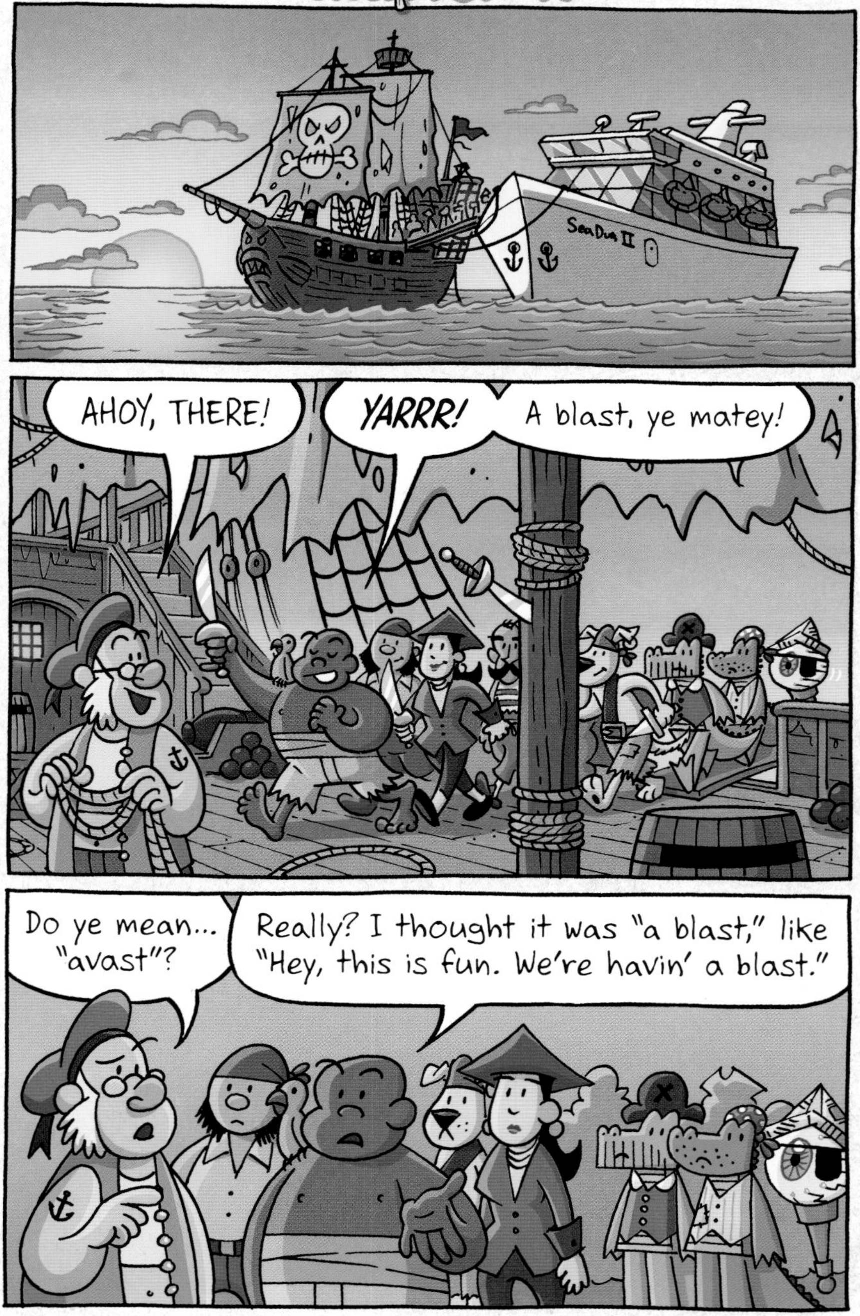
SeaDog II
AHOY, THERE!
YARRR!
A blast, ye matey!
Do ye mean... "avast"?
Really? I thought it was "a blast," like "Hey, this is fun. We're havin' a blast."

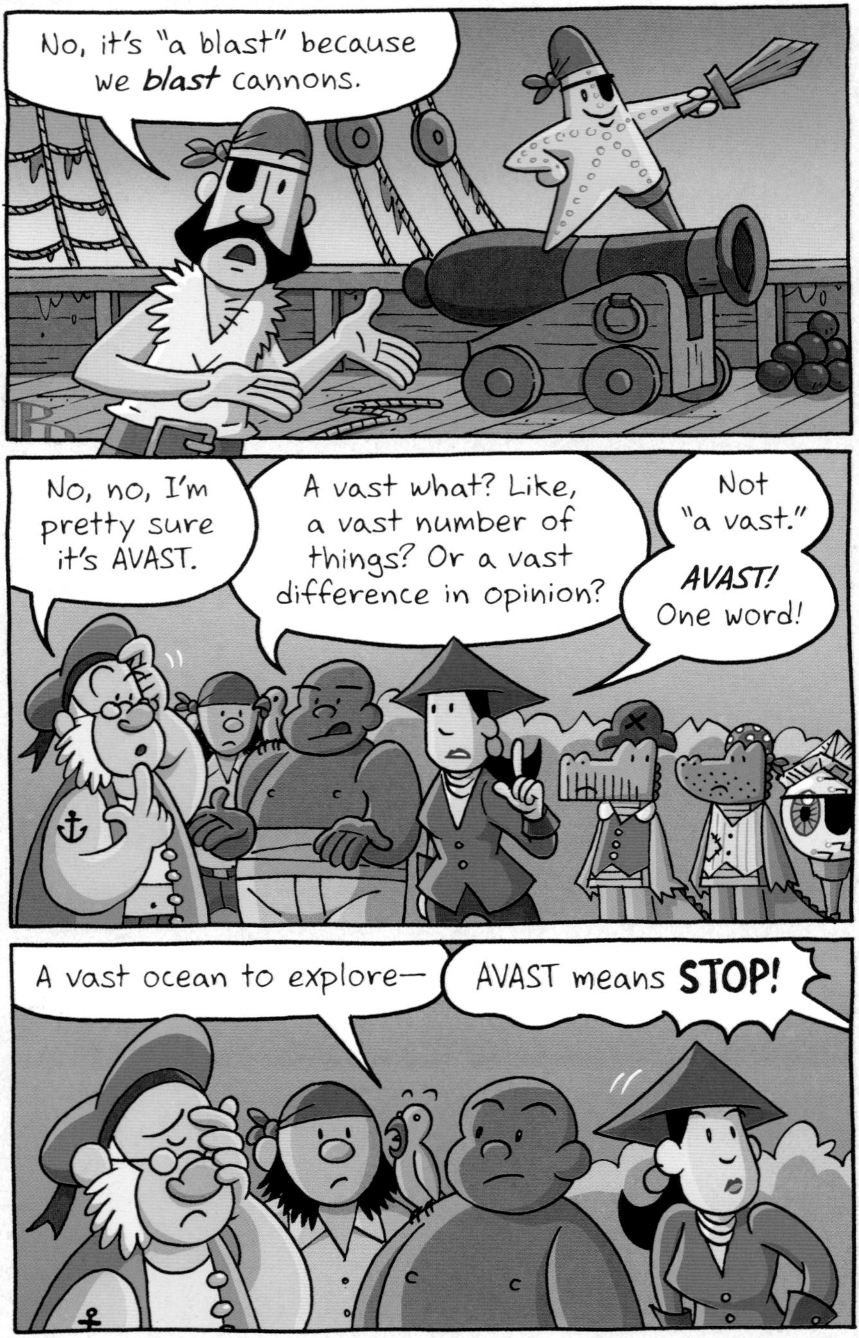
No, it's "a blast" because we **blast** cannons.
No, no, I'm pretty sure it's AVAST.
A vast what? Like, a vast number of things? Or a vast difference in opinion?
Not "a vast."
AVAST! One word!
A vast ocean to explore—
AVAST means **STOP!**

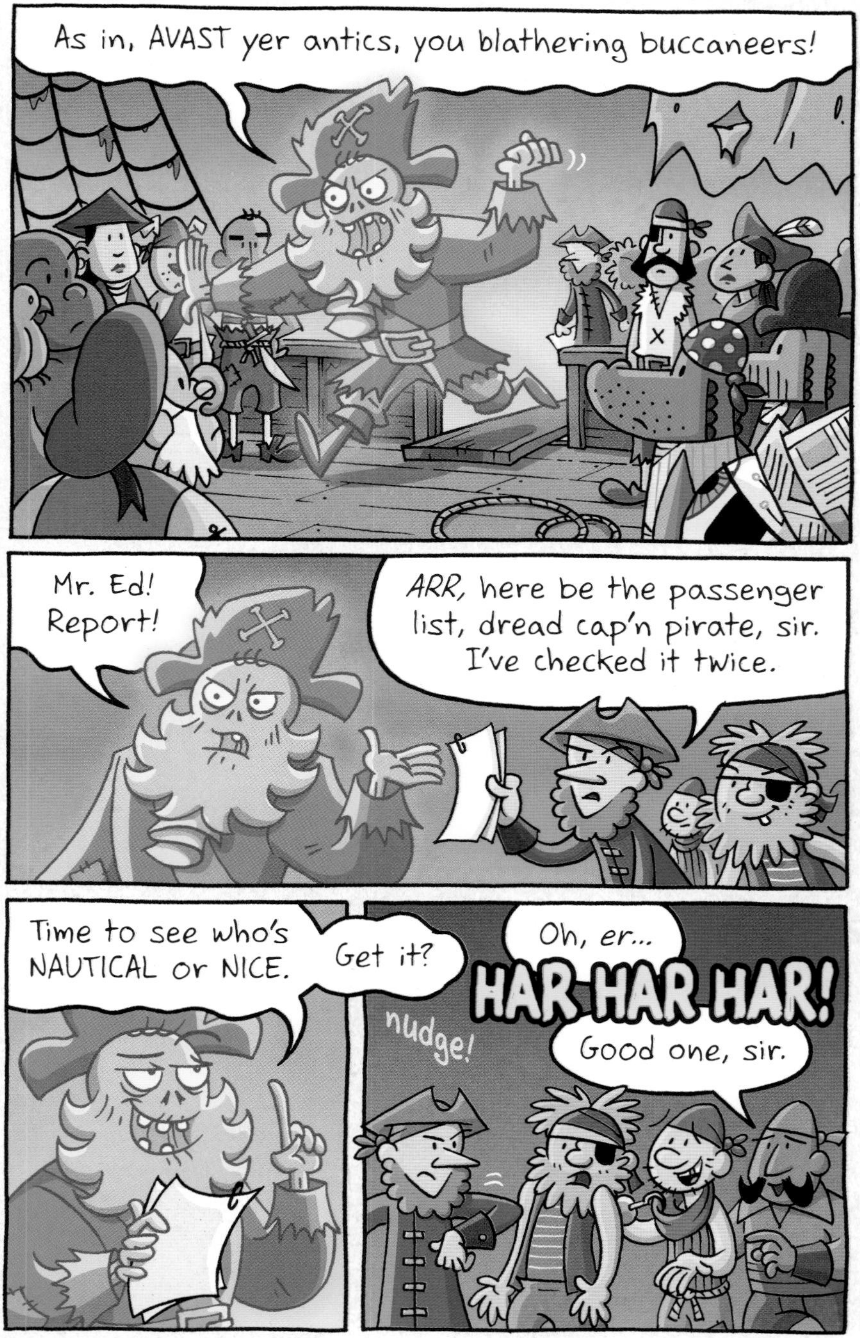

As in, AVAST yer antics, you blathering buccaneers!
Mr. Ed! Report!
ARR, here be the passenger list, dread cap'n pirate, sir. I've checked it twice.
Time to see who's NAUTICAL or NICE.
Get it?
Oh, er...
HAR HAR HAR!
nudge!
Good one, sir.

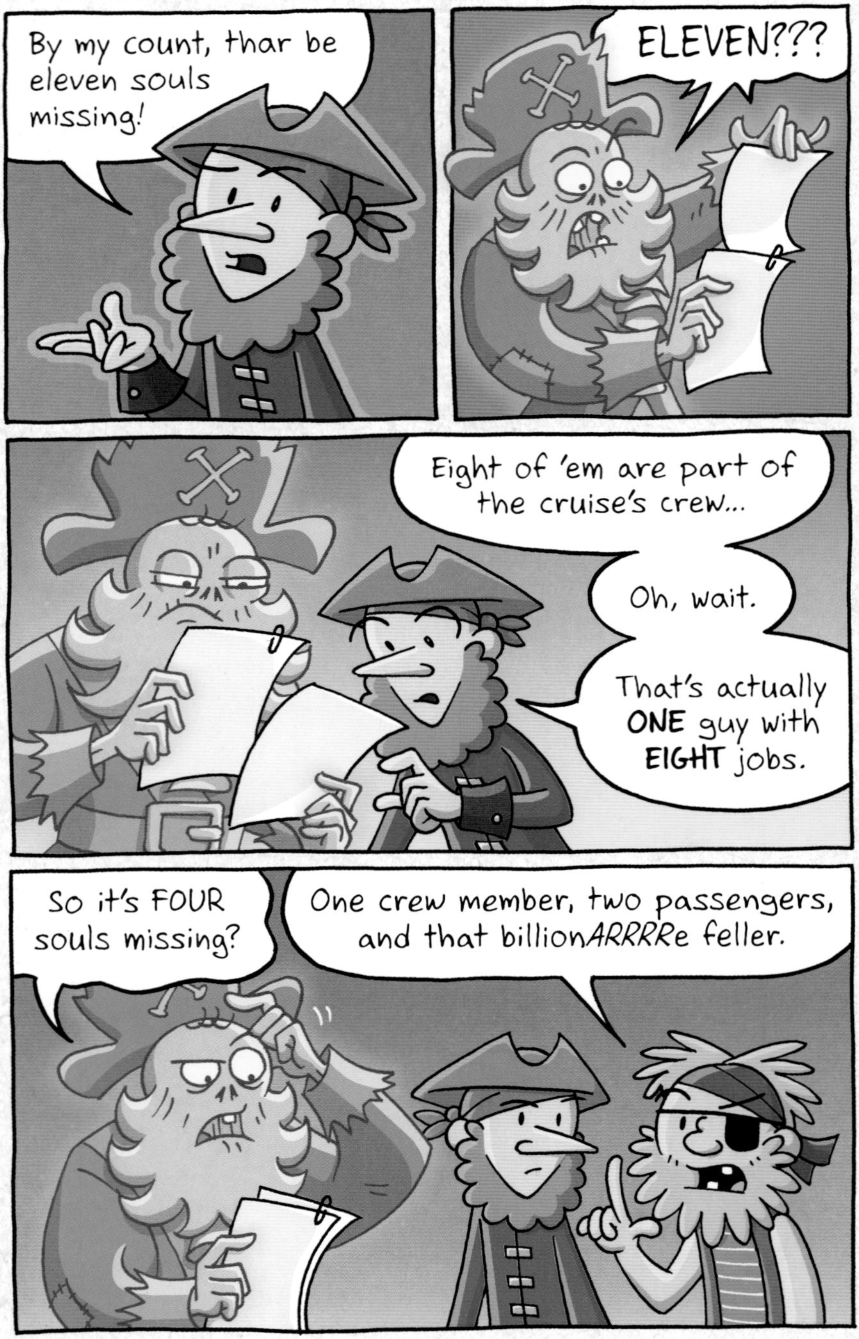
By my count, thar be eleven souls missing!
ELEVEN???
Eight of 'em are part of the cruise's crew...
Oh, wait.
That's actually **ONE** guy with **EIGHT** jobs.
So it's FOUR souls missing?
One crew member, two passengers, and that billion*ARRRR*e feller.

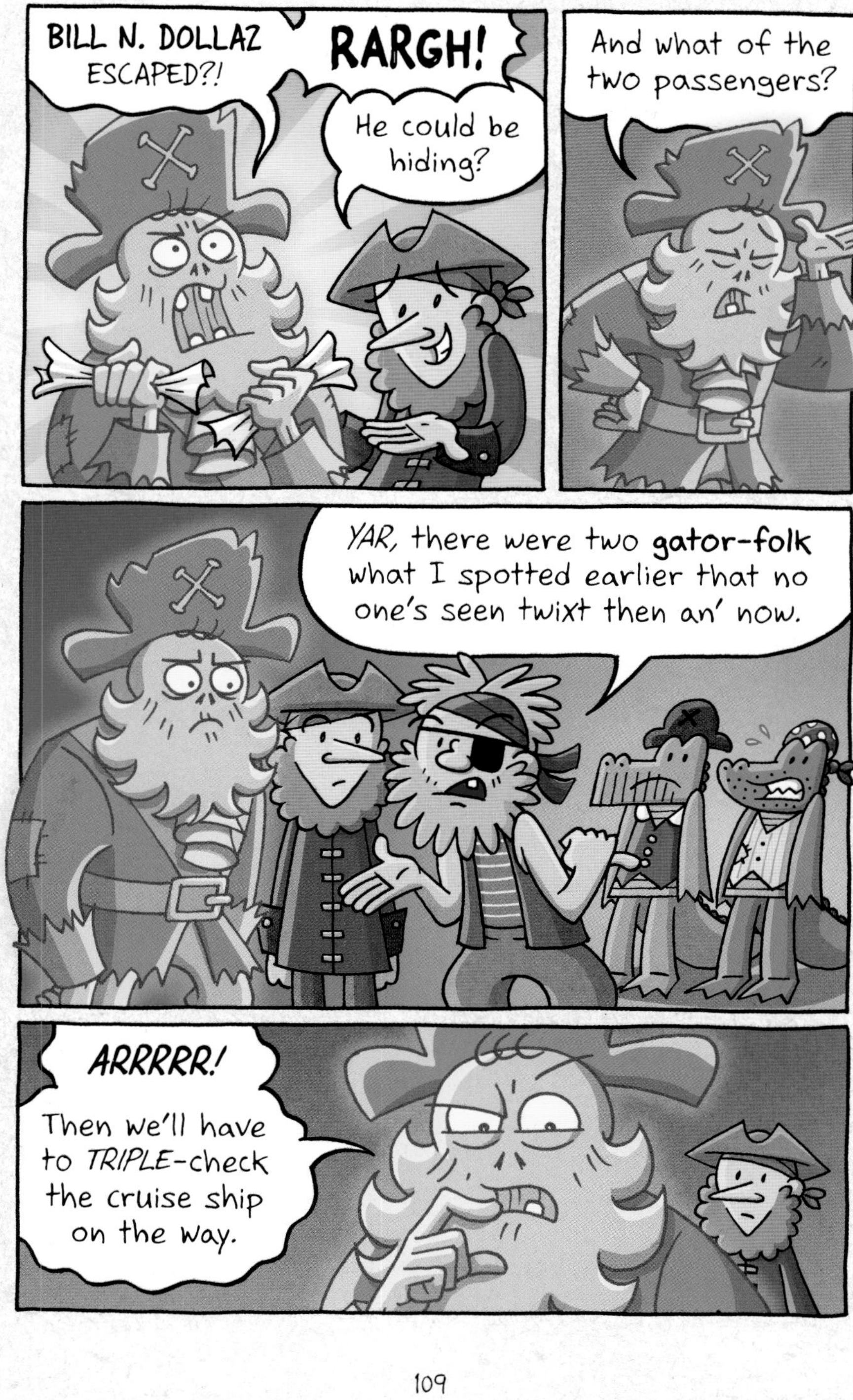
BILL N. DOLLAZ ESCAPED?!
RARGH!
He could be hiding?
And what of the two passengers?
YAR, there were two **gator-folk** what I spotted earlier that no one's seen twixt then an' now.
ARRRRR!
Then we'll have to *TRIPLE*-check the cruise ship on the way.

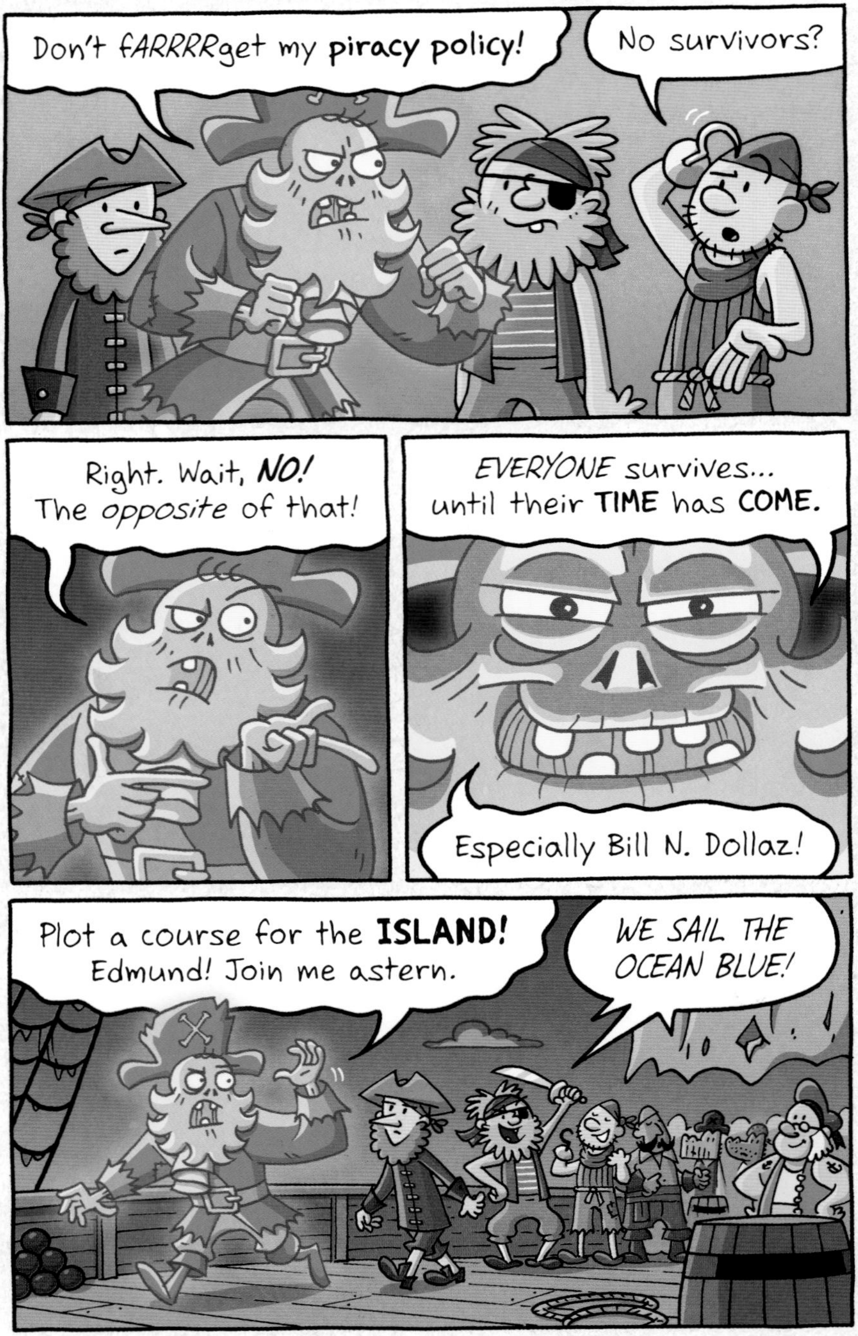
Don't fARRRRget my **piracy policy!**
No survivors?
Right. Wait, ***NO!*** The *opposite* of that!
EVERYONE survives... until their **TIME** has **COME.**
Especially Bill N. Dollaz!
Plot a course for the **ISLAND!** Edmund! Join me astern.
WE SAIL THE OCEAN BLUE!

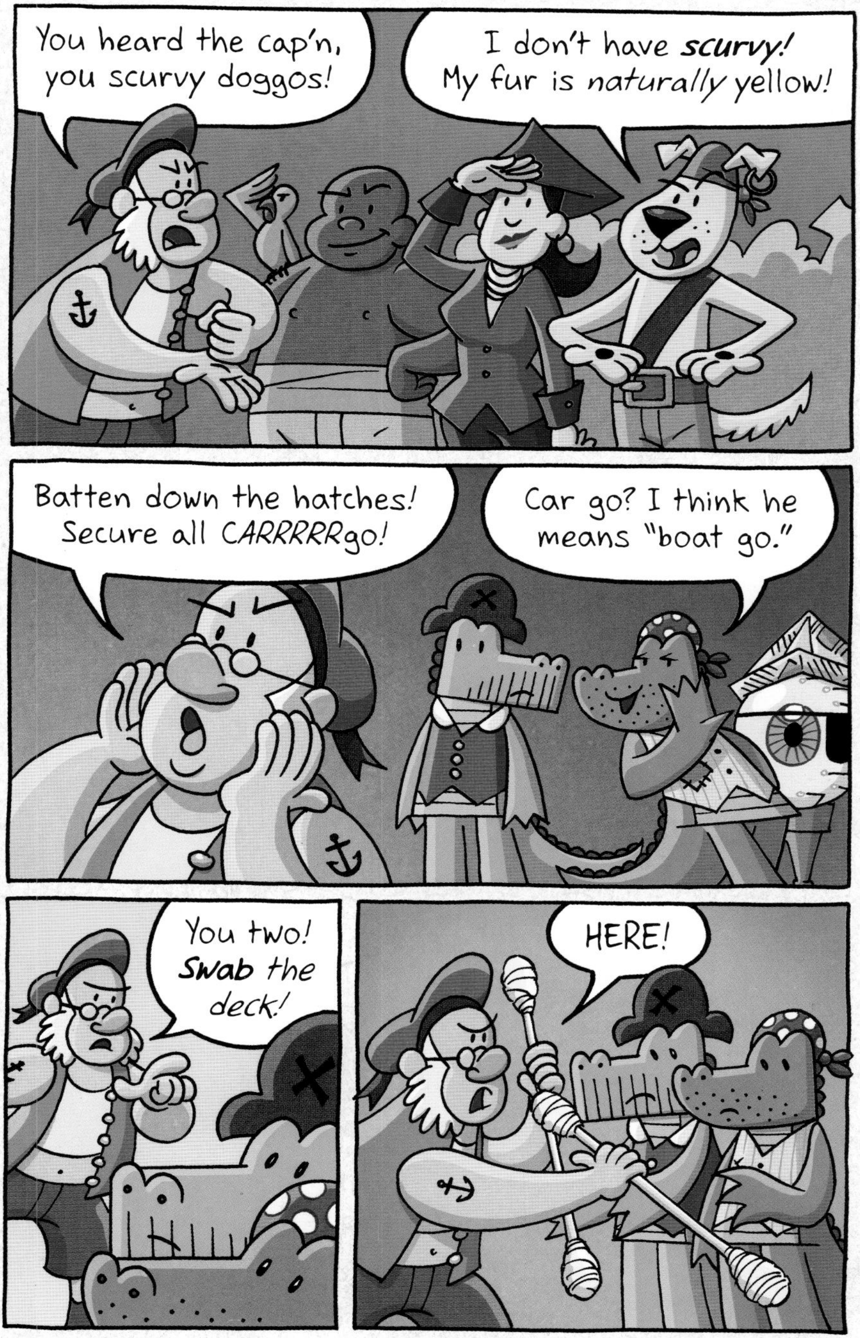
You heard the cap'n, you scurvy doggos!
I don't have **scurvy!** My fur is *naturally* yellow!
Batten down the hatches! Secure all CARRRRRgo!
Car go? I think he means "boat go."
You two! **Swab** the deck!
HERE!

Chapter 12

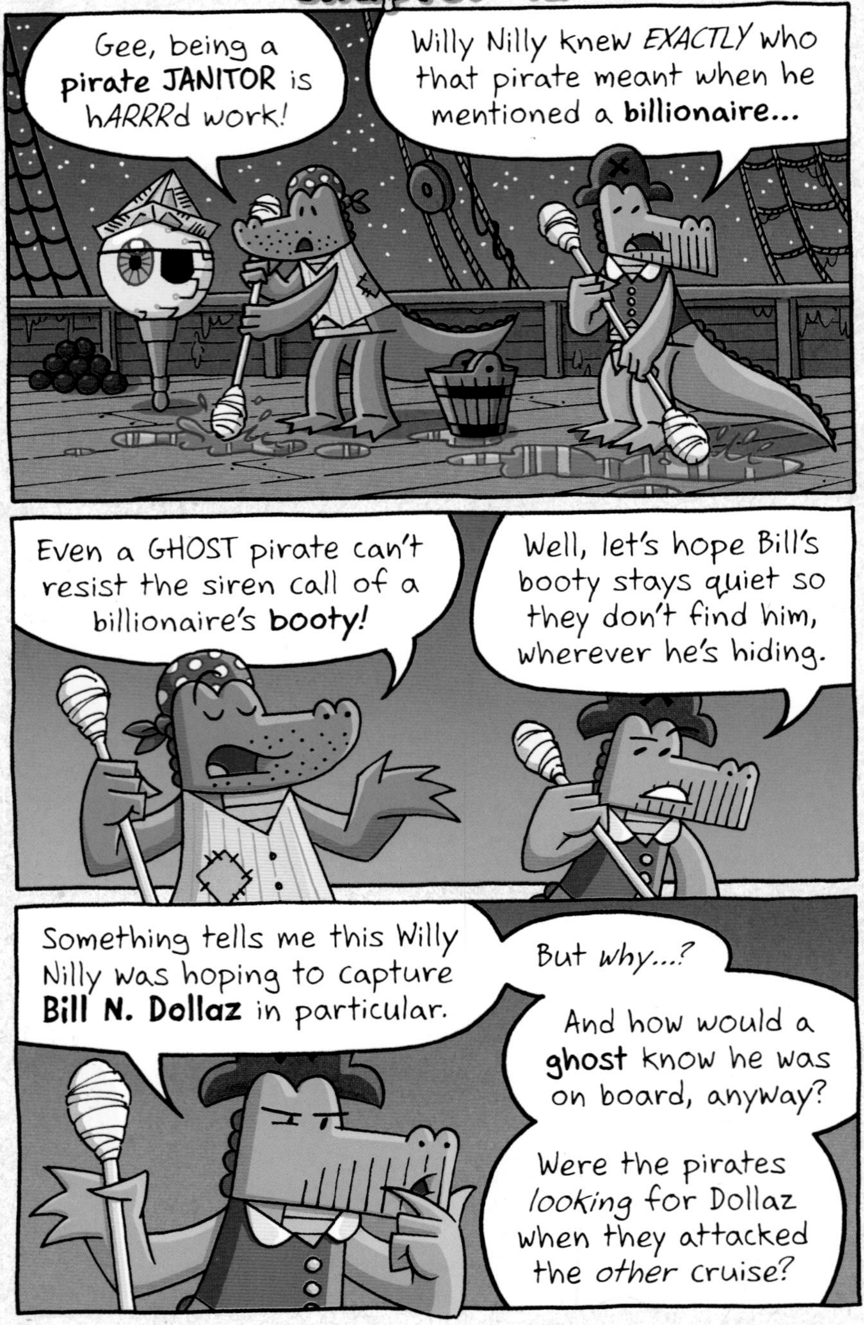

Gee, being a pirate JANITOR is hARRRd work!
Willy Nilly knew EXACTLY who that pirate meant when he mentioned a billionaire...
Even a GHOST pirate can't resist the siren call of a billionaire's booty!
Well, let's hope Bill's booty stays quiet so they don't find him, wherever he's hiding.
Something tells me this Willy Nilly was hoping to capture Bill N. Dollaz in particular.
But why...?
And how would a ghost know he was on board, anyway?
Were the pirates looking for Dollaz when they attacked the other cruise?

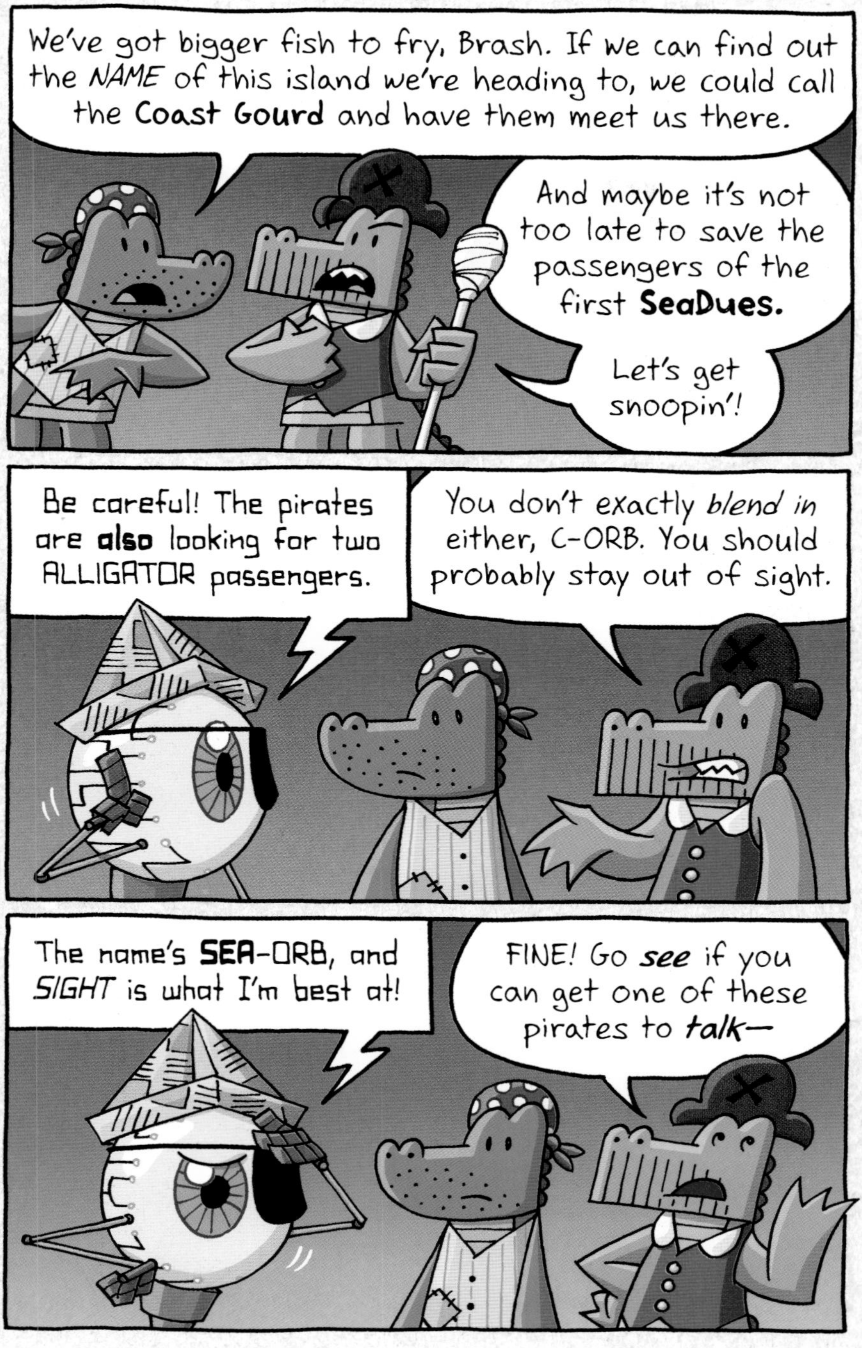
We've got bigger fish to fry, Brash. If we can find out the *NAME* of this island we're heading to, we could call the **Coast Gourd** and have them meet us there.
And maybe it's not too late to save the passengers of the first **SeaDues.**
Let's get snoopin'!
Be careful! The pirates are **also** looking for two ALLIGATOR passengers.
You don't exactly *blend in* either, C-ORB. You should probably stay out of sight.
The name's **SEA**-ORB, and *SIGHT* is what I'm best at!
FINE! Go ***see*** if you can get one of these pirates to ***talk***—

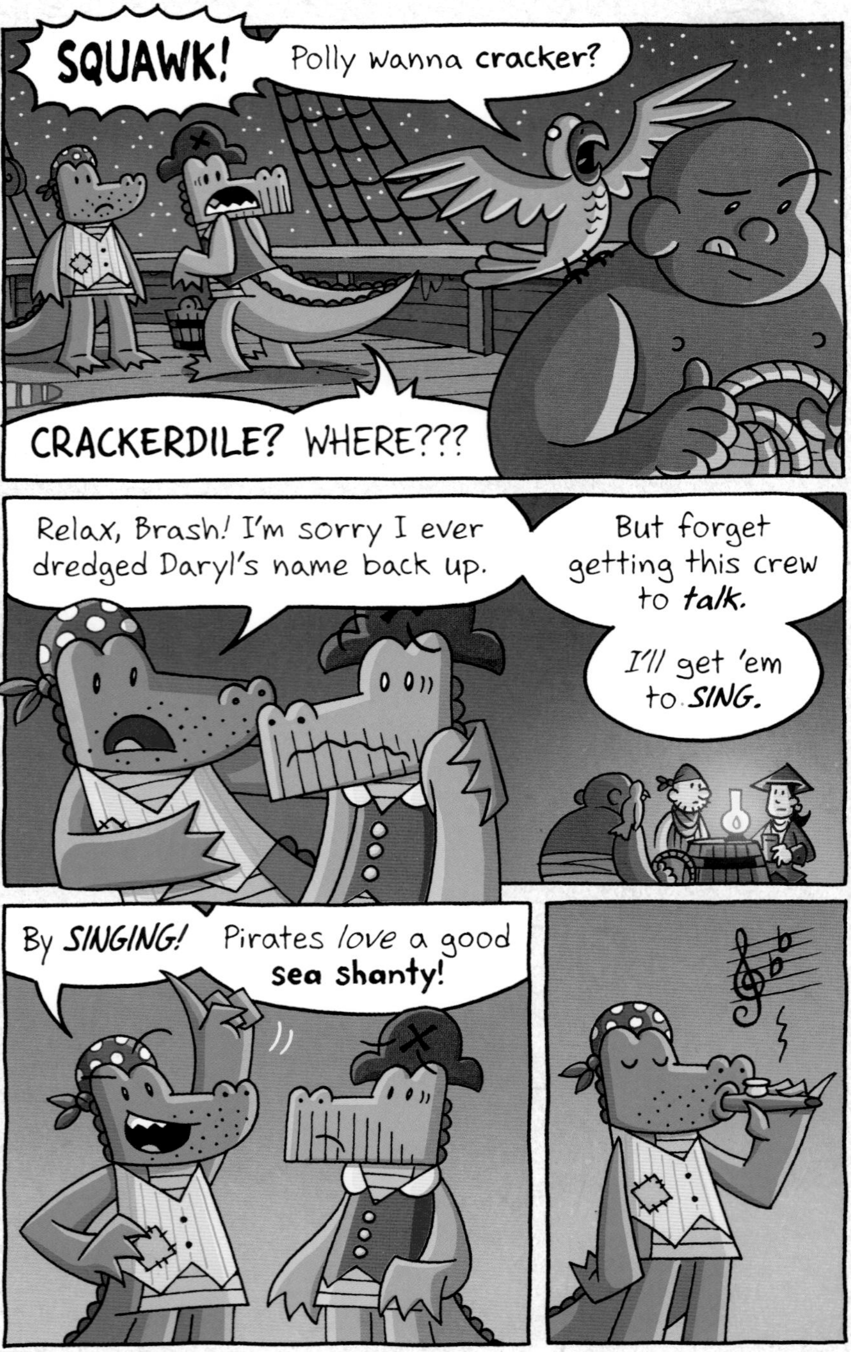
SQUAWK!
Polly wanna cracker?
CRACKERDILE? WHERE???
Relax, Brash! I'm sorry I ever dredged Daryl's name back up.
But forget getting this crew to talk.
I'll get 'em to SING.
By SINGING!
Pirates love a good sea shanty!

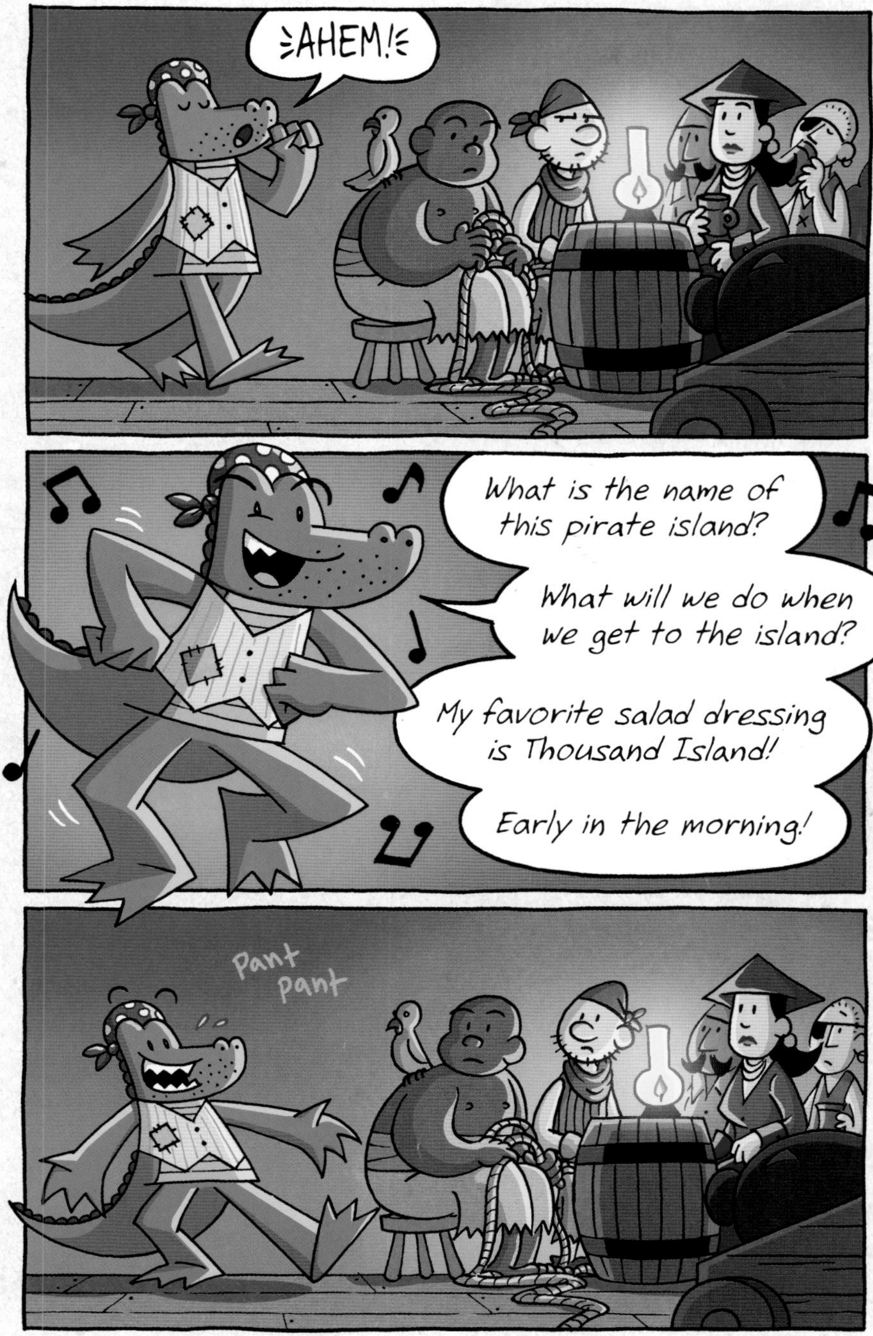
AHEM!
What is the name of this pirate island?
What will we do when we get to the island?
My favorite salad dressing is Thousand Island!
Early in the morning!
Pant pant

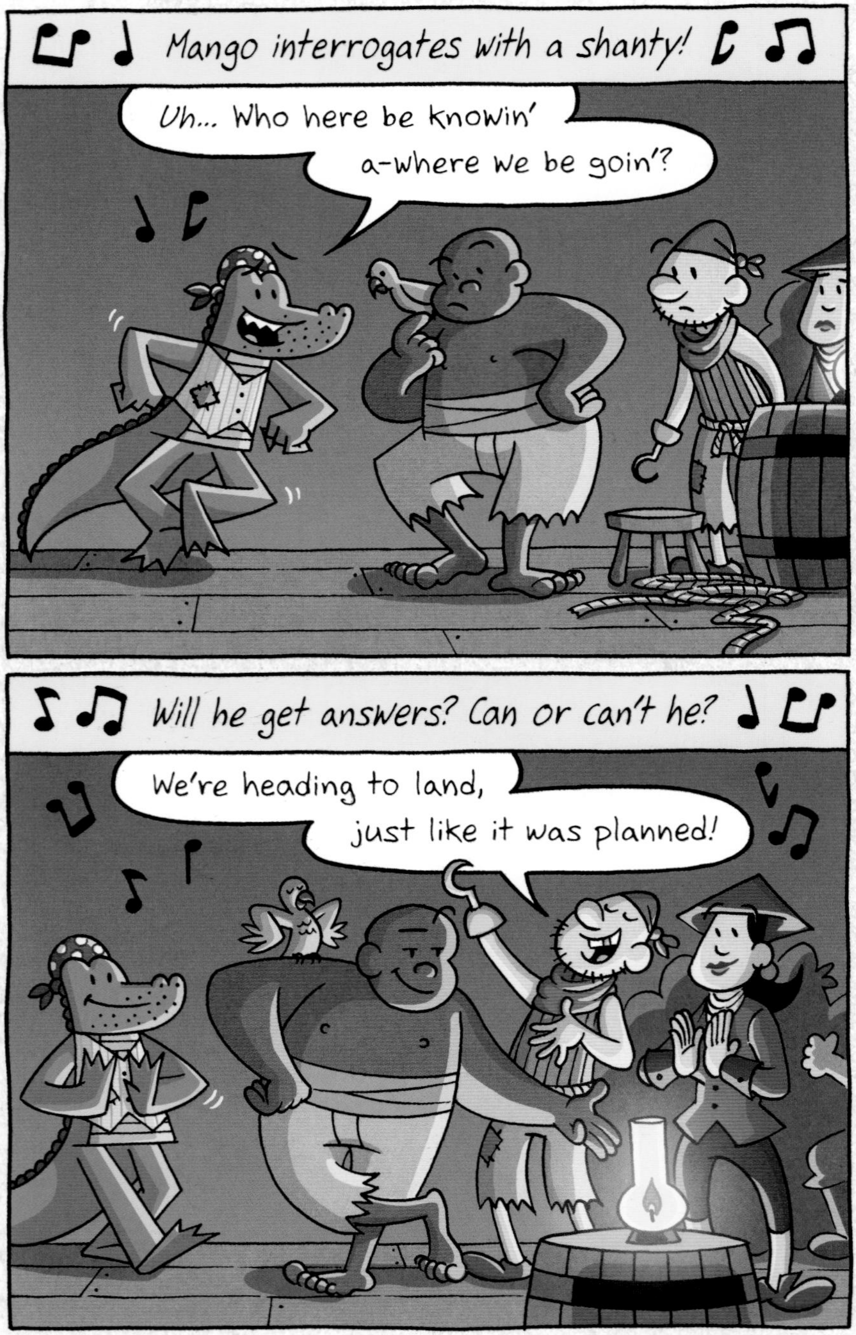
Mango interrogates with a shanty!
Uh... Who here be knowin' a-where we be goin'?
Will he get answers? Can or can't he?
We're heading to land, just like it was planned!

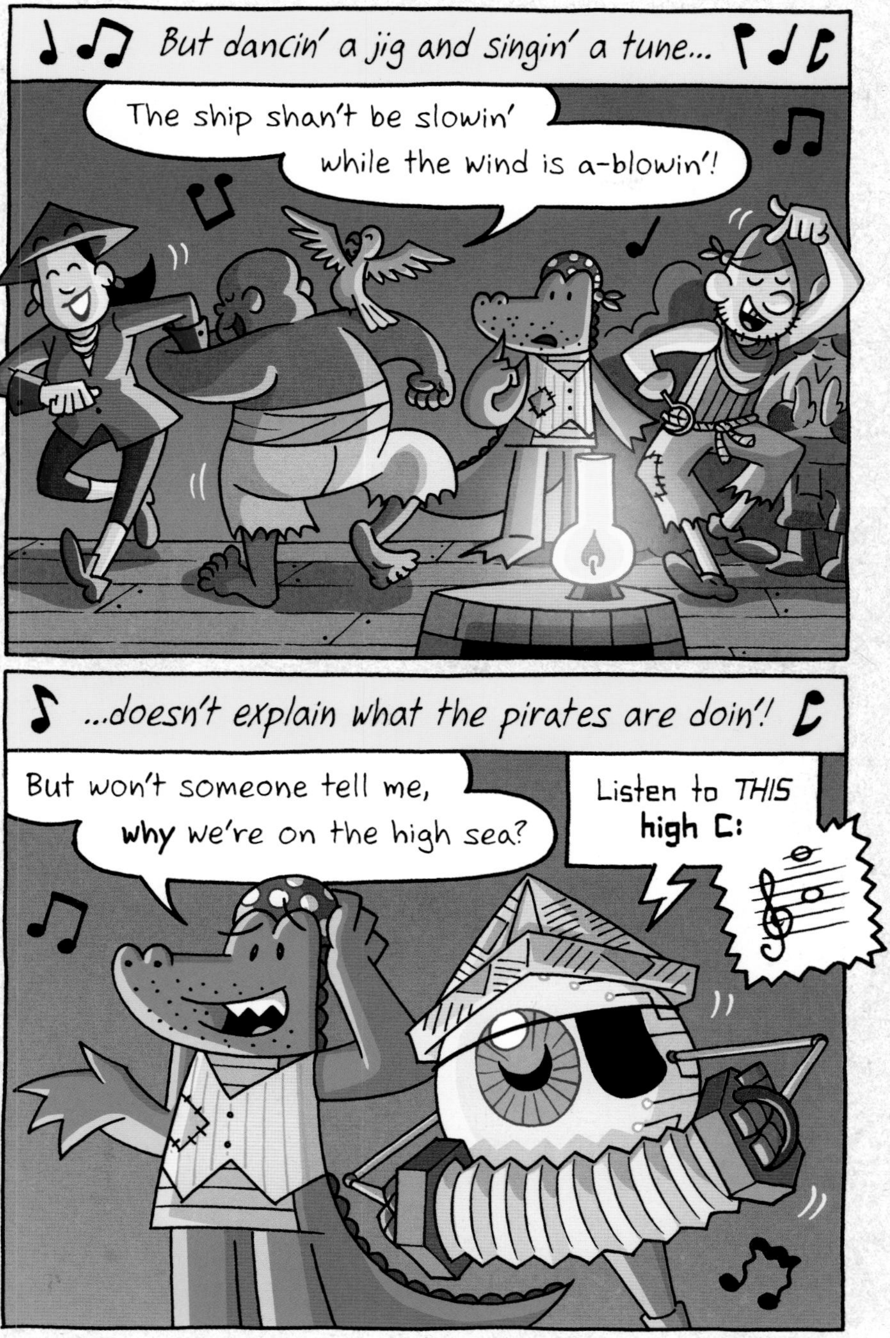
But dancin' a jig and singin' a tune...
The ship shan't be slowin' while the wind is a-blowin'!
...doesn't explain what the pirates are doin'!
But won't someone tell me, why we're on the high sea?
Listen to THIS high C:

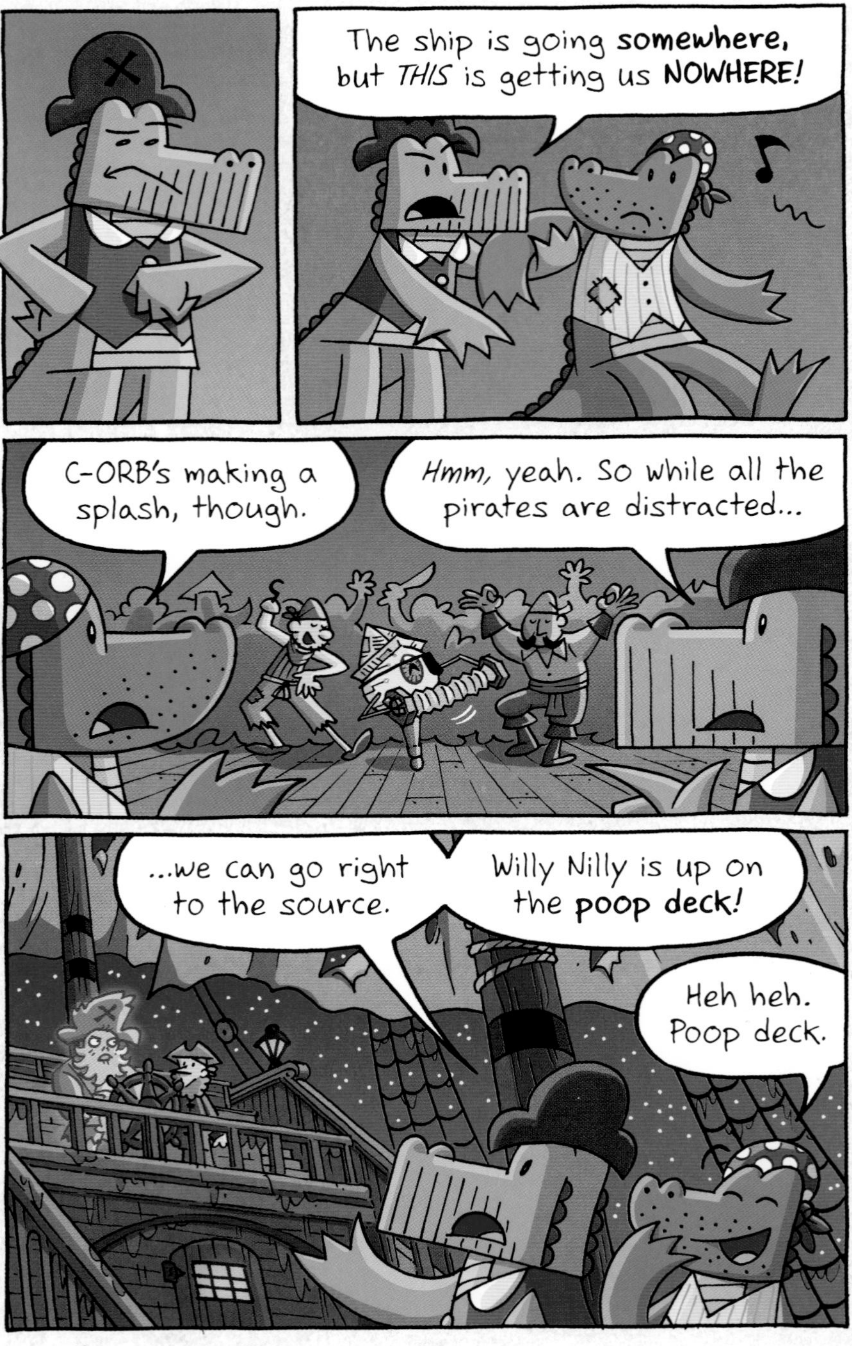
The ship is going **somewhere,** but *THIS* is getting us **NOWHERE!**
C-ORB's making a splash, though.
Hmm, yeah. So while all the pirates are distracted...
...we can go right to the source.
Willy Nilly is up on the **poop deck!**
Heh heh. Poop deck.

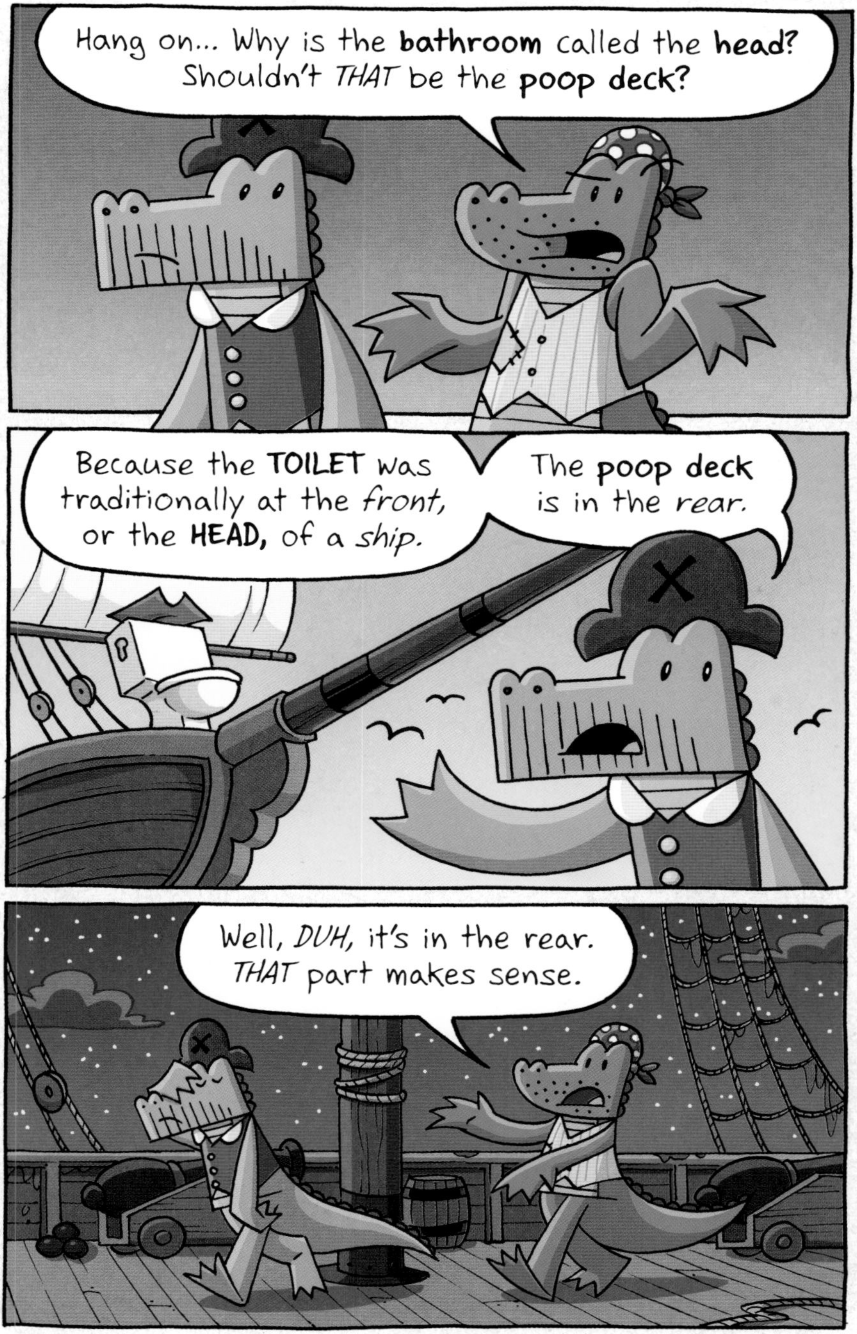
Hang on... Why is the **bathroom** called the **head?** Shouldn't *THAT* be the **poop deck?**
Because the **TOILET** was traditionally at the *front,* or the **HEAD,** of a *ship.*
The **poop deck** is in the *rear.*
Well, *DUH,* it's in the rear. *THAT* part makes sense.

Chapter 13

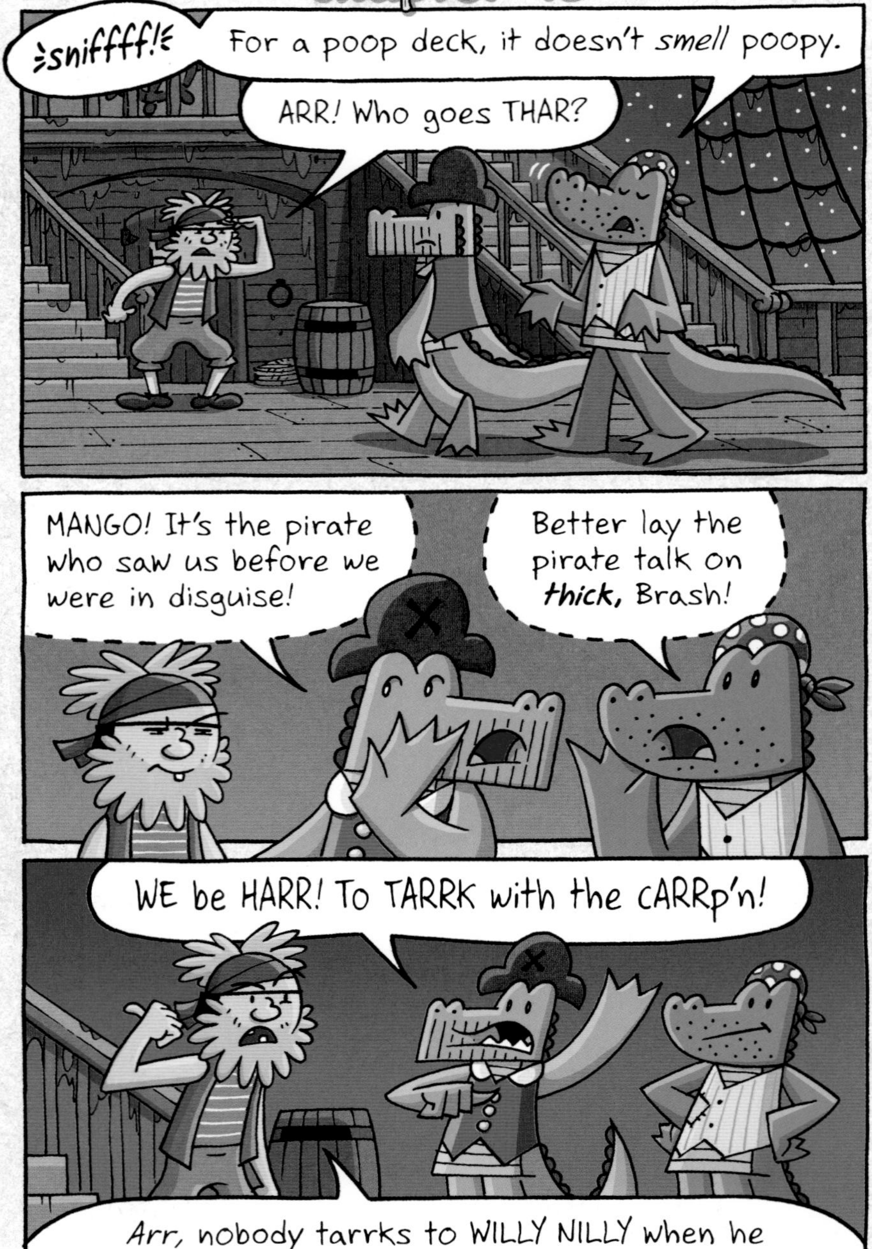

snifffff!
For a poop deck, it doesn't *smell* poopy.
ARR! Who goes THAR?
MANGO! It's the pirate who saw us before we were in disguise!
Better lay the pirate talk on **thick,** Brash!
WE be HARR! To TARRK with the CARRp'n!
Arr, nobody tarrks to WILLY NILLY when he be doin' his captainly duties upon the poop deck!

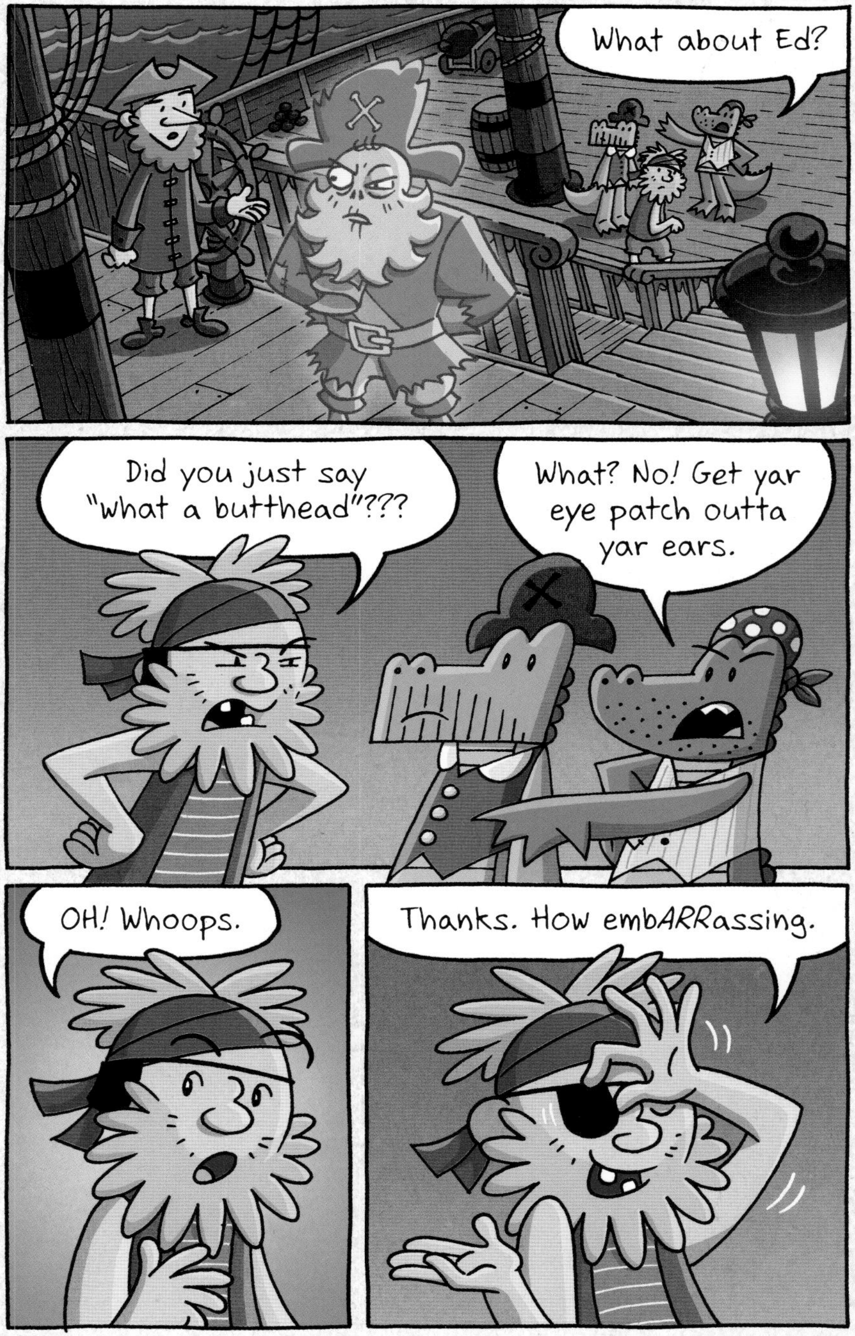
What about Ed?
Did you just say "what a butthead"???
What? No! Get yar eye patch outta yar ears.
OH! Whoops.
Thanks. How embARRassing.

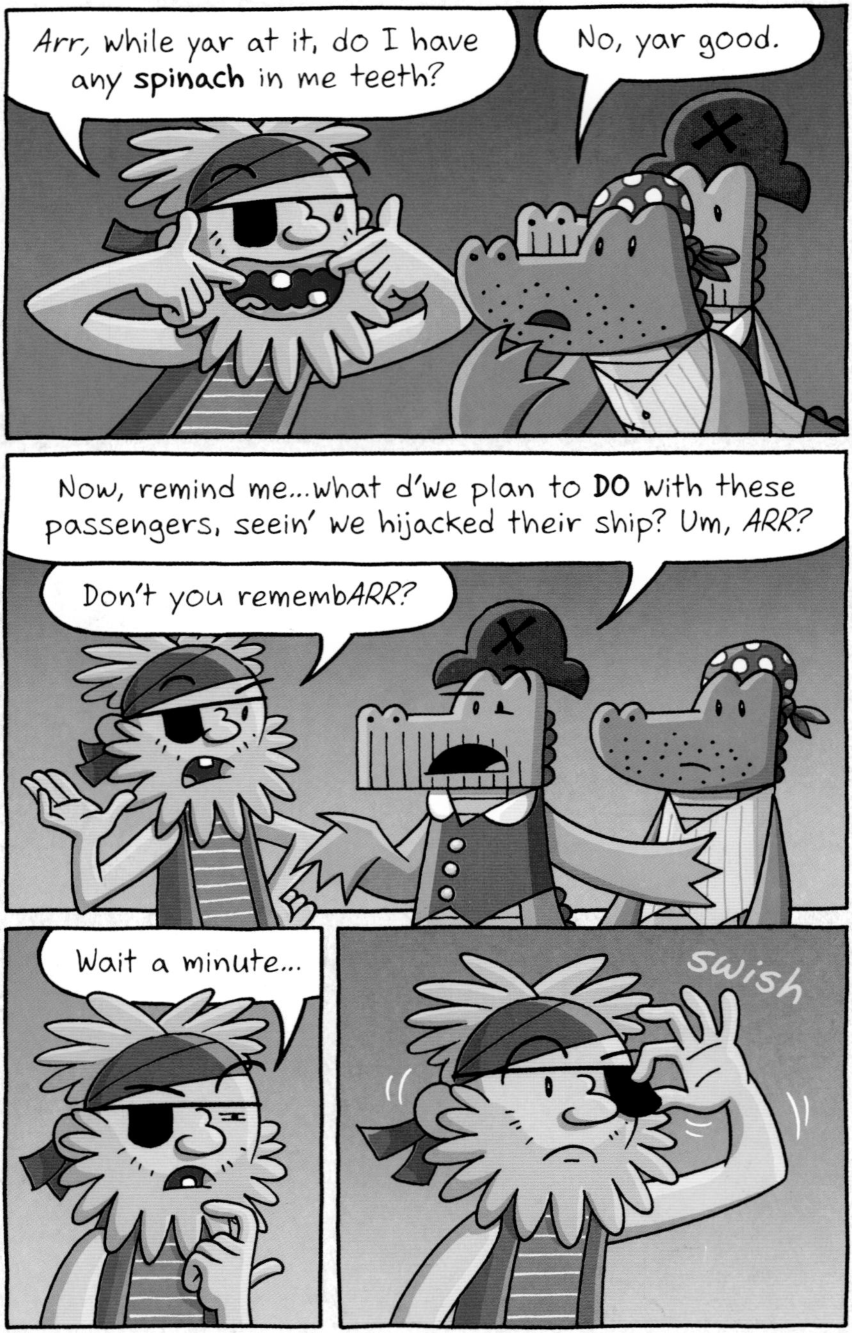
Arr, while yar at it, do I have any **spinach** in me teeth?
No, yar good.
Now, remind me...what d'we plan to **DO** with these passengers, seein' we hijacked their ship? Um, *ARR?*
Don't you rememb*ARR?*
Wait a minute...
SWISH

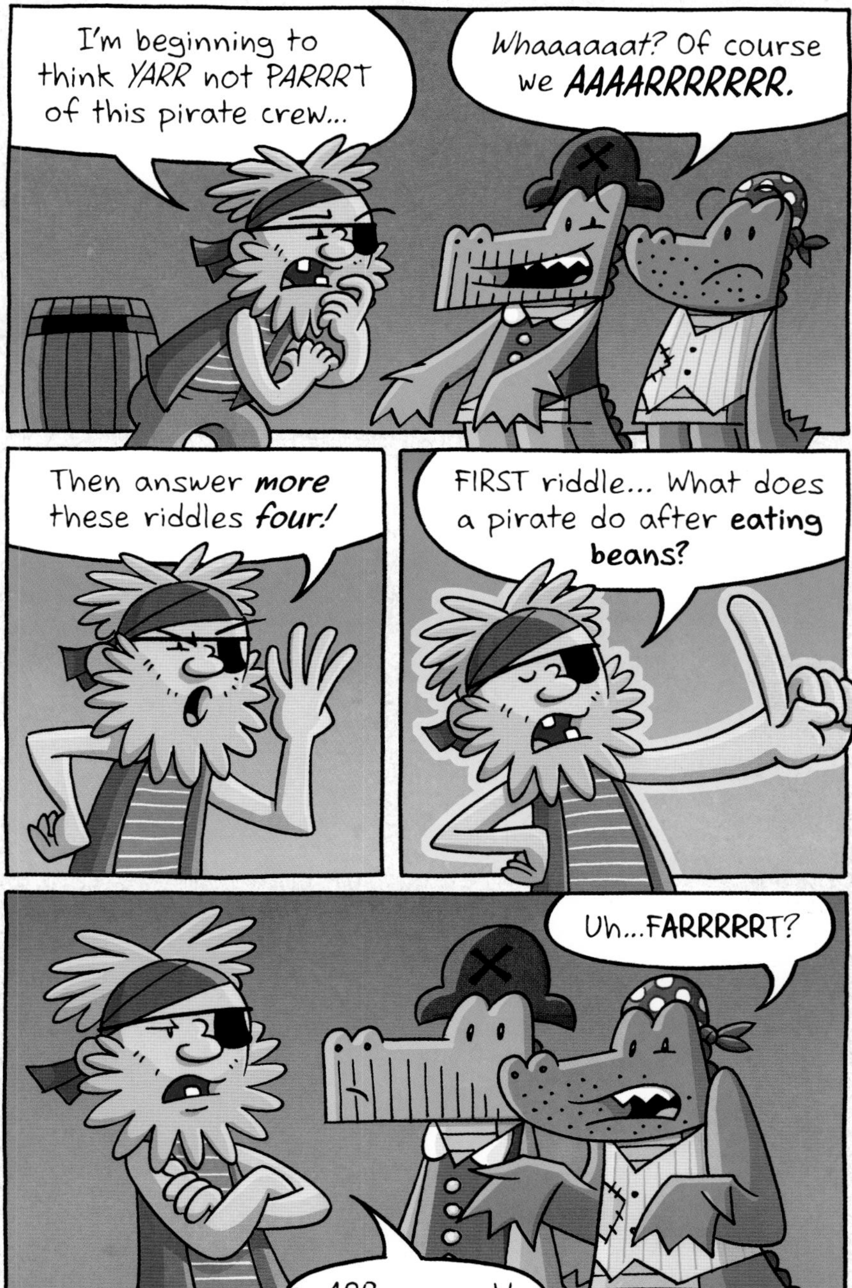
I'm beginning to think YARR not PARRRT of this pirate crew...
Whaaaaaat? Of course we AAAARRRRRRR.
Then answer more these riddles four!
FIRST riddle... What does a pirate do after eating beans?
Uh...FARRRRRT?
ARR, correct!

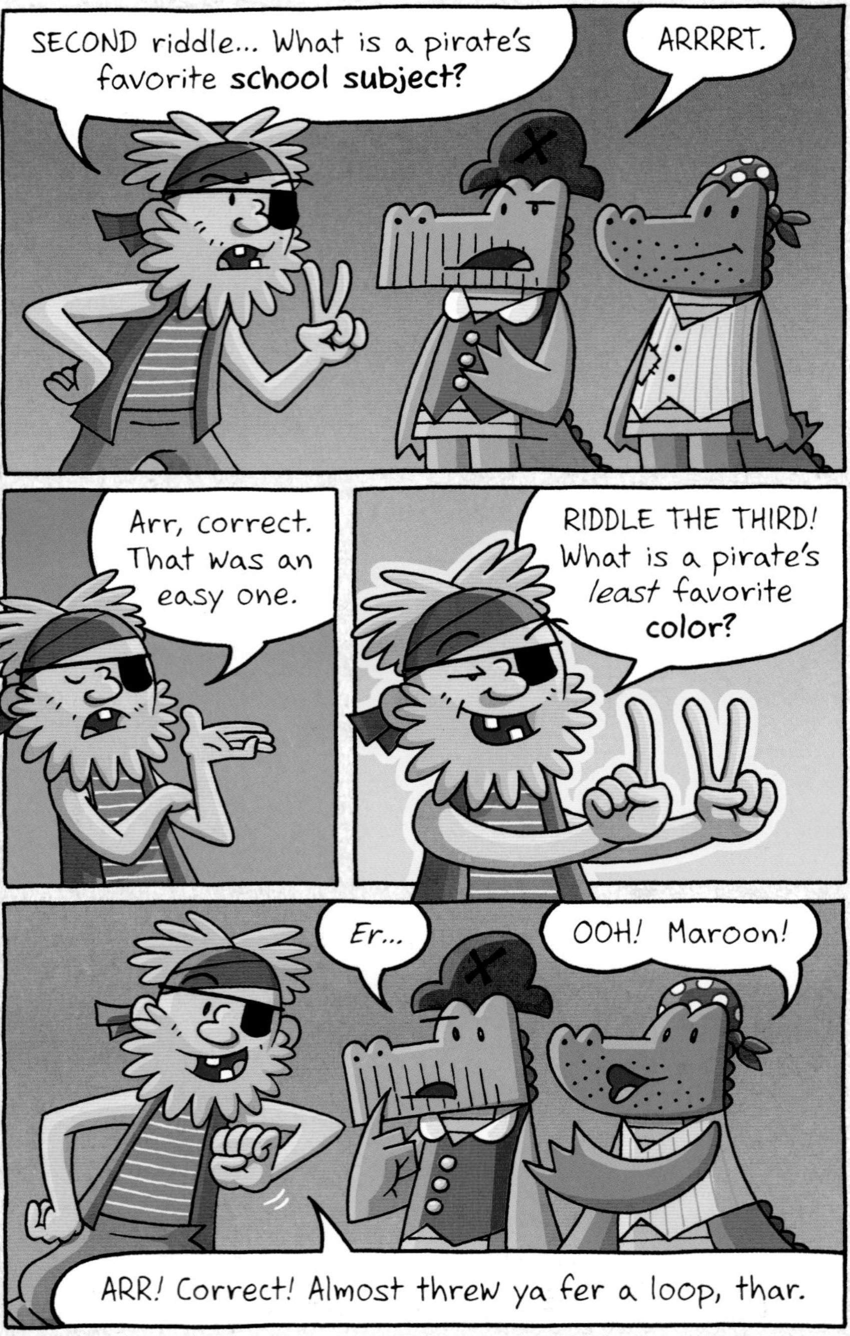
SECOND riddle... What is a pirate's favorite **school subject?**
ARRRRT.
Arr, correct. That was an easy one.
RIDDLE THE THIRD! What is a pirate's *least* favorite **color?**
Er...
OOH! Maroon!
ARR! Correct! Almost threw ya fer a loop, thar.

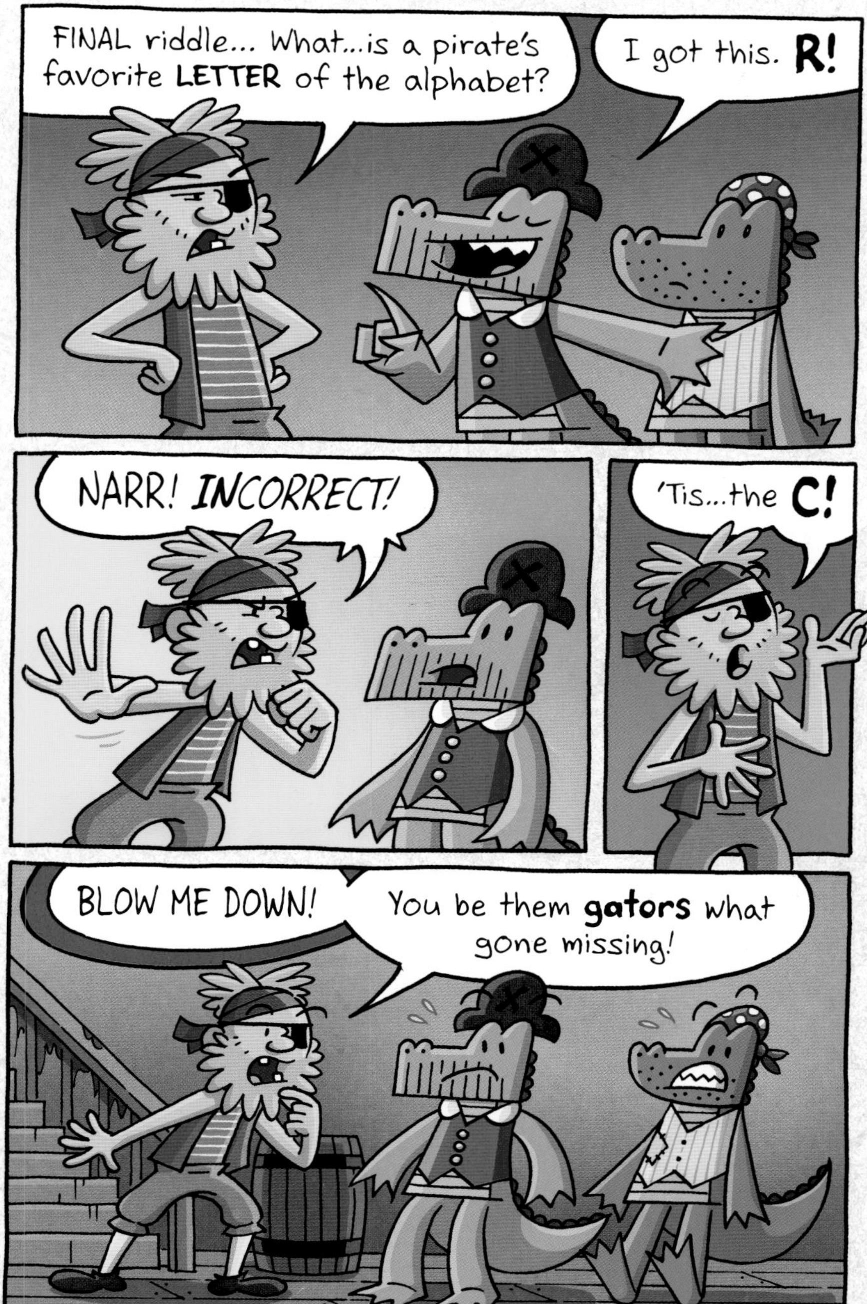

FINAL riddle... What...is a pirate's favorite **LETTER** of the alphabet?
I got this. **R!**
NARR! **INCORRECT!**
'Tis...the **C!**
BLOW ME DOWN!
You be them **gators** what gone missing!

Chapter 14

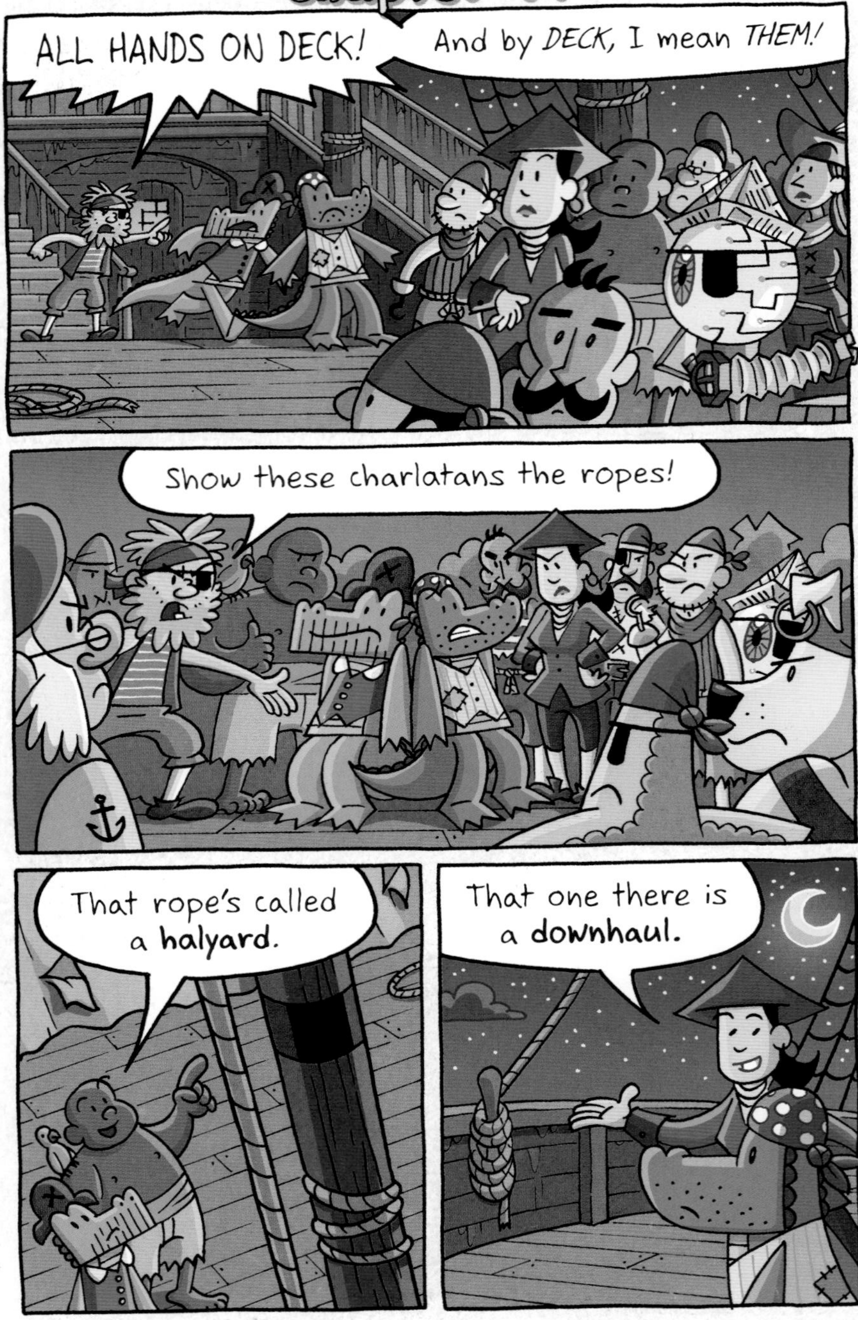
ALL HANDS ON DECK!
And by *DECK*, I mean *THEM!*
Show these charlatans the ropes!
That rope's called a **halyard**.
That one there is a **downhaul**.

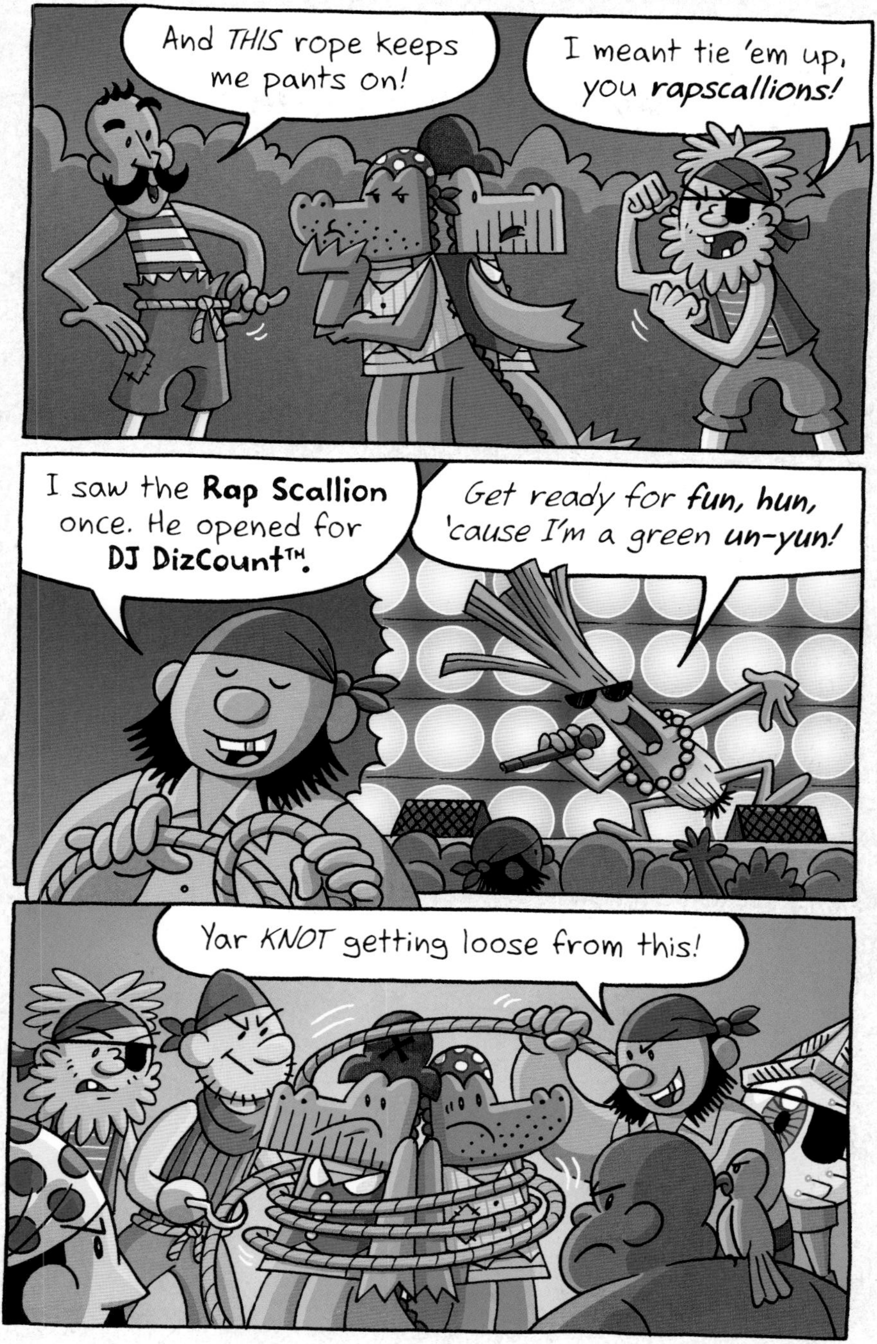
And *THIS* rope keeps me pants on!
I meant tie 'em up, you **rapscallions!**
I saw the **Rap Scallion** once. He opened for **DJ DizCount™.**
Get ready for ***fun, hun,*** *'cause I'm a green* ***un-yun!***
Yar *KNOT* getting loose from this!

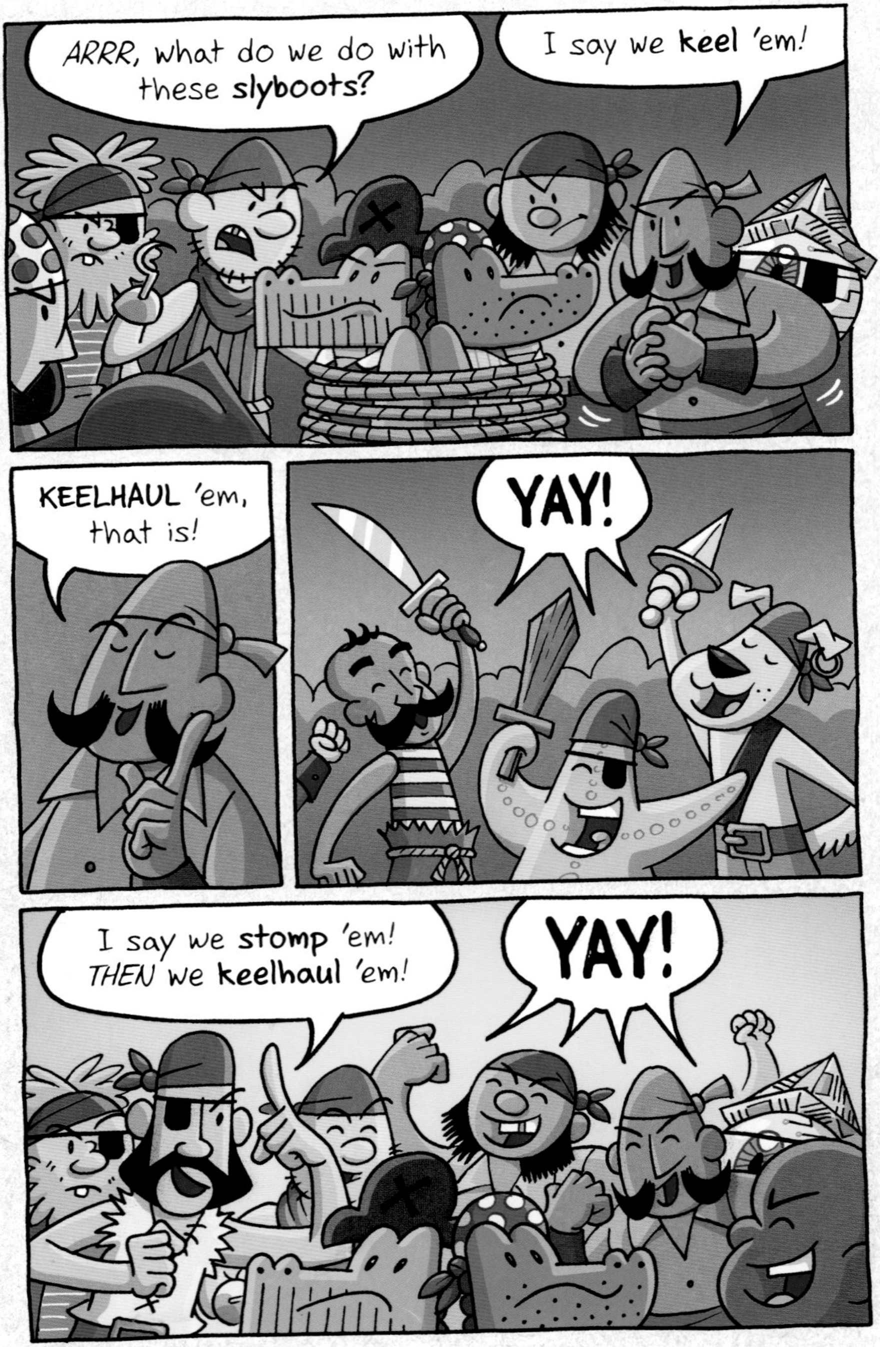
ARRR, what do we do with these slyboots?
I say we keel 'em!
KEELHAUL 'em, that is!
YAY!
I say we stomp 'em! THEN we keelhaul 'em!
YAY!

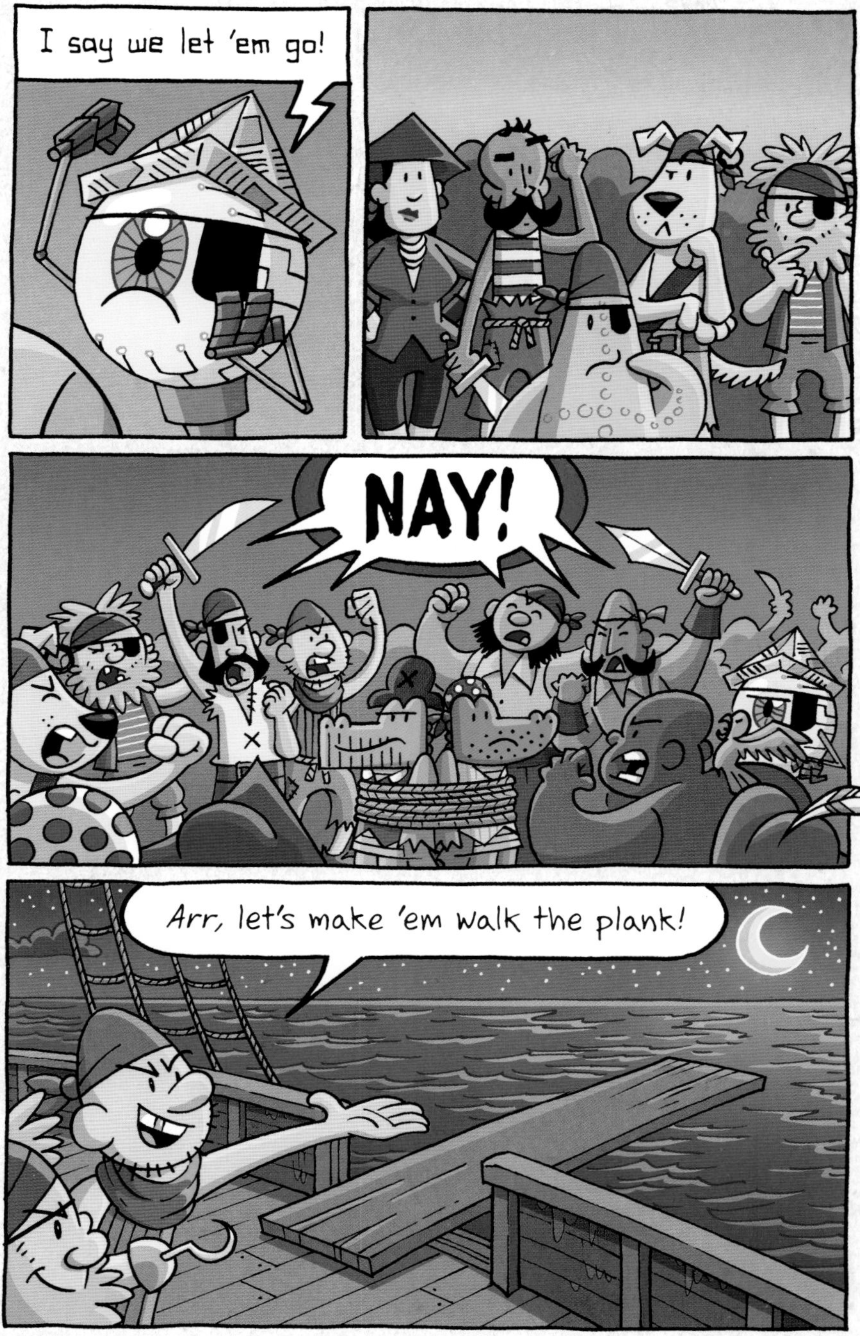
I say we let 'em go!
NAY!
Arr, let's make 'em walk the plank!

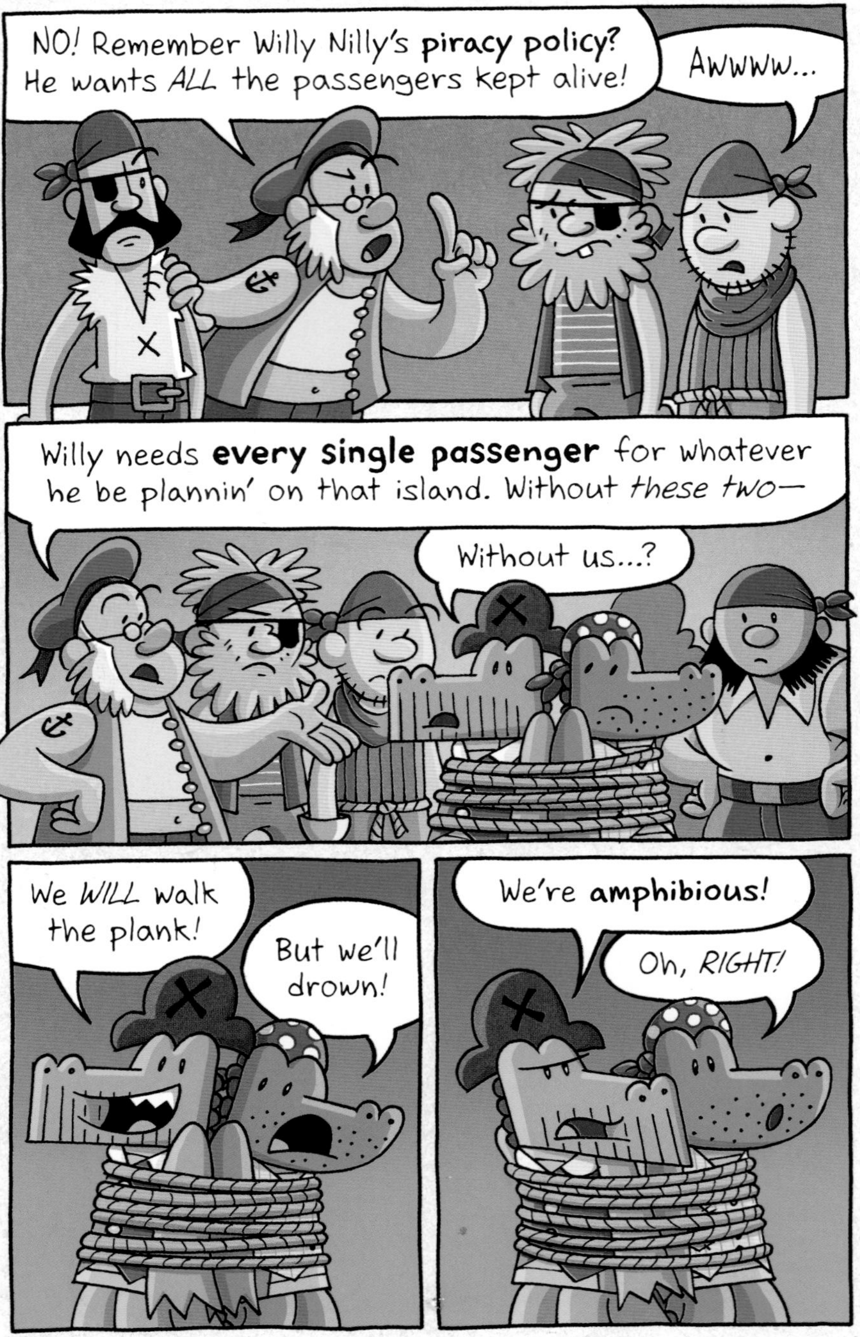
NO! Remember Willy Nilly's **piracy policy?** He wants *ALL* the passengers kept alive!
AWWWW...
Willy needs **every single passenger** for whatever he be plannin' on that island. Without *these two*—
Without us...?
We *WILL* walk the plank!
But we'll drown!
We're **amphibious!**
Oh, *RIGHT!*

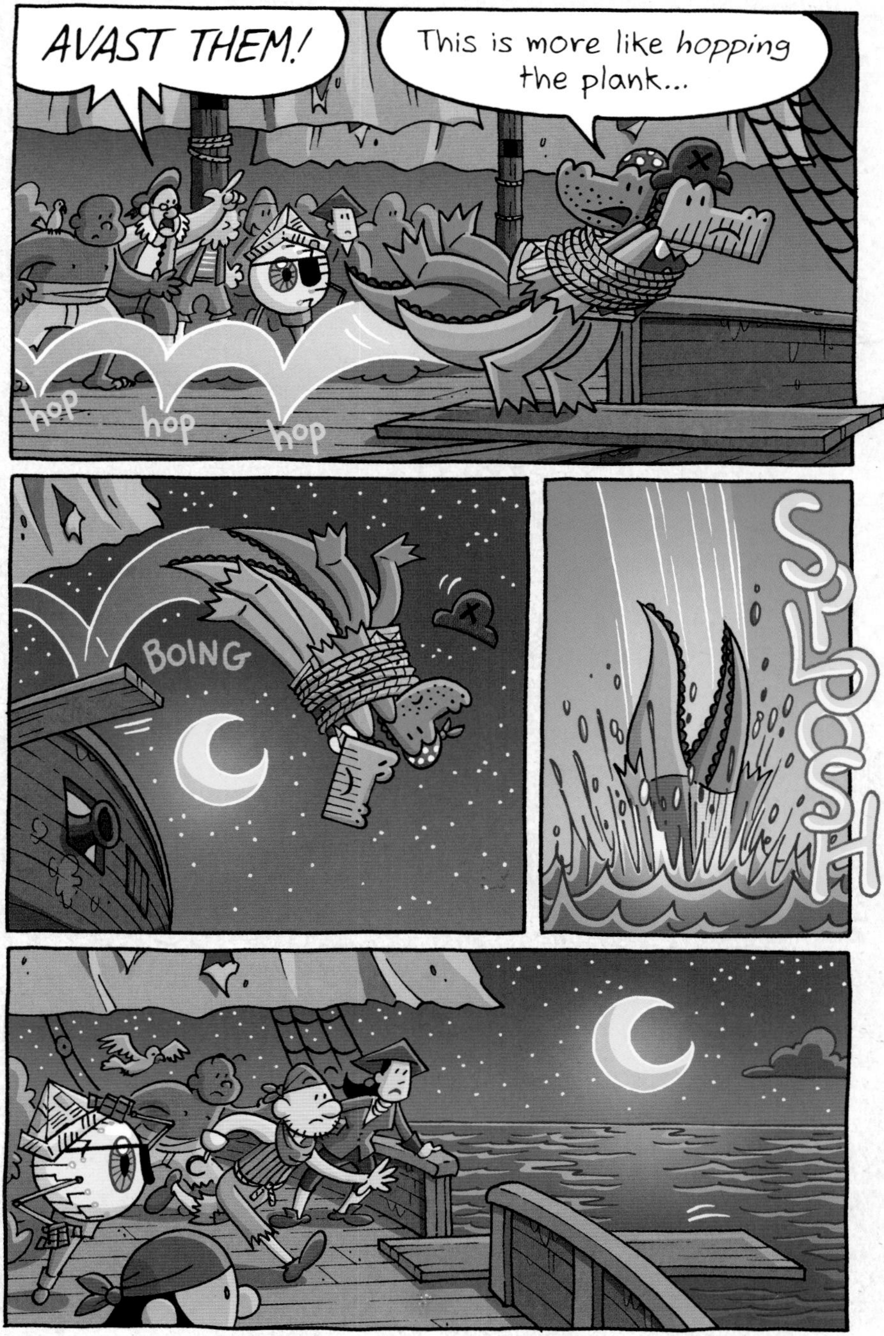
AVAST THEM!
This is more like hopping the plank...
hop
hop
hop
BOING
SPLOOSH

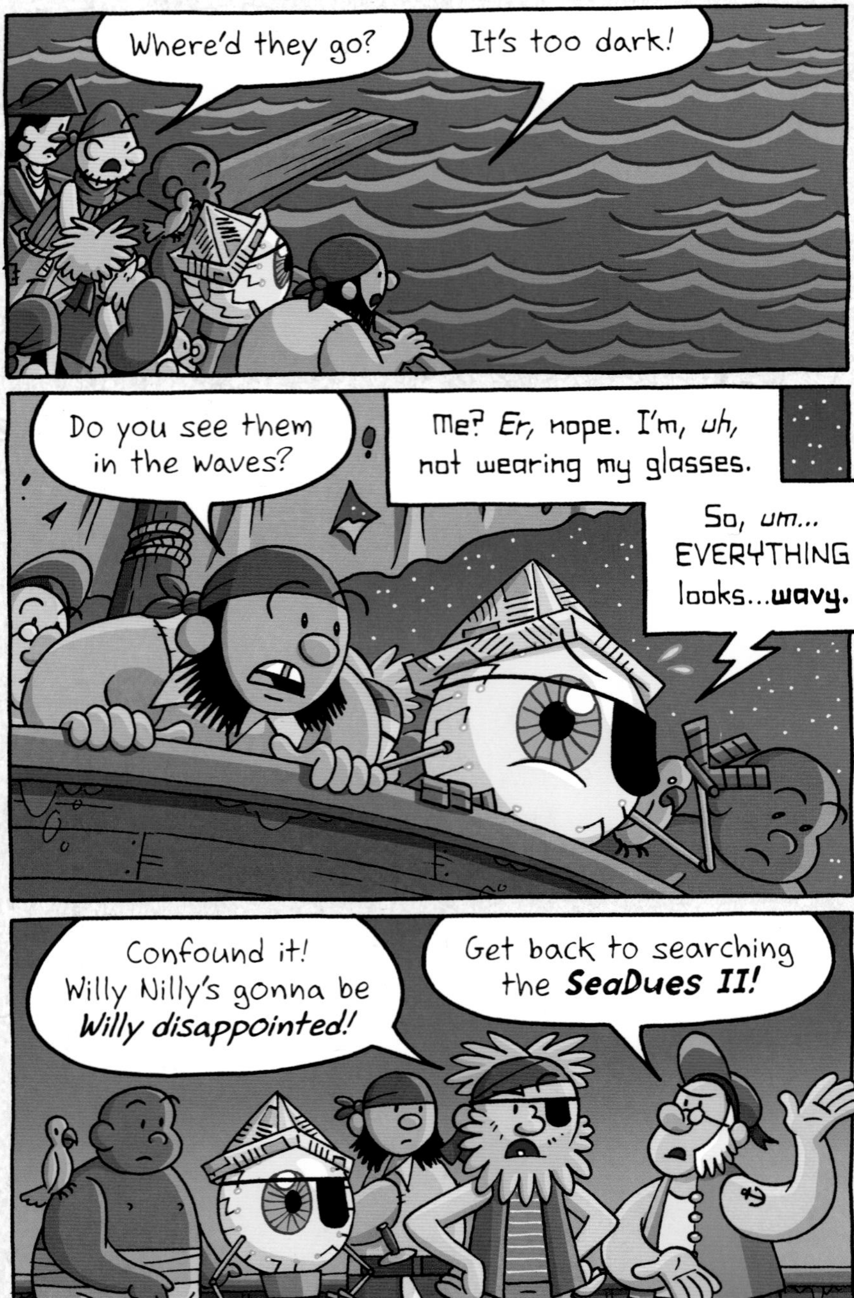
Where'd they go?
It's too dark!
Do you see them in the waves?
Me? *Er,* nope. I'm, *uh,* not wearing my glasses.
So, *um...* EVERYTHING looks...**wavy.**
Confound it! Willy Nilly's gonna be ***Willy disappointed!***
Get back to searching the ***SeaDues II!***

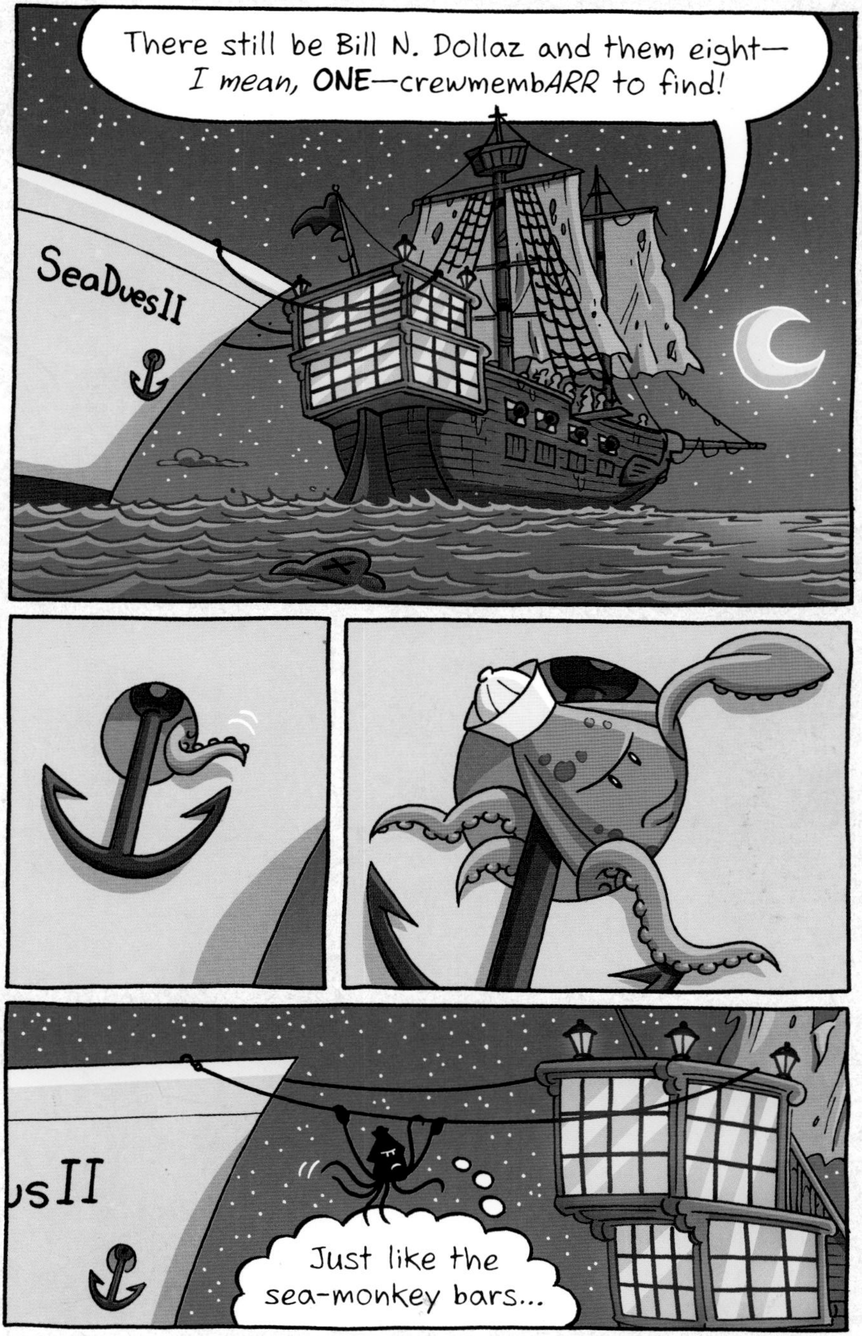
There still be Bill N. Dollaz and them eight—
I mean, ONE—crewmembARR to find!
SeaDuesII
usII
Just like the sea-monkey bars...

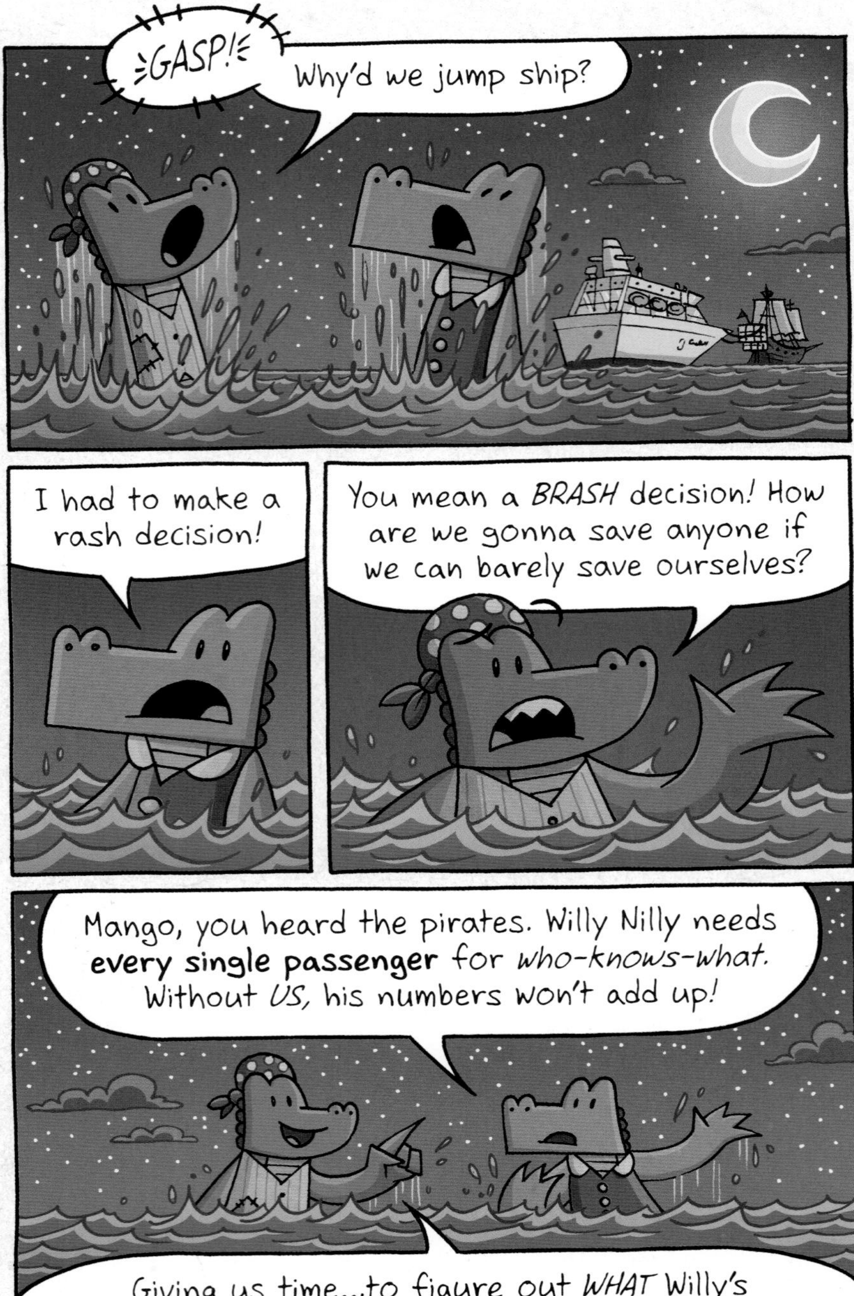
GASP!
Why'd we jump ship?
I had to make a rash decision!
You mean a BRASH decision! How are we gonna save anyone if we can barely save ourselves?
Mango, you heard the pirates. Willy Nilly needs every single passenger for who-knows-what. Without US, his numbers won't add up!
Giving us time...to figure out WHAT Willy's mysterious piratey plan is...and find a way to stop it!

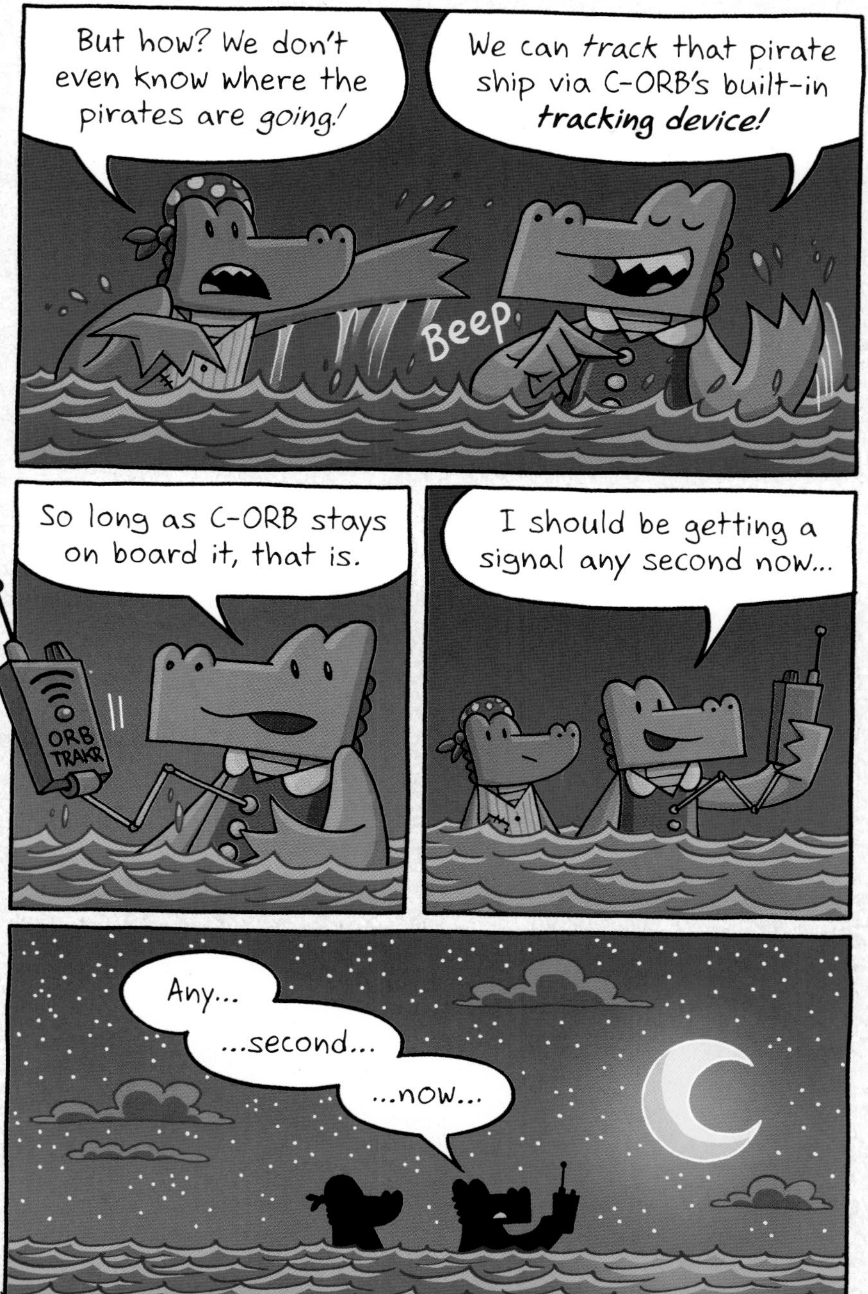
But how? We don't even know where the pirates are *going*!
We can *track* that pirate ship via C-ORB's built-in ***tracking device!***
Beep
So long as C-ORB stays on board it, that is.
ORB TRAKR
I should be getting a signal any second now...
Any...
...second...
...now...

Chapter 15

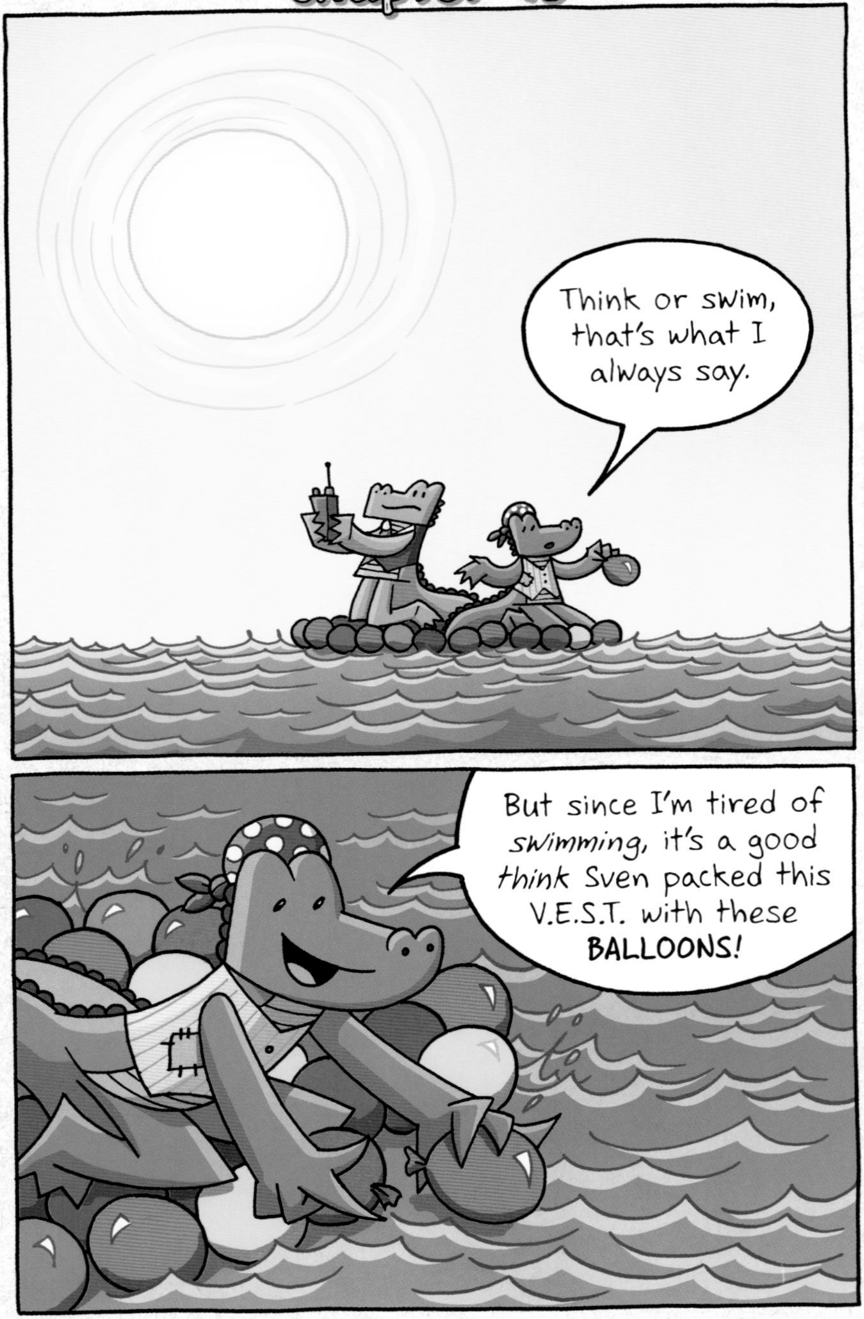
Think or swim, that's what I always say.
But since I'm tired of *swimming*, it's a good *think* Sven packed this V.E.S.T. with these **BALLOONS!**

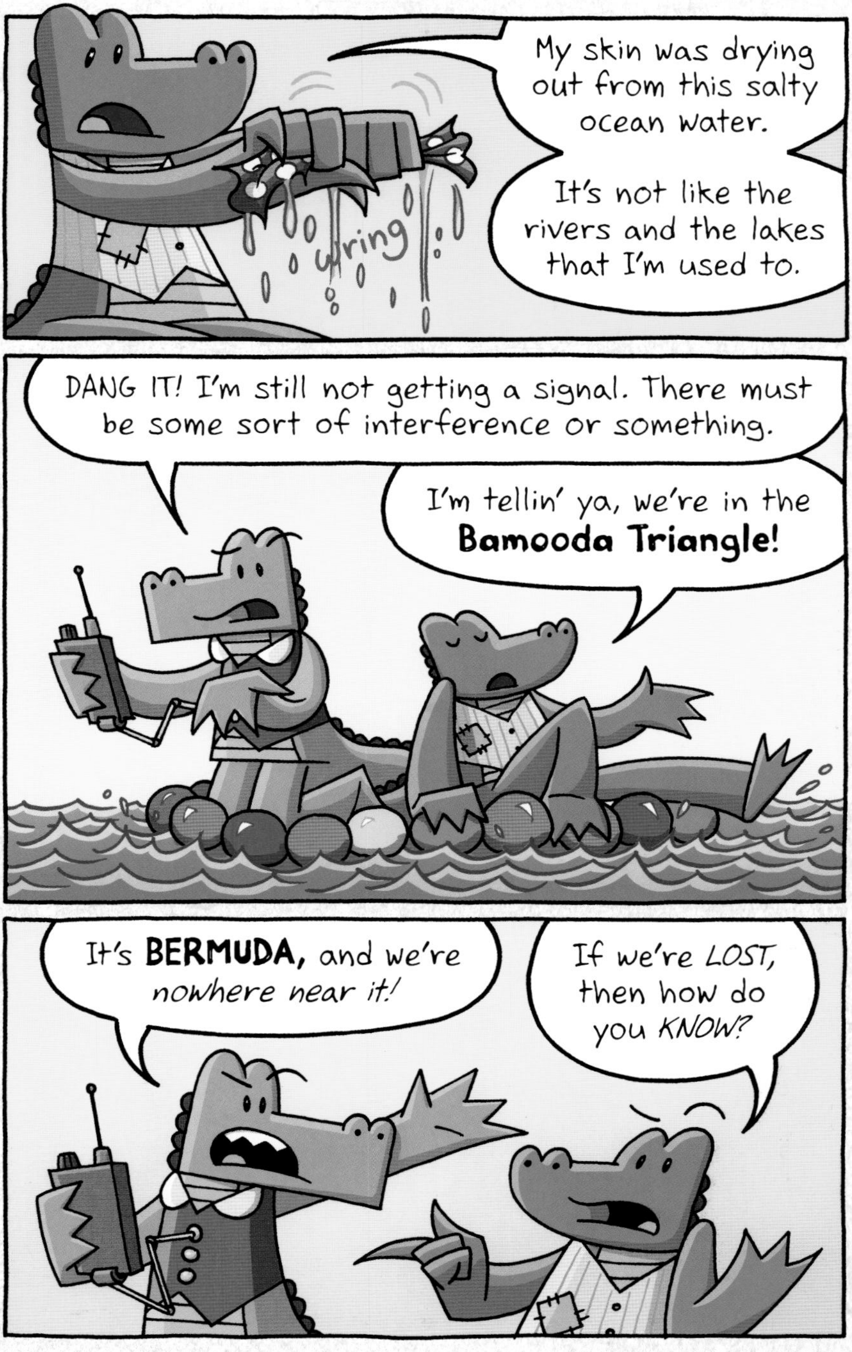
My skin was drying out from this salty ocean water.
It's not like the rivers and the lakes that I'm used to.
wring
DANG IT! I'm still not getting a signal. There must be some sort of interference or something.
I'm tellin' ya, we're in the **Bamooda Triangle!**
It's **BERMUDA,** and we're *nowhere near it!*
If we're *LOST,* then how do you *KNOW?*

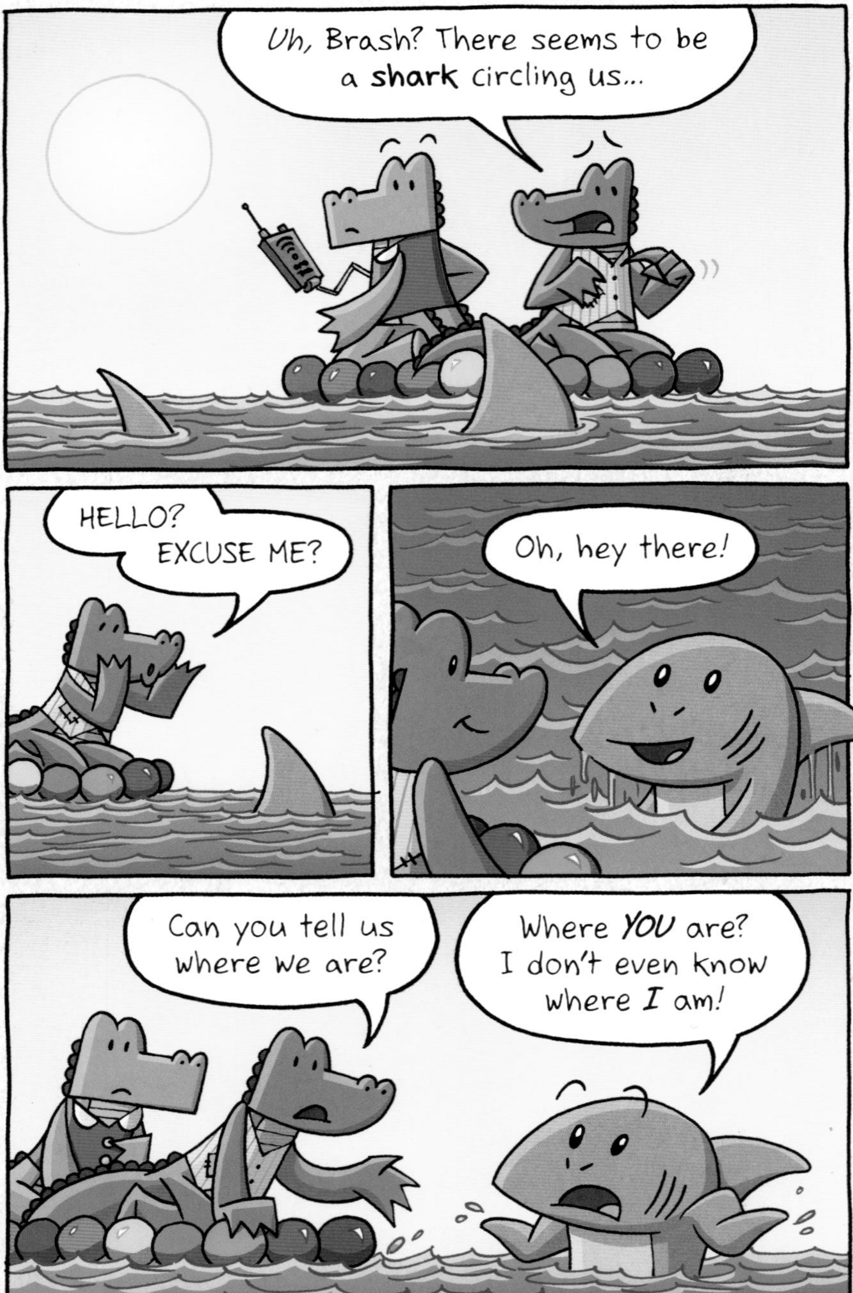
Uh, Brash? There seems to be a **shark** circling us...
HELLO? EXCUSE ME?
Oh, hey there!
Can you tell us where we are?
Where *YOU* are? I don't even know where *I* am!

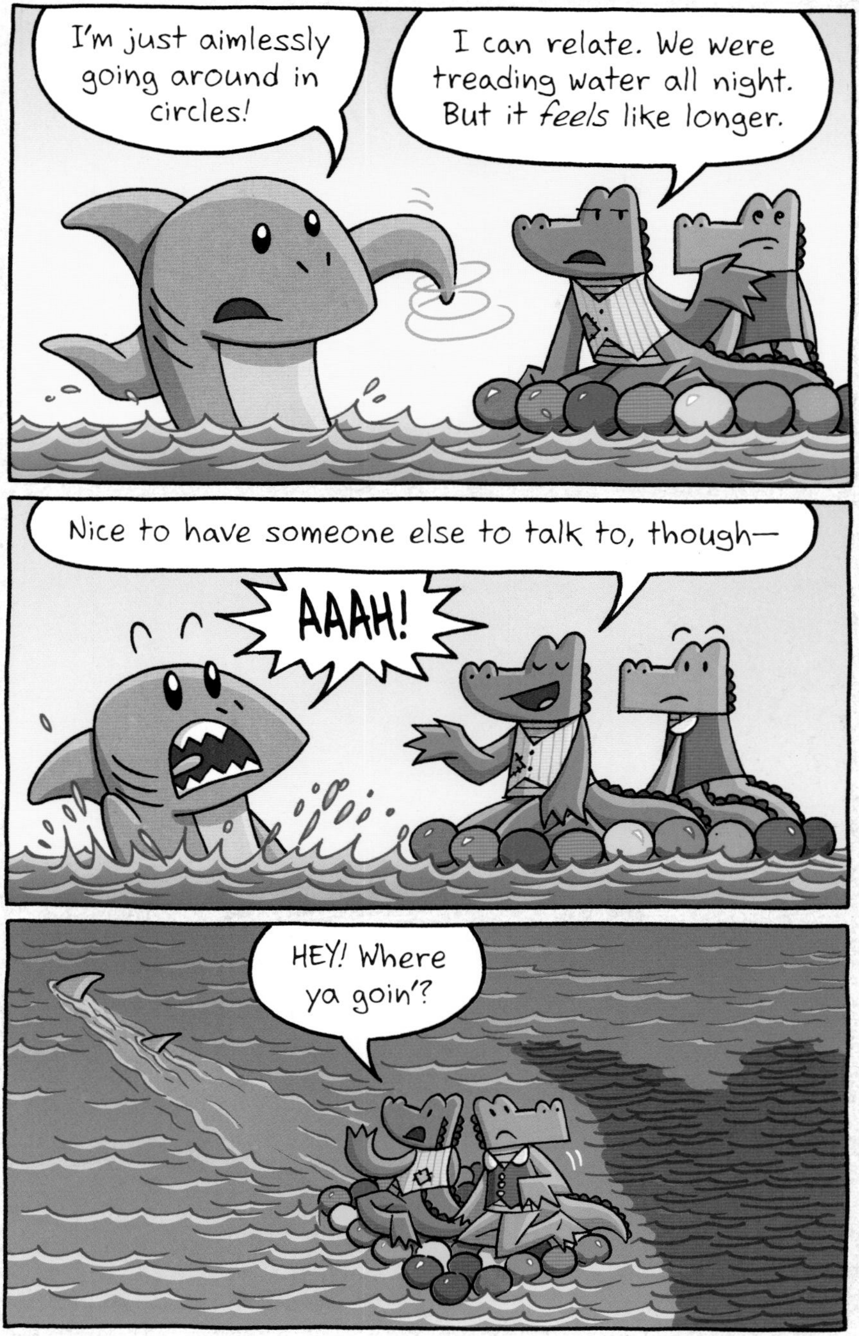
I'm just aimlessly going around in circles!
I can relate. We were treading water all night. But it *feels* like longer.
Nice to have someone else to talk to, though—
AAAH!
HEY! Where ya goin'?

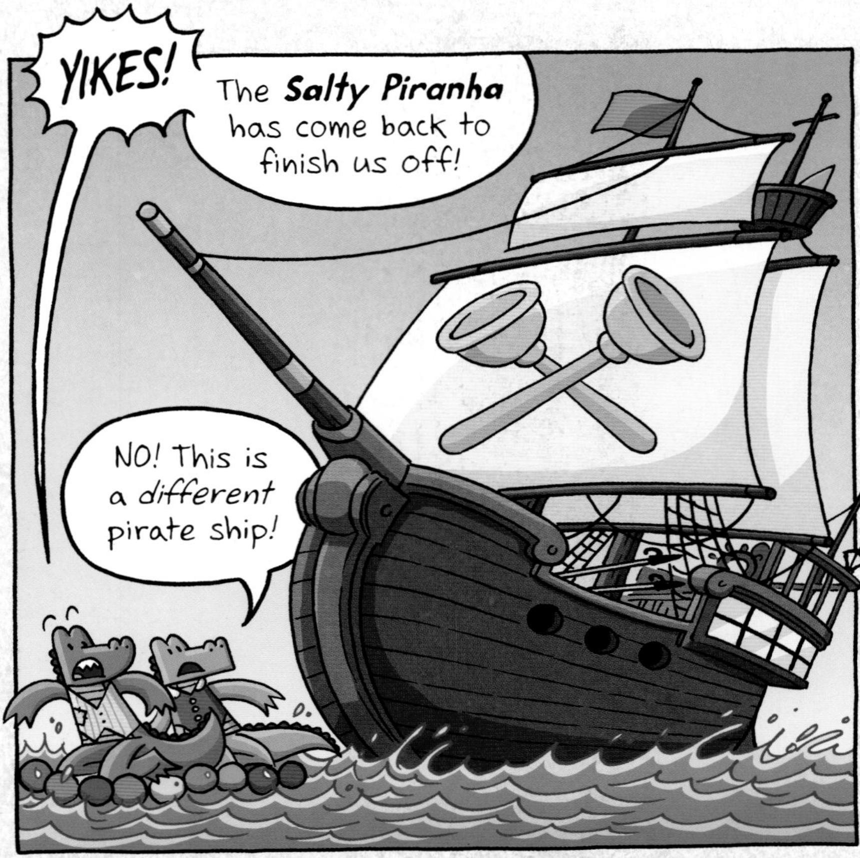
YIKES!
The **Salty Piranha** has come back to finish us off!
NO! This is a *different* pirate ship!

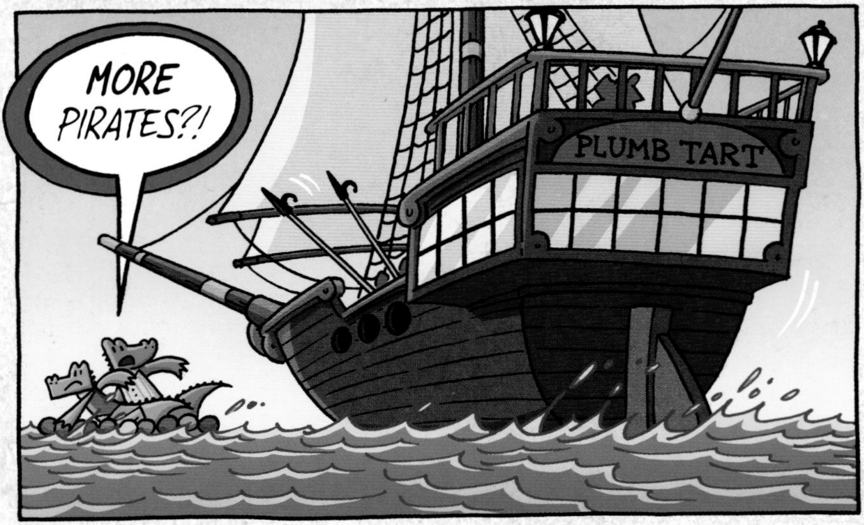
MORE PIRATES?!
PLUMB TART

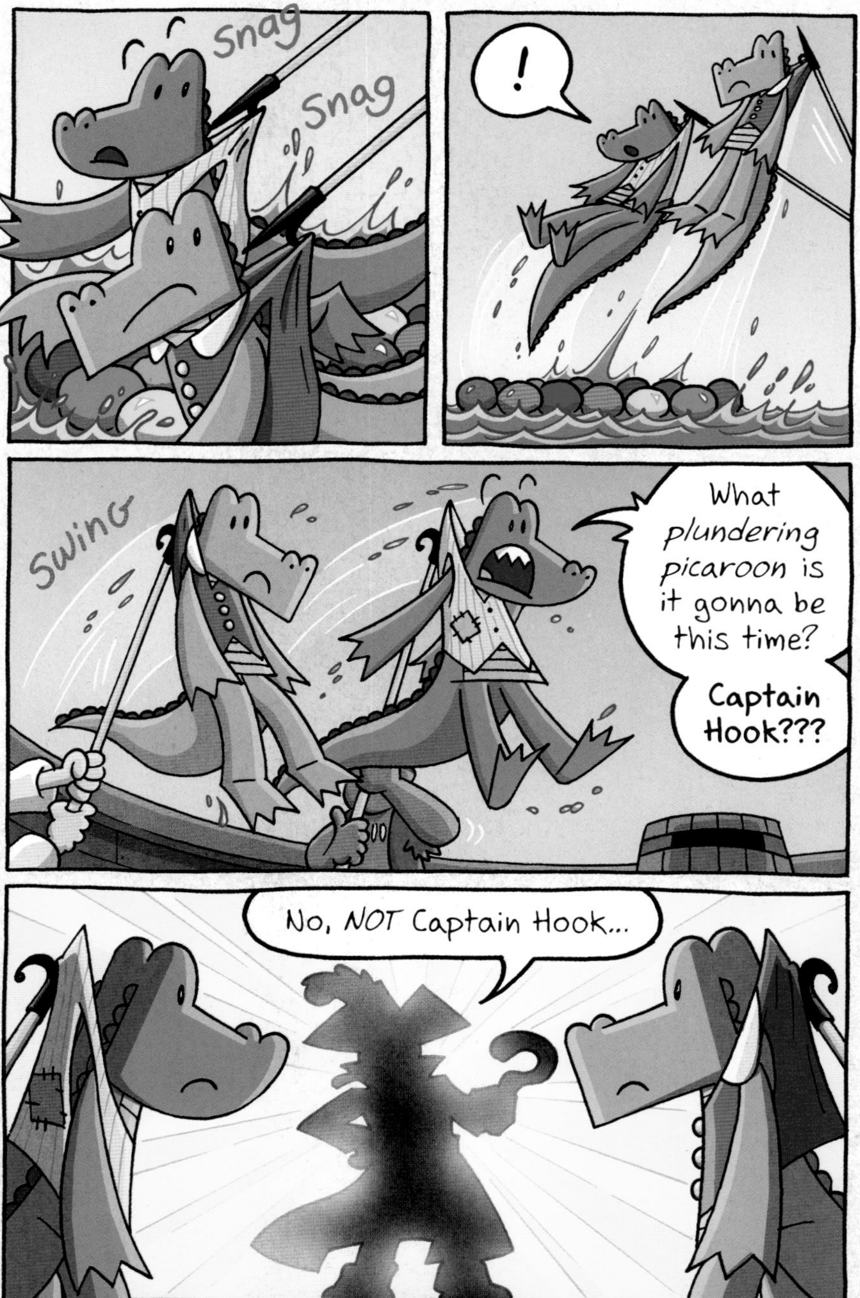
Snag
Snag
!
Swing
What *plundering picaroon* is it gonna be this time?
Captain Hook???
No, *NOT* Captain Hook...

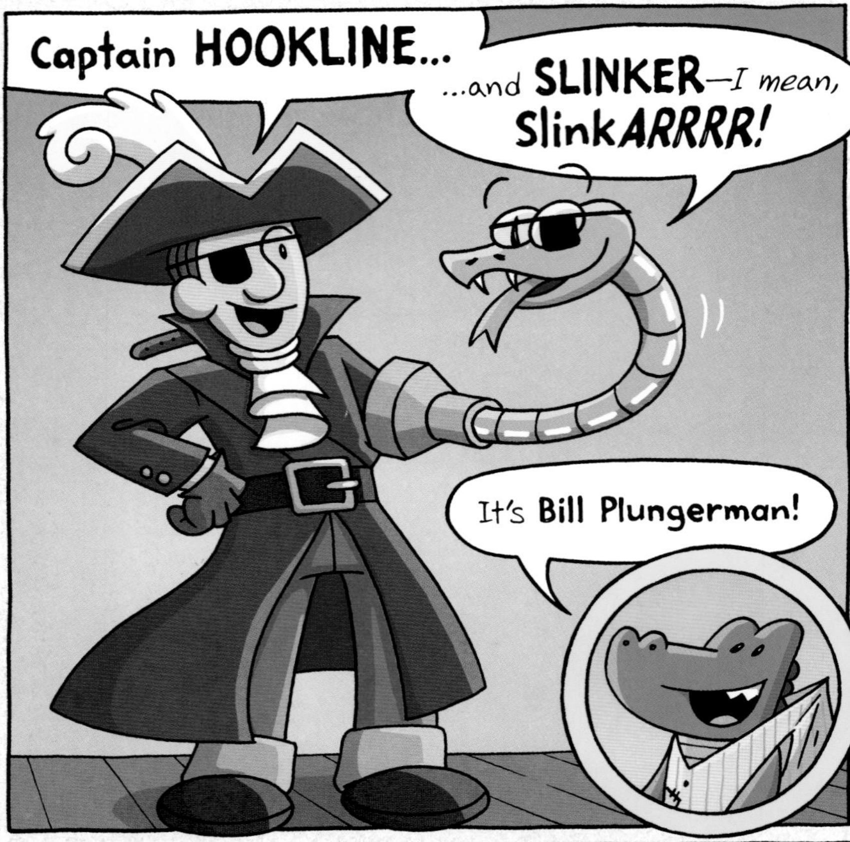
Captain HOOKLINE...
...and SLINKER—I mean, SlinkARRRR!
It's Bill Plungerman!

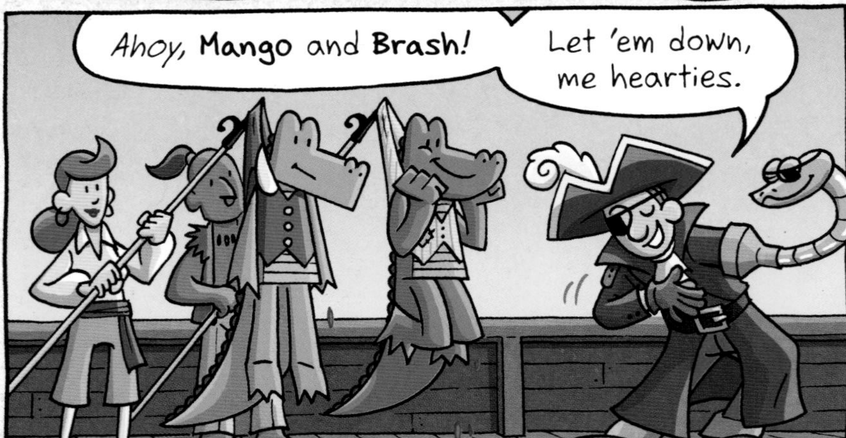
Ahoy, Mango and Brash!
Let 'em down, me hearties.

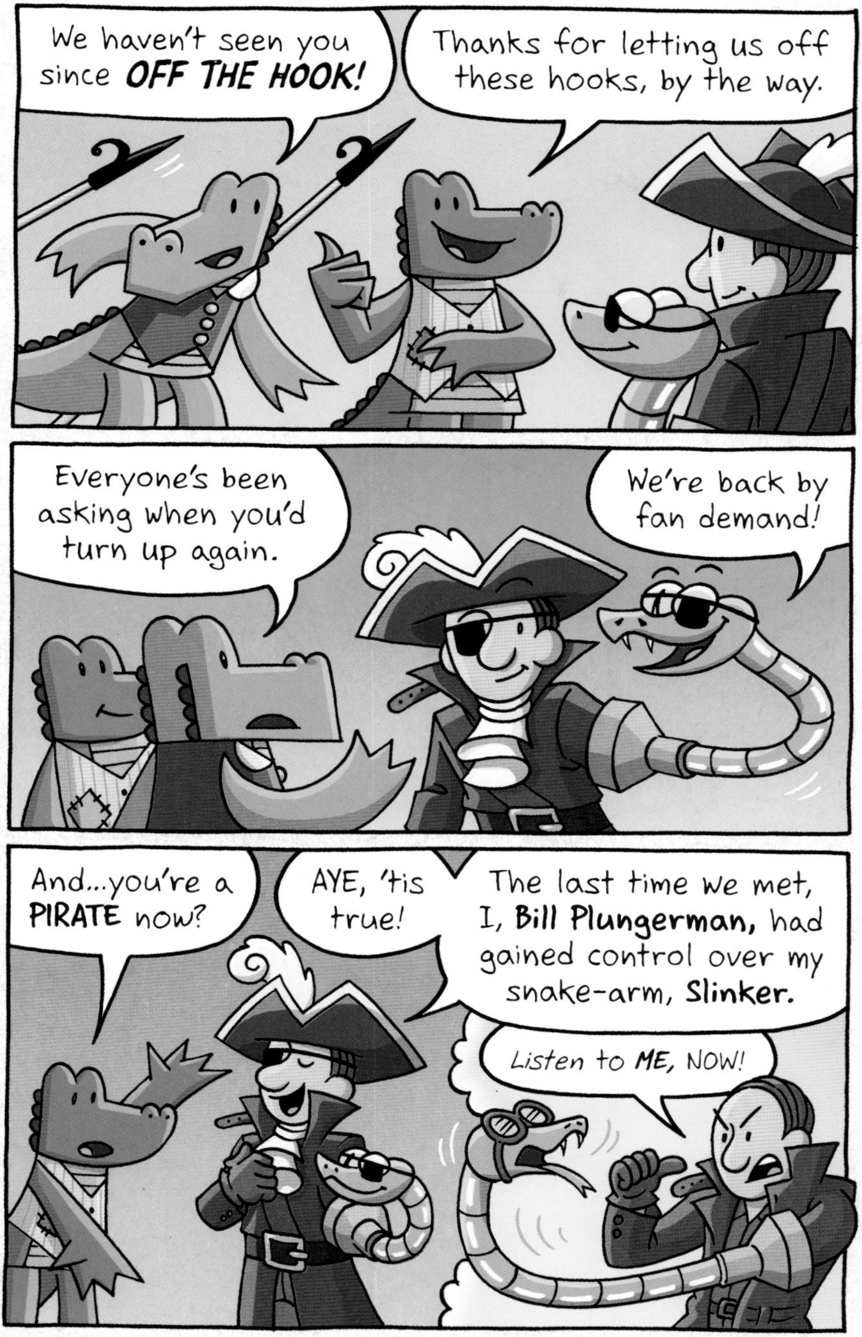
We haven't seen you since **OFF THE HOOK!**
Thanks for letting us off these hooks, by the way.
Everyone's been asking when you'd turn up again.
We're back by fan demand!
And...you're a **PIRATE** now?
AYE, 'tis true!
The last time we met, I, **Bill Plungerman,** had gained control over my snake-arm, **Slinker.**
*Listen to **ME,** NOW!*

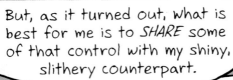

But, as it turned out, what is best for me is to *SHARE* some of that control with my shiny, slithery counterpart.

And what'sss *besssst* for me is to do the *sssame* in return.

Maybe we can... *cooperate?*

By covering *one eye each*, neither of us has the dominant personality...

...allowing us to function as a **codependent organissssm.**

After the eye patches, going **full pirate** seemed like the next logical step.

But not an *EVIL* pirate. We're more of a morally gray, **Robin Hood**—type pirate.

ARRRR!

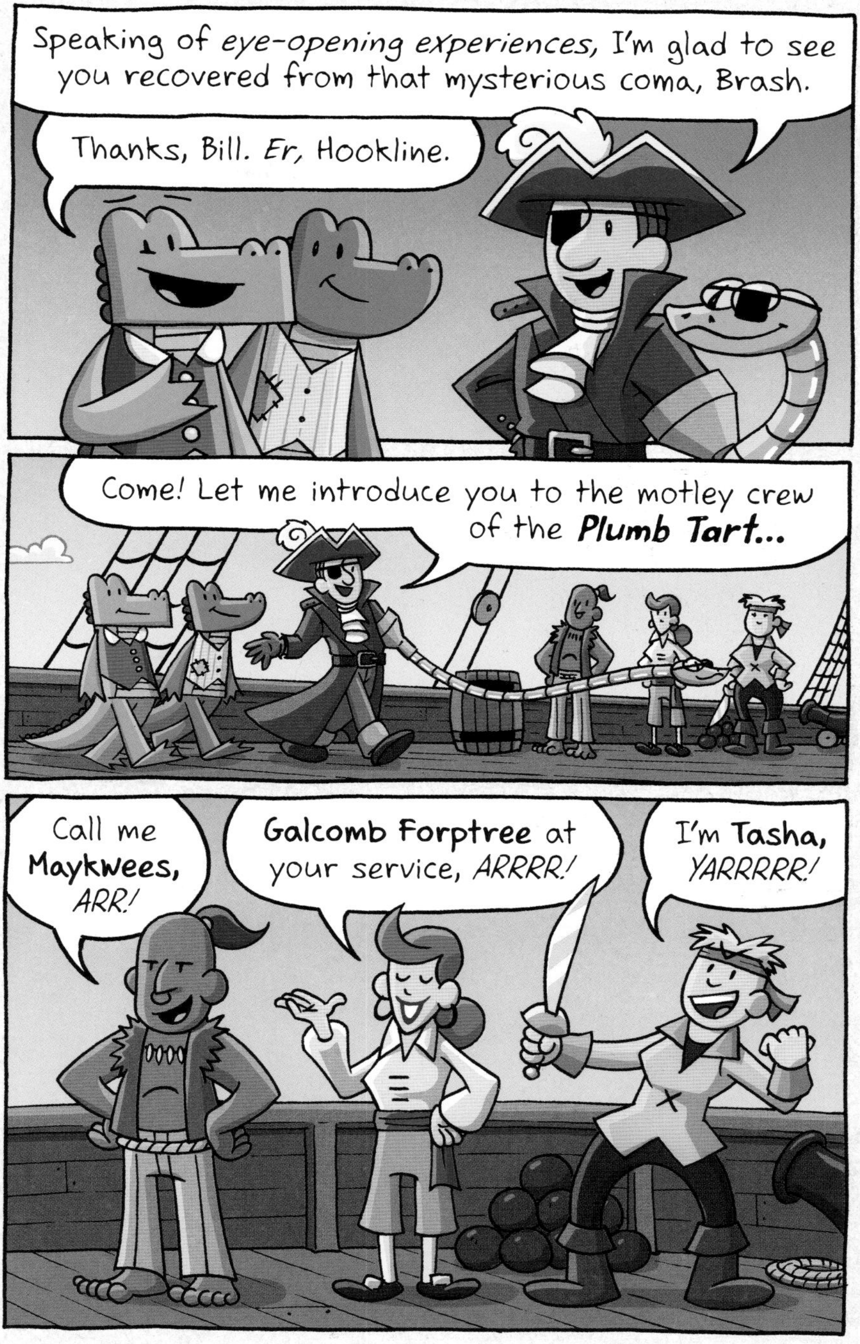
Speaking of *eye-opening experiences,* I'm glad to see you recovered from that mysterious coma, Brash.
Thanks, Bill. *Er,* Hookline.
Come! Let me introduce you to the motley crew of the **Plumb Tart...**
Call me **Maykwees,** *ARR!*
Galcomb Forptree at your service, *ARRRR!*
I'm **Tasha,** *YARRRRR!*

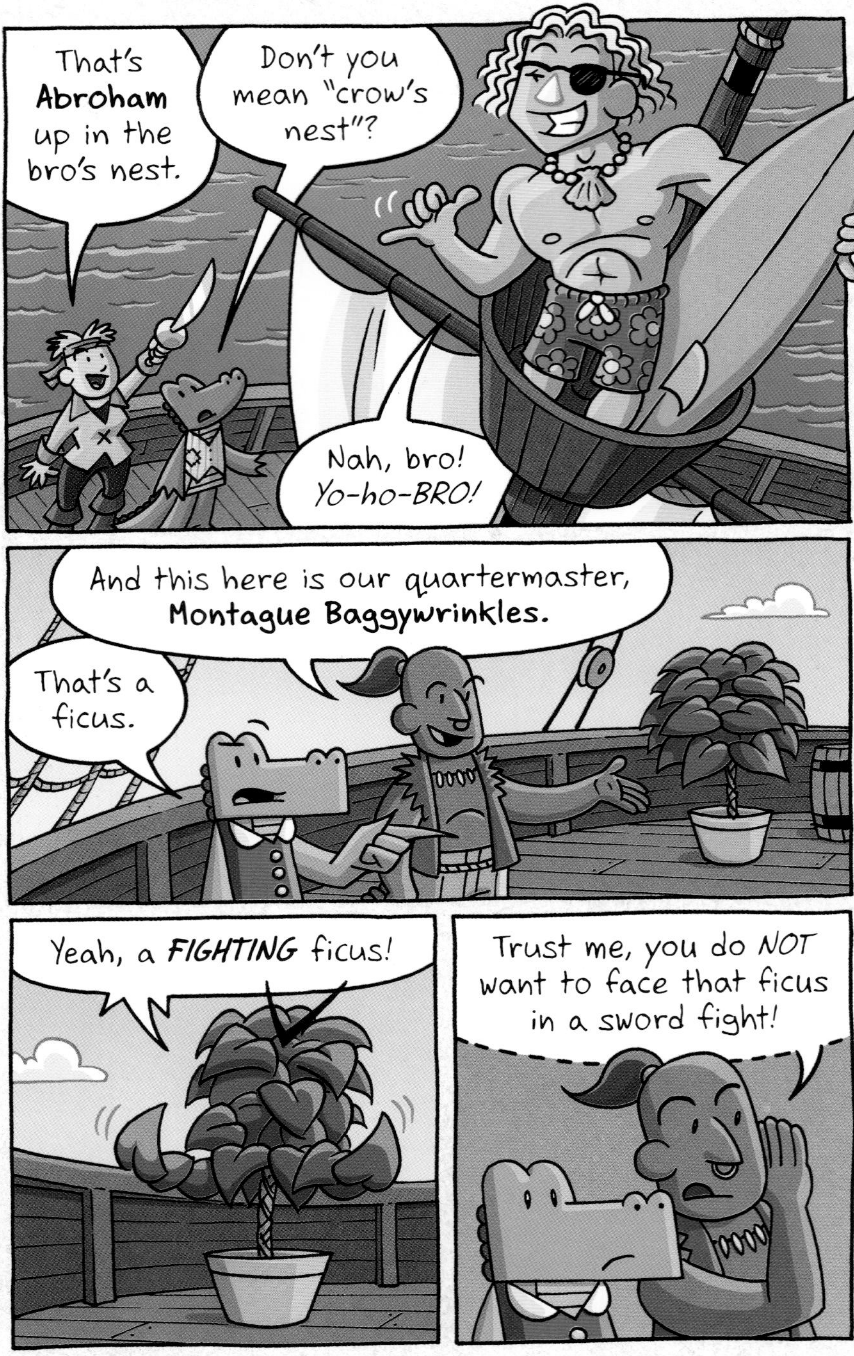
That's **Abroham** up in the bro's nest.
Don't you mean "crow's nest"?
Nah, bro! *Yo-ho-BRO!*
And this here is our quartermaster, **Montague Baggywrinkles.**
That's a ficus.
Yeah, a ***FIGHTING*** ficus!
Trust me, you do *NOT* want to face that ficus in a sword fight!

Chapter 16

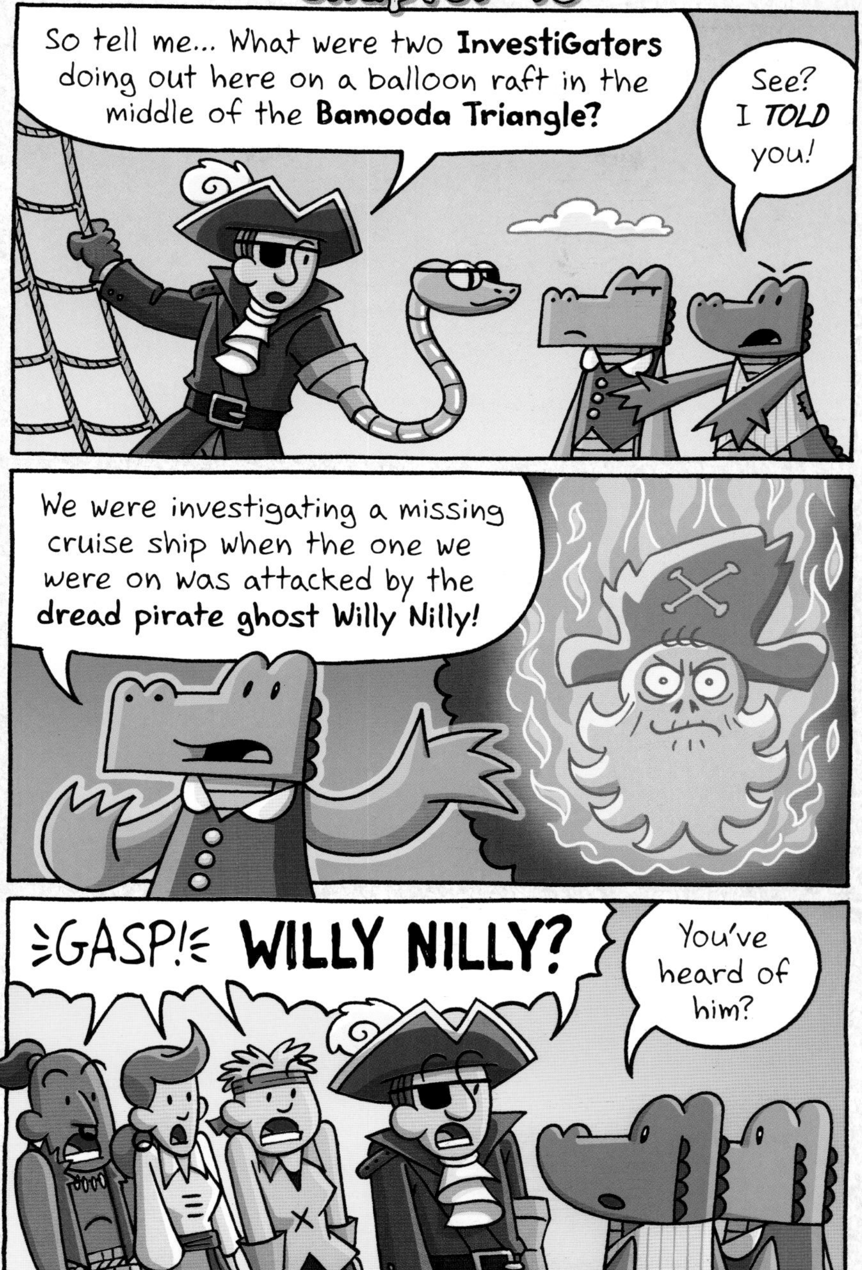
So tell me... What were two InvestiGators doing out here on a balloon raft in the middle of the Bamooda Triangle?
See? I TOLD you!
We were investigating a missing cruise ship when the one we were on was attacked by the dread pirate ghost Willy Nilly!
GASP! WILLY NILLY?
You've heard of him?

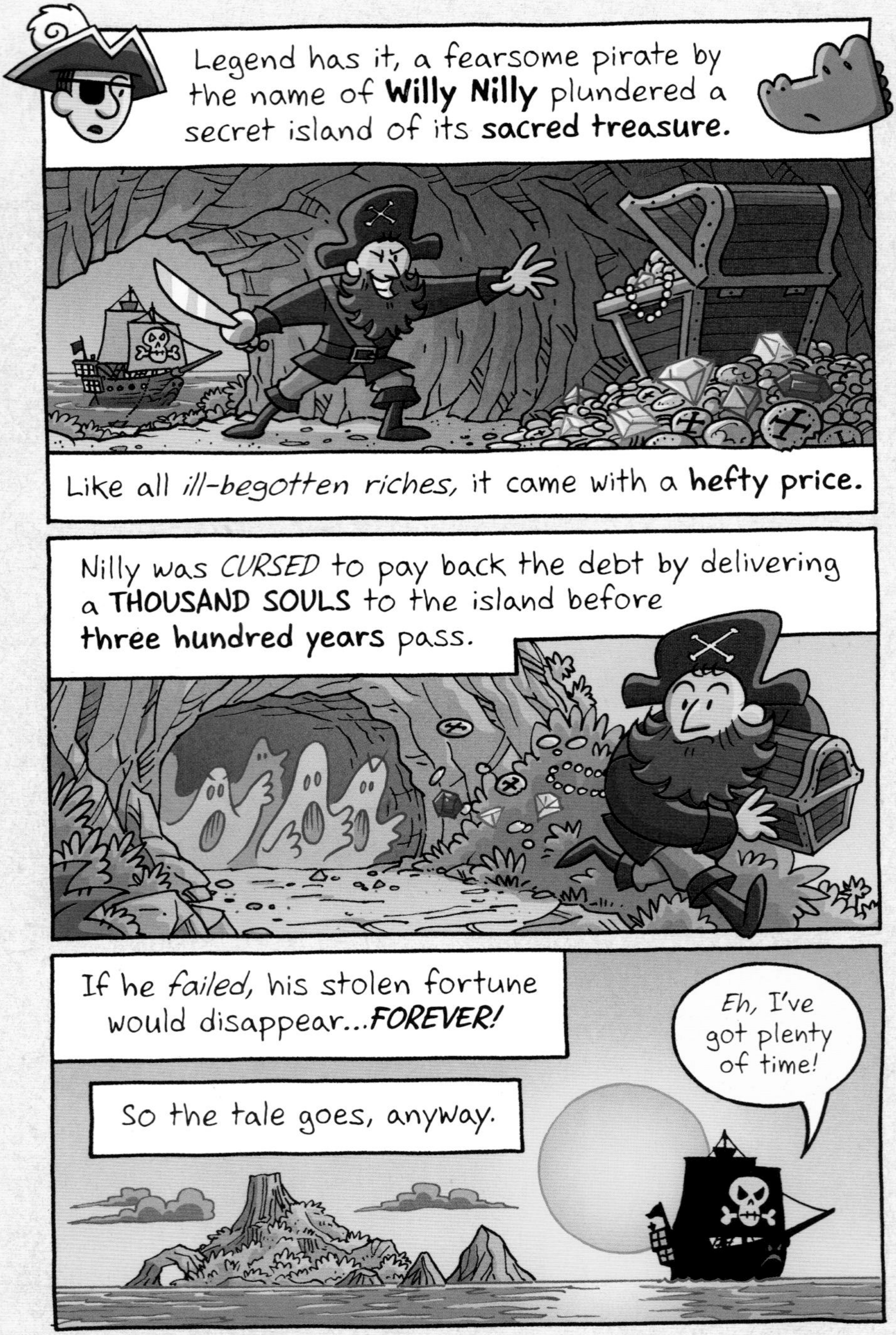
Legend has it, a fearsome pirate by the name of **Willy Nilly** plundered a secret island of its **sacred treasure.**
Like all *ill-begotten riches,* it came with a **hefty price.**
Nilly was *CURSED* to pay back the debt by delivering a **THOUSAND SOULS** to the island before **three hundred years** pass.
If he *failed,* his stolen fortune would disappear...***FOREVER!***
Eh, I've got plenty of time!
So the tale goes, anyway.

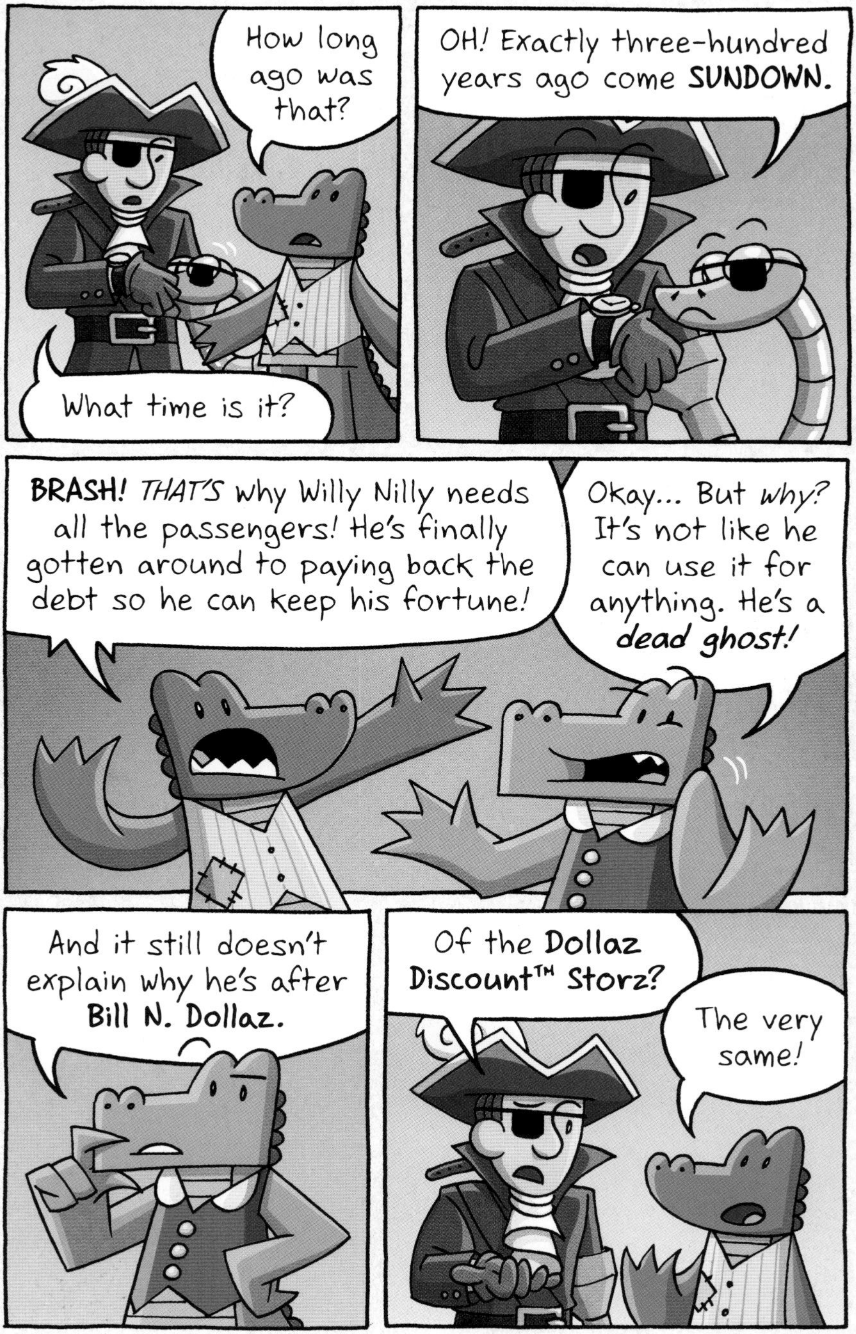
How long ago was that?
What time is it?
OH! Exactly three-hundred years ago come SUNDOWN.
BRASH! THAT'S why Willy Nilly needs all the passengers! He's finally gotten around to paying back the debt so he can keep his fortune!
Okay... But why? It's not like he can use it for anything. He's a dead ghost!
And it still doesn't explain why he's after Bill N. Dollaz.
Of the Dollaz Discount™ Storz?
The very same!

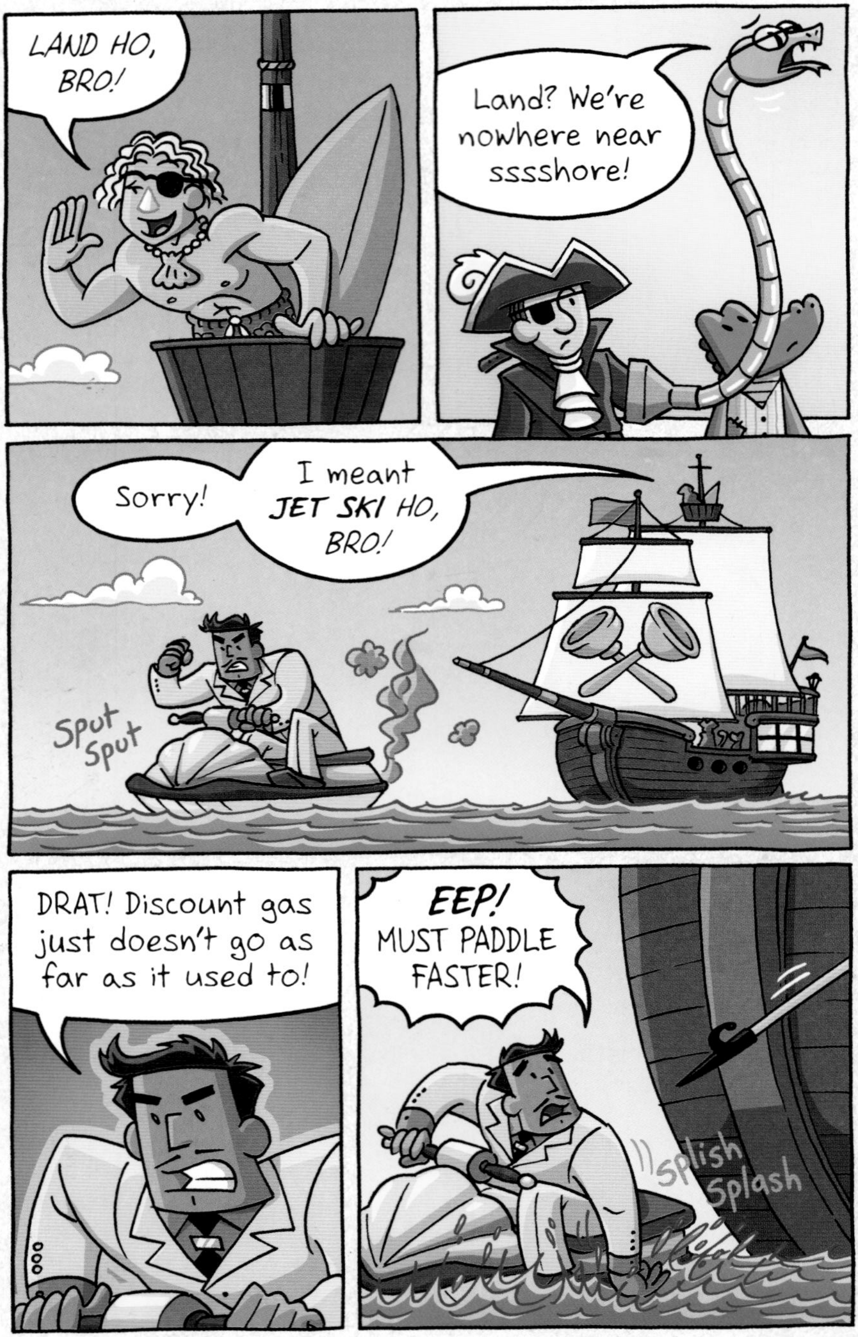
LAND HO, BRO!
Land? We're nowhere near sssshore!
Sorry!
I meant JET SKI HO, BRO!
Sput Sput
DRAT! Discount gas just doesn't go as far as it used to!
EEP! MUST PADDLE FASTER!
Splish Splash

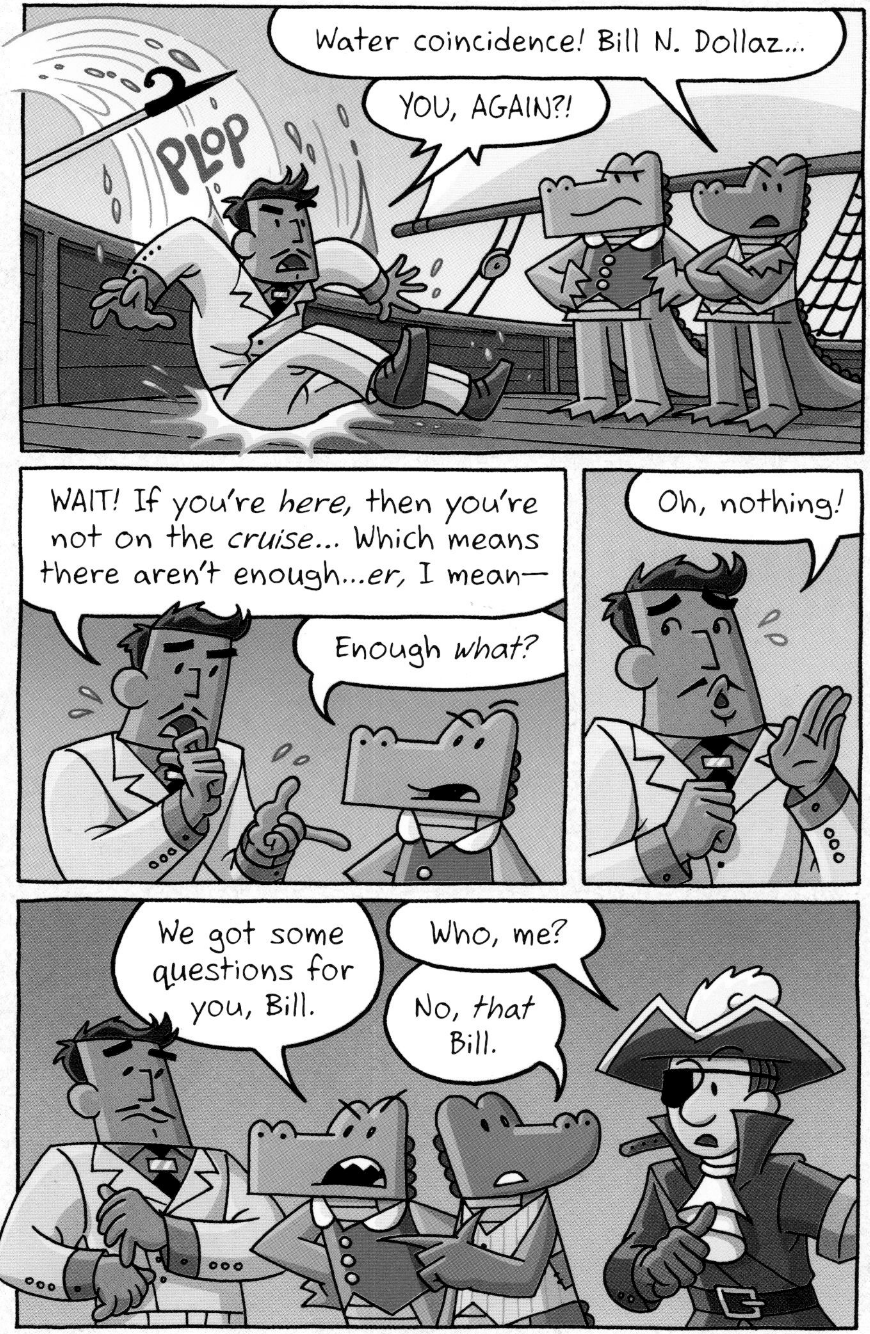
PLOP
YOU, AGAIN?!
Water coincidence! Bill N. Dollaz...
WAIT! If you're *here,* then you're not on the *cruise*... Which means there aren't enough...*er,* I mean—
Enough *what?*
Oh, nothing!
We got some questions for you, Bill.
Who, me?
No, *that* Bill.

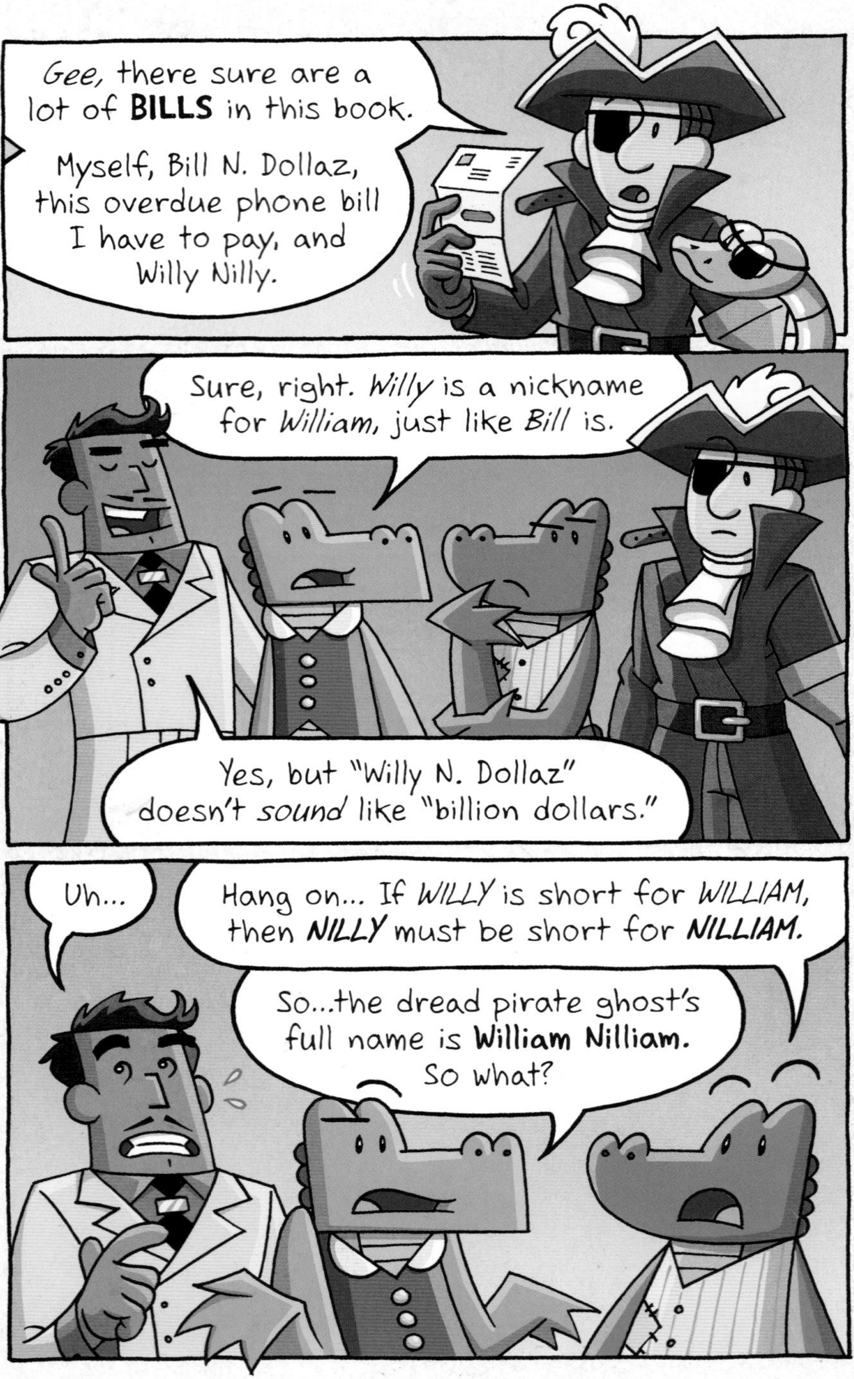
Gee, there sure are a lot of **BILLS** in this book.
Myself, Bill N. Dollaz, this overdue phone bill I have to pay, and Willy Nilly.
Sure, right. *Willy* is a nickname for *William*, just like *Bill* is.
Yes, but "Willy N. Dollaz" doesn't *sound* like "billion dollars."
Uh...
Hang on... If *WILLY* is short for *WILLIAM*, then ***NILLY*** must be short for ***NILLIAM.***
So...the dread pirate ghost's full name is **William Nilliam.** So what?

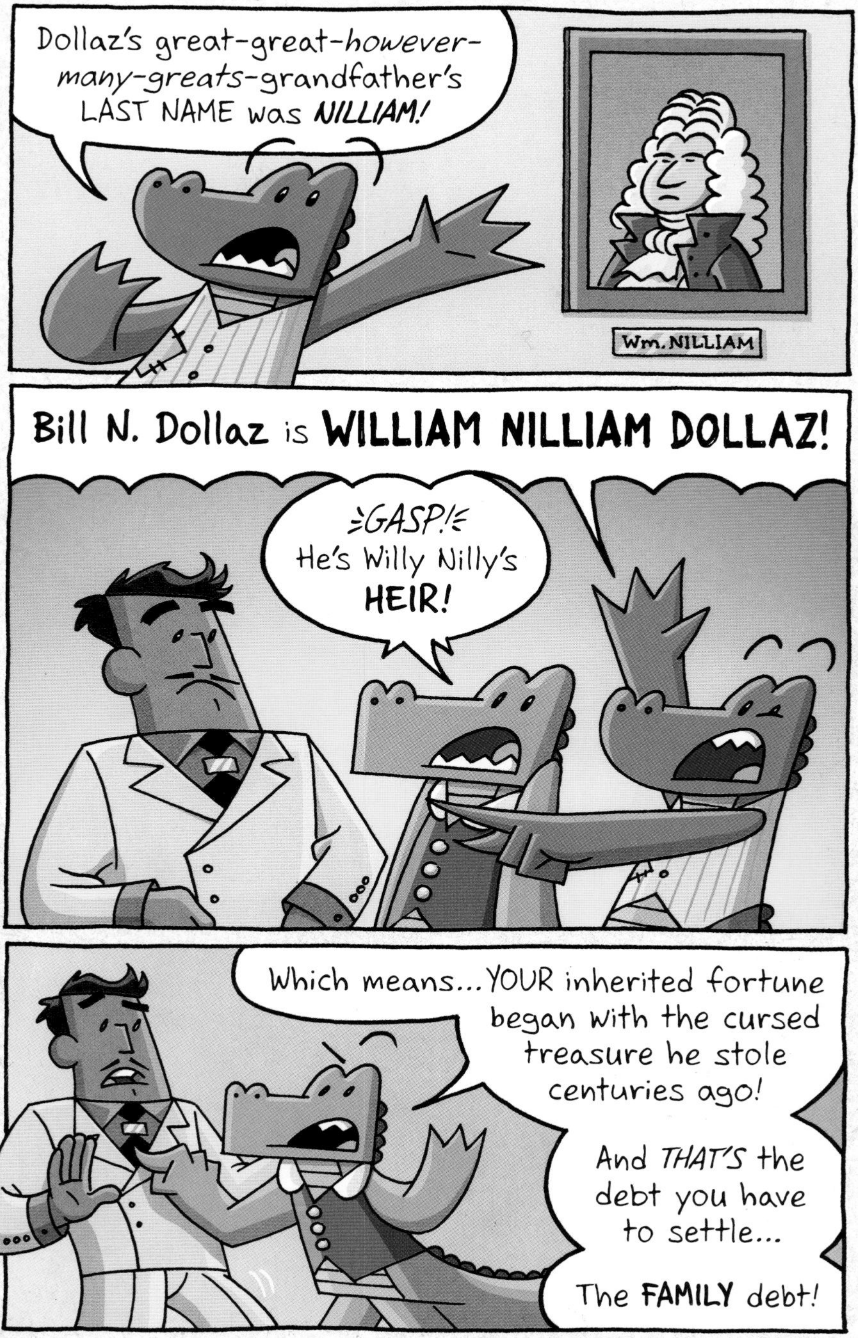
Dollaz's great-great-however-many-greats-grandfather's LAST NAME was NILLIAM!
Wm. NILLIAM
Bill N. Dollaz is WILLIAM NILLIAM DOLLAZ!
GASP! He's Willy Nilly's HEIR!
Which means... YOUR inherited fortune began with the cursed treasure he stole centuries ago!
And THAT'S the debt you have to settle...
The FAMILY debt!

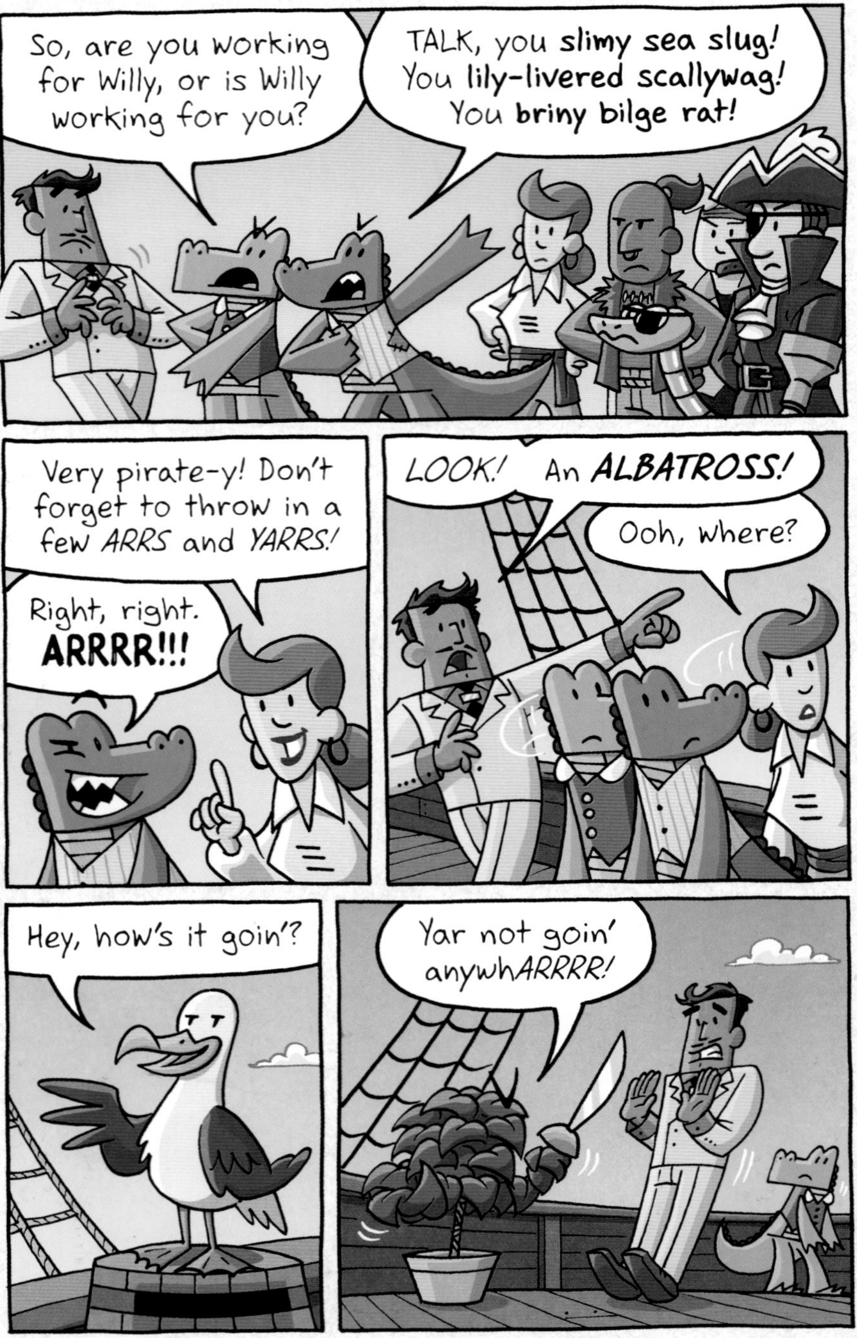
So, are you working for Willy, or is Willy working for you?
TALK, you **slimy sea slug!** You **lily-livered scallywag!** You **briny bilge rat!**
Very pirate-y! Don't forget to throw in a few *ARRS* and *YARRS!*
Right, right. **ARRRR!!!**
LOOK! An ***ALBATROSS!***
Ooh, where?
Hey, how's it goin'?
Yar not goin' anywh*ARRRR!*

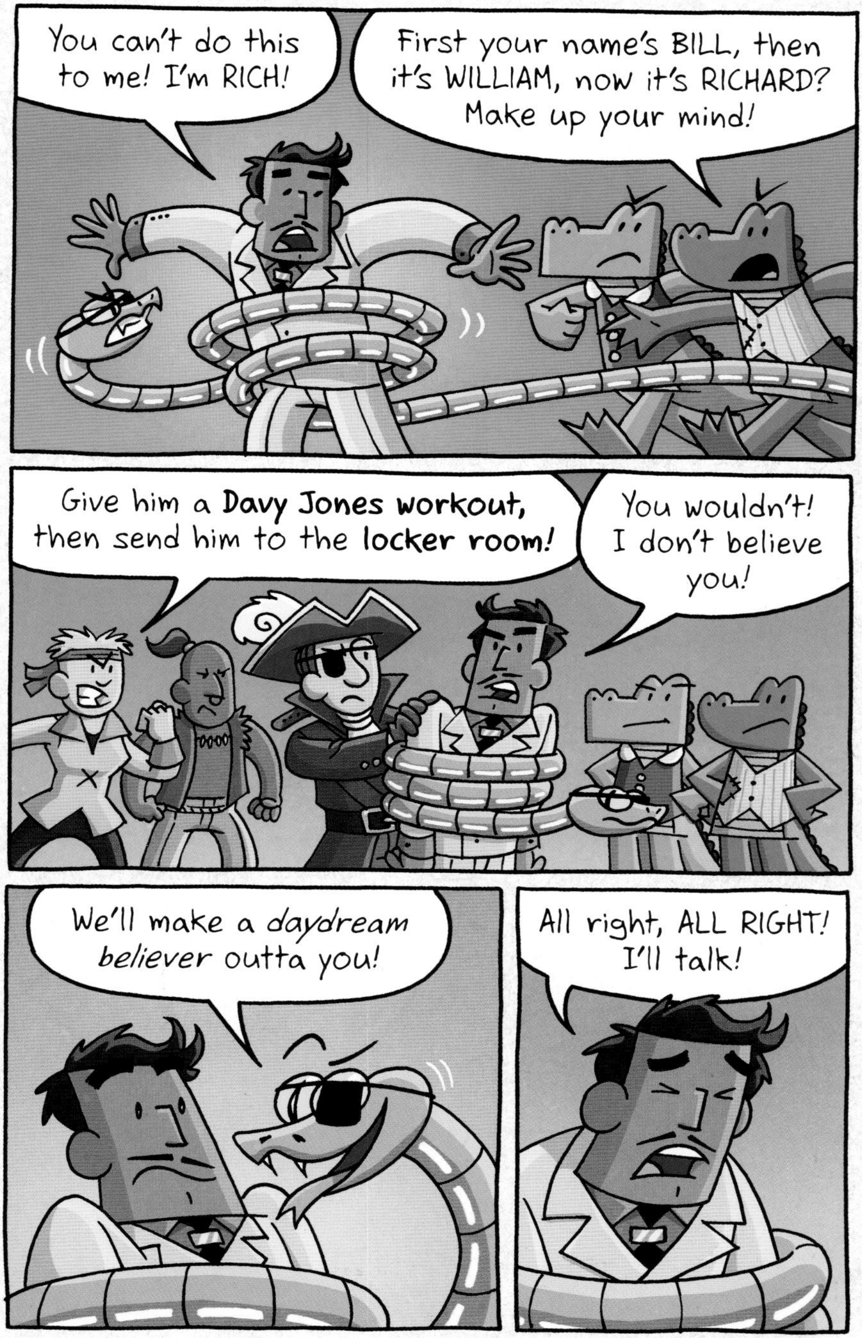
You can't do this to me! I'm RICH!
First your name's BILL, then it's WILLIAM, now it's RICHARD? Make up your mind!
Give him a **Davy Jones workout,** then send him to the **locker room!**
You wouldn't! I don't believe you!
We'll make a *daydream believer* outta you!
All right, ALL RIGHT! I'll talk!

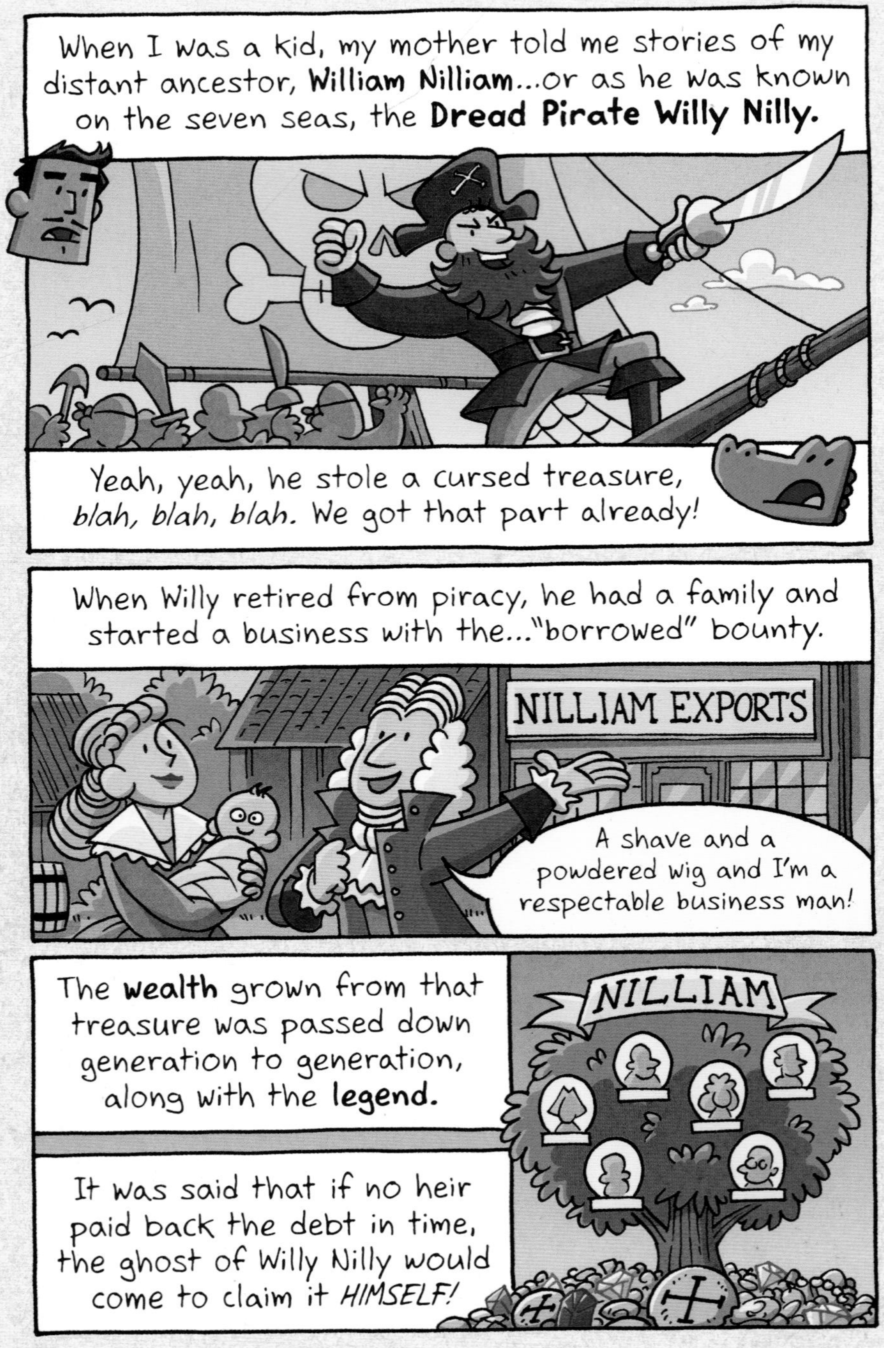
When I was a kid, my mother told me stories of my distant ancestor, **William Nilliam**...or as he was known on the seven seas, the **Dread Pirate Willy Nilly.**
Yeah, yeah, he stole a cursed treasure, *blah, blah, blah.* We got that part already!
When Willy retired from piracy, he had a family and started a business with the..."borrowed" bounty.
NILLIAM EXPORTS
A shave and a powdered wig and I'm a respectable business man!
The **wealth** grown from that treasure was passed down generation to generation, along with the **legend.**
NILLIAM
It was said that if no heir paid back the debt in time, the ghost of Willy Nilly would come to claim it *HIMSELF!*

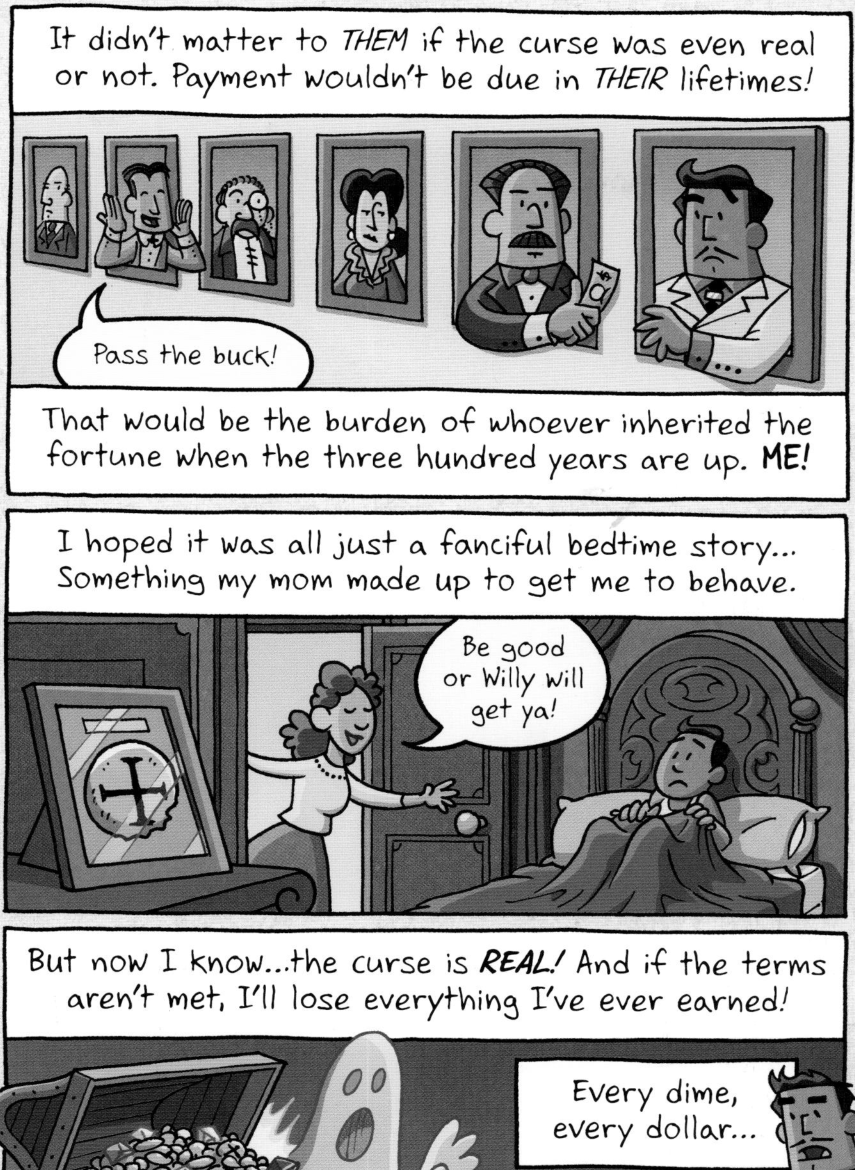
It didn't matter to THEM if the curse was even real or not. Payment wouldn't be due in THEIR lifetimes!
Pass the buck!
That would be the burden of whoever inherited the fortune when the three hundred years are up. ME!
I hoped it was all just a fanciful bedtime story... Something my mom made up to get me to behave.
Be good or Willy will get ya!
But now I know...the curse is REAL! And if the terms aren't met, I'll lose everything I've ever earned!
Every dime, every dollar...
It can ALL be traced back to that centuries-old cursed treasure!

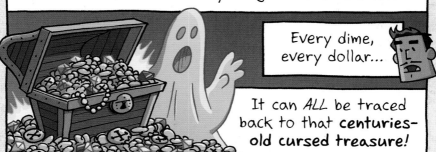

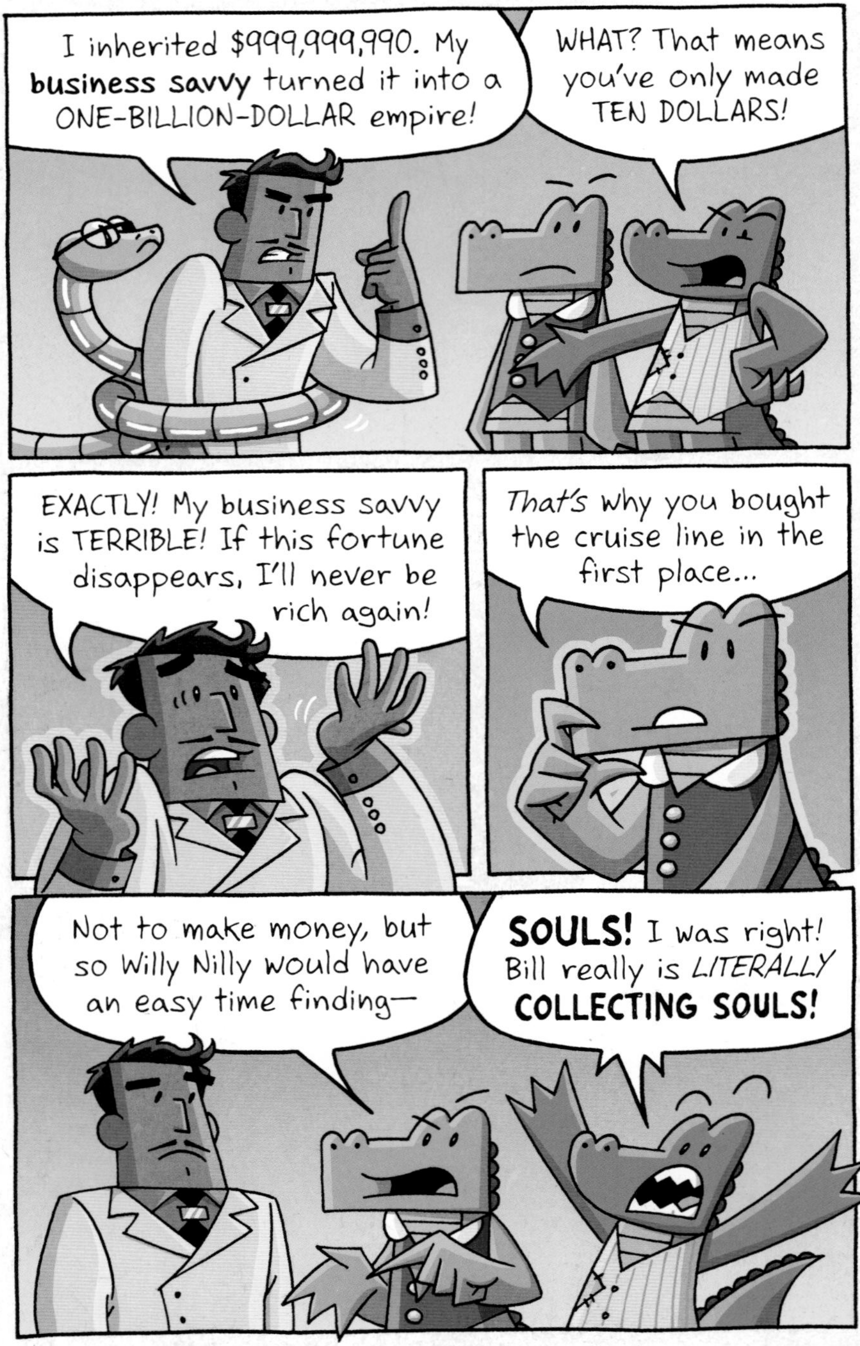
I inherited $999,999,990. My **business savvy** turned it into a ONE-BILLION-DOLLAR empire!
WHAT? That means you've only made TEN DOLLARS!
EXACTLY! My business savvy is TERRIBLE! If this fortune disappears, I'll never be rich again!
That's why you bought the cruise line in the first place...
Not to make money, but so Willy Nilly would have an easy time finding—
SOULS! I was right! Bill really is *LITERALLY* **COLLECTING SOULS!**

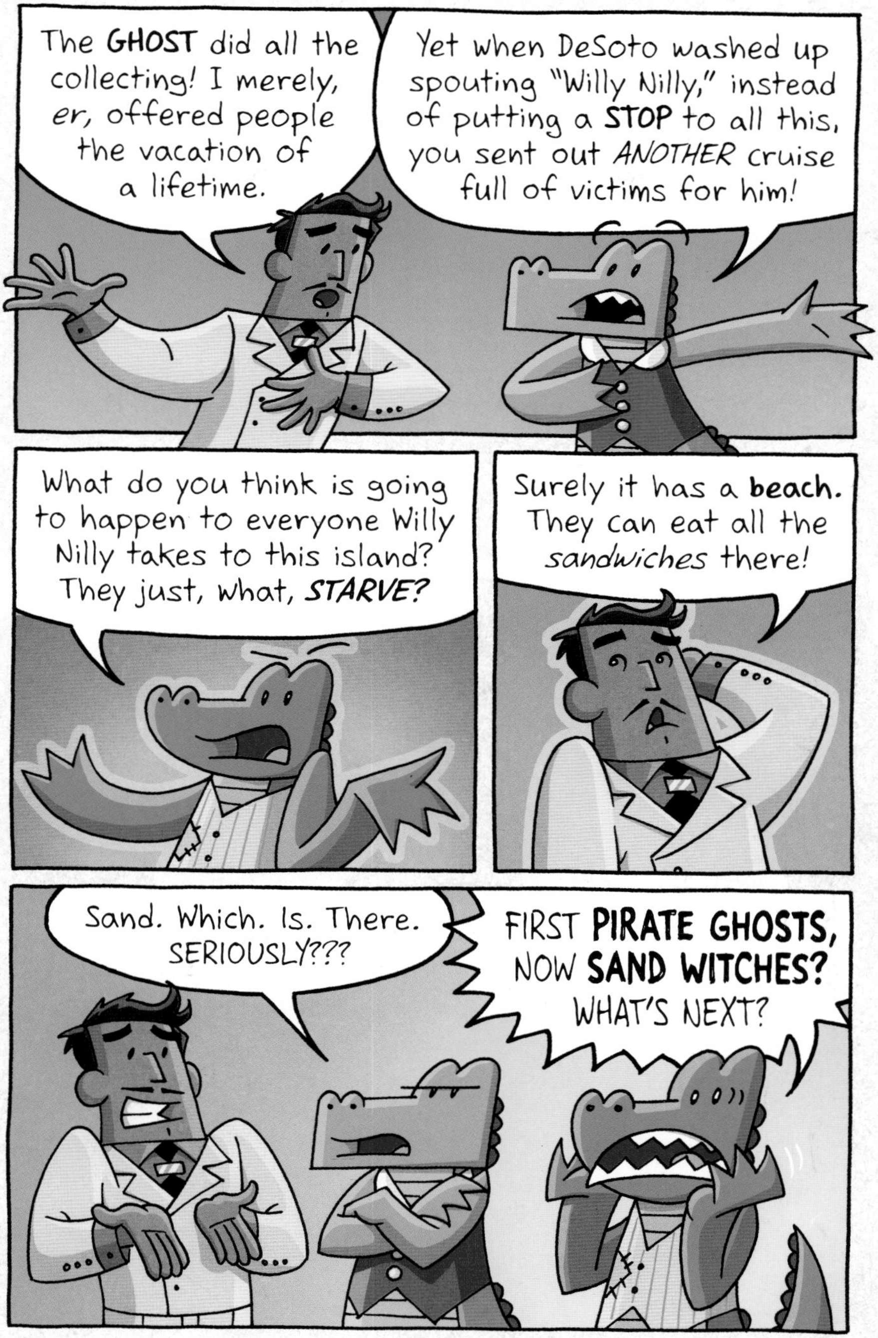
The **GHOST** did all the collecting! I merely, *er,* offered people the vacation of a lifetime.
Yet when DeSoto washed up spouting "Willy Nilly," instead of putting a **STOP** to all this, you sent out *ANOTHER* cruise full of victims for him!
What do you think is going to happen to everyone Willy Nilly takes to this island? They just, what, ***STARVE?***
Surely it has a **beach.** They can eat all the *sandwiches* there!
Sand. Which. Is. There. SERIOUSLY???
FIRST **PIRATE GHOSTS,** NOW **SAND WITCHES?** WHAT'S NEXT?

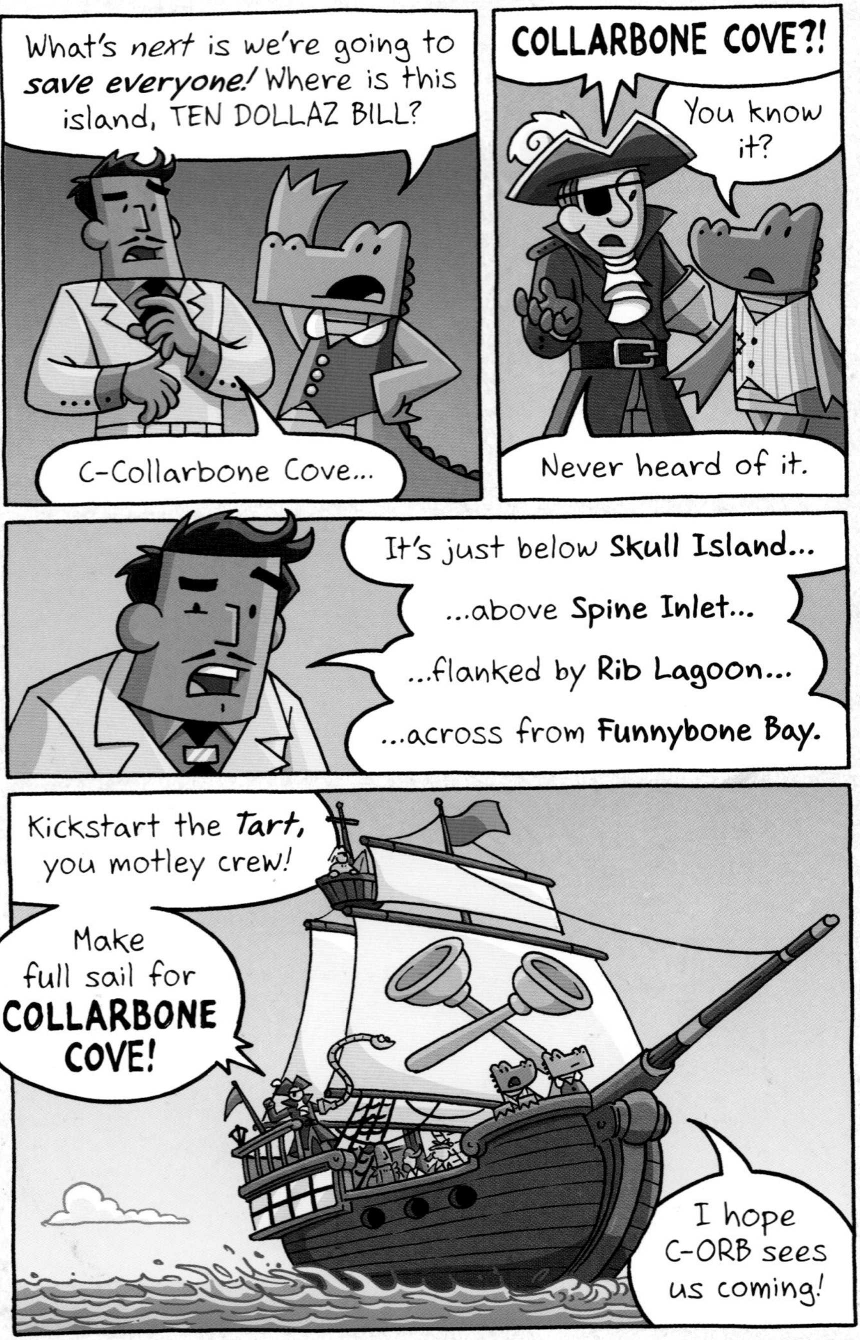
What's *next* is we're going to ***save everyone!*** Where is this island, TEN DOLLAZ BILL?
C-Collarbone Cove...
COLLARBONE COVE?!
You know it?
Never heard of it.
It's just below **Skull Island...**
...above **Spine Inlet...**
...flanked by **Rib Lagoon...**
...across from **Funnybone Bay.**
Kickstart the ***Tart,*** you motley crew!
Make full sail for **COLLARBONE COVE!**
I hope C-ORB sees us coming!

Chapter 17

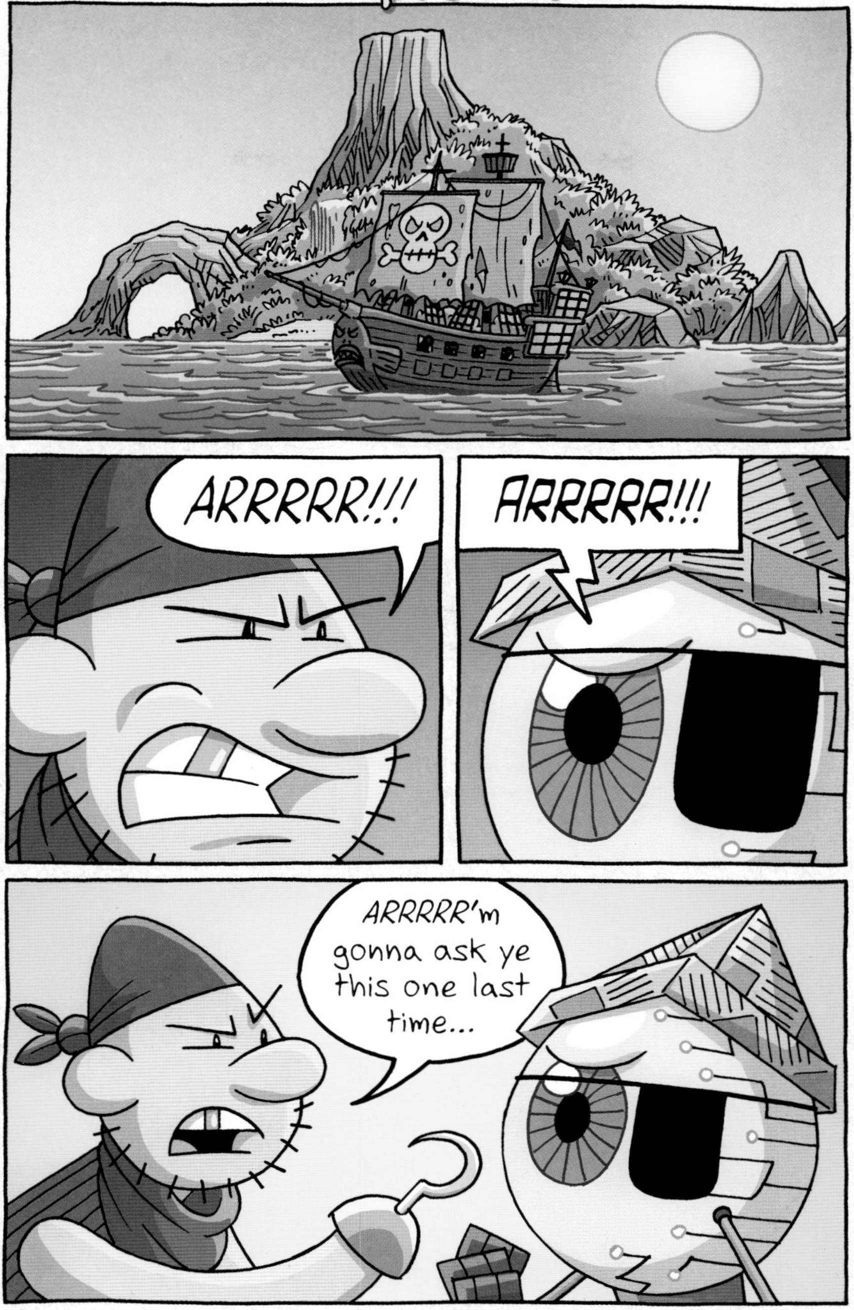

ARRRRR!!!
ARRRRR!!!
ARRRRR'm gonna ask ye this one last time...

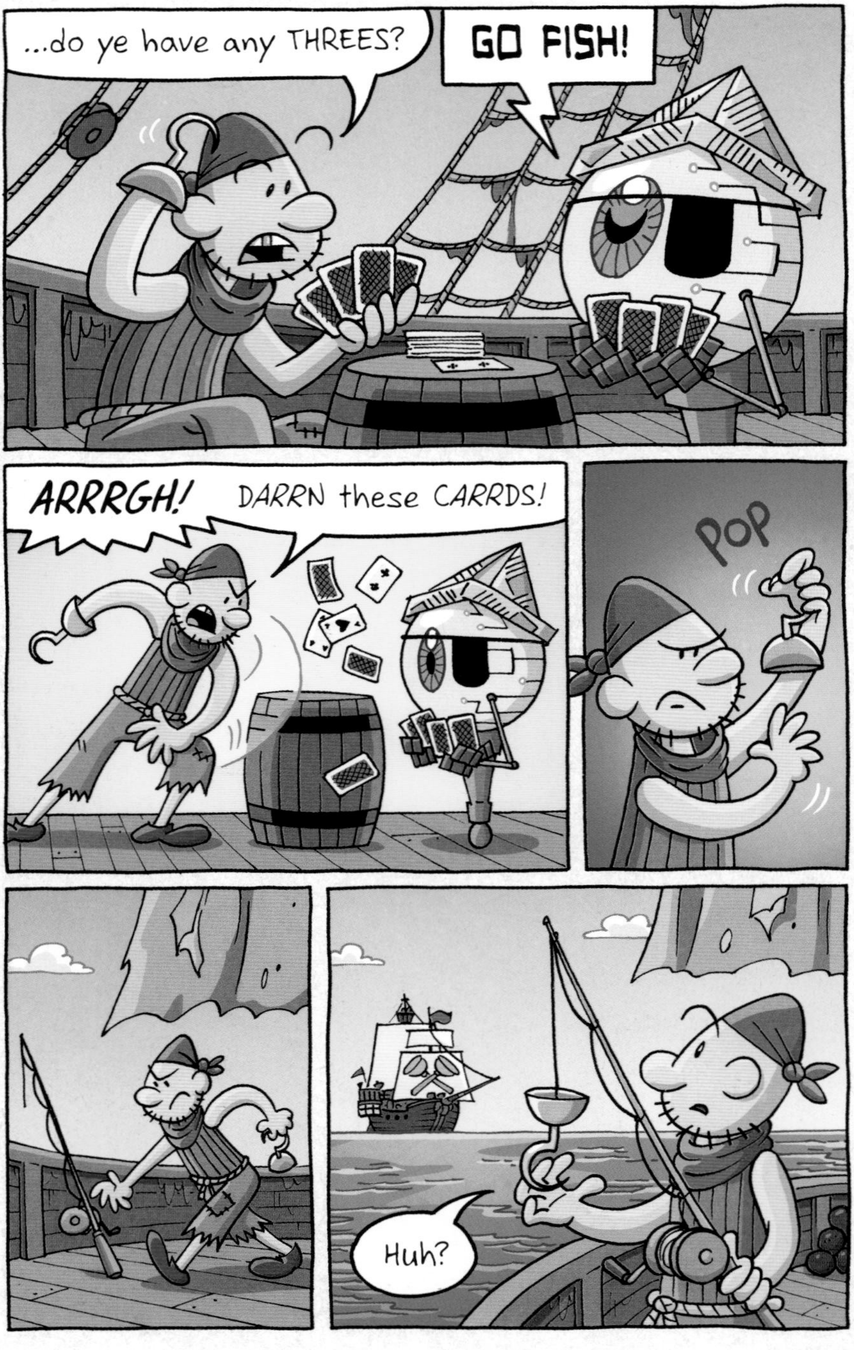

...do ye have any THREES?
GO FISH!
ARRRGH! DARRN these CARRDS!
POP
Huh?

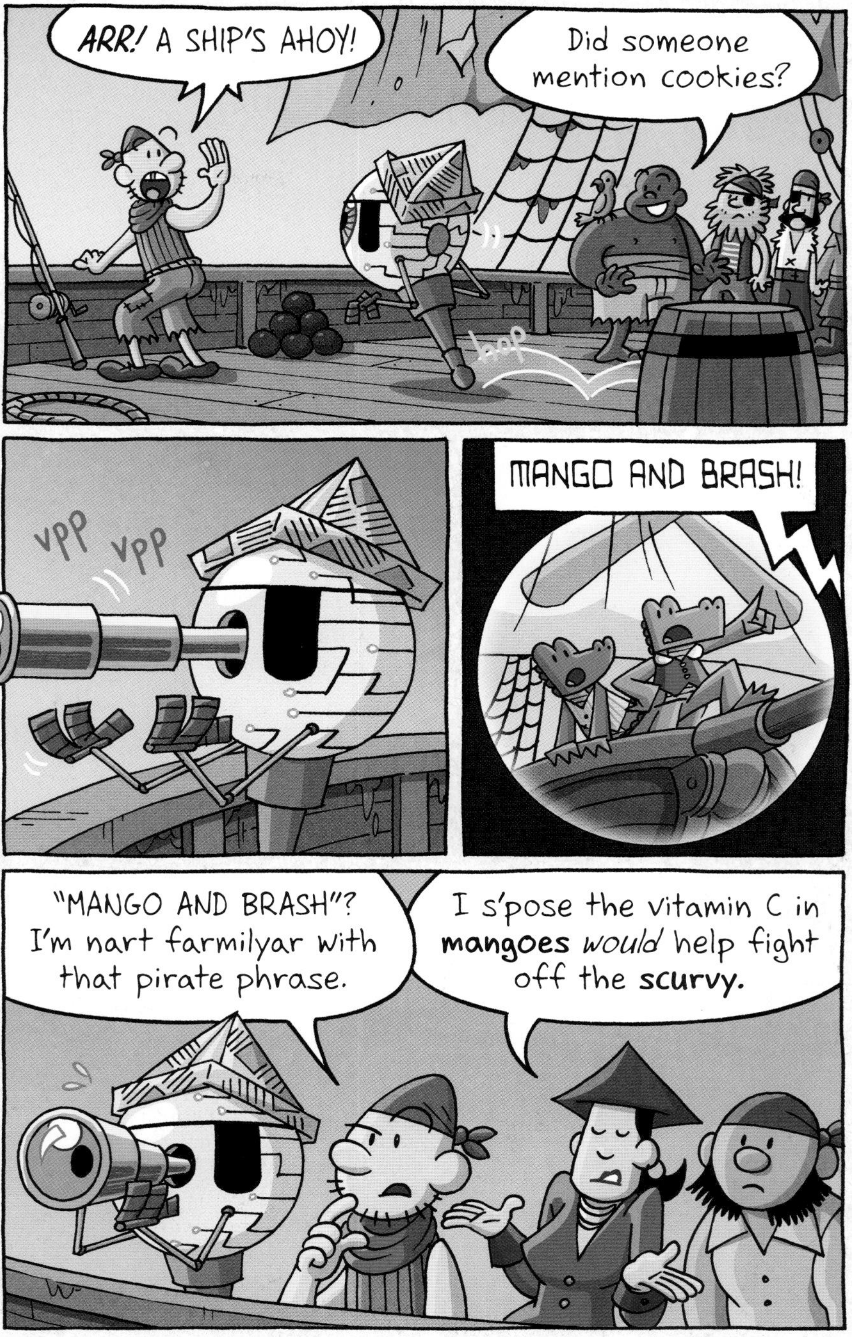
ARR! A SHIP'S AHOY!
Did someone mention cookies?
hop
VPP VPP
MANGO AND BRASH!
"MANGO AND BRASH"? I'm nart farmilyar with that pirate phrase.
I s'pose the vitamin C in mangoes would help fight off the scurvy.

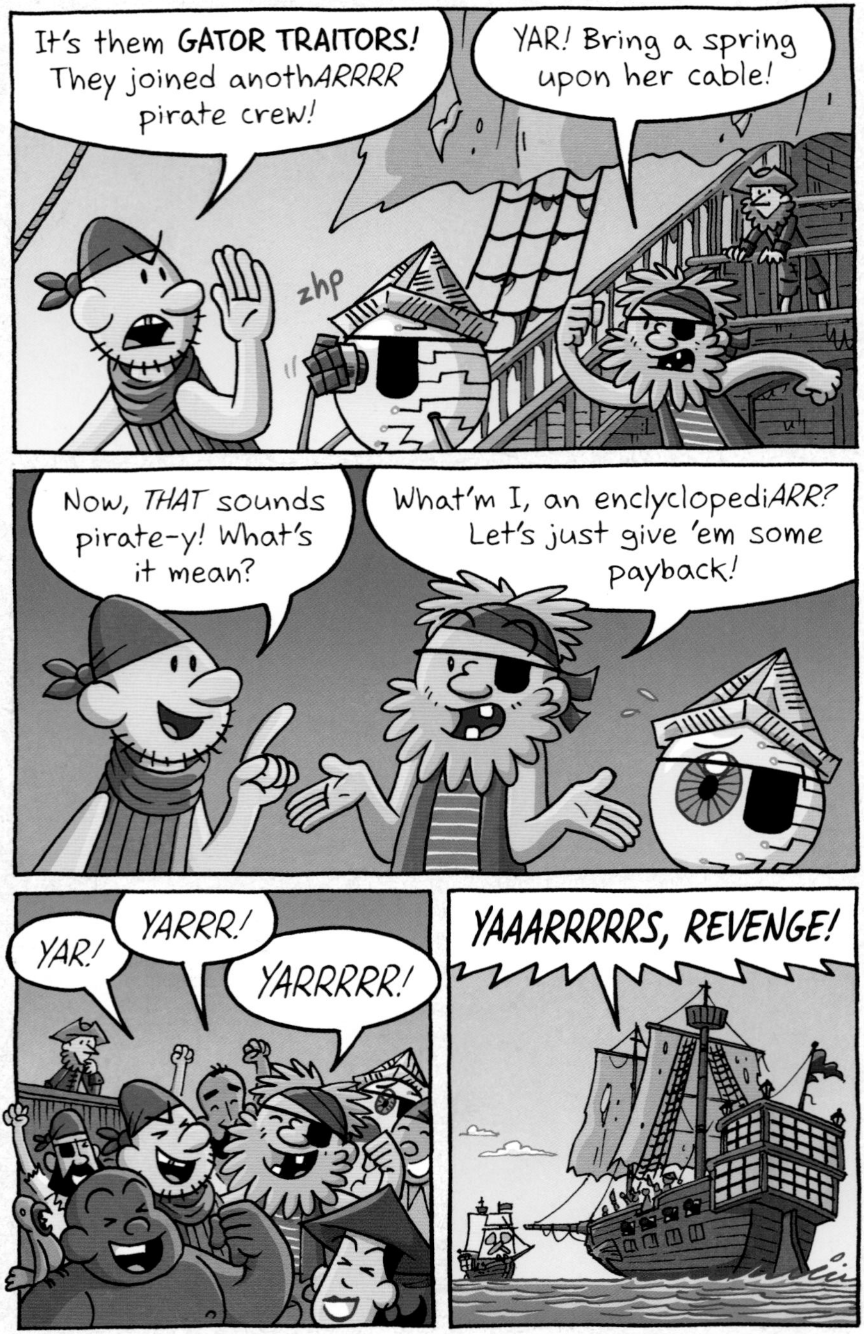
It's them GATOR TRAITORS! They joined anothARRRR pirate crew!
YAR! Bring a spring upon her cable!
zhp
Now, THAT sounds pirate-y! What's it mean?
What'm I, an enclyclopediARR? Let's just give 'em some payback!
YAR!
YARRR!
YARRRRR!
YAAARRRRRS, REVENGE!

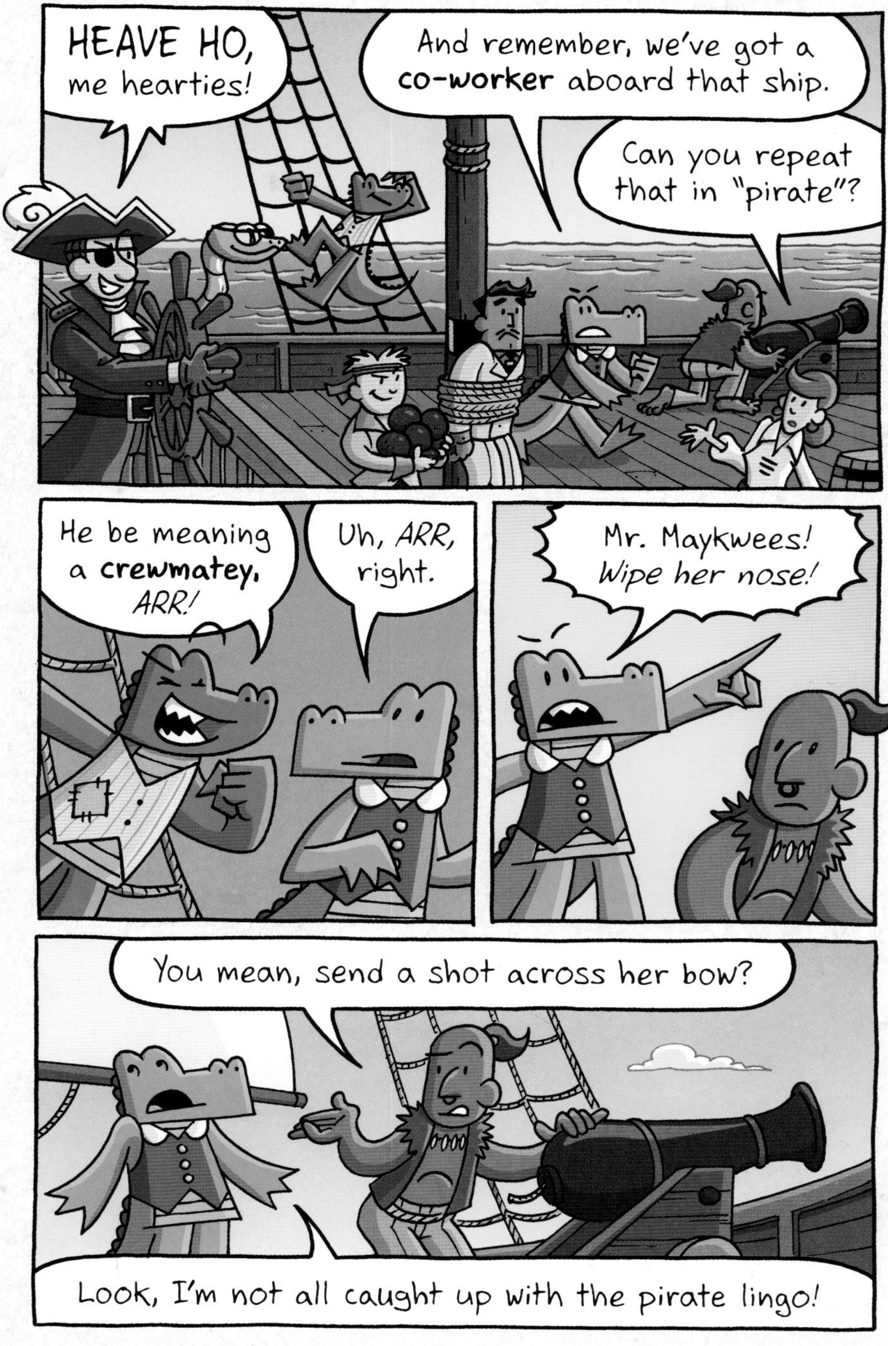
HEAVE HO, me hearties!
And remember, we've got a **co-worker** aboard that ship.
Can you repeat that in "pirate"?
He be meaning a **crewmatey,** *ARR!*
Uh, *ARR,* right.
Mr. Maykwees! *Wipe her nose!*
You mean, send a shot across her bow?
Look, I'm not all caught up with the pirate lingo!

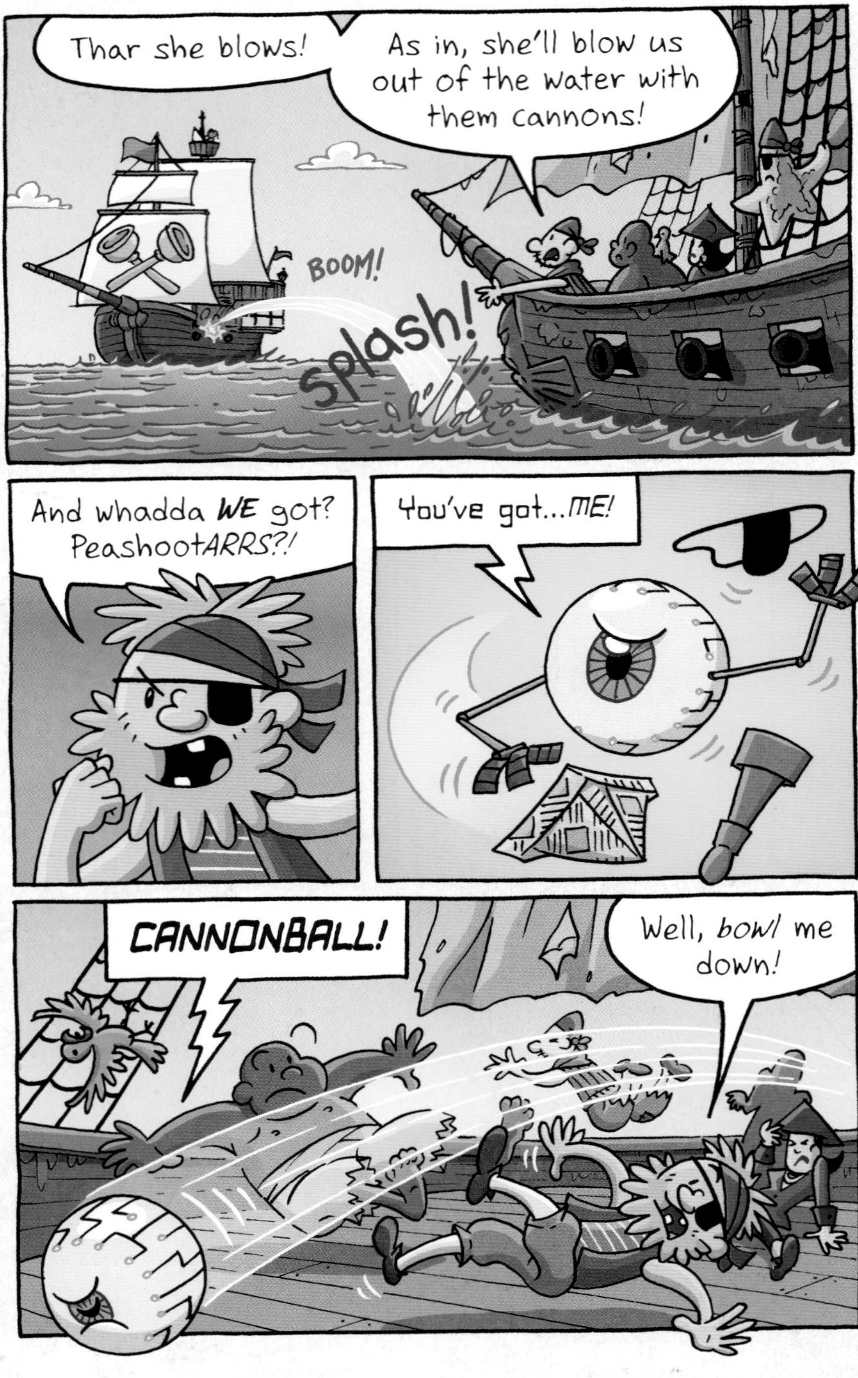

Thar she blows!
As in, she'll blow us out of the water with them cannons!
BOOM!
Splash!
And whadda *WE* got? Peashoot*ARRS*?!
You've got...*ME!*
CANNONBALL!
Well, *bowl* me down!

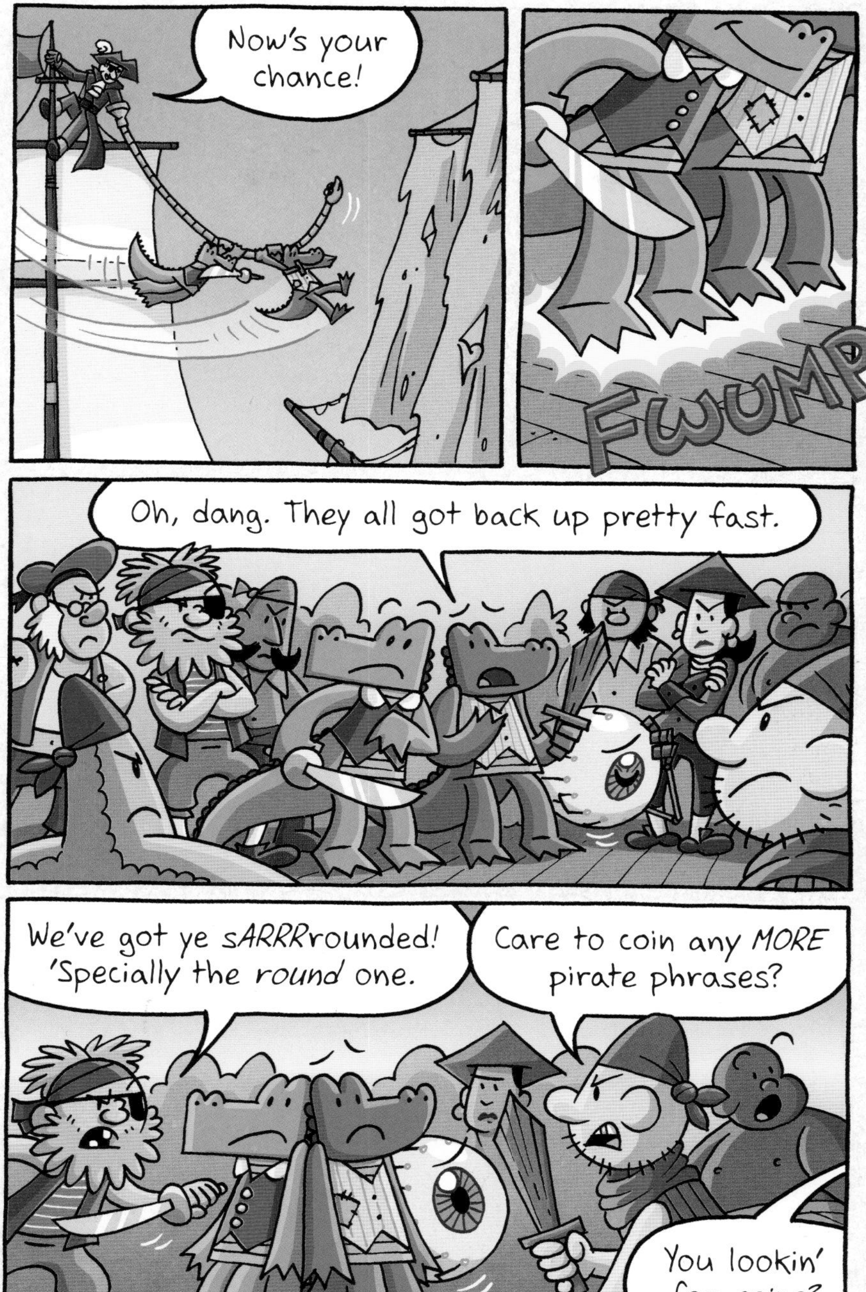
Now's your chance!
FWUMP
Oh, dang. They all got back up pretty fast.
We've got ye sARRRrounded! 'Specially the round one.
Care to coin any MORE pirate phrases?
You lookin' for coins?

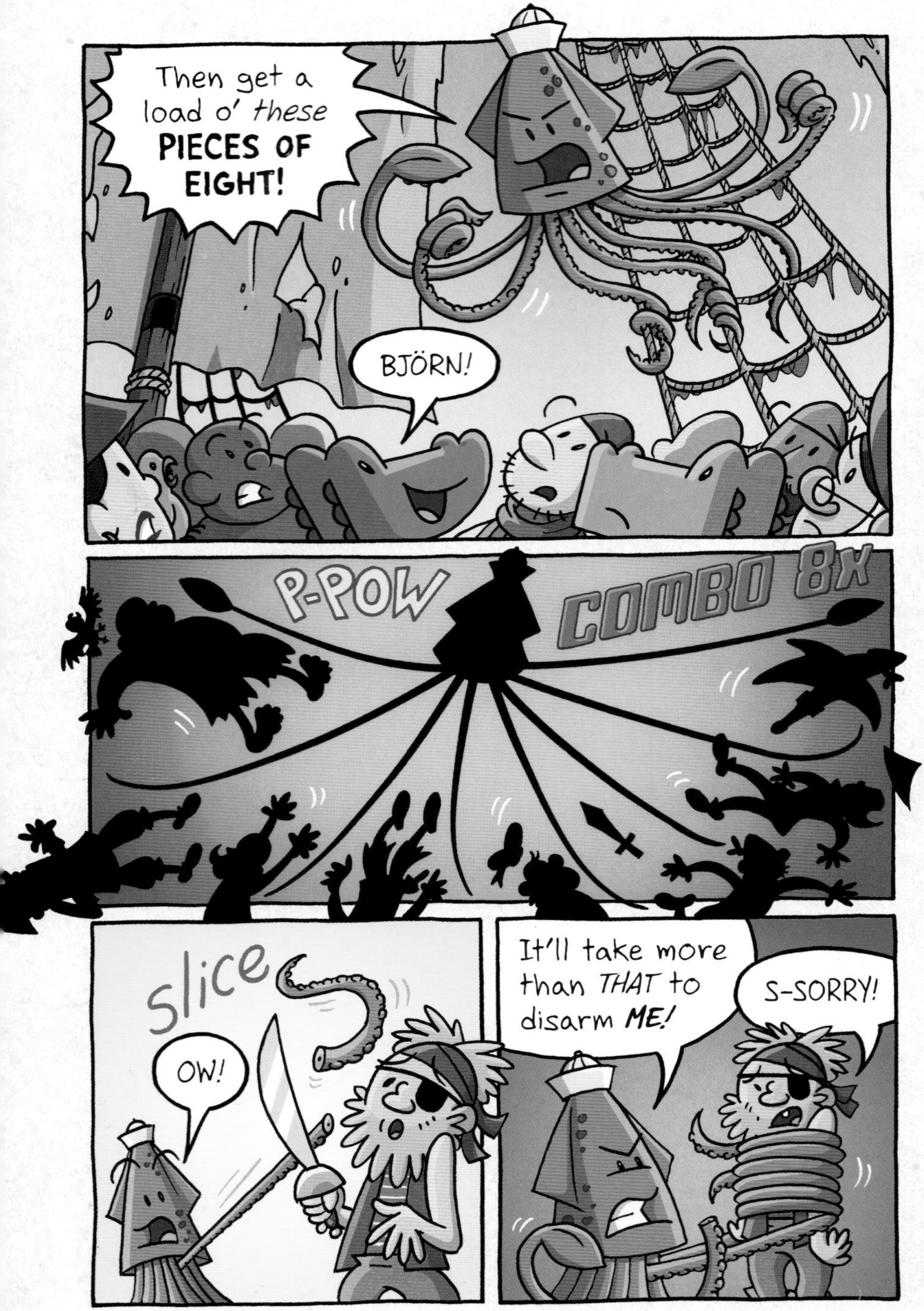
Then get a load o' *these* **PIECES OF EIGHT!**
BJÖRN!
P-POW
COMBO 8X
slice
OW!
It'll take more than *THAT* to disarm **ME!**
S-SORRY!

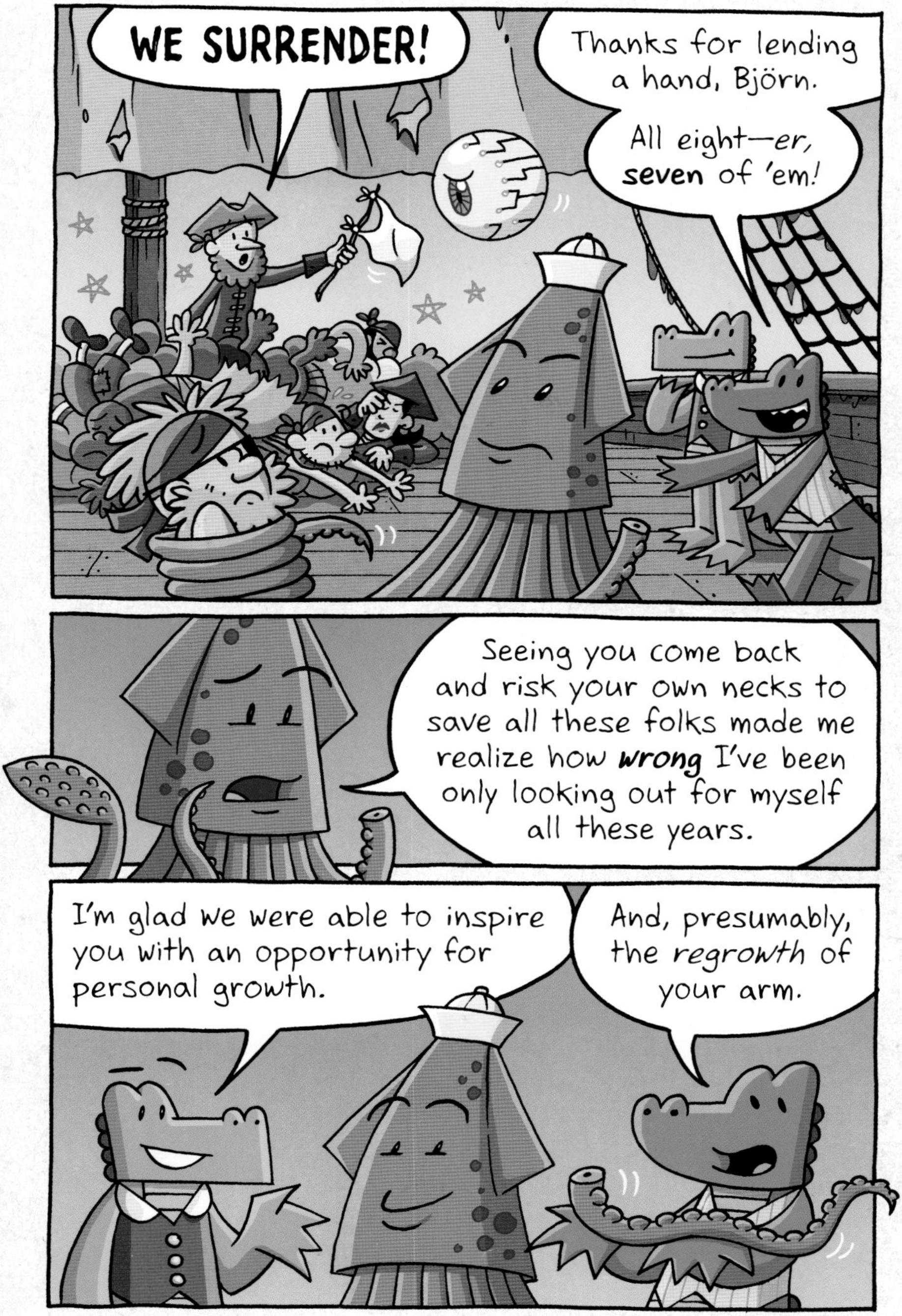
WE SURRENDER!
Thanks for lending a hand, Björn.
All eight—*er*, **seven** of 'em!
Seeing you come back and risk your own necks to save all these folks made me realize how **wrong** I've been only looking out for myself all these years.
I'm glad we were able to inspire you with an opportunity for personal growth.
And, presumably, the *regrowth* of your arm.

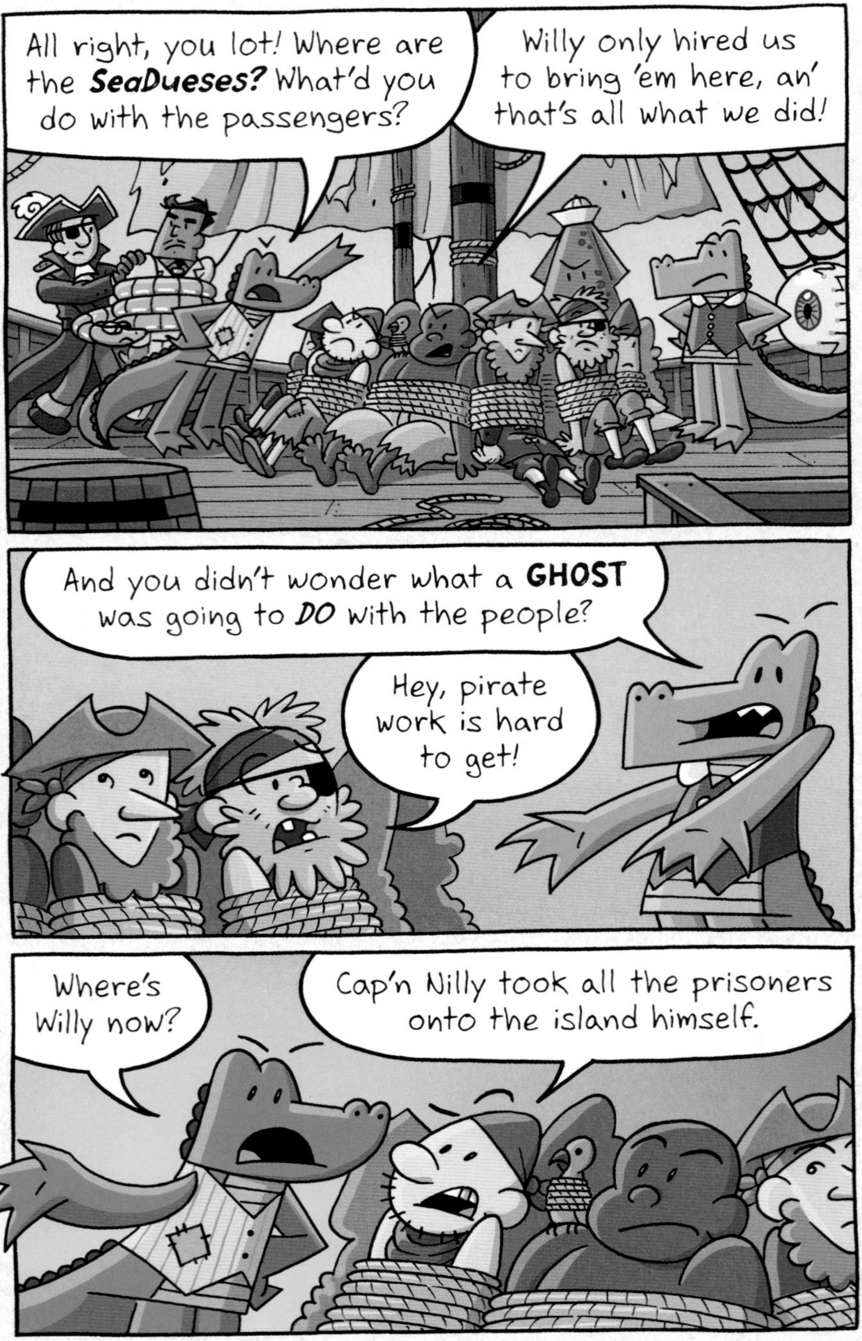
All right, you lot! Where are the **SeaDueses?** What'd you do with the passengers?
Willy only hired us to bring 'em here, an' that's all what we did!
And you didn't wonder what a **GHOST** was going to ***DO*** with the people?
Hey, pirate work is hard to get!
Where's Willy now?
Cap'n Nilly took all the prisoners onto the island himself.

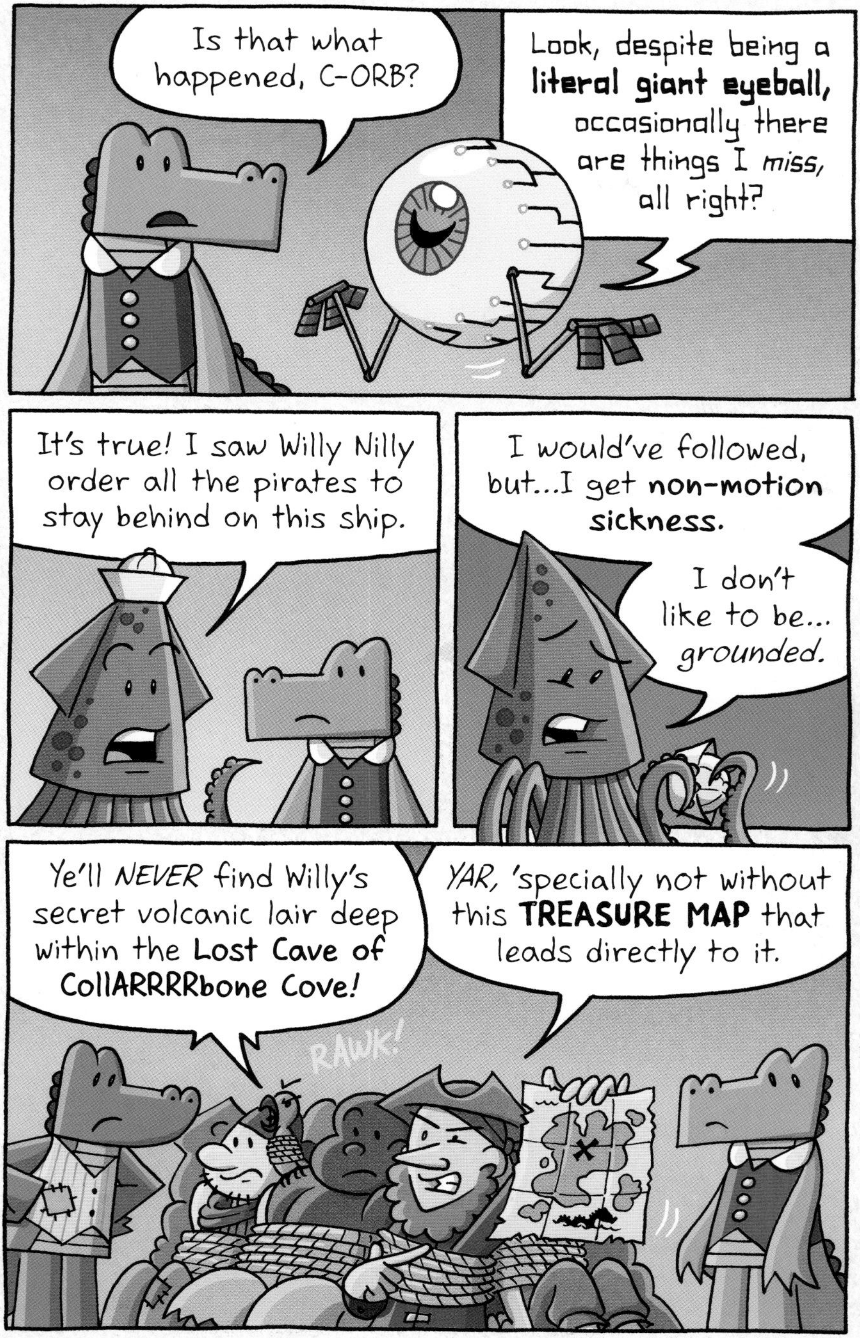

Is that what happened, C-ORB?
Look, despite being a **literal giant eyeball,** occasionally there are things I *miss,* all right?
It's true! I saw Willy Nilly order all the pirates to stay behind on this ship.
I would've followed, but...I get **non-motion sickness.**
I don't like to be... *grounded.*
Ye'll *NEVER* find Willy's secret volcanic lair deep within the **Lost Cave of CollARRRRbone Cove!**
YAR, 'specially not without this **TREASURE MAP** that leads directly to it.
RAWK!

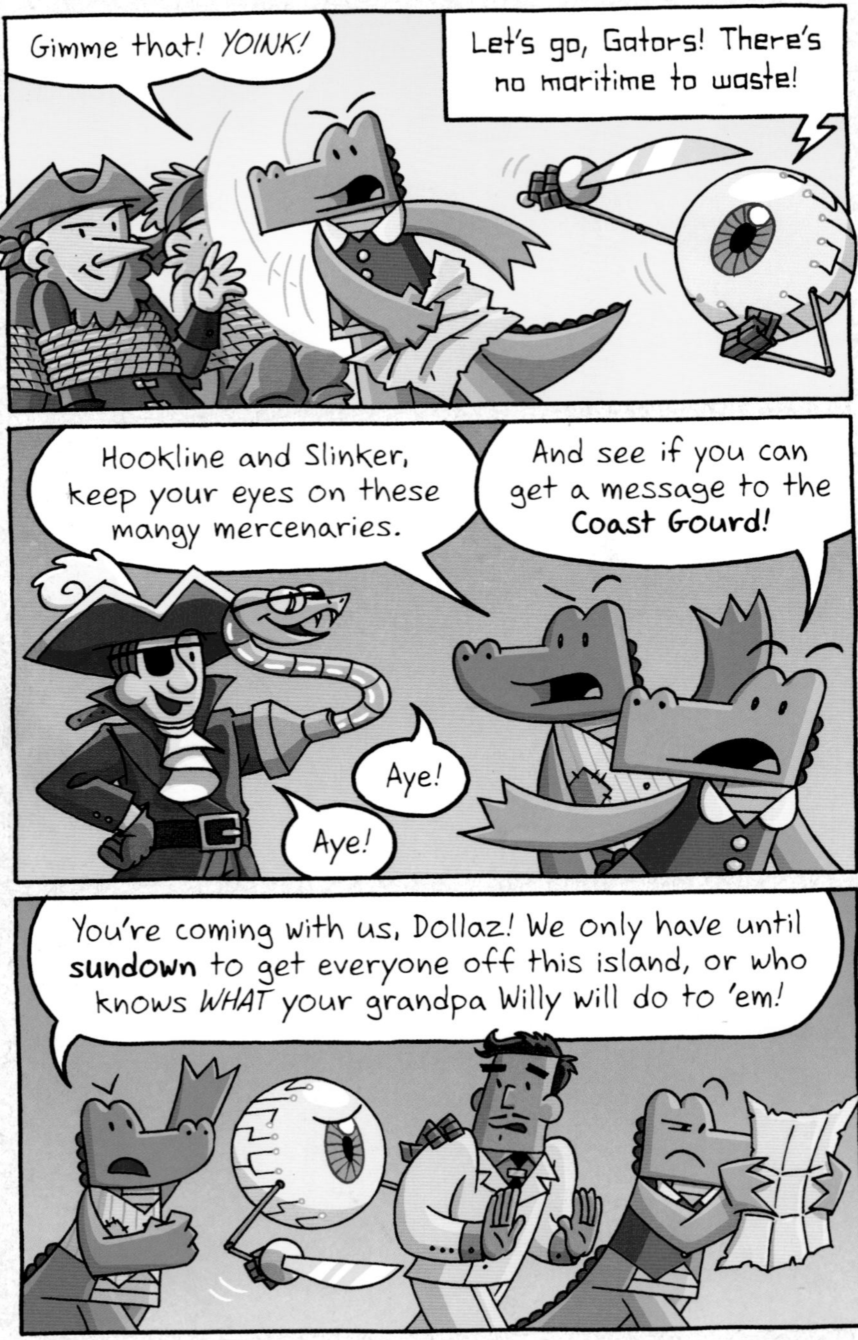
Gimme that! *YOINK!*
Let's go, Gators! There's no maritime to waste!
Hookline and Slinker, keep your eyes on these mangy mercenaries.
And see if you can get a message to the **Coast Gourd!**
Aye!
Aye!
You're coming with us, Dollaz! We only have until **sundown** to get everyone off this island, or who knows *WHAT* your grandpa Willy will do to 'em!

Chapter 18

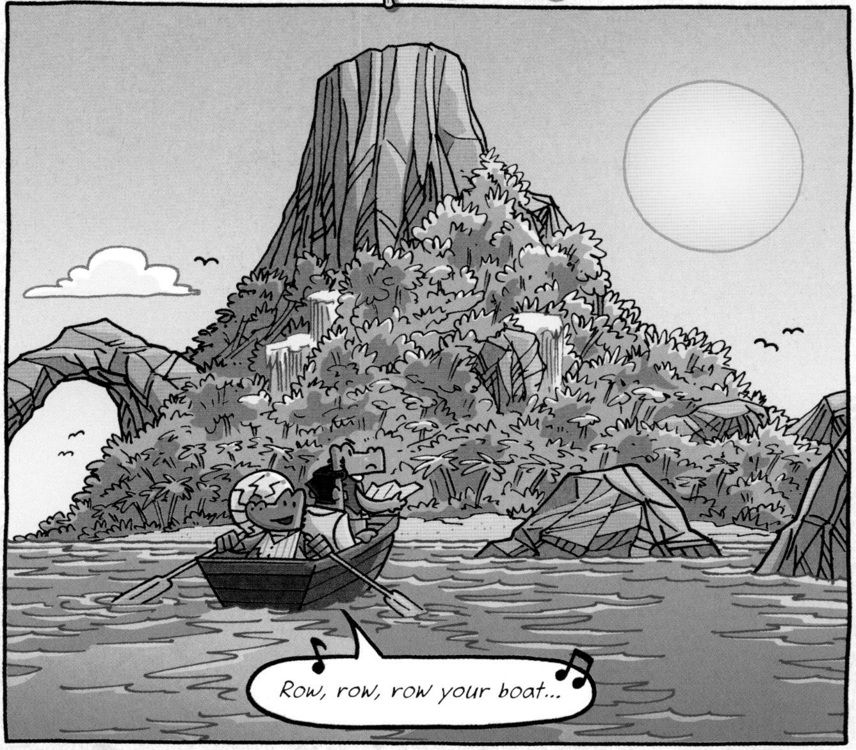

Row, row, row your boat...

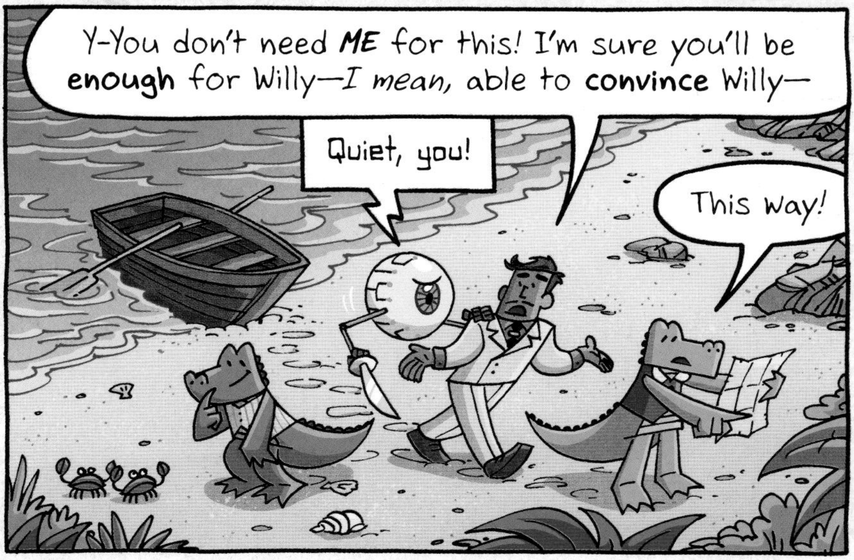

Y-You don't need ME for this! I'm sure you'll be enough for Willy—I mean, able to convince Willy—
Quiet, you!
This way!

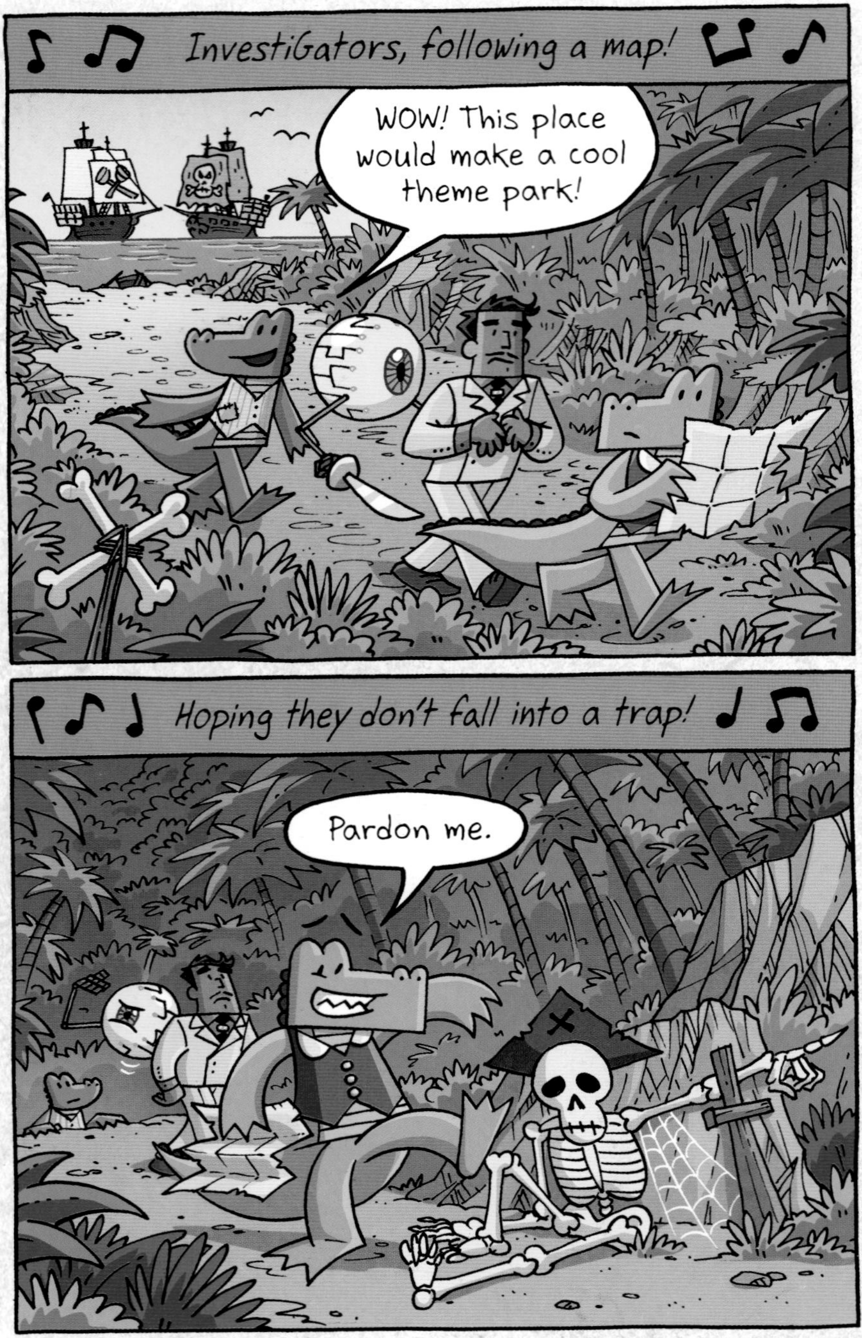
InvestiGators, following a map!
WOW! This place would make a cool theme park!
Hoping they don't fall into a trap!
Pardon me.

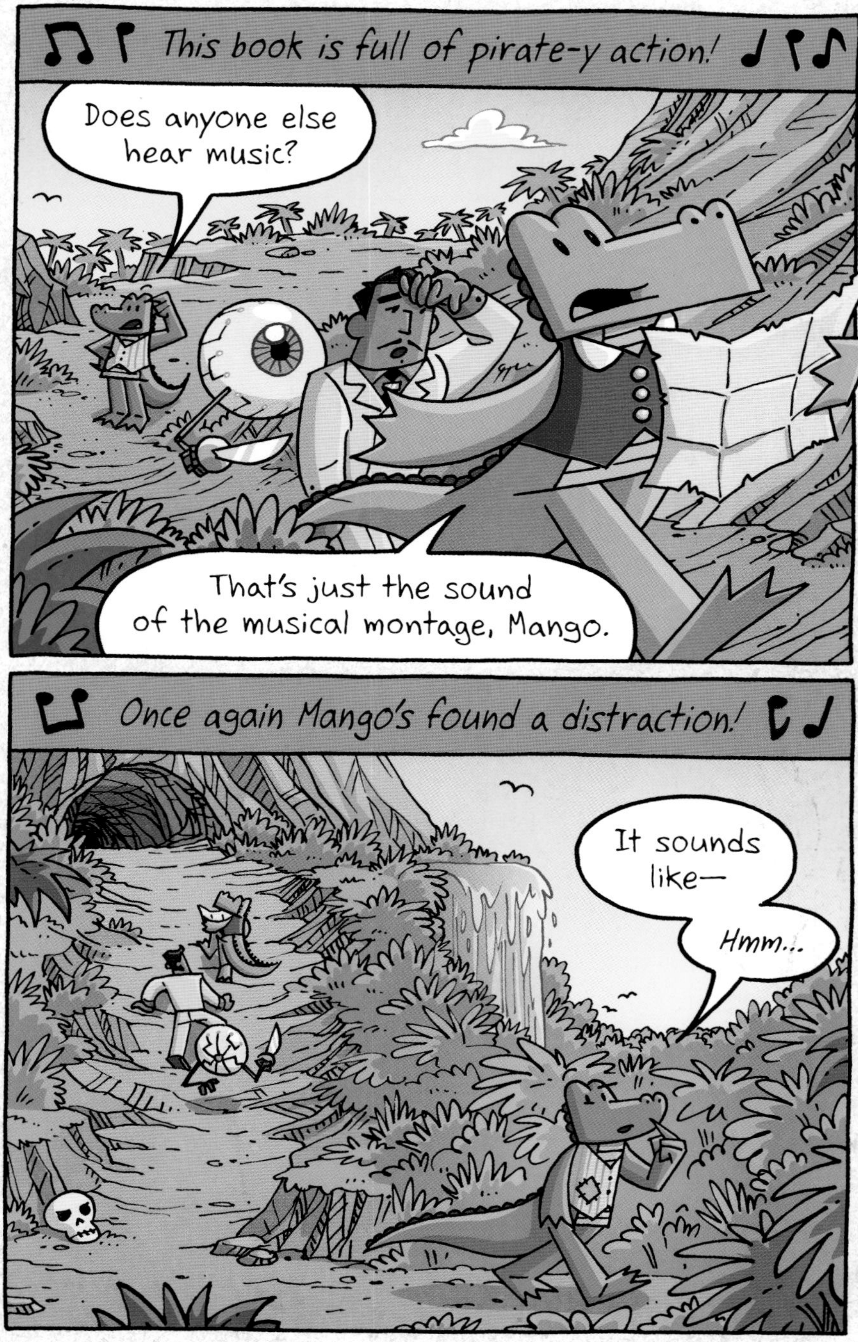
This book is full of pirate-y action!
Does anyone else hear music?
That's just the sound of the musical montage, Mango.
Once again Mango's found a distraction!
It sounds like—
Hmm...

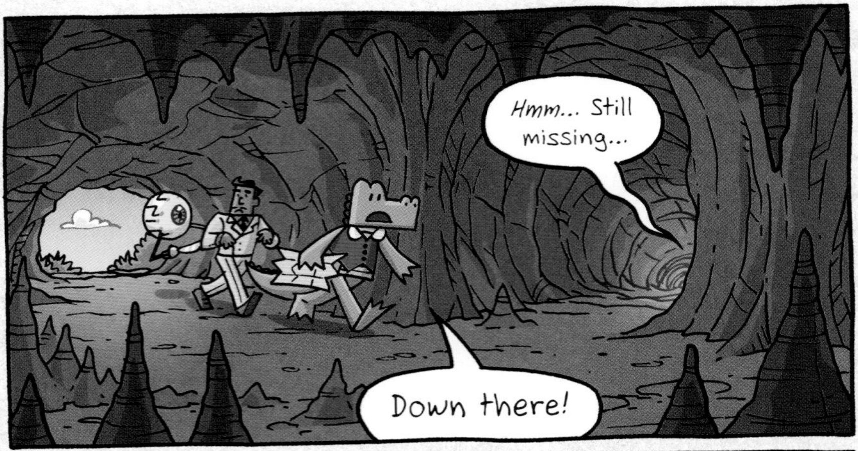
Hmm... Still missing...
Down there!

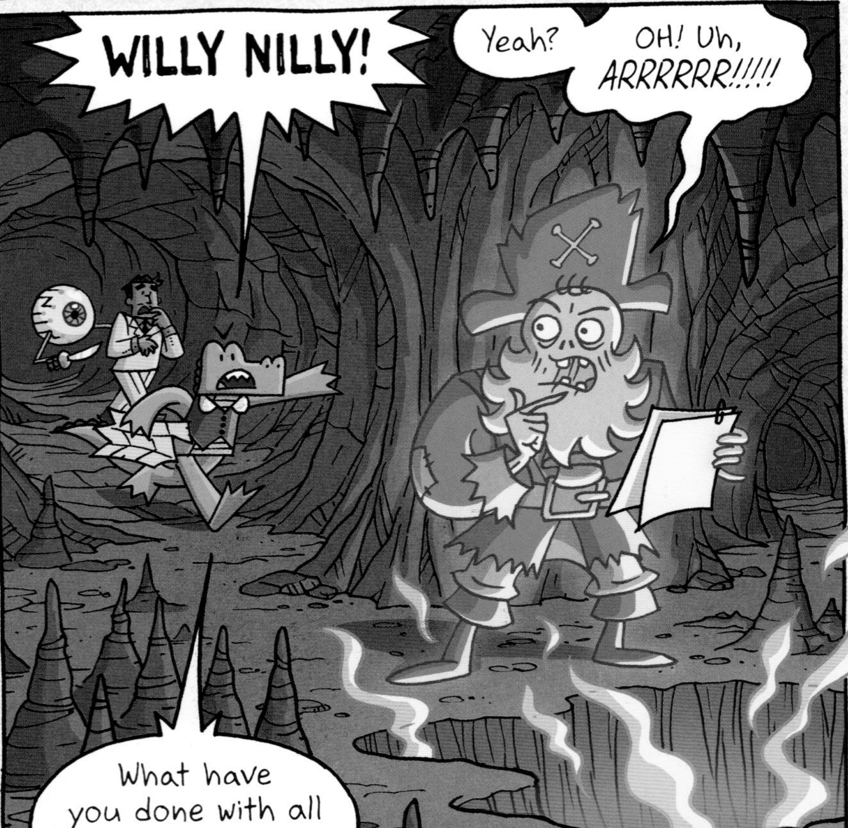
WILLY NILLY!
Yeah?
OH! Uh, ARRRRRR!!!!!
What have you done with all the passengers?

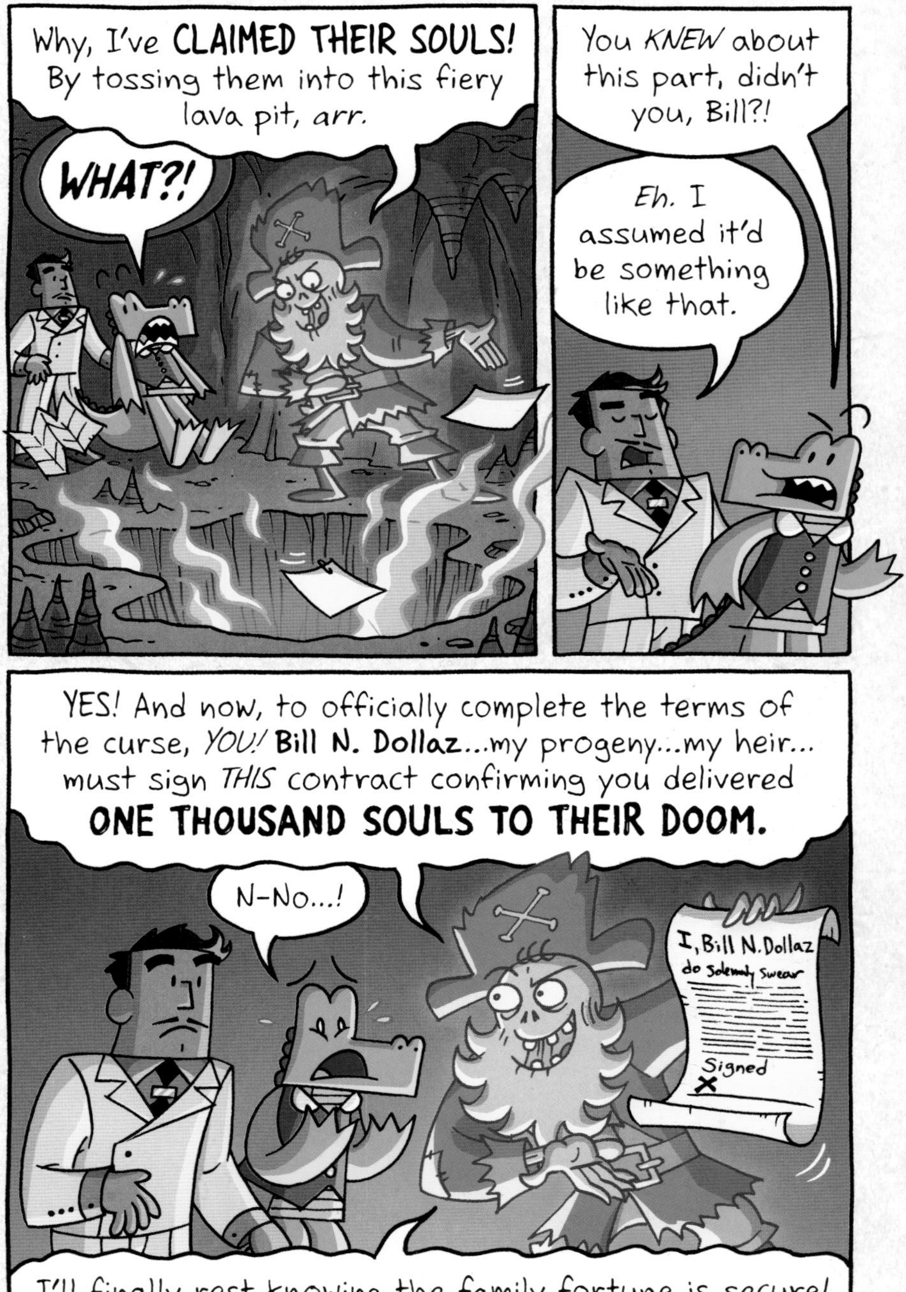
Why, I've CLAIMED THEIR SOULS! By tossing them into this fiery lava pit, arr.
WHAT?!
You KNEW about this part, didn't you, Bill?!
Eh. I assumed it'd be something like that.
YES! And now, to officially complete the terms of the curse, YOU! Bill N. Dollaz...my progeny...my heir... must sign THIS contract confirming you delivered ONE THOUSAND SOULS TO THEIR DOOM.
N-No...!
I, Bill N. Dollaz
do Solemnly Swear
Signed
I'll finally rest knowing the family fortune is secure!

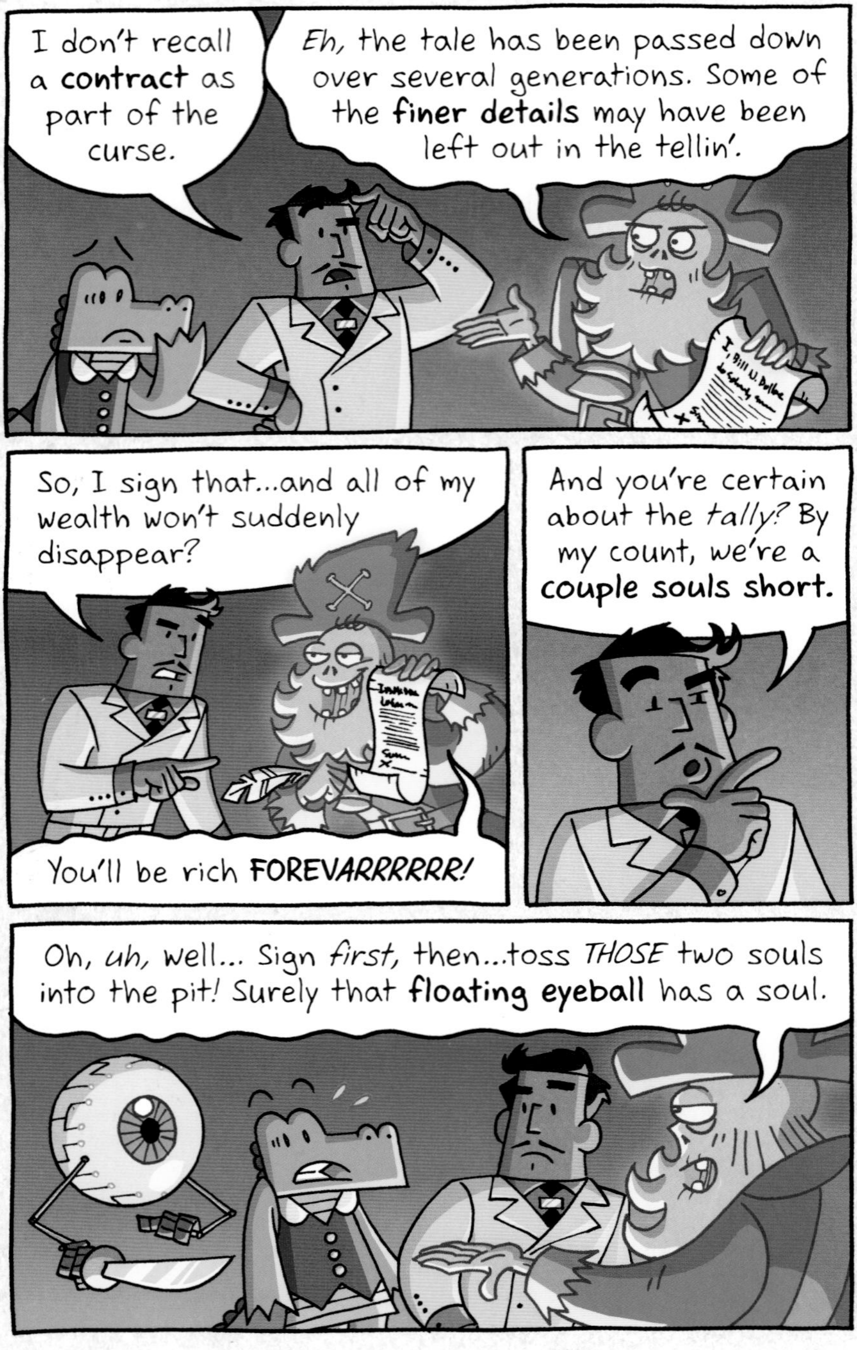
I don't recall a **contract** as part of the curse.
Eh, the tale has been passed down over several generations. Some of the **finer details** may have been left out in the tellin'.
I, Bill U. Dollbe
So, I sign that...and all of my wealth won't suddenly disappear?
You'll be rich **FOREVARRRRRR!**
And you're certain about the *tally?* By my count, we're a **couple souls short.**
Oh, *uh,* well... Sign *first,* then...toss *THOSE* two souls into the pit! Surely that **floating eyeball** has a soul.

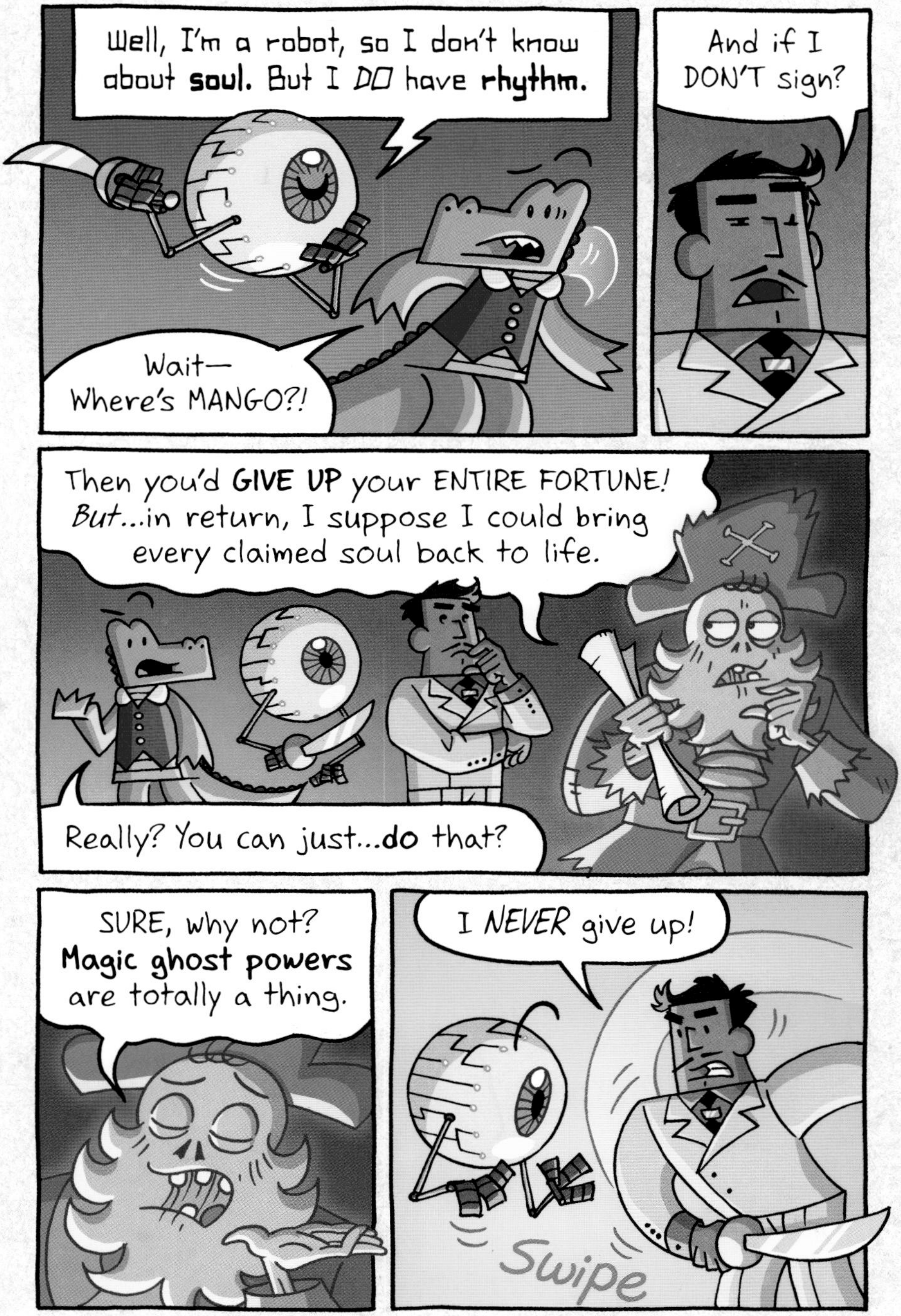
Well, I'm a robot, so I don't know about **soul.** But I *DO* have **rhythm.**
Wait— Where's MANGO?!
And if I DON'T sign?
Then you'd **GIVE UP** your ENTIRE FORTUNE! *But*...in return, I suppose I could bring every claimed soul back to life.
Really? You can just...**do** that?
SURE, why not? **Magic ghost powers** are totally a thing.
I *NEVER* give up!
Swipe

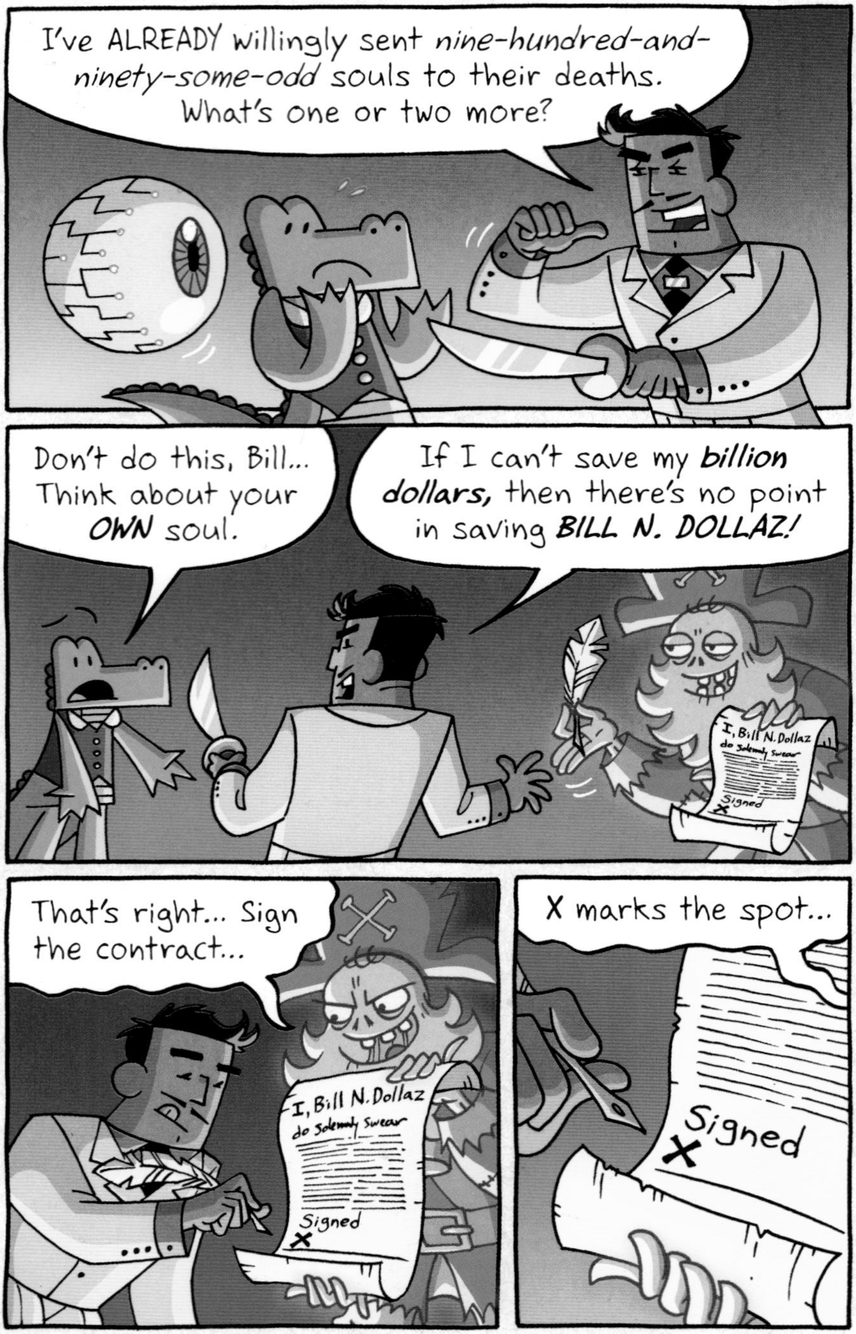
I've ALREADY willingly sent nine-hundred-and-ninety-some-odd souls to their deaths. What's one or two more?
Don't do this, Bill... Think about your OWN soul.
If I can't save my billion dollars, then there's no point in saving BILL N. DOLLAZ!
I, Bill N. Dollaz do Solemnly Swear
Signed X
That's right... Sign the contract...
I, Bill N. Dollaz do Solemnly Swear
Signed X
X marks the spot...
Signed X

AVAST!
MANGO?
What? How did you—
STOW YOUR SPECTRAL SCUTTLEBUTT, GRAMPS!
NO! He didn't sign—
BOOT
YARGH!

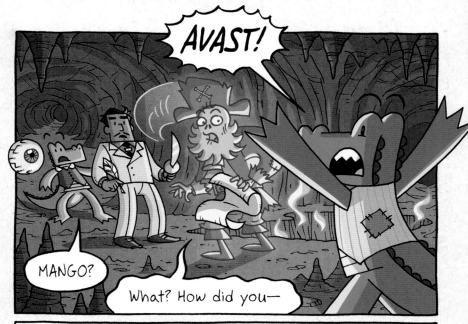

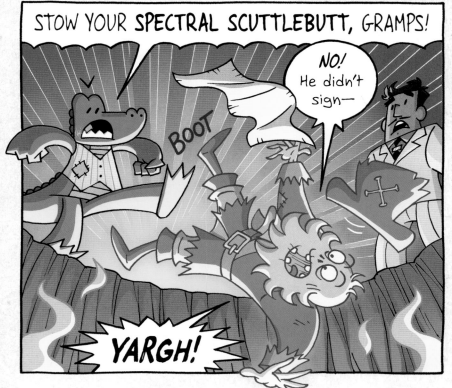

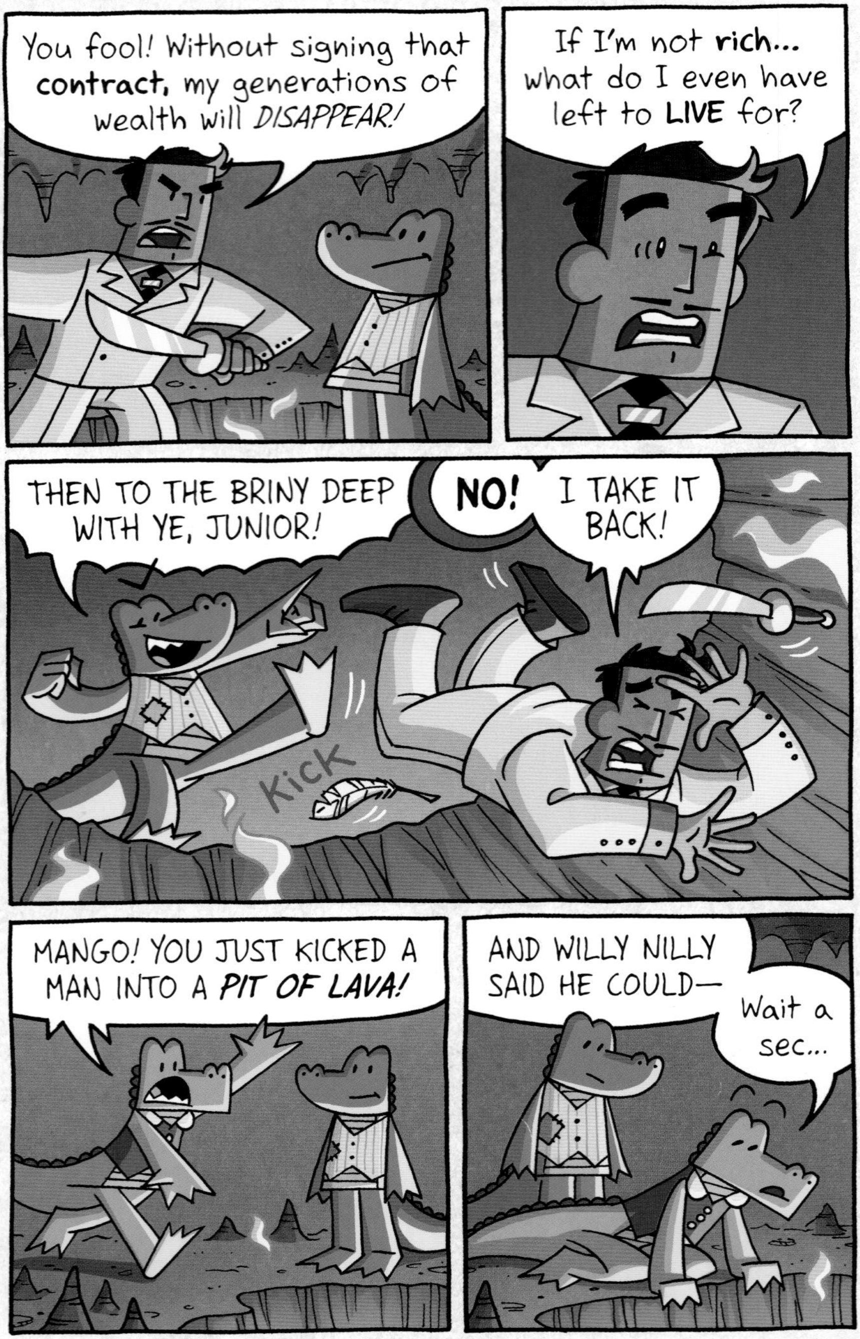
You fool! Without signing that **contract,** my generations of wealth will *DISAPPEAR!*
If I'm not **rich...** what do I even have left to **LIVE** for?
THEN TO THE BRINY DEEP WITH YE, JUNIOR!
NO!
I TAKE IT BACK!
KICK
MANGO! YOU JUST KICKED A MAN INTO A ***PIT OF LAVA!***
AND WILLY NILLY SAID HE COULD—
Wait a sec...

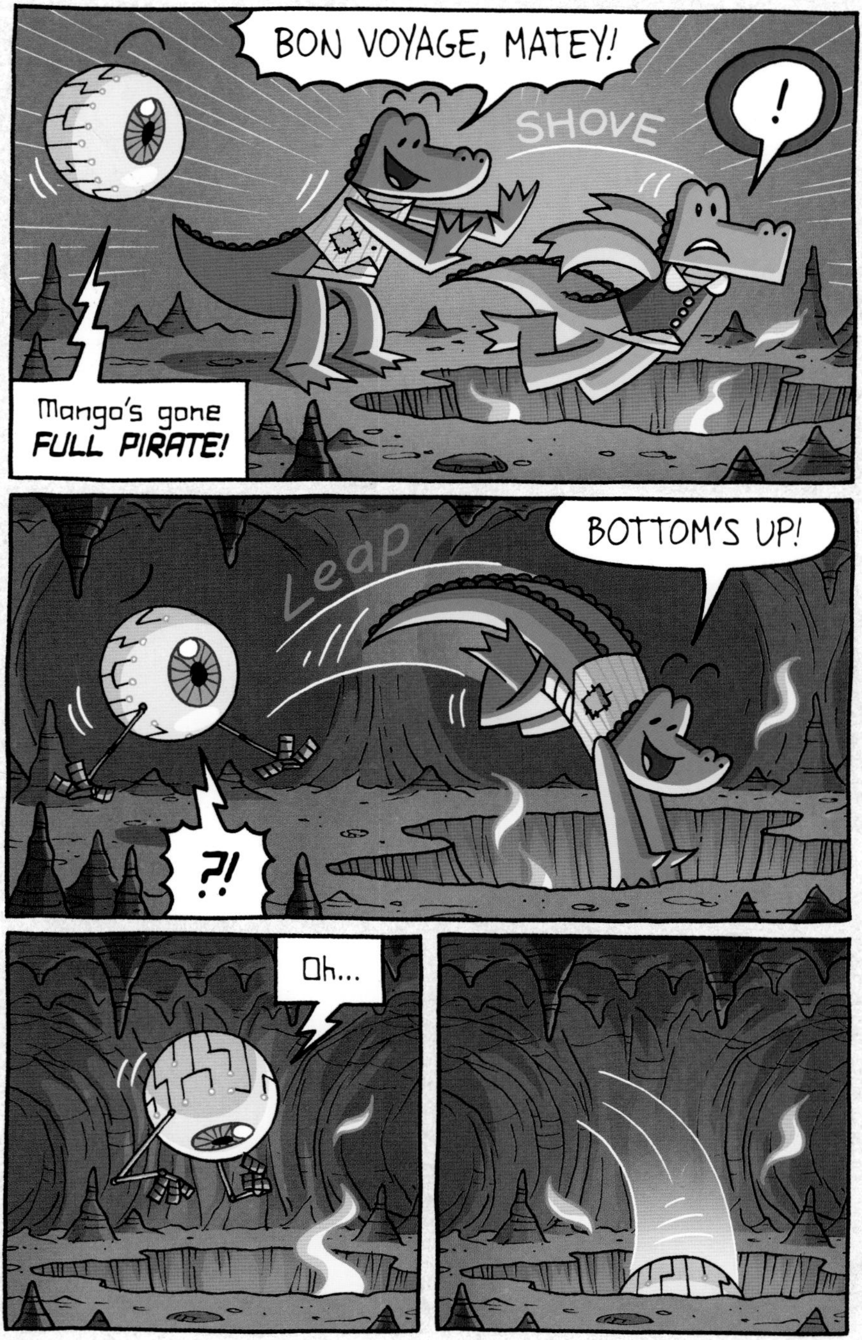
BON VOYAGE, MATEY!
SHOVE
!
Mango's gone
FULL PIRATE!
Leap
BOTTOM'S UP!
?!
Oh...

Chapter 19

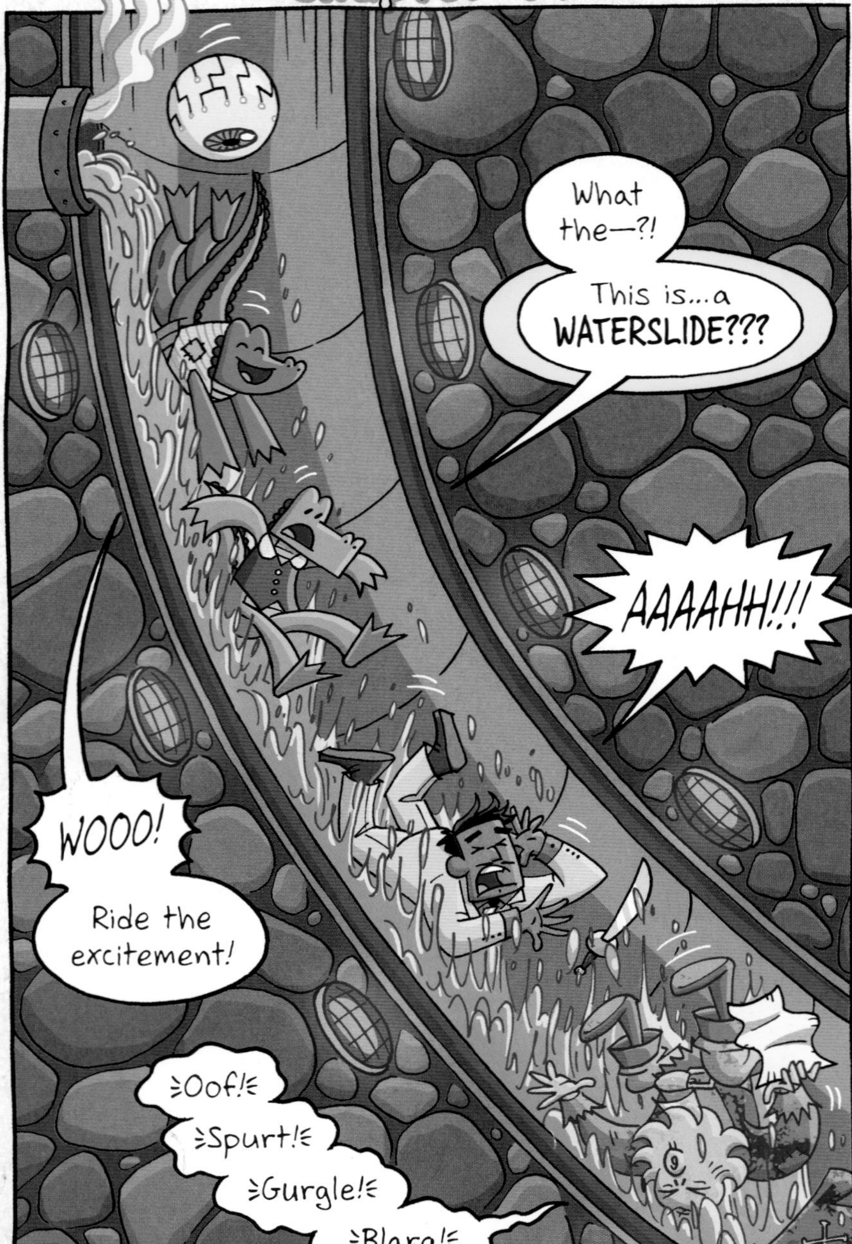
What the—?!
This is...a WATERSLIDE???
AAAAHH!!!
WOOO!
Ride the excitement!
Oof!
Spurt!
Gurgle!
Blarg!

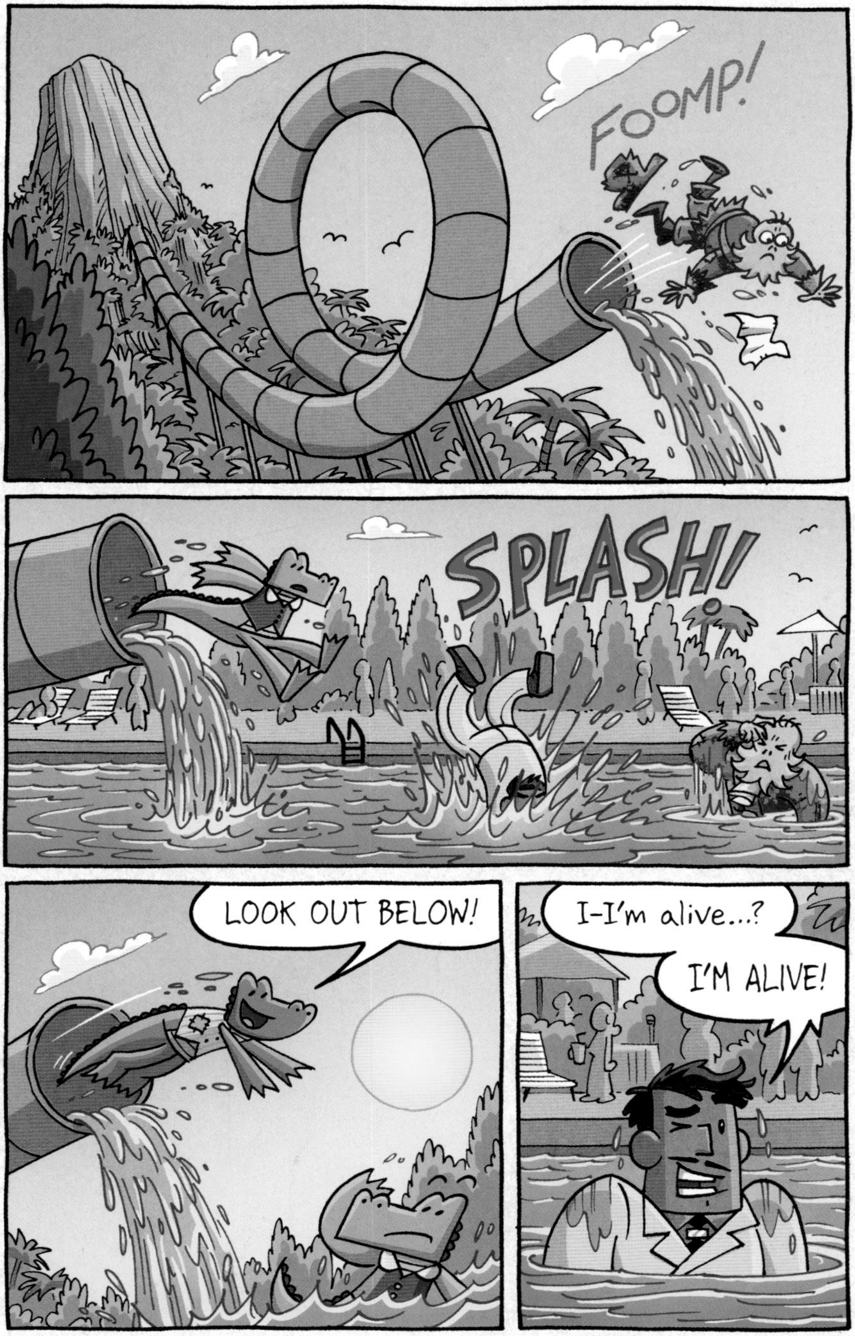
FOOMP!
SPLASH!
LOOK OUT BELOW!
I-I'm alive...?
I'M ALIVE!

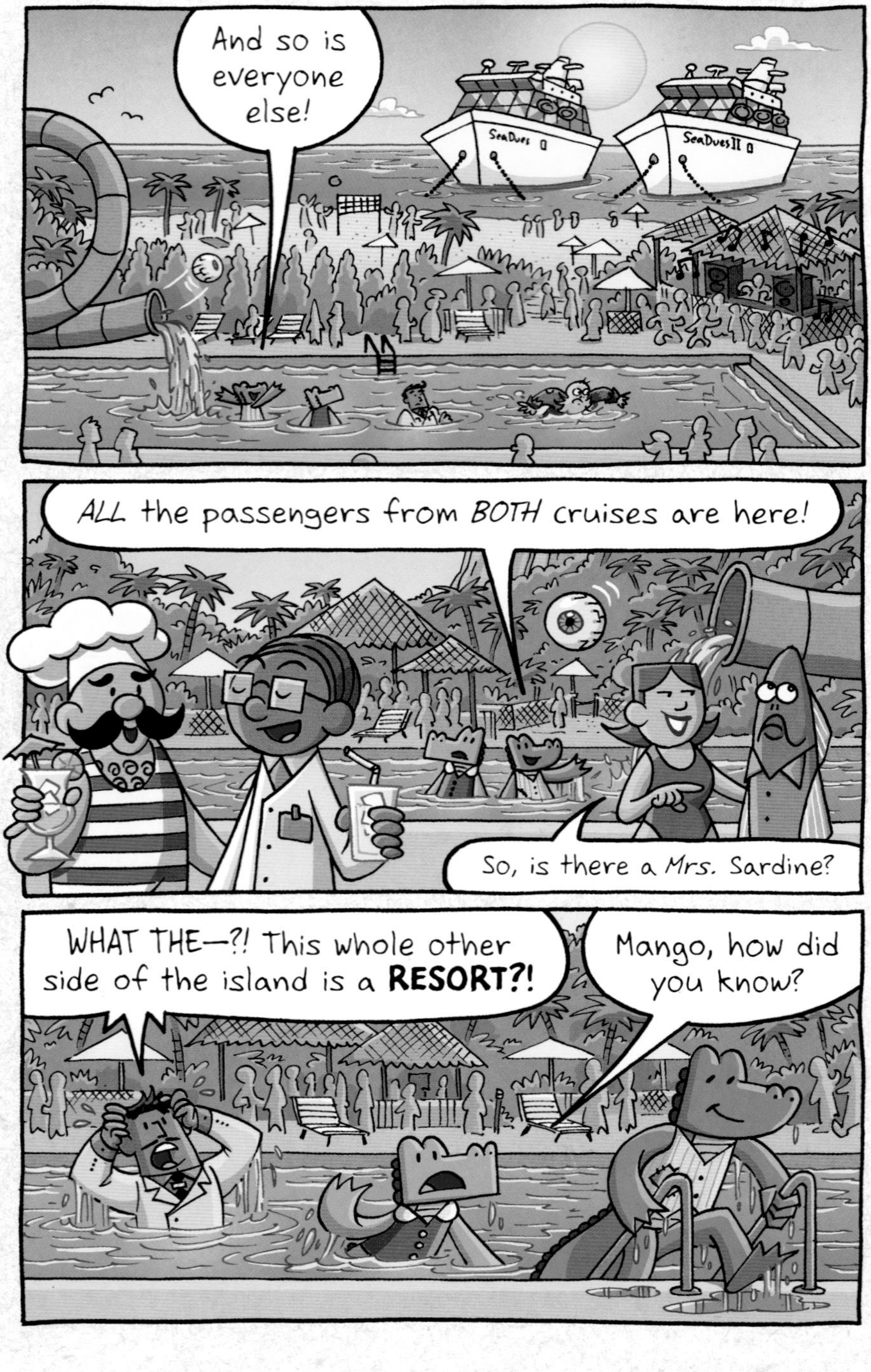
And so is everyone else!
SeaDues II
SeaDues III
ALL the passengers from BOTH cruises are here!
So, is there a Mrs. Sardine?
WHAT THE—?! This whole other side of the island is a RESORT?!
Mango, how did you know?

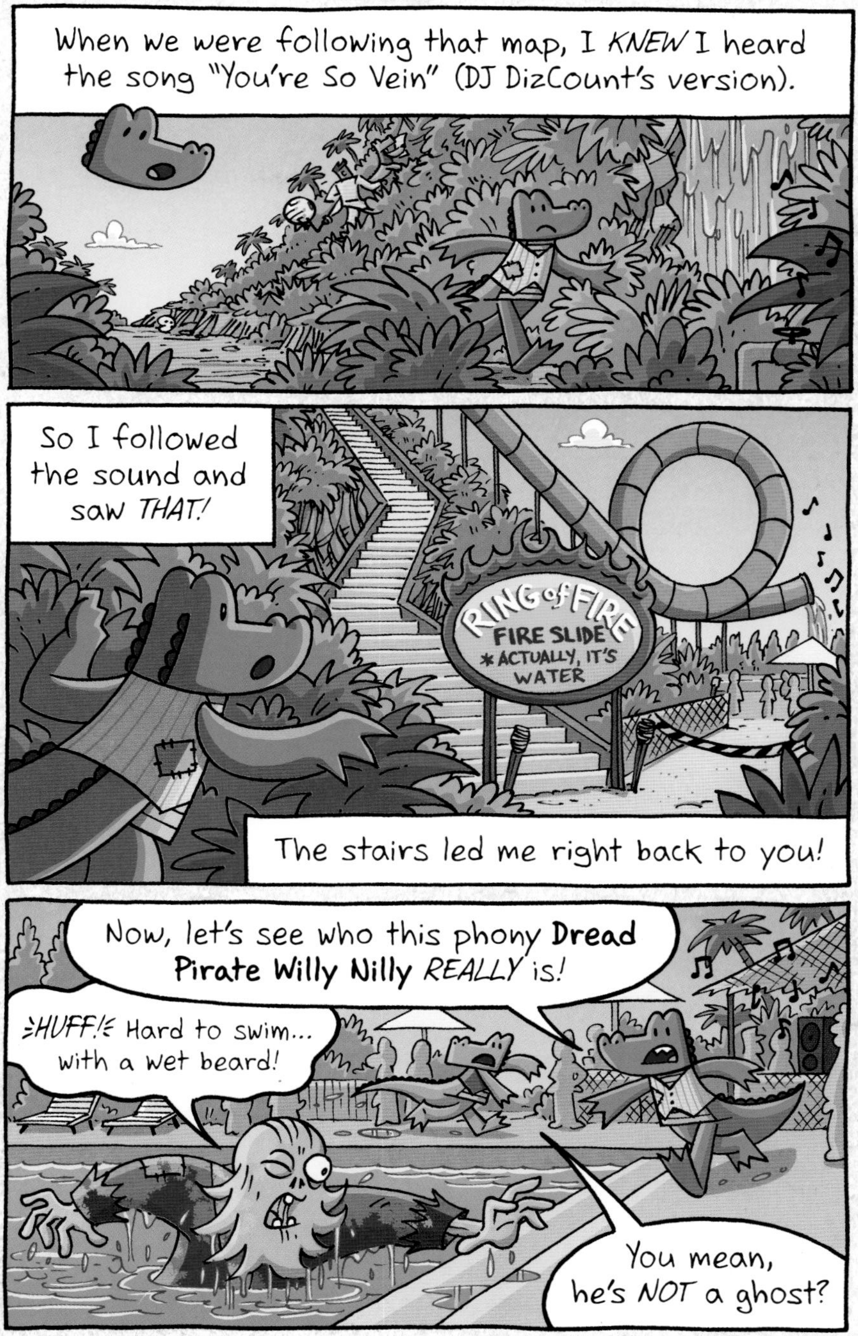

When we were following that map, I *KNEW* I heard the song "You're So Vein" (DJ DizCount's version).
So I followed the sound and saw *THAT!*
RING of FIRE
FIRE SLIDE
* ACTUALLY, IT'S WATER
The stairs led me right back to you!
Now, let's see who this phony **Dread Pirate Willy Nilly** *REALLY* is!
HUFF! Hard to swim... with a wet beard!
You mean, he's *NOT* a ghost?

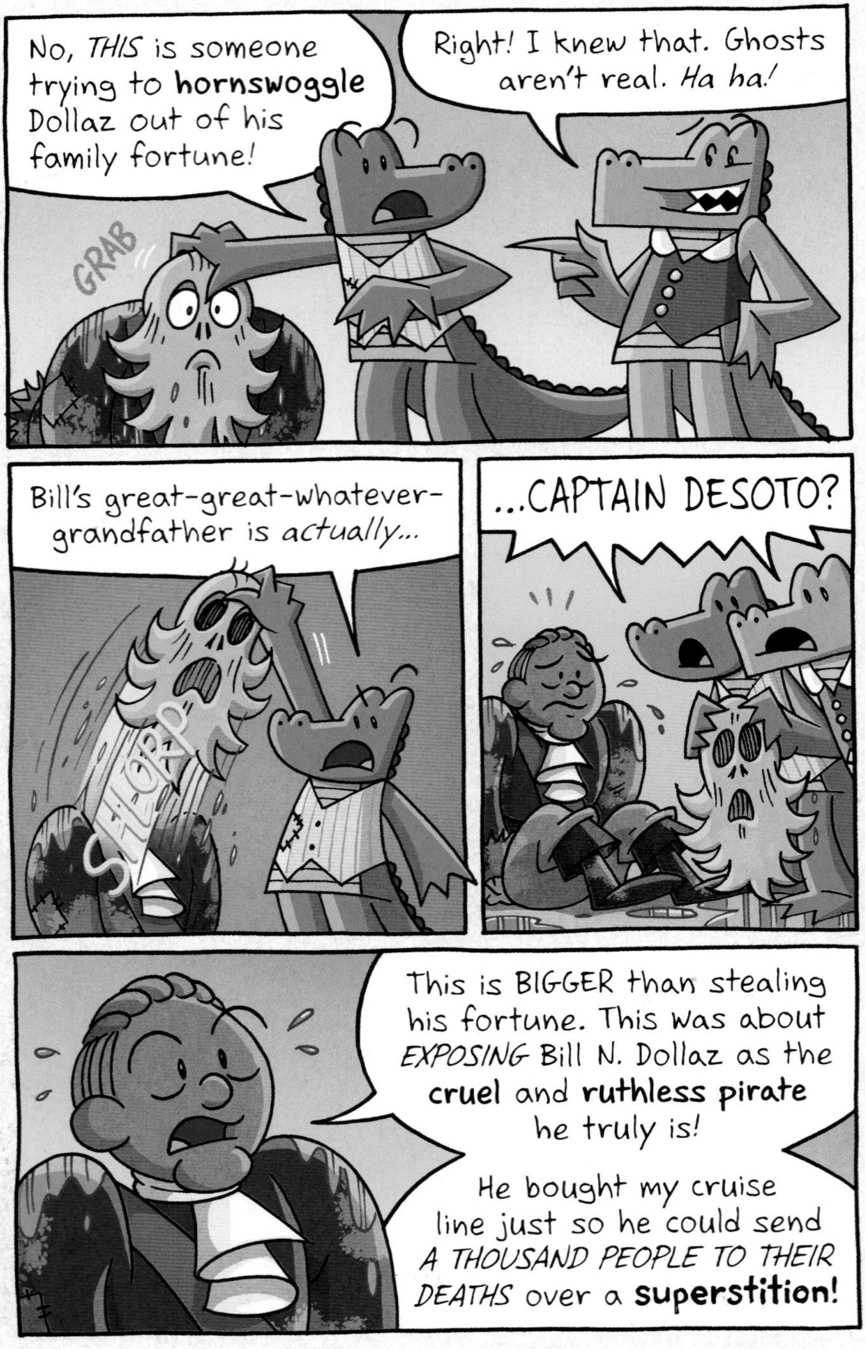
No, *THIS* is someone trying to **hornswoggle** Dollaz out of his family fortune!
Right! I knew that. Ghosts aren't real. *Ha ha!*
GRAB
Bill's great-great-whatever-grandfather is *actually*...
SHLORP
...CAPTAIN DESOTO?
This is BIGGER than stealing his fortune. This was about *EXPOSING* Bill N. Dollaz as the **cruel** and **ruthless pirate** he truly is!
He bought my cruise line just so he could send *A THOUSAND PEOPLE TO THEIR DEATHS* over a **superstition!**

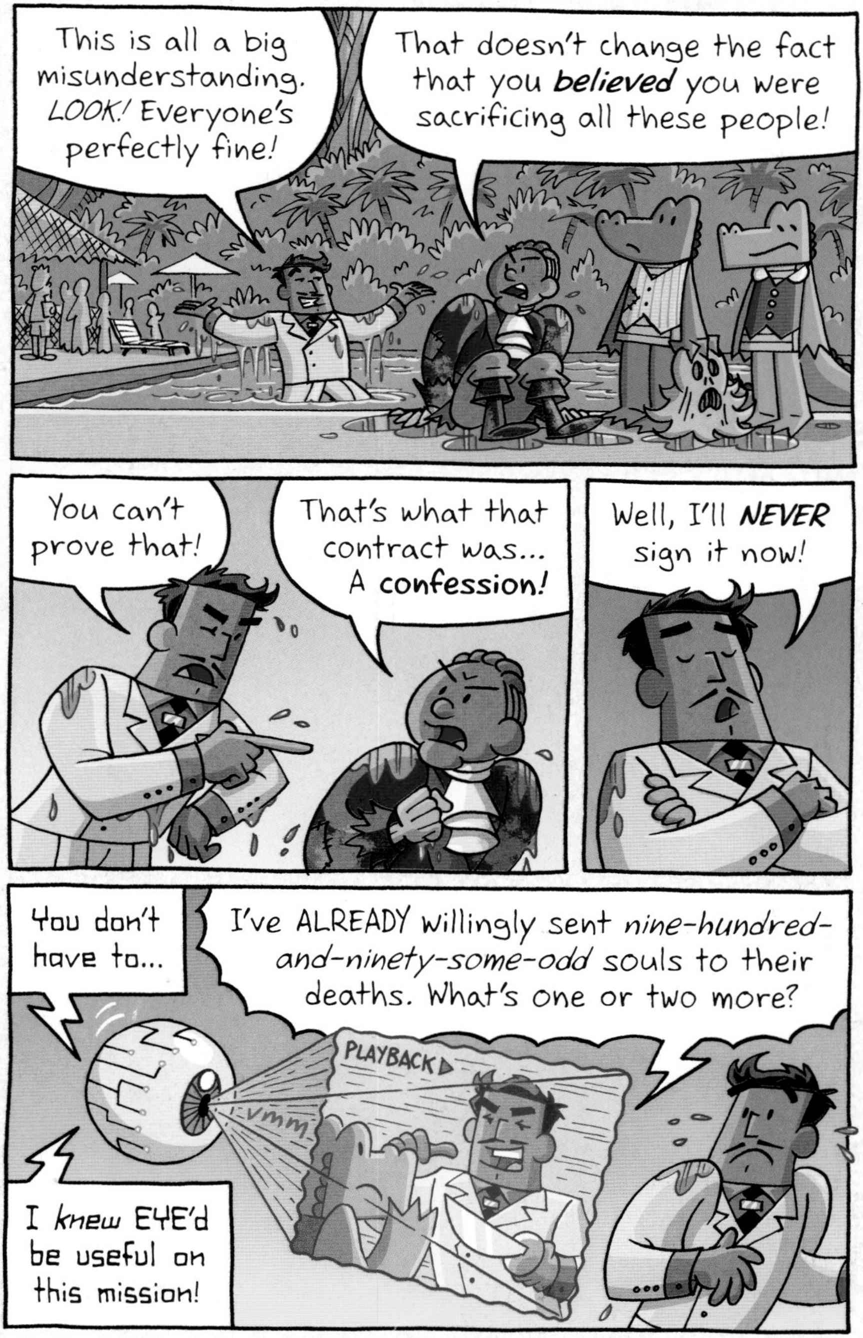
This is all a big misunderstanding. LOOK! Everyone's perfectly fine!
That doesn't change the fact that you believed you were sacrificing all these people!
You can't prove that!
That's what that contract was... A confession!
Well, I'll NEVER sign it now!
You don't have to...
I've ALREADY willingly sent nine-hundred-and-ninety-some-odd souls to their deaths. What's one or two more?
PLAYBACK
VMM
I knew EYE'd be useful on this mission!

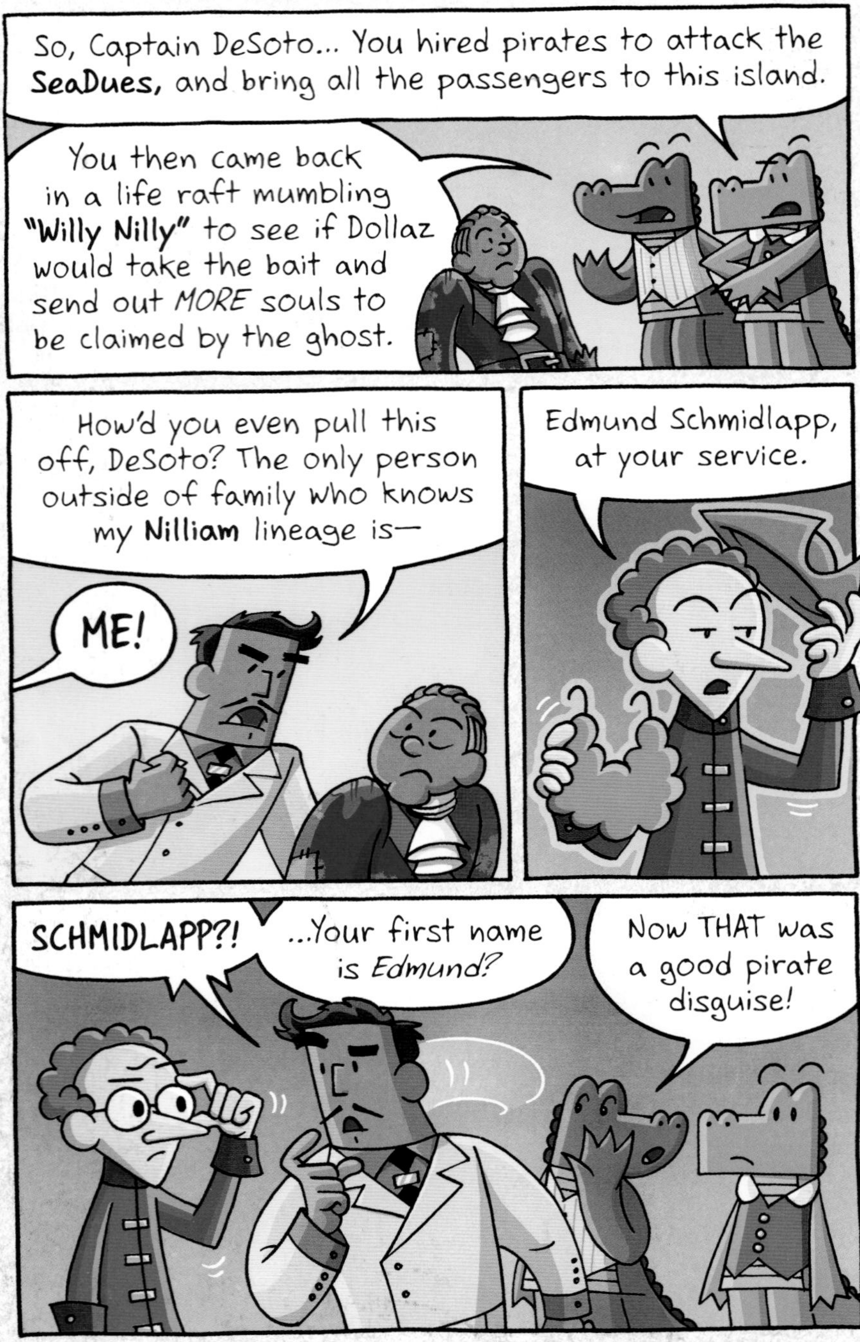
So, Captain DeSoto... You hired pirates to attack the SeaDues, and bring all the passengers to this island.
You then came back in a life raft mumbling "Willy Nilly" to see if Dollaz would take the bait and send out MORE souls to be claimed by the ghost.
How'd you even pull this off, DeSoto? The only person outside of family who knows my Nilliam lineage is—
ME!
Edmund Schmidlapp, at your service.
SCHMIDLAPP?!
...Your first name is Edmund?
Now THAT was a good pirate disguise!

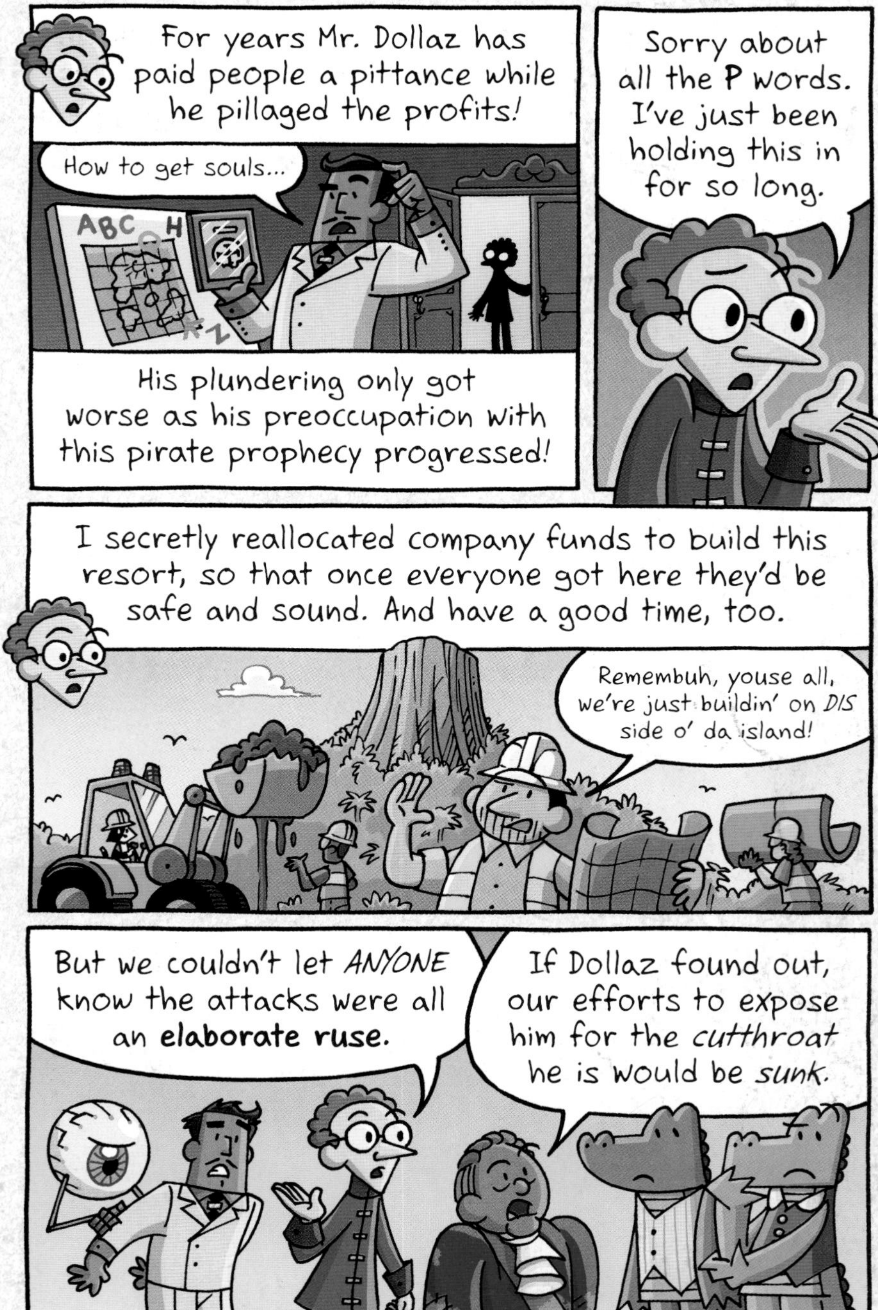

For years Mr. Dollaz has paid people a pittance while he pillaged the profits!
How to get souls...
ABC
H
Z
His plundering only got worse as his preoccupation with this pirate prophecy progressed!
Sorry about all the P words. I've just been holding this in for so long.
I secretly reallocated company funds to build this resort, so that once everyone got here they'd be safe and sound. And have a good time, too.
Remembuh, youse all, we're just buildin' on *DIS* side o' da island!
But we couldn't let *ANYONE* know the attacks were all an **elaborate ruse.**
If Dollaz found out, our efforts to expose him for the *cutthroat* he is would be *sunk.*

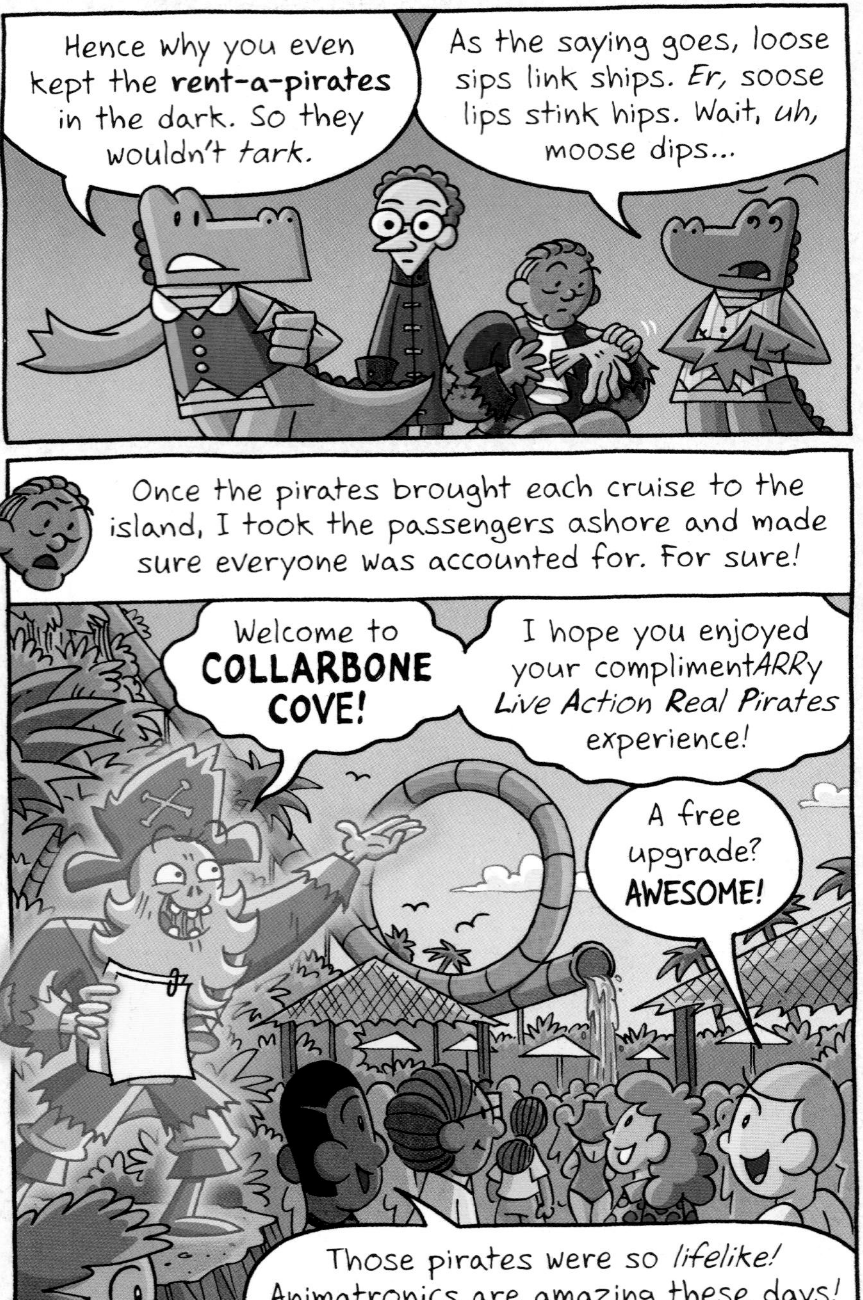
Hence why you even kept the **rent-a-pirates** in the dark. So they wouldn't *tark.*
As the saying goes, loose sips link ships. *Er,* soose lips stink hips. Wait, *uh,* moose dips...
Once the pirates brought each cruise to the island, I took the passengers ashore and made sure everyone was accounted for. For sure!
Welcome to **COLLARBONE COVE!**
I hope you enjoyed your complimentARRy *Live Action Real Pirates* experience!
A free upgrade? **AWESOME!**
Those pirates were so *lifelike!* Animatronics are amazing these days!

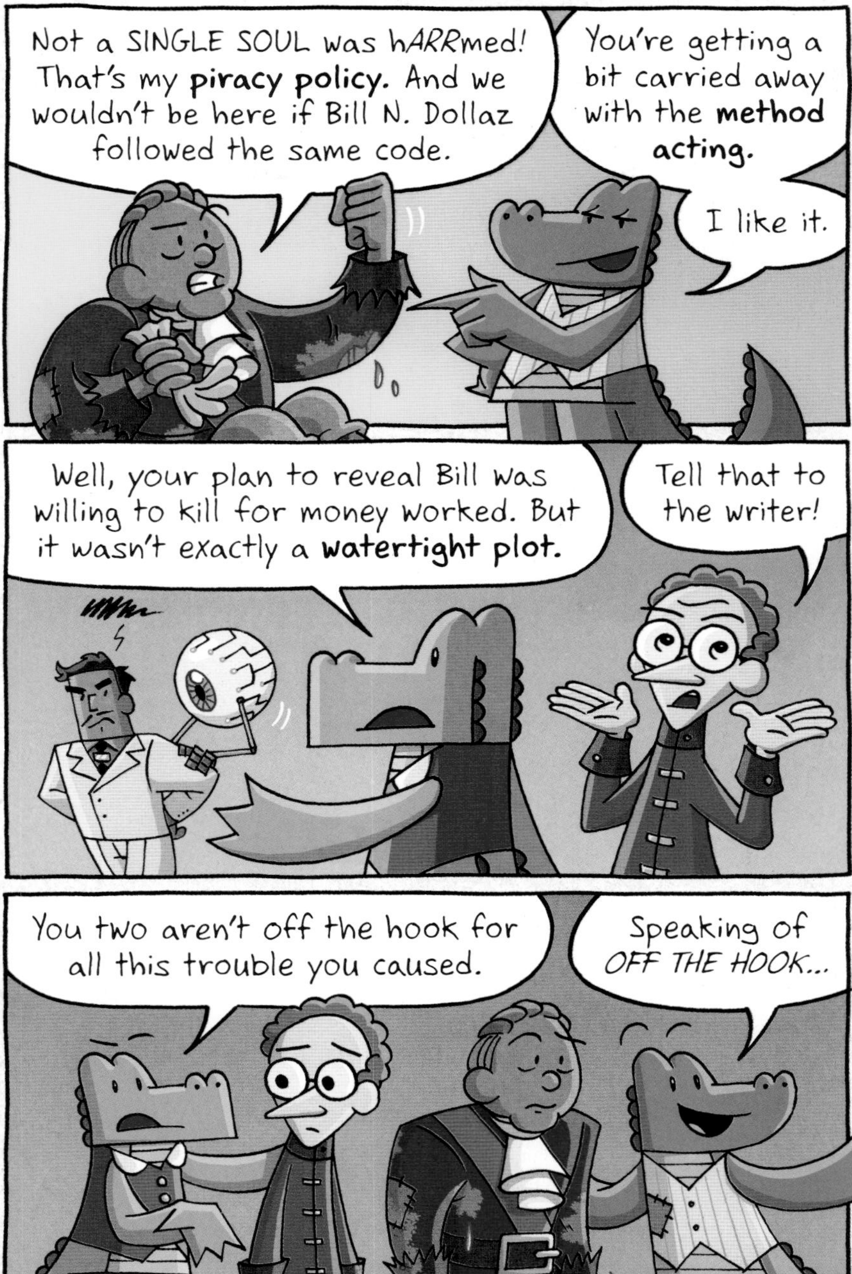
Not a SINGLE SOUL was hARRmed! That's my **piracy policy.** And we wouldn't be here if Bill N. Dollaz followed the same code.
You're getting a bit carried away with the **method acting.**
I like it.
Well, your plan to reveal Bill was willing to kill for money worked. But it wasn't exactly a **watertight plot.**
Tell that to the writer!
You two aren't off the hook for all this trouble you caused.
Speaking of *OFF THE HOOK...*

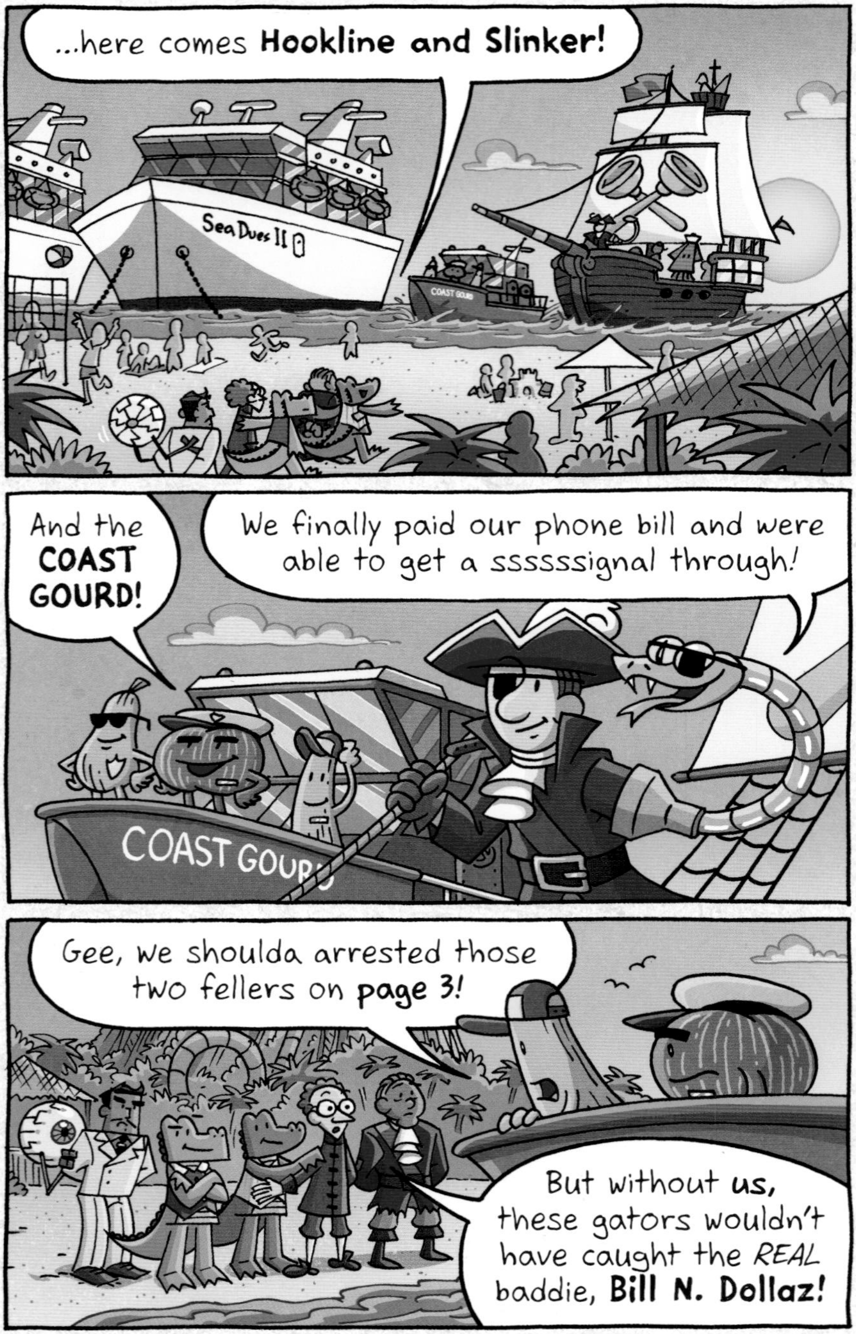
...here comes **Hookline and Slinker!**
Sea Dues II
COAST GOURD
And the **COAST GOURD!**
We finally paid our phone bill and were able to get a ssssssignal through!
COAST GOURD
Gee, we shoulda arrested those two fellers on **page 3!**
But without **us,** these gators wouldn't have caught the *REAL* baddie, **Bill N. Dollaz!**

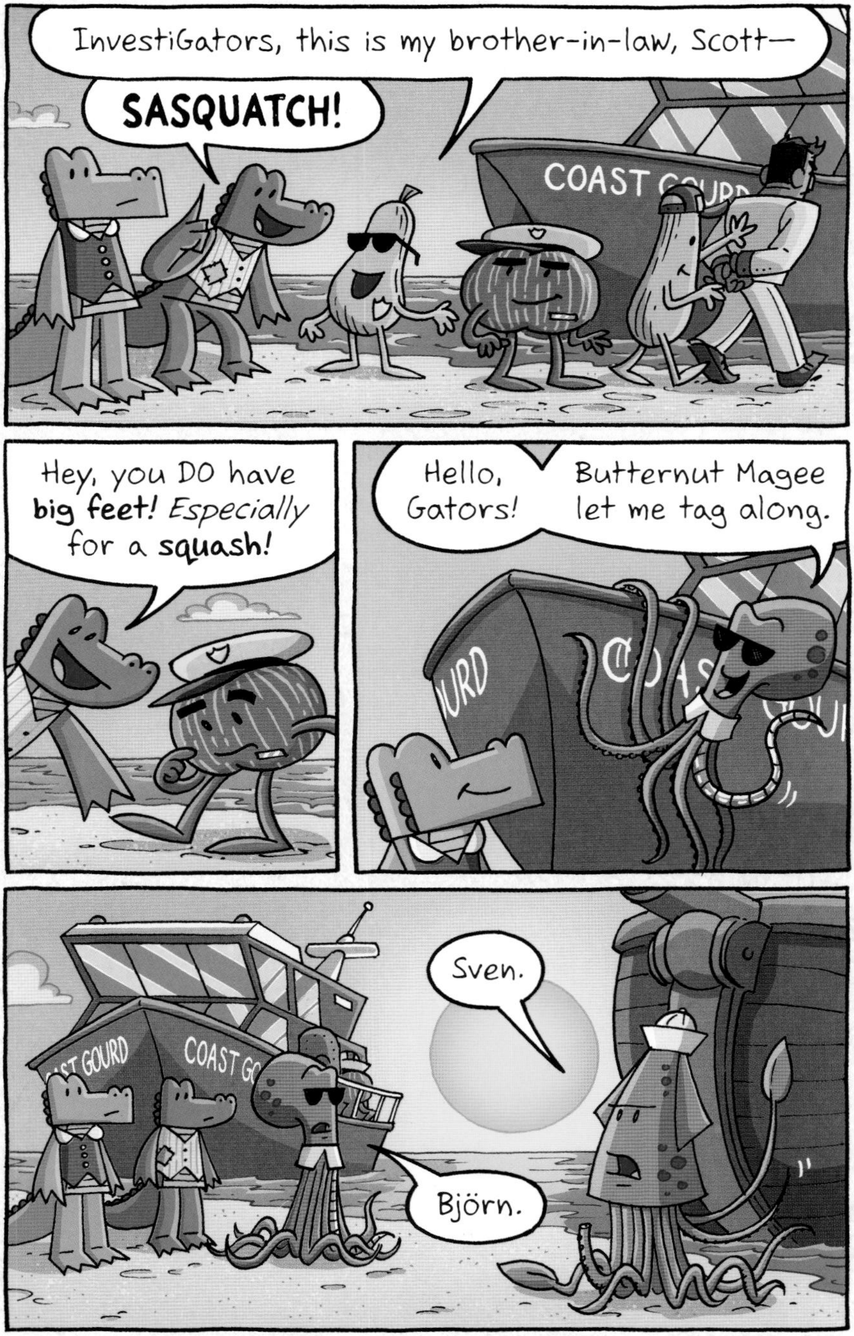
InvestiGators, this is my brother-in-law, Scott—
SASQUATCH!
COAST GOURD
Hey, you DO have big feet! Especially for a squash!
Hello, Gators!
Butternut Magee let me tag along.
Sven.
Björn.
COAST GOURD

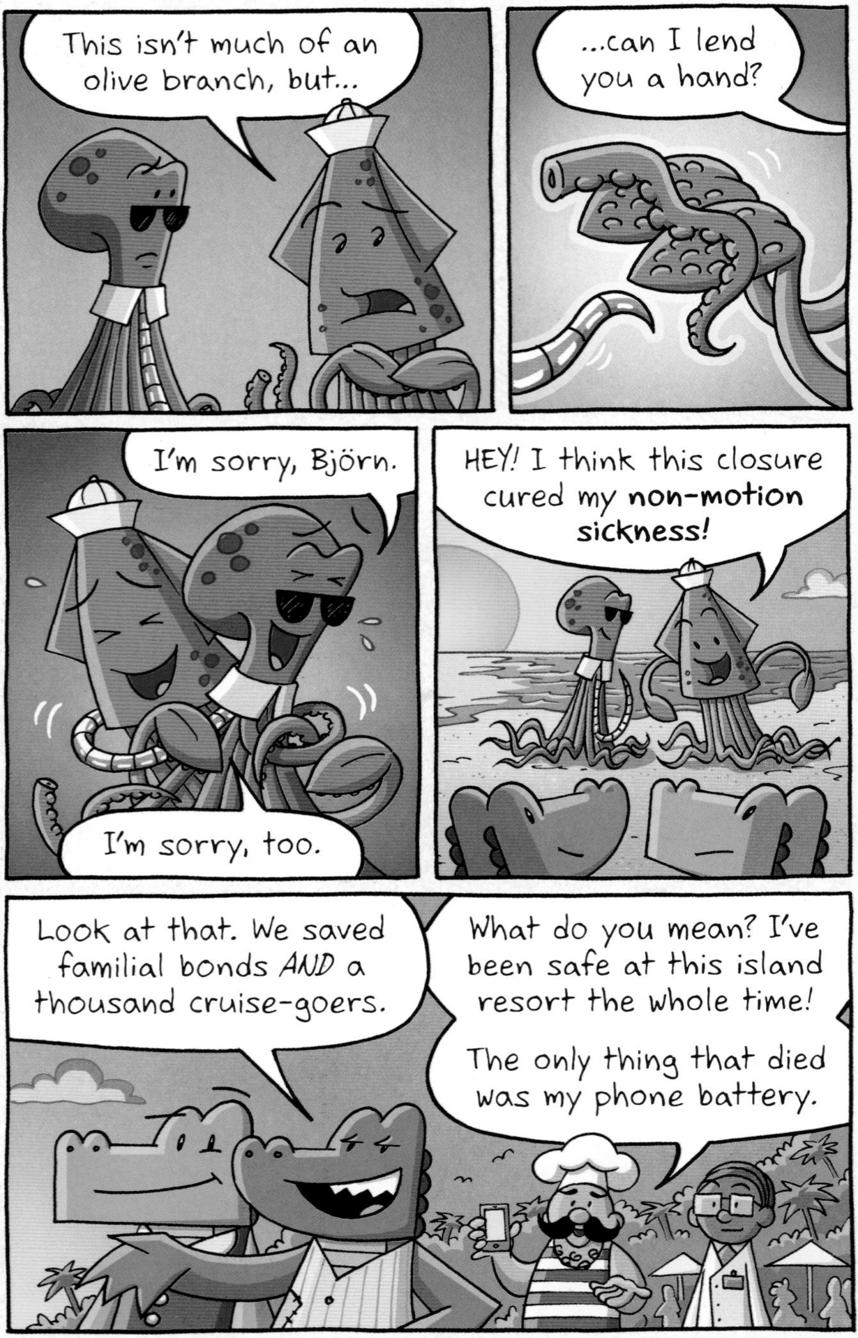
This isn't much of an olive branch, but...
...can I lend you a hand?
I'm sorry, Björn.
I'm sorry, too.
HEY! I think this closure cured my **non-motion sickness!**
Look at that. We saved familial bonds *AND* a thousand cruise-goers.
What do you mean? I've been safe at this island resort the whole time!
The only thing that died was my phone battery.

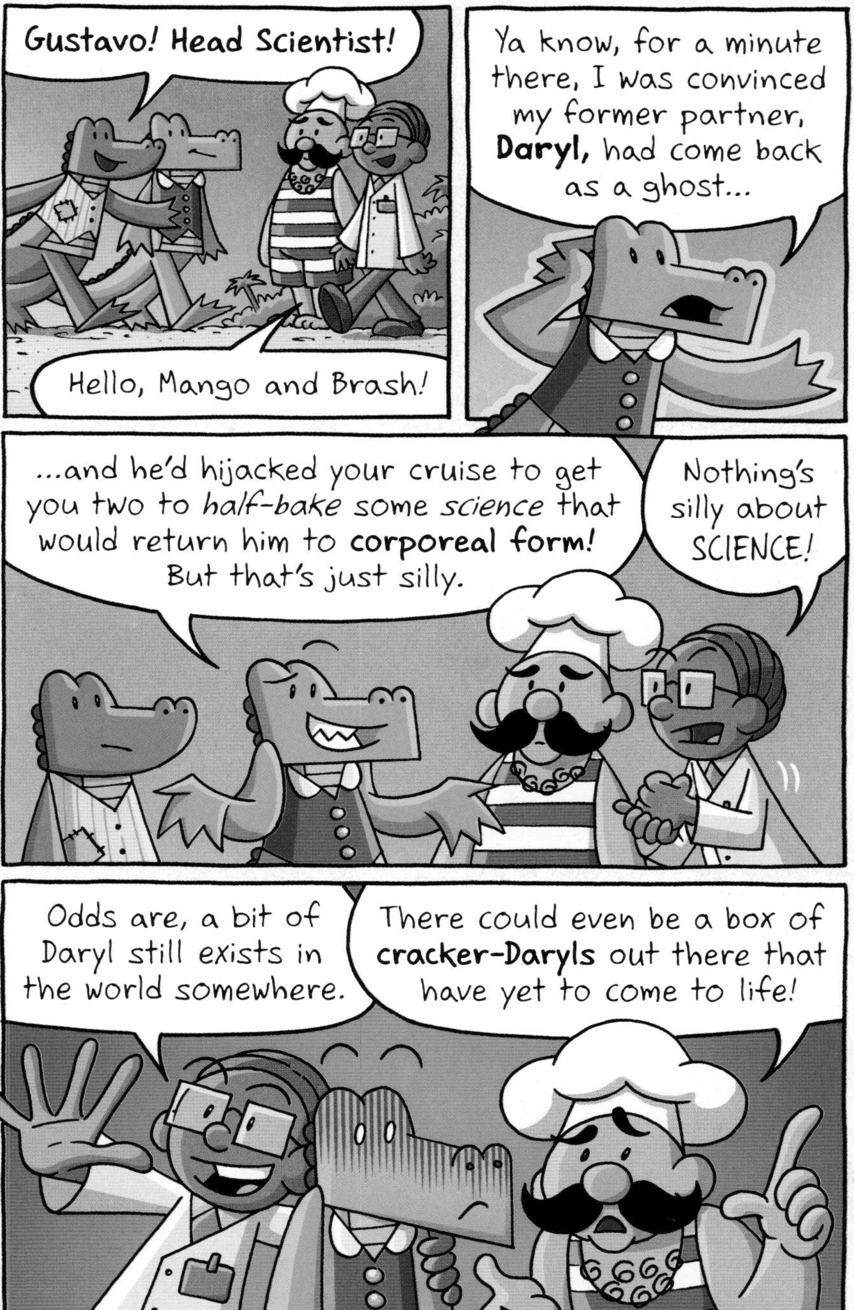
Gustavo! Head Scientist!
Hello, Mango and Brash!
Ya know, for a minute there, I was convinced my former partner, **Daryl,** had come back as a ghost...
...and he'd hijacked your cruise to get you two to *half-bake* some *science* that would return him to **corporeal form!** But that's just silly.
Nothing's silly about SCIENCE!
Odds are, a bit of Daryl still exists in the world somewhere.
There could even be a box of **cracker-Daryls** out there that have yet to come to life!

Epilogue

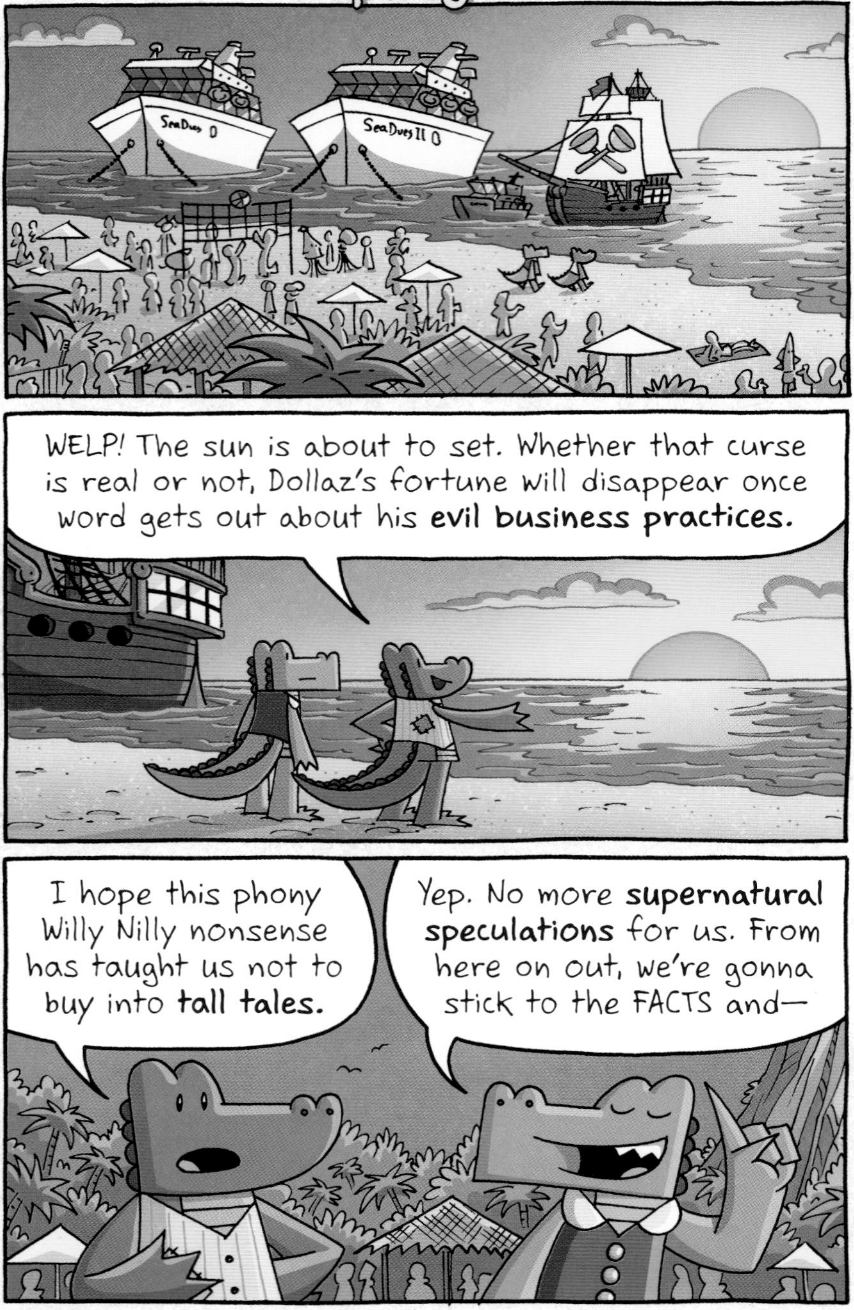
WELP! The sun is about to set. Whether that curse is real or not, Dollaz's fortune will disappear once word gets out about his **evil business practices.**
I hope this phony Willy Nilly nonsense has taught us not to buy into **tall tales.**
Yep. No more **supernatural speculations** for us. From here on out, we're gonna stick to the FACTS and—

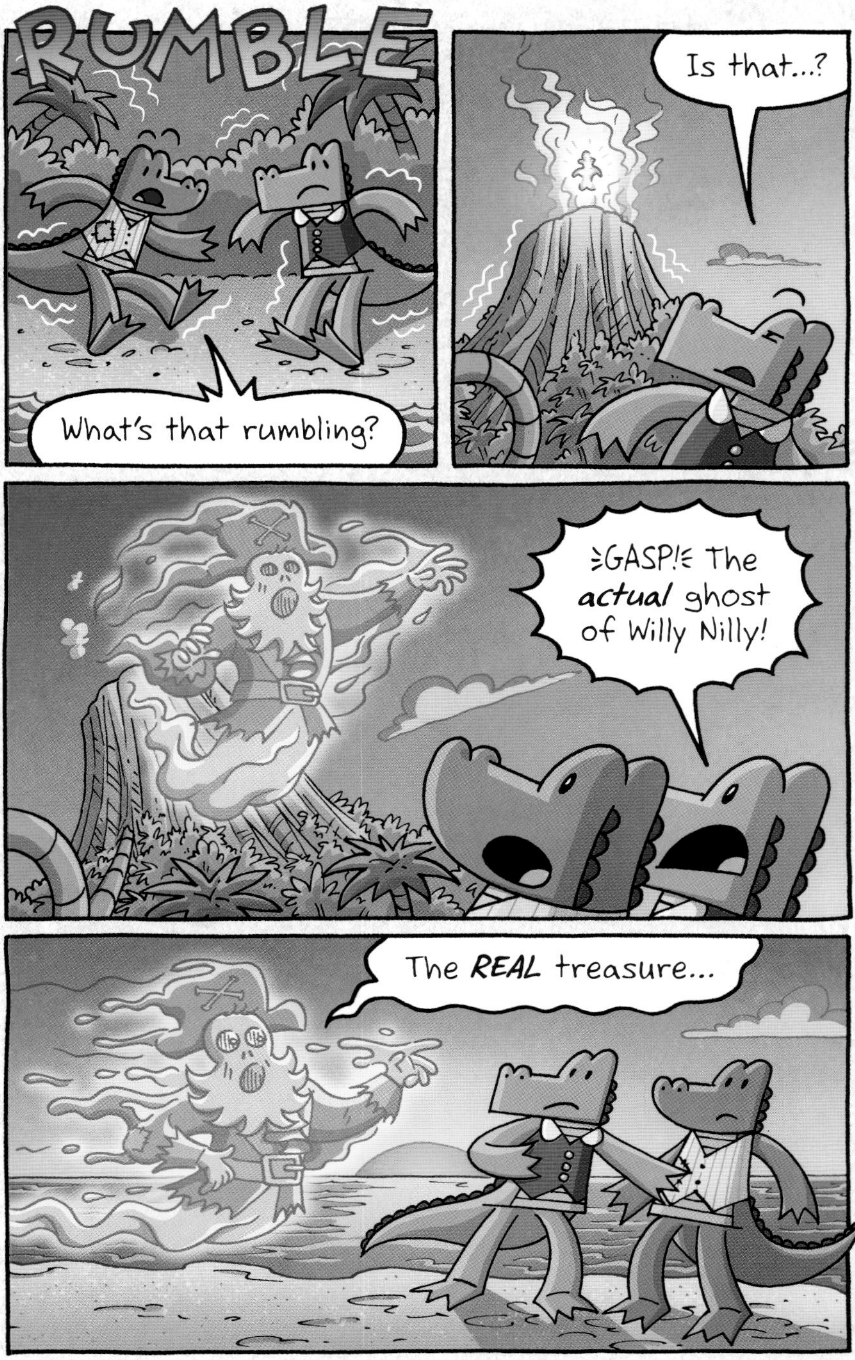
RUMBLE
What's that rumbling?
Is that...?
GASP! The *actual* ghost of Willy Nilly!
The *REAL* treasure...

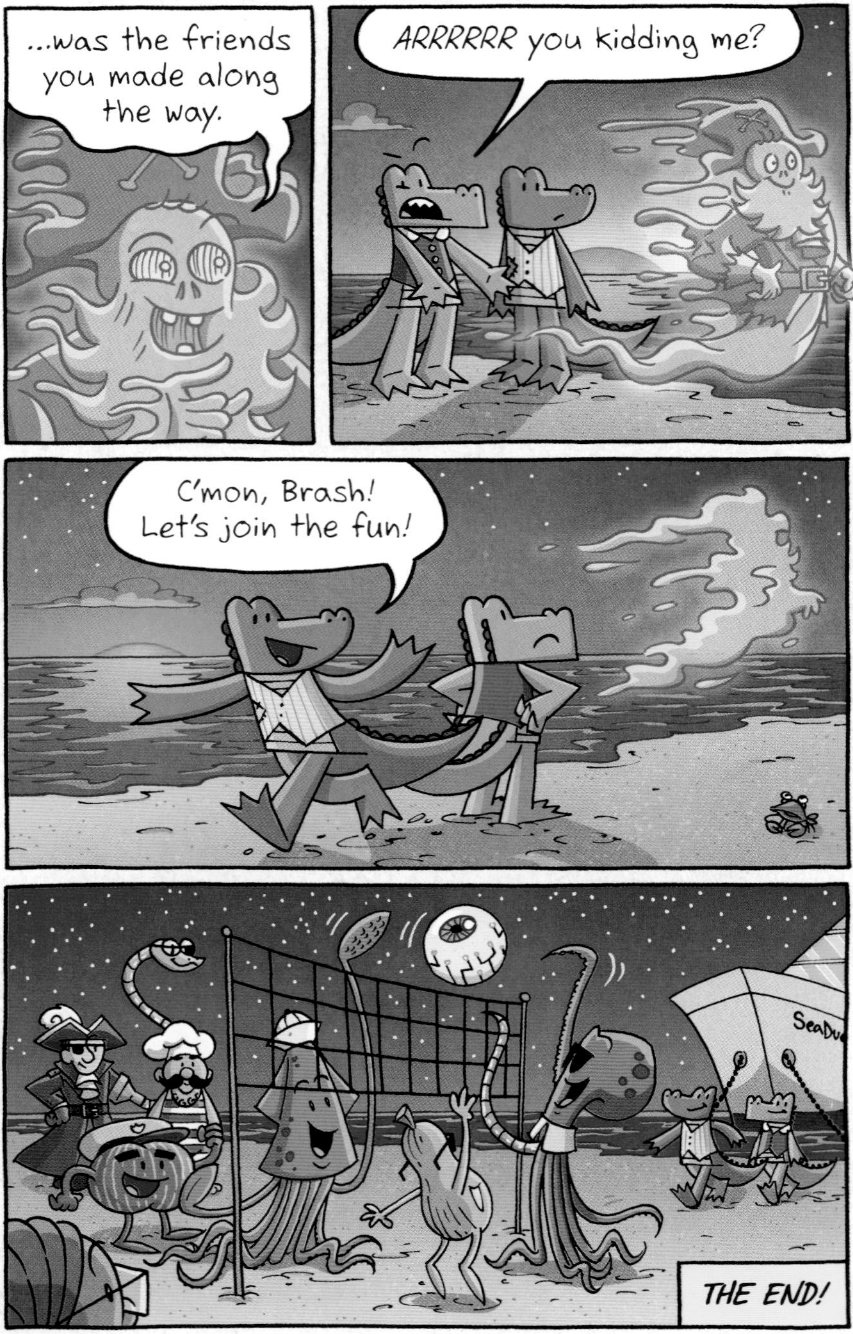
...was the friends you made along the way.
ARRRRRR you kidding me?
C'mon, Brash! Let's join the fun!
SeaDu
THE END!

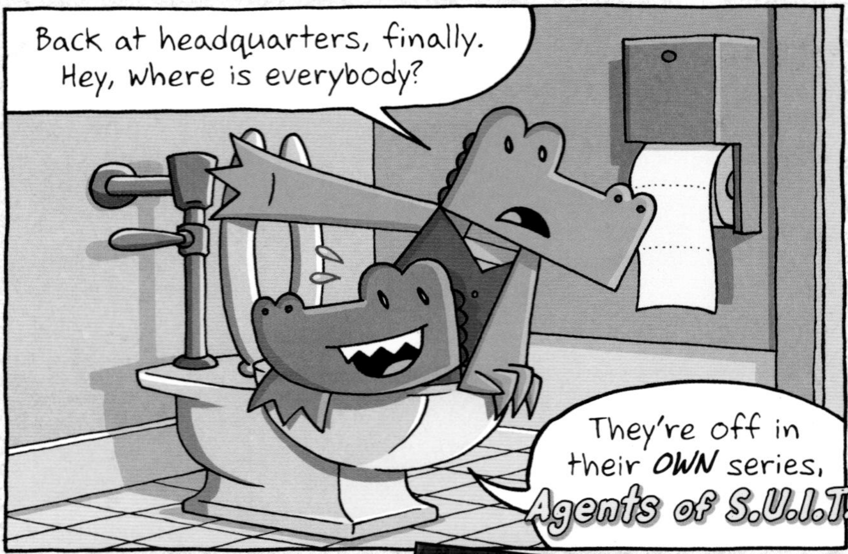
Back at headquarters, finally. Hey, where is everybody?
They're off in their *OWN* series, Agents of S.U.I.T.!

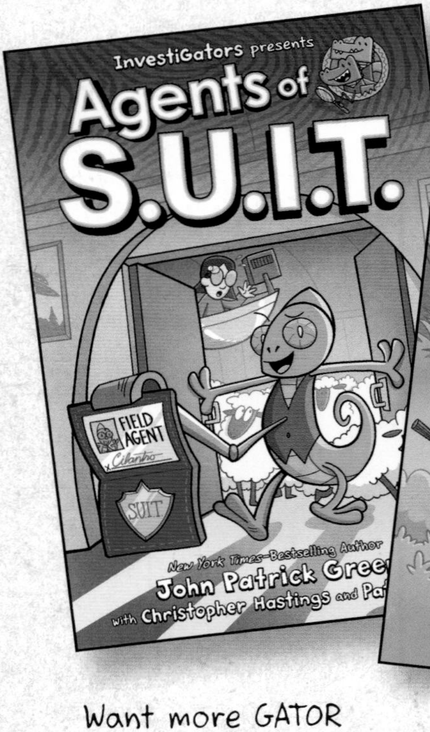
InvestiGators presents
Agents of S.U.I.T.
FIELD AGENT
Cilantro
SUIT
New York Times–Bestselling Author
John Patrick Green
with Christopher Hastings and

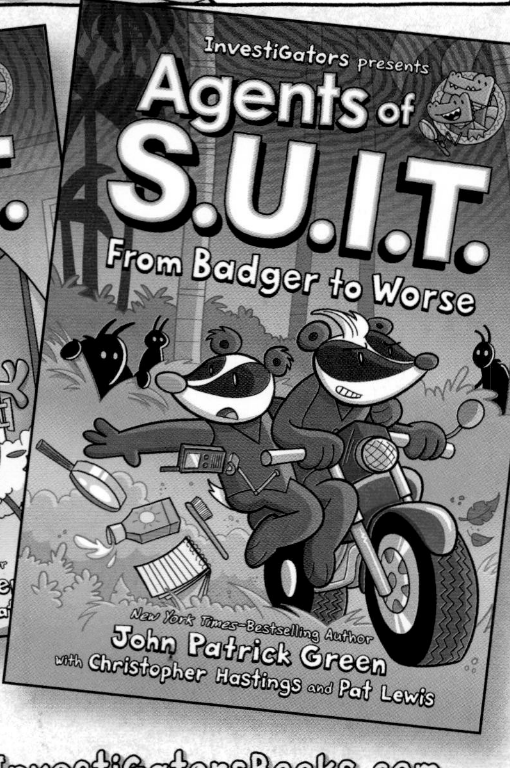
InvestiGators presents
Agents of S.U.I.T.
From Badger to Worse
New York Times–Bestselling Author
John Patrick Green
with Christopher Hastings and Pat Lewis

Want more GATOR fun and news? Visit **InvestiGatorsBooks.com**